D1551174

WITHDRAWN

FACE VALUE

By
RON POWERS

THE NEWSCASTERS

FACE VALUE

RON POWERS

DELACORTE PRESS/NEW YORK

Published by
Delacorte Press
1 Dag Hammarskjold Plaza
New York, N.Y. 10017

Copyright © 1979 by Ron Powers

All rights reserved. No part of this book may be reproduced or
transmitted in any form or by any means, electronic or mechanical,
including photocopying, recording, or by any information storage
and retrieval system, without the written permission of the
Publisher, except where permitted by law.

Manufactured in the United States of America
First printing

Designed by Oksana Kushnir

LIBRARY OF CONGRESS CATALOGING IN PUBLICATION DATA

Powers, Ron.
  Face value.

  I. Title.
PZ4.P88932Fac   [PS3566.O93]   813'.5'4   79–773
ISBN 0–440–01649–5

FRANCIS BRANCH/BOOKMOBILE

cap. 3

For Honorée

I have met them at close of day
Coming with vivid faces . . .
All changed, changed utterly:
A terrible beauty is born.

—William Butler Yeats,
"Easter 1916"

Prologue

Bobby Lee Cooper's immortal soul floated over America's Friendly Skies like a phosphorescent, alabaster album cover.

It brooded above the grieving continent, thickening the August air and turning the afternoon Drive Time into a funereal crawl. Disc jockeys wept through scheduled commercial breaks. Women in supermarkets, strangers, locked eyes in unspoken communal bereavement.

Tastee-Freezes closed their windows. The President of the United States, a fellow Southerner and "a longtime fan," issued a condolence to Cooper's mother. Leadoff men knelt, staring vacantly, in their on-deck circles as Moments of Silence were observed. Sources were reached for comment. The Man in the Street (who had sputtered Daddy-disapproval when Bobby Lee was unleashed on a sexually torpid nation twenty-two years earlier) faced the camera with his familiar expression of bewildered hang-dog pain and said how awful it was. (The Woman in the Street, recalling long-ago nascent orgasms, wept.) Film at eleven.

He had died in Las Vegas in the hot afternoon, possibly the greatest entertainer America had ever known; died before a scheduled rock'n'roll revue at Caesar's Palace; died with his Southern troll's leer gone puffy but the leer long since disarmed; the forbidden rhinestone pistoning hips long since domesticated into twin batons at the head of Middle America's unending Thanksgiving Day Parade.

Died drooling half-dissolved violet capsules of barbiturate, with his heavy blown-dry head resting inside a plastic wastepaper basket in the bedroom of his hotel suite in Las Vegas: uncomprehending, in his first rush of sweet nonexistence, that his greatest triumphs as an American celebrity were still to come.

America keened.

In Chattanooga, Tennessee, Bobby Lee's ancestral city, a sixteen-year-old girl lowered her head and plunged into the path of an oncoming Toyota Celica Gt LiftBack. ("You asked for it—you got it: Toyota.") She was clutching Bobby Lee's latest LP hit, *Bobby Lee Live From Jerusalem's Wailing Wall.*

At 30 Rockefeller Center in New York Tom Brokaw's voice caught a bit as he led off the *NBC Nightly News* with the announcement, "Bobby Lee Cooper died today. He was forty-two . . ."

In suburban Melrose Park, Illinois, the thirty-nine-year-old wife of a tree surgeon got stiff on Southern Comfort (Janis's drink), had a coughing-and-crying fit until the tears streamed down the rouged rinds of her cheeks, and began throwing Mark Evans pantsuits into her suitcase for the long drive to Chattanooga. She took the Monte Carlo, which had the eight-track stereo. She was one of the three hundred thousand who went.

In San Antonio, Texas, a woman caller swooned after revealing to all-night call-in host Art Snow that her horoscope had the same ascendant sign as Bobby Lee's and that she had predicted his death. Art Snow's keen sense of the moment in history took over from there. He immediately dedicated "the remainder of my show" to "the memory of Bobby Lee," and began playing Bobby Lee's greatest hits as a "tribute" to the dead rock'n'roll star.

Art Snow was exactly the seventy-ninth radio personality in America to mobilize a "tribute" to Bobby Lee Cooper. The honor of first "tribute" was claimed (and subsequently publicized in a seventy-five-thousand-dollar ad campaign) by a fifty-thousand-watt rocker in Chicago, which was on the air with its "tribute" at 3:30 in the afternoon, just forty-seven minutes after the bulletin announcing Bobby Lee's death came over the United Press radio wire.

The four major networks called emergency staff meetings to organize prime-time specials on Bobby Lee. CBS and NBC each planned "salutes." (NBC changed its "salute" to a "tribute" after learning of CBS's plan.) ABC planned a "tribute" but changed it to a "wide world of." CBN planned a "farewell salute."

The *Las Vegas Tattler* hit the streets with a front-page photograph of the wastebasket in which Bobby Lee Cooper's head had come to rest. Under the twenty-four-point caption line, DEATH WASTEBASKET, was the by-lined account of the bellhop who had recovered the wastebasket and sold it to the *Tattler* for twenty-five thousand dollars. At 8:12 P.M. the bellhop was contacted by a booking agent for *The Stanley Siegel Show*.

Bobby Lee's longtime friend and patriarchal manager, the legendary C. W. "Hoss" McCullum, held a press conference on the front porch of his antebellum estate fourteen miles outside Chattanooga. His beefy face flushed and perspiring, his white Stetson clutched reverentially in one large paw, the old man leaned heavily on the baluster, his head bowed, his lips moving silently.

Below him, cowed into a self-conscious hush like a stump congregation, stood the Chattanooga press corps. They pointed their minicams and their directional mikes, all the latest RCA issue, up toward the bowed hulk of Bobby Lee Cooper's discoverer and the architect of his fame, and waited for the old man to find words.

At last McCullum lifted his head. His mouth was a scar of sorrow.

"Ladies and gen'mun of the press," he said in his deep, courtly drawl, "this is . . . *indeed* a tragic occasion, not only for Bobby Lee's momma and his millions of friends aroun' the world. It is a tragic occasion for the Yew-ninet States of America.

"Bobby Lee Cooper *was* the American Dream. He . . ." here the old man swung his Stetson in a helpless gesture. ". . . he sang his songs and he loved his momma and he made three hundred forty-seven million dollars. And you cain't ask more of any man.

"Now, I trust that you all will excuse me in my hour of personal sorrow. Good Lord in His inf'nite wisdom done seen fit."

C. W. "Hoss" McCullum bowed briefly to the Chattanooga press corps, many of whom already were mentally rehearsing for the national shot, and shuffled heavily toward the front door of his mansion.

Once inside, McCullum quickened his gait. He strode directly upstairs to his study. In an oak-paneled room decorated with photographs and souvenirs tracing the career of Bobby Lee Cooper, McCullum lifted a silver telephone and dialed an unlisted number.

A moment later McCullum spoke to the president of a Connecticut marketing firm. The firm's name was Images, Inc.

In his deep, courtly drawl C. W. "Hoss" McCullum dictated the particulars of an agreement with the president of Images. The agreement designated Images as the sole licensing agent for Bobby Lee Cooper's name and likeness. Under the terms set down by McCullum, Images would become the authorized subcontractor for Bobby Lee Cooper posters, T-shirts, statuettes, rubber masks, and any other commercial products bearing the Cooper name.

In return for the privilege, the president agreed to sign a contract compensating C. W. "Hoss" McCullum in the amount of one million five hundred thousand dollars.

McCullum put the silver telephone down and was busy for a moment paring the tip off a Havana Montecristo with a Gillette blue blade. When he had the cigar going, McCullum picked up the receiver again and telephoned another unlisted number—this one in Beverly Hills.

"Mr. Bookmaster? This here's C.W.," he said in his deep courteous drawl. "Har yew? Yeah, that was a pity. I tole that damn fool boy to stick t' Di-Gel. I . . ."

McCullum fell silent for several long minutes. By the time he spoke again, his Montecristo had gone out. Some of the color had drained from his face. With the perspiration that dampened his silver hair and the haunted look that had come into his eyes, C. W. McCullum resembled not so much the lovable backwoods impresario as he did a cocker spaniel that had been thrown into a very deep pond to drown.

"Well, Ah surely didn' mean no disrespect t' the boy . . ."

Another silence.

"Ah *know* he was a valuable commodity . . ."

A very long silence.

"Mr. Bookmaster, Ah tried to get that boy int'sted in politics, Ah talked mahse'f blue in the face, even if'n he was still with us, there just ain't no way he'd . . ."

Silence.

"Wellsir, those Summer Olympics are still two yee-ahs off, seems to me you could . . . nossir. Nossir, it *ain't* none of my business."

McCullum listened a little longer. He licked at a fleck of tobacco on his fleshy lower lip. Then he said:

"Nossir. Ain't nobody knows. I don't even have your number wrote down, like you said."

Then he said:

"You won't have t' do that, Mr. Bookmaster."

Then he whispered:

"Please."

In Manhattan, in the darkness of a small Second Avenue bistro named Stitch's, a thirty-three-year-old actor named Robert Schein sat alone at the bar smoking L&M Long Lights and drinking Benedictines. Schein was watching, without particularly absorbing, Walter Cronkite's coverage of Bobby Lee Cooper's death on a television set mounted on a shelf above the bar. "The passing of this still-young man, a fixture in the panoply of popular music for nearly the last quarter-century, has cut as deep a wound in America's heart as the passing of John F. Kennedy in 1963," Cronkite was intoning. On the screen there was footage of Cooper's last concert—a heavy-bellied figure in white, lumbering about a stage like a bewildered upright bear, eyes squinted shut, a hand microphone held to his sneering, puffed mouth.

Schein exhaled smoke through his nostrils and studied the image of Cooper.

Now the CBS footage shifted to another face, a face that at first seemed to be an androgynous mirror-image of Cooper. It was the face of a heavy-jowled woman, beaded with sweat, her eyes squinted shut, her lipsticked mouth contorted into a voluptuous sneer. The woman held up a fragment of scarlet, and buried her face in it, twisting her head from side to side. Schein thought he saw a flash of tongue. The scarlet fragment was one of Bobby Lee Cooper's scarves. The woman was a fan.

"His fans were among the most devoted of those of any entertainment figure . . ." intoned Cronkite. Schein thumped his glass down on the bar.

The owner of Stitch's, a raw-faced little man named Al Gnagy, looked up sharply. He put down a shot glass that he was wiping and came over to where Schein was sitting alone on his stool.

Gnagy put his skinny elbows on the bar and leaned across to look into Robert Schein's eyes, the way a trainer will look into the eyes of his fighter.

"Hey," said Gnagy. "Don't go gettin' drunk. You got two and a half hours to go before we start the comedy acts. I don't want you to go out there and puke on my customers. That's not my idea of comedy, you understand?"

Two humorless ice-blue eyes stared back at Gnagy. For a long moment the little proprietor thought he saw violence in the eyes. The rest of Robert Schein's face remained expressionless. It was the vacantly handsome face of a young Republican commuter: a wheat-wave of blond hair, the mouth thin and wide and bloodless.

Gnagy stood there waiting for this Schein to say something. Fucking actors, he hated them. Faggots. He should have kept this place what it was, a bar, the hell with bringing in comedy acts.

"Just don't throw up on anybody," he said finally.

Three-and-one-half hours later, at 10:45 P.M. on the night of the day that Bobby Lee Cooper died, the phantasm that came to be embedded in the American consciousness as "Robert Schein" was born.

Part One

 "Where's Teller?"

"Day off."

"Beep the fucker."

"I can't beep him."

"Why can't you beep him?"

"He doesn't wear his beeper."

The dispatcher might as well have announced that Mark Teller didn't wear pants. Morris Kitman, for one of the few times in his life, was shocked.

He ceased pacing the WRAP-TV newsroom, which at this moment was a chaos of scrambling reporters, screaming assistant producers, and jangling telephones, and gaped down at the dispatcher.

Morris Kitman was the *WRAP-Around News* assignment editor. Right now he was busy deploying reporters and crews to cover New York's reaction to the death of rock'n'roll legend Bobby Lee Cooper. But the dispatcher's statement had stopped him in his tracks.

Kitman stood motionless in the eye of the babbling newsroom swarm, one small white hand resting on the edge of the Communications Desk, near a random, half-empty jar of Hi-Ho soy sauce.

The dispatcher met Kitman's incredulous gaze with a pursed

expression. The expression meant to tell Kitman, "What do you expect? He's not one of us, not really. He's not broadcasting. He's print. What the hell does he know?"

All of that was lost on Kitman. The single fact of Mark Teller's not wearing his beeper, just at this moment, was filling his intellectual universe. Morris Kitman had dealt with a lot of strange people in his years as a New York television newsman, a lot of serious moonbeams. But he had never yet met an on-air personality who was disinclined to wear a beeper.

Kitman shook his head and looked up at the wall clock above the bank of TelePrompTer typewriters. Something slippery turned over in his stomach.

It was 4:28 P.M. on Thursday afternoon, August 17, exactly thirty-two minutes away from the start of WRAP's two-hour afternoon newscast. The first Cooper bulletin had broken on the wires a scant forty-five minutes ago, sending the fifteen-million-dollar-a-year electronic journalism complex into a state of activity not unlike that of an ant colony threatened by a butane lighter. It was the biggest news bombshell since the capture of Son of Sam. Bigger than Sadat. Bigger than the Panama treaty thing. Ed Kurtis, the WRAP news director, had immediately summoned his staff into an emergency meeting to improvise an appropriate response: a special two-hour "theme" newscast. The *WRAP-Around News* department prepared to throw out its scheduled news budget and attack the Cooper story from every conceivable angle.

Bracing himself at the head of a scarred Formica table that nearly filled a tiny conference room, glancing at notes scribbled on the back of a Common Cause press release, the squat, balding news director had issued orders to the dozen-odd producers and editors gathered around the table.

"Stagg will handle the headline story from the anchor desk. Have Art Sand rewrite it from the wires; I guess he's the best writer we got. Jesus. Tell him to make it come from Stagg's heart. I want him visibly shaken."

"He *is* visibly shaken, Ed. Hell, I think half the time Stagg thought he *was* Bobby Lee Cooper."

"All right, just don't let him ad-lib anything. You remember what happened when he ad-libbed on the rape story last month. We damn near lost our license. Just tell him to read it exactly like Sand writes it."

Kurtis blew his nose on the back of a piece of carbon paper and looked at his notes again.

"All right, where were we? I want every videotape crew we've got on this story. Have Sean Murphy take a crew and go on over to Macy's; I want him to get reactions from people on the street. Tell him to find a lot of old broads who used to get off on Cooper in the fifties. Sensitive, human side. Bawling broads. That type thing."

"Ed, we've been monitoring Two, Four, and Seven. They're all sending crews over to Macy's. Hell, they'll all end up interviewing one *another*."

"All right." Kurtis waved a hairy forearm. "Send him to Bloomingdale's then. Somewhere. Hey, I got it. Send him to Rockefeller Center! We'll get our hand down the back of NBC's pants." Kurtis's heavy black eyebrows drew together in what he evidently considered a conspiratorial wink. The effect was frightening.

"Arroz will do the black and the Latino reaction; bleeding-heart stuff. Maybe he can put something together on the effect of black rhythms on Cooper's style, or vice versa."

"The blacks *hate* Bobby Lee Cooper. They thought he was a racist. When his death came over the wires, our phone clerks did the Bus Stop."

"Far as that goes, the blacks hate Carlos Arroz. So do the spicks. They know his name's Carl Rice, he lives in Westchester and balls Senator Kaufman's old lady." Affirmative chuckles went around the conference table.

Kurtis put his knuckles on the edge of the table. There was a simian menace to his posture as his dark eyes darted from face to face. The faces were amused, relaxed. Typically, his staff regarded the crisis as an occasion for a smart-ass derby.

"THIS SHIT STOPS!" Kurtis bellowed. The men around the table jerked in unison.

When Kurtis spoke again, his voice carried the lull of sweet reason.

"I could give a shit about the numbers," Ed Kurtis said, spreading his hands. "I'm a newsman, I don't know from the ratings. Right? Normally, I don't even allow a ratings book in my office. I go where the news is. I don't even keep up on whether we're Number One or Number Four."

His voice sank to a whisper.

"But goddammit, gentlemen. There are more television sets in this fuckin' city than there are toilets. Bobby Lee *Cooper* just died. People know him who don't know the governor of this state. Four, maybe six fuckin' million people are going to watch the news tonight."

Kurtis's voice was rising again.

"I'd like to think that some of 'em will be watching *us*! Toward that end, I want Cooper's fuckin' hood puss all over that screen. I want Cooper and Alpo, Cooper and Wesson Oil, Cooper and Nescafe, Cooper and Burger King! When the Colonel tunes us in, I want him to entertain the notion that tonight, for once, we just might be picking ourselves up off the goddamn carpet and at least give WCBS a run for their money; they're down to a nine share, not that I have any notion what that means.

"Bobby Lee Cooper's the story of the year. We're gonna run with it. We're either a serious news organization or we're not! Foster, what was our lead story today supposed to be?"

"New disclosures on the Vietnam war policy. Former CIA guy here in town says he can prove Nixon made a secret deal with Thieu."

"Stick it in the hole. Cooper's our lead. Morris, here's the rest of the assignments I want. Lafontaint at City Hall, with crew. Mayor's reaction. Jennifer has contacts in the record industry; I want somebody to talk to her about Cooper's impact on the Beatles, number of Gold Records, sorry to see him go, that sort of thing. Teller will do a commentary, in-studio. Maybe Bannister can whip up a health piece, kind of drug that killed Cooper, Cooper didn't get any exercise, warning to middle-aged males, that sort of thing. Maybe the sports department can find out whether Cooper played high school ball, earned a letter, phone interview with his grizzled mentor, if he's still alive. Anybody else who's free, send 'em out on the street for reactions. Anybody have any questions?"

An assistant producer cleared his throat. "The weather," he said.

Kurtis leaned on his knuckles and squinted hard at the man.

"The *weather*?"

"Yes. We're covering everything else about Cooper. Maybe we should get our meteorologist to find out whether his croaking will affect the five-day forecast."

Another little ripple of giggles went around the room. Kurtis started to say something violent, but Morris Kitman spoke up quickly to head it off.

"Ed," Kitman said, "I don't know whether Lafontaint is going to go along with being pulled off his beat to help cover the Cooper story. He already thinks you don't take him seriously enough as a political correspondent."

Kurtis turned his attention to the assignment editor.

"He doesn't, huh," said Kurtis. He leaned down. "Well, you tell him this, Morris. Tell the son of a bitch that if he doesn't do what I tell him to do, we'll go on the air tonight and disclose that his real fucking name's Lipschitz."

That was all forty-five minutes ago. Now, with just thirty-two minutes left before the newscast, Morris Kitman had accomplished most of the impossible. He had relayed Kurtis's orders to everyone concerned. The *WRAP-Around News* team was mobilized and fanning out through the city, setting up its minicams for "live reports," its cream-and-orange WRAP ACTION VAN hurtling through traffic, its sound men and light men belted and strapped with equipment like infantry, its clear-eyed, manly, tousled reporters applying last-minute touches of Max Factor No. 2. Everyone was in action.

Everyone, that is, except Mark Teller. The young pop-culture critic was nowhere to be found.

"You've tried his home number?" Kitman asked the dispatcher mechanically. The dispatcher's pursed, unchanging expression suggested that the very question had assaulted his professional integrity.

"And he doesn't wear a beeper," Kitman mused. He grasped a shiny lapel with one small white hand and stared reflectively across the moiling newsroom.

"Must be some kind of Communist."

He had passed the afternoon walking in New York, fists in his jean pockets, scenting and listening to this strange new enveloping urban garden as much as looking at it. A year in New York had not dulled Mark Teller's sensory curiosity about the city; his small-town midwesterner's impulse to scout it like a trapper.

It was one of those commonplace paradoxes peculiar to the Age of Communications that Teller, without any organic connections to New York, without having ingested its patterns and rhythms, without even being able to visualize the shape of Manhattan Island in his head, had become a spokesman for the city: an arbiter, in fact, of its trends, its entertainments, its iconography, its phrasing, its sexuality, its "style."

(Not that New York *had* any of the aforementioned, not as qualities that stood for the city at large, or even a substantial chunk of its population. That fact made Teller's job, and the jobs of people like him, somewhat easier.)

Teller was the pop culture critic for WRAP Television, flagship station for the Continental Broadcasting Network. He had held the job for three months. Before that, he had written a daily column tapping the same vein for the flamboyant tabloid *The New York Messenger*. Before that, he had covered a professional football team for a couple of midwestern papers. He was one year short of his thirtieth birthday. None of it made any sense.

No sense, at least, to Teller. For the time being he was content to regard it all as an uproarious joke; a sort of goofy acting out of some beery southern improvised satire on a pilgrim's progress: takes an ole boy from the Ozarks, by God, to tell those aht-dam' easterners all about their fancy fag discos and what color pants ole Liza wore to the ball.

The hell of it was that Teller was extremely good at what he did. His columns and commentaries were marked, discussed by the shrewd and knowing brokers of pop, the agents, public-relations people, the marketers and merchandisers, the impresarios and the managers of image, most of whom paid Teller the important homage of despising him.

Some of the despising, unbeknownst to Teller, came from his own superiors at WRAP. He had demanded, as a condition of his employment, that the field of "pop culture" be expanded to include the media—specifically, television itself. When Mark Teller put the television business in his cross-hairs, the reverberations usually went all the way up to the executive suite.

So far, there had been no attempts to curtail him.

In style and in content, Mark Teller was a maverick in the New York media world.

He seldom joined the wolf pack for film screenings at the Trans-Lux, the openings at the Whitney or the Public Theater or the Bottom Line. He was not among the luncheon fixtures at Café des Artistes or the Four Seasons. He was not on the guest list of the beautiful, crushed-velvet-and-cocaine parties that purred low into lost SoHo mornings, parties rendered into folklore on the pens of Reed and Suzy and Smith.

He did not drink at Elaine's. He had never followed Greta Garbo down 49th Street.

"You behave like an outsider," Jennifer Blade had told him once. She did not mean it as a compliment. (Jennifer seldom meant anything as a compliment.) Teller was, if anything, a minor mystery figure in New York's media circles: a demirecluse, friendly enough, affable, but apart.

Some days he ran in New York.

He ran seriously, stretching it out around the reservoir in Cen-

tral Park, a white kerchief holding back his brown locks, wrists
held high, flash of brown sharp knees, gliding abstractedly past all
but the most determined of the Adidas-coutured stockbrokers and
lawyers on the track. Seven years out of Ozark State College, where
he'd been a cross-country man, Teller was still flat in the belly,
rawboned and slim-faced. The sprawl of curly brown hair and the
offhand grin suggested a doggy, distracted collegiate affability.

There was a relentless concentration, a skeptical probing intensity behind the innocent brown eyes. Running, for Teller, was less
a competitive sport than an activity most compatible with the
incessant, churning patterns of his mind. He was a chronic day-
dreamer, architect of mystagogical fantasies, the energies of his
perceptions sucked inward until the exterior world was all but
blotted out.

This fantasizing—rich, languorous, fierce in projected color and
detail, sexual, reminiscent—alternated with spells of coldly intense, disciplined analysis of the fantasies. Running was something
to do with his body while this inner dialogue played itself out.

But not today.

Today was a rare day for walking in New York, under the hot
clean sun that burned along the shimmering telescoped stoplights
of Upper Madison Avenue and brought up the heavy soup smell
of Manhattan; the accumulation of vapors that had gathered on
the city's surface forever, unwashed by winds and impervious to
the passing of populations: ripe garbage, gasoline fumes, building
soot, the melting ridges of animal manure, the occasional wisp of
sachet from old women: sulfur, the electric smell that floated up
out of the subways, liquor-vomit, dead things. Each odor fresh and
distinct and insistent to Teller's nostrils, keyed to the secret, in-
formative, clean aromas of the Ozark hunting fields.

He didn't mind the crowding, insistent odors. They were part of
the enormous joke he enjoyed on days like this one; the joke of
being *here*. An Ozark boy here in New York, telling the most
sophisticated people in the world about themselves.

He glanced at his watch. Time to head for the Commerce
Center.

Caught by the glare of the sinking sun, the Six Captains stood in
fierce silhouette facing the Commerce Center's gray facade. Mark

Teller could never approach the building at sunset without stopping for a moment to stare at them.

Cupreous needles of light glinted from the line of a patrician nose, the tip of a bronze goatee. It was meant to be an awesome and elegant sight, an empyrean testimony to mercantile grandeur: the bronze busts of six captains of American industry, executed in heroic style, each head four times life size, each mounted on a concrete pillar, twenty feet above the sidewalk. The busts had been commissioned upon completion of the fortress that was the Commerce Center in 1932.

Teller often wondered whether the architect had meant for the row of busts to be contemplated at this hour, at sunset. In this red hour of truth, the effect was something quite different from elegance.

In silhouette the heads of the Six Captains looked like the heads of six vanquished warriors impaled on stakes. The effect was barbaric.

He leaned his lanky frame against the building near the three glass revolving doors that formed the entranceway. Thirty stories above him, he knew that the *WRAP-Around News* was drawing toward its 7 P.M. close. He had managed to spend one fine day at large in New York, speaking to no one, avoiding headlines, scenting and listening to the city, feeling its heavy presence, himself in it. Now, in a few minutes, Jennifer Blade would be down from the studio. Jennifer Blade. His Jennifer Blade. The notion still stunned him.

Teller slapped his hands to his chest, feeling his sweat-damped western shirt. Jennifer would be tailored and immaculate, as usual. He kept a Qiana shirt upstairs in his locker. Maybe he should dash up, sprinkle some water on his body, and change. Maybe in a minute. His gaze lingered on the second of the Six Captains, a railroad baron. A reverie formed, a fantasy of the railroad baron days of the 1880s, forging the link between Chicago and San Francisco . . .

"I understand they were the first six anchormen hired by WRAP."

He spun around. Jennifer Blade had come up behind him. Tall, honey-haired, ironic Jennifer Blade, sensational Jennifer Blade, long-limbed, deeply tanned, her deep broadcaster's voice almost

mannish, but sexy in a husky, challenging way; Jennifer, all bracelets and sunglasses, leggy in her cream-colored hopsack dress.

Surprised at her uncharacteristic banter, Teller ransacked his
brain for a witty reply. But Jennifer's mood had already begun to
darken. Her jawline had hardened, an unmistakable danger sign.

"Where have you been?" she asked with contempt in her voice.
"Kurtis has been trying to find you for the last four hours. Bobby
Lee Cooper died today."

For a moment Teller stood silent before Jennifer Blade. He felt foolish. It was characteristic of her to throw him into mute confusion with one swift, unforeseen rebuke.

"Cooper died?" he repeated finally.

"Yes, and Kurtis would have liked you to help us cover it. Haskell did a beautiful commentary on Seven. Why don't you wear your beeper? Do you think you're better than the rest of us?"

She was rummaging in her handbag for a cigarette, not looking at him, her tone clipped and impersonal. This was one of Jennifer Blade's patented surprise attacks, carried out, as always, with what Teller suspected was ruthless glee. The best ones, the most destructive, were of the type now being launched: besides Jennifer's personal irritation, they conveyed a second-hand judgment of failure from some higher authority—in this case, the WRAP news director and, probably, half the staff as well.

Teller the Newspaper Interloper, the Dilettante Slumming in Television, was a familiar rap.

He spread his hands toward Jennifer, who was cupping hers over her cigarette. "Look," he said. "All right. I fucked up. How did Cooper die? Do you think I should run up and see Kurtis?"

20 RON POWERS

She waved the match out with a violent, mannish snap of her fingers, gazing over his shoulder. She inhaled a puff of smoke, lips parted. She studied him for a moment, her great brown eyes glazed with detachment.

"Cooper died of a drug overdose in Vegas," she said, again with the note of cool contempt in her voice. "Barbiturates, in case you're interested. I don't care whether you go see Kurtis or not. No, wait until tomorrow, you're too late now anyway. He's busy. Come on, let's go have dinner."

He had met her on the day he joined the *WRAP-Around News* team back in June. With characteristic abruptness, she had marched up to his desk, extended a long arm, and announced: "I am Jennifer Blade. I liked your work on the *Messenger*. This place is the pits. You'll probably last about one ratings-period. Do you want to have a drink after the news?"

Teller didn't need to be told that the woman standing over him was Jennifer Blade. She possessed one of the most recognized and striking faces in a city in which beautiful women television reporters were commonplace. (She had already graced the covers of *The New York Times Magazine* and *Us.*)

But Jennifer's was not the mannered, self-conscious beauty of her envious colleagues—a look sculpted around Cinandre coiffure and Estée Lauder eyeshadow and Hermès scarf arranged just so.

Such preoccupation with image was not Jennifer Blade's style. Hers was a challenging, artless sort of beauty. Her face was dominated by huge, restless deep-brown eyes and a generous mouth—a curiously mobile mouth that conveyed most of Jennifer's emotions. In moments of self-absorption or stress, she had a habit of pursing her lips toward one side of her face. It gave her a sort of lopsided, little-girl appeal that was mostly unsupported by her personality.

Her skin, winy dark from years of southern California summers, was drawn tightly over fine cheekbones; the supple hollows above her jaw were as perfect as a model's. Her hair was thick and honey-blond, and she let it cascade unattended below her shoulders.

Teller, who liked to tell himself that looks were not decisive in his choice of women, was instantly mesmerized by that face—by its intimations of a deep and penetrating intelligence coupled with an offhand eroticism.

Her body was deceptive. Dressed, she appeared almost thin, the wrists corded and strong from tennis; hands and feet large, the toes turned slightly in. But those regions of her body hidden from the business world were like a secret rain forest, lush and darkly inviting. Her legs were long and delicately muscled. Her breasts Teller could only think of—he was not sure he understood the association —as biblical. Something of the elemental desert-woman in them; they sloped in a heavy, generous parabola above her elongated torso, their fullness easily camouflaged by her silken Giorgio shirts in the summer, her tweeds and turtlenecks in the winter.

Teller knew about her only what he had read in the *Us* cover story: she was twenty-four, young for a television reporter at a major, network-owned station—but Jennifer Blade was a special case. She was the daughter of Sterling Blade, the West Coast baron of made-for-TV movies. The elder Blade had built a fortune with a string of long-running cop- and western-series in the 1960s— series drenched in blood, heaving bosoms, crashing helicopters, and screeching car chases, punctuated with occasional flecks of dialogue, along the lines of, "*Freeze!*" and, "I'm asking you for the last time, Jenner—where's Trish?"

He had invested his wealth into a fifty-million-dollar production studio, which he built on an abandoned ranch north of Los Angeles. The studio, Blade City, was a wonder of television technology and cost-efficiency. Blade built it on a gamble that made-for-television movies would be a staple of TV in the seventies—and he was right.

The Blade TV movie was a ratings winner. In fifteen years he had come to dominate American television programming as surely as any network executive—and his influence reached across the continent into the executive suites of the network headquarters at Rockefeller Center, 51 West 52nd Street, 1330 Avenue of the Americas, and Commerce Center Plaza—the headquarters of the four networks.

Blade, without a second thought, had wielded his influence to commandeer his daughter an on-air assignment at *WRAP-Around News* immediately upon her completion of a master's degree in communications at U.C.L.A.

But if Jennifer had secured her job through special privilege, she retained it through merit. Her most bitter rivals among the city's television newswomen found it hard to deny her ability. She brushed past her colleagues' surface attempts at news coverage and established herself as a tough, knowledgeable, digging reporter.

Jennifer Blade had an instinct for power. And the powerful people whom she sought out, the state assemblymen and police captains and producers and corporate vice-presidents, the very ones who winced under her blunt and ruthless questions, sensed the power that was in Jennifer Blade.

Their drink after the news had been a success. She had suggested a discreet downstairs bar on 56th Street, polished brass and oak—not one of the several whooping media watering holes along Broadcast Row.

"Please forgive the sunglasses," she had laughed, as soon as she had shaken out her hair, summoned the waiter—by name—and ordered a Pernod. "I think they are hideously affected, but if you don't wear them people will grab at you on the street. You'll find out—if you last." She smiled quickly to cover what Teller sensed was a persistent trace of mockery. "We may as well be doing soap opera news. God, my purse is a mess. Do you have a match? Why'd you leave the *Messenger*? I loved your stuff there. Are you trying to get rich?"

Teller held out a lighted match and regarded Jennifer. Her every other remark, it seemed, was barbed. "If I told you why, you'd probably laugh at me."

"Don't hand me that bullshit." The bantering tone had abruptly disappeared from her voice. "Come on. Let's hear it. Why'd you leave the *Messenger*?" She turned her head aside to exhale smoke, but kept her gaze squarely on him.

Teller studied his hands for a moment as they toyed with his frosted stein of beer.

"Better question: Why'd I ever *join* the *Messenger*? I'm a fish out of water, Jennifer. I'm your basic sportswriter. God put me on earth to ask coaches with clipboards what the turning point of the game was. Hell, I'm still learning about Pop. A year ago I thought Meatloaf was a linebacker for the Chicago Bears."

She grimaced. "You were an athlete, weren't you? A runner?"

"Yeah. At some drinkwater college . . . how the hell'd you know *that*?"

Jennifer remained poker-faced behind her sunglasses. "You were saying. About the *Messenger*."

"I was saying. Let's see. Sportswriter. Oh, yes. Ever hear of an All-Pro defensive end named Swearingen?"

"Sure."

He looked at her in surprise. Somehow, women were not supposed to know about defensive ends.

"Mr. Swearingen was my ticket to the *Messenger*, in a strange way. He owned a disco back in Ohio. He was the featured vocalist in it. One of those insane coincidences. I wrote some articles. He got embarrassed."

"You criticized his singing?"

"He criticized mine. The Syndicate had front money in his establishment. I found out about it . . . printed it."

"So Swearingen threatened to break your legs and you used them to get you to New York."

"That's a rotten thing to say and it isn't true." His voice turned cold with irritation. She had a natural talent, he saw, for the putdown.

"*Sorry*. But I mean, that is the natural conclusion one would draw."

He shrugged. "That's the hell of it. It wasn't Swearingen who put the heat on me. It was my newspaper."

"The Mob was into your newspaper?"

"Interesting idea. Might have spiced up the coverage. No, fact was the sports editor was shocked at my stories. Shocked that *I wrote them*. Said my stuff was bad for the 'image' of sports. Warped little kids' minds. Type of thing."

"You're kidding."

"Have you ever been around a sports department? Ever seen a groupie in polyester?"

"Some of them are great reporters."

"Some of them are. The rest of them think of Vietnam as an unconfirmed rumor. Drugs? Don't ask them. The sixties haven't happened yet. They think the great ideological choice facing the free world is the Tastes Greats against the Less Fillings. They're starmakers, Jennifer. They live in the reflected light of the heroes they create. They don't want to print anything you couldn't find on the back of a bubble gum card." He sighed and took a deep draught of his beer. "But I bore you."

"Don't be silly. That linebacker . . . Swearingen . . . your stories got him barred from the National Football League, didn't they?"

Teller set his glass down hard. "You're incredible. That was three years ago back in the Bible Belt. How could you possibly know about that?"

"I'm a reporter. I check out things that interest me. Anyway, the story made the papers all over the country. I remember reading about it at U.C.L.A. I was following the Rams then. In fact I knew some of the guys. They loved it when Swearingen got kicked out of the league. He was not only kinky with the Mob, he played *very* dirty football."

Teller stared at her speculatively. He had never known a woman her age with such an ease of access to random information. Her remarks here, at the bar, confirmed a feeling he'd had about her from watching her reports on *WRAP-Around News*: a feeling of a profound worldliness, an almost instinctive capacity for probing the undercurrents of the world around her, a gift for *knowing* who was hot, who was important, and who was soon destined to become so.

And she had run with the L.A. Rams. Why did that information produce a twinge of jealousy? He had hardly known her for an hour.

"Anyway," he went on, "the upshot was they yanked me off sports. Nudged me over to a padded cell in the features department. Told me I had a 'flair' for 'bright writing.' Took away all the pointed instruments. Told me to write nice upbeat pieces about famous celebrities. Well, most of my 'bright writing' went into résumés. One was to *The New York Messenger*. That's how I got here."

"Writing about famous celebrities."

Teller winced and looked away. "Implacable force of history," he muttered. "Is anybody writing about anything else? Well, it wasn't too bad until Adolph Grade took over."

"Ah, yes," said Jennifer. "Dear Adolph. The Canadian Comet. Adolph is an ass, but he has more imagination than any American publisher I know of."

"You call what he does to newspapers 'imagination'? It seems to me that he's all but destroyed the *Messenger*."

Jennifer's mouth shifted to one side as she regarded the ember of her cigarette. "He's increased the circulation by seventy-five thousand in eleven months. I wouldn't call that 'destruction.' "

"But, Jesus, look what he's done to the contents. That used to be a writer's paper. Now it's UFOs and orphans and 'Sex Secrets of Anwar Sadat.' "

"You're complaining? That sort of stuff paid your salary. *Is that why you quit?*"

Teller sighed ruefully. "You're close. You remember the celebrated rapist who was all the rage a few weeks ago?"

Jennifer laughed. " 'Rising Son'? Sure. I interviewed his mother after he was caught. If I was a man and had a mom like that, I'd be a rapist, too. She probably stage-managed his nickname."

Teller wished this hadn't gotten as far as it had. But he had blundered along too far with his story to turn back now.

"You remember the sketch?" he asked.

"The sketch?"

"The composite sketch. The, uh, police artist's sketch that ran in the *Messenger*. The one that was drawn from the descriptions of the victims."

Jennifer stared blankly at Teller for several seconds. Then she sat upright, hands flying to her mouth, and emitted a loud shriek of hilarity. Several patrons at the bar turned their heads to gape.

"HIS PENIS!" Jennifer crowed, clapping her hands in glee. Teller shut his eyes.

"You resigned because of the *penis*!" Jennifer's voice seemed to reverberate through the bar. "Oh, Mark, how absolutely *chaste* of you. My God, you *are* a straight arrow after all, aren't you? That's a wonderful story. That's a real inspiration to us all."

Teller felt his face burning. "Look," he began angrily, "it wasn't that I was *shocked* by the goddamn *penis*. But I don't think a newspaper . . ."

Jennifer's jawline had developed a hard edge.

"You've got a lot to learn, Teller. That drawing was a great publicity stunt. Do you think the *Daily News* or the *Post* would have held back if they'd thought of it first?

"And don't think you've walked into some kind of garden of virtue at WRAP. If Ed Kurtis could think of a way to put a prick on the air and not lose his license, he'd do it." She gave a humorless snort. "I guess he *has* done it, in a way, with Lon Stagg as anchorman. But you've got to come down off your moral high horse if you're going to cover what you're covering in this city, Mark. People don't want to be preached to. And there *is* that side of you. You're a good writer and a lousy moralizer. It'll be interesting to see which side of you wins out."

Despite her open and amused contempt for his peculiar sensibilities, Jennifer Blade made it clear (she made everything clear; subtlety was not among her aptitudes) that she was attracted to Teller. The logic of it baffled him. It was not that he was unsuccessful with women. On the contrary, women were drawn to his boyish good looks, his lean runner's body, his obvious intelligence and his innate gentle nature, and tended to romanticize him.

But Jennifer Blade! Her, he imagined consorting with senators. With rock stars. With potentates of oil-rich Middle Eastern emirates. With the goddamn Los Angeles Rams. Jennifer Blade was not a romanticizing woman.

And yet . . .

Four days later, on a golden Thursday evening, Jennifer presented herself at Teller's west side apartment for a dinner of cold lobster salad and Montrachet. She looked fresh and young, almost girlish, in faded jeans, a striped polo jersey, scuffed canvas shoes, and—always, with Jennifer, a discordant note—thick white sweat socks.

In her right hand she carried an overnight bag.

Teller would always remember, with bittersweet affection, that the last articles of clothing to fall away from her body on that first, golden, humid evening were the white sweat socks. He would remember watching them tease the insides of his legs as they both sat in their jeans, naked to the waist, facing each other on Teller's sofa, sipping the last of the wine—Teller aroused and astonished at the directness of her sexuality (the Ozarker in him had braced for the usual circuitous gallantries of seduction); Jennifer, with an orange patch of fading sunlight illuminating one bare shoulder—ironic, mysterious, amused.

On the bed, surrounded by the dim shelves of Teller's books, his writing desk in shadow, one of his matted photographs (an Ozark valley in spring) tinged with a dull orange ribbon of sunlight, soft Coltrane humming on the stereo, Jennifer had lain with her shoulders off the edge of the mattress, her thick hair piled beneath her on Teller's bare floor.

Crouched above her, he had wanted to explore the damp dark body that seemed to unfold for him with infinite languid ease; had wanted to luxuriate in the leg-flesh now taut, now pliant and humid to his touch; had wanted to kiss the elongated soft torso, to contemplate the biblical breasts stretched back, but inviting, against her rib cage; had longed to feast for hours in the secret rain forest. But . . .

"Come into me!" her whisper was harsh. "Now!"

She had screamed once and drawn him tightly with her strong thin arms locked at the small of his back, and in the violent rush of his orgasm he had catapulted himself down on top of her, so that the two of them had tumbled, limbs locked, like erotic wrestlers, crashing to the bedroom floor.

When his breath had returned to normal and the blur passed from his eyes, he could see that she was laughing silently, propped up on her elbows, her head resting against the side of his bed:

"That was fantastic. Where are my cigarettes?"

"Why did you come here? Why the hell are you interested in me?"

Her cigarette ember glowed. "Would you think I was handing you a line if I said you were different?" Two thin fingers pinched the inside of his knee. She giggled.

His own hand kneaded the luxuriant curve of her thigh. "I bet you say that to all the guys. Seriously. I don't understand it. You could have any man in New York."

"And probably will. Ouch! Kidding, Teller. Don't ask so many questions. Just enjoy it. I'm the best you'll ever have, Buster."

"Seriously. Why?"

He heard the long exhalation of cigarette smoke in the dark next to him.

"Because you just might become very, very good in this city. Very powerful. If you stop moralizing. And that intrigues me. And you're nice. Hell, I don't know, Teller. Who's to say about sex?"

"How about you, Jennifer? What's going to happen to you?"

Even in the darkness, he knew that her jawline was hard and her deep-brown eyes cold and fixed.

"I'm going to become the first anchorwoman for the Continental Broadcasting Network. And God help anybody who gets in my way. You or anybody else, Mark."

That was all three months ago. Since then, their affair had grown sexually intense, Jennifer's lovemaking insistent, abrupt, and at times almost touching a certain concealed violence in her character.

But the tender moments, since that first night, had become rare. Irritability punctuated by sexual need—that was the cycle of Jennifer Blade's response toward Teller.

Now, in the taxi, speeding east on 66th Street toward Second Avenue, Jennifer Blade was silent. She had positioned herself well over on the far side of the seat, to herself, her legs crossed away from Teller, one elbow resting on her lap. She smoked a cigarette and stared out the window.

Teller was never comfortable with the angry silences of women, but Jennifer Blade's silences were more lacerating than any he could remember. There was something almost vicious about them. The very skin on her face seemed to freeze and harden; it was as though she had retreated inside herself to some brittle chamber of the mind. The aggressive aspect of her silences made it difficult, but not impossible, to perceive in them a terrible anguish, a private struggle with an ancient raw wound.

Conversation in these circumstances was not promising, as Teller had painfully learned. But a long, hot summer evening stretched ahead. He determined to make an effort.

"So Bobby Lee Cooper died," he intoned, looking out his own window, keeping his voice deadpan. "I'd call that a pretty shrewd career move."

The effect of this remark on Jennifer was cataclysmic. She whipped about to face the startled Teller, her honey-blond hair brushing across her face. She had been holding a cigarette between her lips in the center of her mouth, and she kept it there; it bobbed as she lashed at him through clenched teeth.

"Bobby Lee Cooper was a great artist and a hell of a man," she raged at him, spitting little puffs of smoke with each syllable. "What the *hell* right have you got to make jokes about his dying?"

Once again, Jennifer Blade had caught Teller speechless. He gaped at her with a grin of disbelief.

As monomaniacal as they were in their loyalty, Cooper's fans, Teller had always believed, comprised the Great Unwashed—the people who watched reruns of *Hee Haw* and memorized fried chicken jingles and sent in their six ninety-nine for the *Great Sounds of the Sixties*.

But now Teller realized he had not given Bobby Lee his complete due: his admirers included the educated, sophisticated, worldly Jennifer Blade.

"A great artist," he repeated at last, searching the blazing brown eyes beneath Jennifer's tortoise-shell sunglasses. "Bobby Lee Cooper was about as great an artist as Tommy Leonetti. What was *great* about him was the flacks around him; they merchandised him like Alka-Seltzer. Jesus, Jennifer, you ought to know that. You've been around show business."

He braced for a probable Jennifer Blade response—a shriek of vitriol followed by her bolting from the cab. Instead, she sat studying him impassively, motionless except for a characteristic nervous twitching at the corner of her mouth. The woman was unfathomable.

They both lurched as the taxi bounced across Park Avenue just ahead of a red light.

Teller sighed and sank back in his seat, gazing up at the taxi's ceiling. He raised his hands, balled them into fists, and let them fall into his lap.

Jennifer's unexpected admiration for Bobby Lee Cooper had made Mark Teller jealous of a corpse.

"Listen," he said after a minute. "If you want an apology for stepping on your toes, you've got it. I didn't know you were a fan of his, for Chrissake. But if you expect *me* to shed tears over a greaseball hillbilly who . . ."

"Don't hand me any of that greaseball hillbilly crap! Look who's talking!" Jennifer was stabbing her cigarette out in the door handle's tin ashtray. "Don't let your meteoric rise to eastern media stardom go to your head, Mark. There's still a lot of hick in you, and a lot of people are beginning to notice it."

"Jennifer . . ."

"Oh, don't worry, lover, it's considered endearing. So far. You're very lumberjack, and the women adore you. So far. The point is, you don't understand Pop as much as you think you do. You don't grasp, for instance, that you're riding pretty much the same kind of image-trip that Cooper was on. Oh, you're different. He was all groin and you're all head. He was a rock'n'roll star, you're a minor cult figure in SoHo and the Upper East Side. But you're an outsider, and it shows. You *are* from the sticks. That's part of your charm, and it was part of his charm. It's not what you say or what you sing, it's whatever fantasies you can tickle in people's heads."

"I understand that." He wasn't quite sure he did.

"I'm sure you do. But let's get back to Bobby Lee, lover. You were surprised when I said I admired him. Don't be naive. I got off on his music. Sure, I know all about the glitter and hype. That's how my father made his fortune. But I love it. Most American women do. They love the illusion. It's *sexy*, lover. And let's face it"—her voice sank to a whisper—"Bobby Lee was an incredible hunk."

Teller had been staring straight ahead, through the scratched Plexiglas divider toward the onrushing buildings of 66th Street. His fists had clenched again as he tried to fight back the irrational rush of jealousy. At Jennifer's last words, he turned to glare at her, and he saw that once again, this most enigmatic of beautiful, changeable women had changed. Her features had softened with her voice. And though her words were mocking, her manner was sexual.

"It's like with Sinatra—she leaned toward him and laced his ear with a sudden wet tongue—"you know I'm turned on by Sinatra" —again, the tongue; Teller felt a white heat rise in him and he shuddered—"you know I know the stories, how he has had people beaten up"—he felt the weight of her large left hand above his knee—"how he's tight with unsavory people"—again the tongue; the hand slid higher on Teller's tight denim—"how he calls newswomen two-dollar whores"—she took his wrist with her free hand and placed it on her own knee, under the hopsack; Teller, in delirium, felt the shock of cool flesh and he realized for the first time that Jennifer was not wearing hose, she must have removed them at the studio—"I'd still go anywhere to hear him sing"— Teller's hand thrust deeply into cool enveloping thigh—"he turns me on, his world turns me on, power turns me on"—lips whispering inside his ear, now, the thin strong fingers of her left hand fluttering expertly at his crotch—"and that's why I turn on to you, darling"—more tongue; thighs parting—"even though I hate you sometimes when you're a moralizing klutz"—his ear a buzz of moist erotic murmurings, his vision red; Teller arched his sweating back upward from the taxi seat—"because you have power and I'm going to see to it that you come . . ."

"Aaaaaaaaaaaaahhhhhhhhhhh!" roared Teller as the taxi screeched to a halt at the corner of 66th and Second Avenue. The driver, thinking, "holdup," whirled around and yelled, too: "Aaaaaaahhhhhh! . . . what the *hell*?" his eyes bulged in their oily sockets.

When the red maze cleared from Teller's vision, he turned to see a prim, composed, crisp Jennifer Blade sitting on the seat next to him, knees primly together.

". . . a long way," she was saying, as though concluding a casual thought begun long ago. "Mark, I think you need a handkerchief. We're here, Mark. Mark, *pay the man!*"

Stitch's at 9 P.M. resembled the inside of a grotesque department-store dollhouse, in that cacodemonic hour after the store has darkened and the dolls come to life.

It was a comic Valhalla; the corporeal fantasy of a bloated child strung out on Scooby's Laff-a-Lympics and Count Chocula.

Jennifer took three steps inside and planted her feet. Teller, following close behind, bumped into her.

"My God. Mark, this is a lunatic ward. Let's get out of here."

Teller lowered his lips to Jennifer's ear.

"Shhhh. Line of duty. Come on, let's have a drink at the bar anyway."

The bar itself, with its polished L-shaped counter, its gleaming rows of bottles stacked beneath an ancient oak-frame mirror, was the only recognizable element in what once had been a modest east side neighborhood bistro. The rest of the place had been festooned with the frantic paraphernalia of comic overkill.

Everywhere were icons to the Great God Yuk: smiling red lips splashed on the walls, disembodied violet grins—visual aids, the familiar figurative nudge in the ribs that accompanies much of commercial American mirth. Laughter not canned as much as aerosolized, spray-painted into the woodwork—the place was heavy with howls and hee-haws, good nature unnaturally preserved like butterfly wings.

For Stitch's was serious about its product. The way Al Gnagy looked at it, it was a question of supply and demand. He was a businessman providing a commodity the public wanted; if the public wanted laughter, or Laffs, they could find it at Stitch's—cost-efficient, high-inventory, fast-turnover Laffs, emanating like jelly beans from the lips of his mostly youthful stable of "talent": aspiring comedians who would work for nearly nothing, or nothing. One-liners. That was what these kids could stand up there and spout all night, one-liners. Gnagy had no particular love for his entertainers, pathetic asses most of them, but as a businessman he had a certain respect for the one-liner. It was the perfect distillation of humor as he saw it, the distinctive American touch: to strip an idea of all its nonessentials, round it out, eliminate the elements of surprise and mass-produce it cheaply for a market that didn't care much for nuances or subtle touches. Bob Hope as the Henry Ford of humor.

"This is the most depressing place I've ever seen in my life," said Jennifer under her breath. She was examining a comic cocktail napkin on the bar in front of her—something about a tee martooni lunch.

"Just don't make eye contact with anybody," he grunted under the whirr of a drink mixer. "We're surrounded by starving comedians. We're fresh meat. We're an audience."

Jennifer turned to her left and surveyed the elongated room: a few small tables, empty save for one group of fat young women in black silk blouses smoking cigarettes and snickering in a way that suggested cruelty. Behind them was the plasterboard partition that divided the bar from the comedy stage. With Jennifer and Teller at the bar, several stools apart, sat three men: a skinny Gene Shalit look-alike in thick glasses and a frizzy Jewish Afro, a leathery middle-aged hipster in West Coast denim and, in the corner at the foot of the L, a sullen, vacant-faced young man studying a Benedictine bottle between his hands, his blond hair illuminated by an imitation candle on the wall.

"I don't see anybody I'd want to make eye contact *with*. Why are we here?"

"I told you. Line of duty. I've been thinking about doing a piece on this place."

Jennifer regarded a cluster of framed, signed glossy photographs under the mirror—Rodney Dangerfield, Marty Allen, Joan Rivers. "Wonderful," she said. "That's just the sort of news judgment that got us where we are now, fourth place in an exciting three-station ratings race. You're catching on to the *WRAP-Around* style, Mark."

"Just keep your sunglasses on and don't raise that famous voice of yours. These savages would cut their mothers' tongues out if it would get them a shot on television."

"Well, they're normal in one respect." Jennifer withdrew a cigarette from her purse, lighted it, snapped the match out, and exhaled smoke through her nose. Teller judged that the novelty of the place had, for her, expired.

"Charlie Byrd is at Sibi. We still have time to make the first set."

"Hey, Jennifer—I'm serious. Line of duty."

She smoked in silence.

After a minute Teller said, "You really did dig Bobby Lee Cooper."

"Yes, I really did."

"Well . . . I'm sorry the guy died." The thought reminded him again of his blunder of the afternoon, of being out of touch when he was needed at the station.

"I just don't want to go in to see Kurtis empty-handed tomorrow, Jennifer. Sometimes a dive like this can surprise you. Sometimes a talent turns up. Two light drafts," he told the soiled shirt of the bartender in front of them.

"Besides, look at it this way. We've entered a time capsule. This place is an honest-to-God subculture. Most of these people are doing stand-up comedy the way Milton Berle did it. This is living nostalgia."

"Nosssstalgia," said a jazzy staccato voice on Teller's right. "Nossssstalgia's not what it used to be."

Teller glanced to his right. The middle-aged customer, four stools away, sat grinning at them. His mouth was twisted into a Jimmy Durante ain't-I-a-card grimace. But his flint eyes remained flat and hard: the shrewd eyes of the journeyman comic, eyes that had sized up the faceless faces in the crowds from the polyester lounges of Las Vegas to the rhinestoned rows at Grossinger's.

He was perhaps forty-five. He had the seamed, soft-leather face of a serious boozer. His sandy hair, thin and askew at startled angles, reminded Teller of an old photograph of Nelson Algren. There was a restless intelligence in the flint eyes. Teller saw that although the comic recognized neither him nor Jennifer, he understood that they did not just happen into Stitch's.

Teller gave the man a curt nod and started to turn back to Jennifer.

"The comedy of today is the jazz of yesterday."

It was a challenge, an invitation. The comic was working him. Flattering him with an aphorism, an intellectual's one-liner.

Despite his better judgment and Jennifer's protesting squeeze on his arm, Teller turned to face the man.

"Wyler's the name." A thick right hand came up. Teller took it, surprised at the strength of the grip. He remained silent.

"Same name as the director," Wyler pointed out after a speculative second, his flint eyes darting now to Jennifer's face. "I know 'im. He helped me out on the Coast. When I'm out there, I always call 'im up, I always get right through. Yeah, I know all those guys." Wyler's right knee jiggled under the bar. Teller had a sudden image of pay telephone booths inside bus stations at night. Of hair oil and furtive Certs.

"You were saying about jazz and comedy."

"Oh, yeah . . . the hell was I? . . . oh, yeah. Hey, I used to be in jazz. I used to be a clarinetist, right? Wanna see sump'in?"

With a quick motion, Wyler flashed a walking stick that had been resting under the bar. Wyler unscrewed the top third of the walking stick. He placed the end between his thin lips and blew a quick and delicate arpeggio.

"That's fantastic," whispered Jennifer.

"Yeah," said Wyler. He glanced down at the makeshift flute, turned it over in his hands, then let it drop into his lap. "Yeah, I used to do a lot of gigs with the big bands; Charlie Parker at the London House in Chicago, places like that."

"The London House is now a Burger King." Jennifer's chin was cupped in her hand, and she was looking at Wyler with interest now. Teller glanced at her with his usual incredulity at her depth of random information.

"You got it, baby," said Wyler. "That's why I'm a comic. You can't swing with a Whopper." Jennifer nodded. "Yeah, the jazz spots all dried up, that little box up there"—he pointed at the TV screen above the bar—"helped knock it off, and now it's doin' the same thing to comedy. No minor leagues, right? You understand where I'm comin' from? No little spots, no clubs anymore, where a kid can work on his material."

"Isn't that what this place is supposed to be? Don't they call it a comedy workshop?"

Wyler snorted. "Comedy workshop. Fuckin' comedy *sweat*shop. Pardon my French," this with a nod to Jennifer, who wrinkled her nose amiably. "Kids come here, they come right out on a conveyor belt from their parents' rec rooms in Newark; they come right outta Plywood, Minnesotasville, where they been watchin' television since they was *weaned*. Right outta the hothouse. They grew up on Dick Van Dyke and Fred Flintstone, and maybe last night they seen David Brenner guest-host Johnny Carson. They do a few lines in front of the bedroom mirror, and all of a sudden they're goddamn *celebrities*. They don't know nothin', they don't read the papers, they don't have any opinions to wise off *about*, but see, it don't matter. They grew up on television jokes. It gets in your blood, it's like jazz used to be, it's the *way* you talk to one another, man."

He drummed his fingers on the bar. "Where you people from?" He made it sound offhand. But Teller had seen the hard flint eyes probing, sizing them up, and he knew that the man sensed what they were about.

"Upper East Side." And then, as though the thought just struck him, "Did you hear about Bobby Lee Cooper? He died this afternoon."

"No shit." Wyler stopped drumming his knuckles. He seemed genuinely moved.

"He couldna been more'n forty, forty-two years old. Where'd it happen?"

"Las Vegas. His hotel suite. Drug overdose."

"Jesus." Wyler's cocky facade evaporated. He sat staring at the floor, swinging one scuffed boot in a thoughtful circle. There was real pain in the boozy, soft-leather face. It occurred to Teller that Wyler may have sensed a preview of his own obituary.

The next voice was Jennifer's.

"I'd call that a real good career move, wouldn't you?"

Wyler looked up sharply. His seamed face split into a wide grin.

"Ha ha *ha* ha ha ha!" He slapped the bar hard with the open palm of his hand. " 'Good career move!' Jesus, I gotta remember that for the act. That's terrific!"

The bartender reached for their empty beer glasses. "Show starts in about five minutes, folks. You want another round, you can take it inside with you."

"Hey, I gotta run," said Wyler. He slid off the stool. "Ciao. 'Good career move.' Jesus."

After he was gone, Teller pivoted slowly on his stool to gaze at the inexplicable woman next to him.

"I thought . . ." he began.

"I liked him," said Jennifer. "I wanted to cheer him up. God, Mark, I grew up with that kind of man around the house all the time. Daddy's friends. Not friends, I guess. Yes-men. They all dress alike, they all crack the same jokes, they all smoke the same cigars, they're all going somewhere. They're all going to make it big in Vegas, because they know all the lines, they know the right agents, they have connections. They never make it. But they never break down. They never get old. They're crude and macho, and I guess I admire them. I think that if I were a man, I'd be one of them."

Teller gazed into her eyes behind the smoked glasses, then shook his head.

"Let's go see the show."

Teller did not expect the comedy at Stitch's to rival Monty Python's Flying Circus.

He was not prepared, however, for the horror show that ensued.

The stage was a small raised wooden platform lighted by a single, remorseless beam. Teller thought of a police lineup. A floor microphone stood at center stage. At stage left a thin kid in a white T-shirt hunched over the keyboard of an upright piano. When the chairs under the audience had stopped scraping, the kid lifted two vampire's claws and played a fanfare.

Onto the stage stalked a moon-faced man whose dark brow hung over his eyes like a football helmet. He was dressed in the aggressive spiff of a conventioning barber: a tight-fitting green body shirt with Donald Duck faces printed on it, and knife-creased navy slacks. His pig eyes, set close together, glittered under the cavern of his brow as he surveyed the audience.

He snatched the mike out of its cradle with a let's-get-down-to-business gesture. His left hand smoothed the cord back as he squinted at the piano player.

"How do you like the *house orchestra*, laze an' gen'men? How 'bout a hand for Bruce, *okay!*"

Two or three people clapped. Jennifer folded her arms and sank deeply down into her chair. "I don't believe this," she announced quietly.

"My name's Johnny Sticka, I'm your master of ceremonies, we got a great show for ya tonight." The moon-faced figure paced back and forth across the little stage flicking the mike cord out behind him. His voice was hitting the low modules like a deejay's. "Little later on, we'll be passing out *free cocaine*, heeeeeyyyyyy!" He froze and shot one arm into the air, in the manner of a trapeze artist who had just accomplished a triple somersault. The audience sat stupefied until it dawned on some of the more alert members that this was a cue to laugh.

But Sticka seemed miffed by the pause; he brushed the polite chuckles aside by bellowing into the mike.

"Got a great lineup of comedians for ya, laze and gen'men, one guy couldn't make it tonight, he swallowed *nineteen razor blades and threw up! Okay!*"

Jennifer, whose head was resting on the top of her chair, rolled it to stare up at Teller in silent accusation. Her mouth was a tight line.

"Not too hot so far, huh?" whispered Teller. He glanced into the darkness around him. He could see upturned, expectant faces, the smiles already half on . . . these people were *waiting* to laugh, waiting politely until they understood it was time.

"We're gonna have a contest after the show," brayed the emcee. "The winner gets to ball an albino *midget!* Okaaaayyyyy!" Silence, then a few respectful, nervous titters. A withering glance. "This must be a masochist's field trip," he whispered.

Jennifer did not remove her gaze from the ceiling. Her head still resting on the back of her chair, she let out a long hiss of breath.

"Don't you get it, Teller? These people *want* to like the show. Look around you. They're all Plymouth dealers. If they can pretend the scene is groovy, that means *they're* groovy. Oh, God. Why do I bother?" She crossed her arms.

Johnny Sticka thrust his heavy-browed face in the direction of Jennifer's murmured voice. "Heeeeeyyyyy," he bawled with bogus good humor. "We got a lady inna audience who wants to say a few words! Excuse me, ma'am, for talking while you're inter-ruptinnnnnng!"

"Drop dead, you pitiful creep." Jennifer's cool voice floated out on a note of authority that hushed the entire room.

For a moment Johnny Sticka stood there on stage holding his hand microphone as though it were a cigar that had just exploded in his face. He opened his mouth, then thought better of it. "Heeeyyyyy, we're gonna keep it rolling right along. Let's begin our Comic Cavalcade with a sensational young act . . . direct from Trenton, New Jersey . . . "

The ensuing forty-five minutes made Wyler's barstool assess-ment of Stitch's seem charitable. The "comedy workshop" that unfolded resembled a group-therapy session as conducted by the Mad Hatter.

The succession of pallid post-adolescents who swaggered on-stage, smirks pasted on their domestic faces in approximation of worldly amusement, were not only hopeless.

They were interchangeable.

And the audience loved them. Embraced them with a whooping mother-love, the hollowness of its laughter echoing the hollowness of the repartee.

There were endless parodies of television newscasts—the outer frontier of experience, Teller gathered, for most of the per-formers. The temperature in Los Angeles was always "high." The Boston anchorman sounded like a Kennedy. The Miami anchor-man sounded like a hood.

"Women are really making strides in a lot of areas," began a mustachioed cherub, his head revolving in an am-I-right? gesture. The audience poised for the zinger. Apparently, the zinger eluded the mustachioed cherub—either that, or the line *was* the zinger, because his next utterance was, "Let me ask you a question: Have you ever driven a car totally stoned? RIGHT?"

Teller kept shifting his large frame in his chair. He wanted it to end. The day had gone out of control, and this was the final mock-ery, this assault of doggy, banal wit: the braces-on-teeth jokes, the Bar Mitzvah jokes, the limp parodies of television. It was a loser's enclave, and God, what was he doing here with Jennifer Blade? Jennifer Blade, who had spoken of being charmed by Walter Matthau's whimsy in the emberglow of "A"-list barbecues at her father's glittering ranch.

A kid who looked like a former college linebacker came onstage and made some jokes about retarded children. The audience laughed nervously. The hulking kid asked the table of eight where they came from. Somebody at the table said New Jersey. "New Jersey," said the ex-linebacker, "New Jersey's sort of the *Poland of the United States!*"

"Hey, hey, great," said Sticka.

Wyler was up next. Now, for the first time during the evening, Stitch's was charged with an air of crisp comic professionalism.

Wyler's material was not the greatest. But he knew timing. He knew how to let rhythm and pacing cover the mildewed edges of his act. He stood before the microphone, one knee bent in, one hand on his hip, the other smoothing back his shock of hair. He talked rapidly with his eyes closed, as though communing with an inner voice, almost like a musician calling up old familiar rhythms, and his act was good. Nothing for the ages. But solid, economical, commercial stand-up comedy.

He talked about the cops in New York City—"I'm in Times Square in my car, and a hairy arm reaches out and yanks me out the door. And I don't care how tough you are, you gotta be scared of a hooker that mean!"

He talked about the dogshit problem around Times Square: "The dogs are so bad, the hookers wear hip boots. But if you own a dog and you don't clean up, the law will step in."

He talked about the new postage stamp honoring a recent president—"It never caught on 'cause too many people spit on the wrong side." He did some fast, accurate topical humor, taken from the front-page story of the week.

The audience sat on its hands.

When his act was over, Jennifer was the only one in the room clapping after the perfunctory applause died down.

"They don't even know when they're getting entertained, the dopes. All right, Teller, I'm ready." She leaned down to grope for her purse on the floor.

Johnny Sticka was back onstage.

"*Bill Wyler,* laze and gen'men," he brayed, holding his right arm aloft. Billy'll be appearing at the *men's room* at the *Port Authority! Okay!*"

"You can't carry his union card, you little cretin," muttered Jennifer from below the table. Teller winced; that was loud enough to hear, and he really didn't want this day of blunders to end with a confrontation. God, that would be about all Kurtis would need.

But Sticka didn't hear, or again was pretending not to hear. "We're gonna keep it rolling right along, laze and gen'men," he was booming into the mike. "Our last act of the evening, last but not least . . . our piano player's on *speed*, laze and gen'men, *okay*! Our last act of the evening, direct to Stitch's from a sensational week at the *Brooklyn Public Library* . . . let's have a big hand for *Robert Schein!*"

Teller looked at his wristwatch. Ten forty-five. "Might as well sit through the last act," he whispered to Jennifer. She shrugged and nodded.

The comedian now making his way out of the darkened wings bore no resemblance to the assembly line of comics who had preceded him. He was somewhat older than the faceless suburbanites, but younger than Wyler. Teller put his age as somewhere short of thirty-five.

The man didn't prance, he didn't scoop up the microphone. He took up his position with the understated grace of an actor walking onto a dramatic stage. The spotlight illuminated a wheat-wave of blond hair.

"He's the guy at the end of the bar," whispered Jennifer. "He was knocking back the Benedictines pretty good. Let's see if he's smashed and grosses all these children out, I hope."

The comic Schein stood poised at the microphone, his fingers absently working the microphone's level-ring. There was no anxiety in his face, none of the suppressed audience-terror they'd seen so often tonight. But neither was there any hint of Wyler's quick, penetrating street wisdom. It was the noncommittal, casually handsome face that one sees in the blurred background of an ad for Teacher's or After Six.

Several seconds had gone by now, and the room had grown quiet. Schein had not moved—save for his fingers working and reworking the level-ring. His clothing gave no clue to the type of comedy he might specialize in; it was neither sloppy-affecting, nor funky, nor Vegas, nor brittle-hip. He wore a soft-gray sports jacket, a dark, knitted tie, and a blue shirt.

Some nervous titters now broke the heavy silence in the room—as though the audience were unsure whether it should be appreciating some subtle joke, some awfully laid-back put-on.

Schein's face was expressionless. There was no comic twinkle in the eyes, no playful smile at the corners of his mouth to indicate what he might be up to. He was a statue except for the slowly twisting and untwisting fingers; he appeared almost in a trance. The effect on the audience was hypnotic. No one spoke.

Even Jennifer seemed caught up in the unexpected suspense. The frozen moment stretched into twenty seconds. Thirty. Forty-five. A minute. Someone cleared his throat. Someone else suppressed a giggle.

Robert Schein collapsed.

The movement was so sudden that everyone in the room sucked in breath at once. Schein's knees went rubbery; he began to weave in oblong circles—and then he went down like a rag doll, his entire body going soft and wavy. He lay sprawled on the stage on his back, still clutching the microphone, which he had pulled over on top of himself.

The audience's first reaction had been a collective gasp; its second, an instant later, was even more stunning.

The room convulsed.

Everyone was laughing, applauding. Roaring. Guffawing. This was not the anxious forced laughter that Teller and Jennifer had heard all evening, desperate sycophantic yuks. This laughter was pure, it was a release. It danced around the room in shock waves. Teller and Jennifer looked at one another—and realized that each was wearing a sheepish grin. They looked back toward the stage. The laughter was subsiding, finally, and one or two people were starting to wonder whether it was, in fact, a routine. "Is he all right?" a girl whispered to her date.

But now Schein was back on his feet—to a renewed round of applause and whistles. He had sprung up so quickly that the move, like his collapse, had taken everyone by surprise; it was as though invisible wires had pulled him upright.

Schein's expression had not changed. He stood frozen for a few seconds, regarding the audience with the same enigmatic stare.

Then he took a step to his left, away from the microphone, bowed deeply from the waist, raised his right hand in a salute, and was gone.

In the taxi headed for Jennifer's apartment, Jennifer plucked Teller's amorous hand from the cool skin of her leg.

"None of that. You have to go home and be fresh for your court-martial in the morning."

"I don't know why the hell I can't leave a suit or two at your place."

"Tacky. What would I tell my other lovers?"

"That isn't funny, Jennifer."

"Oh. Look who's saying something isn't funny. What about the evening you just dragged me through?"

"You know what I mean." Teller, who had never before felt possessive toward the women in his life, detested Jennifer's sexual banter. He wasn't sure it was entirely banter. She knew it, and enjoyed toying with his jealousy.

She lighted a cigarette. "Well, which one of those comedic masterminds are you going to make a star?"

Teller was staring out the window; he wanted to pursue the subject of their relationship. He always wanted to pursue the subject of their relationship. It was a bothersome subject. And a futile pursuit.

"I don't know," he said absently. "I thought maybe I'd see if I could get a camera crew down and film that last guy do his collapse."

"*What?*" Jennifer lurched forward. "And ignore Wyler? Oh, Mark, that's a crime."

Teller snorted. He was in no mood to indulge Jennifer Blade her whims.

"Wyler didn't get a single laugh from the crowd. The other guy, Schein, brought down the house. Besides, it'll look good on film."

"You're really going to do that."

"I really am, yes."

Jennifer sat back in the far corner of the seat and folded one arm across her waist, clutching her elbow. With her free hand she smoked for a minute. Her deep-brown eyes were slitted in thought. Teller saw the jawline harden.

"Just like God, this business," she said finally. "It scares me sometimes. If we don't create 'em, they don't get created. They don't exist." She gave a cold laugh and looked sideways at Teller.

"I wonder if poor Wyler'll ever know he missed his big opportunity because you didn't get laid tonight?"

The Commerce Center was an unlikely setting for a broadcasting network headquarters.

But then, CBN was an unlikely broadcasting network.

A squat old sandstone fortress of thirty stories, nearly as thick as it was high, the Center lacked the Art Deco dash and thrust of Rockefeller Center, which housed NBC. It could in no way match the soaring high-rise insolence of the ABC building at 54th and Sixth, nor the fastidious gray Saarinen sweep of CBS headquarters, with its famous address —51 West 52nd.

Not even its location conferred on the Center the dignity of an American communications pantheon. Far from Broadcast Row, it rose like a hulking panhandler above the low storefronts and truck-rumble of Ninth Avenue in the 60s. Its ponderous ornamentation, the Six Captains, fixed their blind stares at its stained gray sandstone walls, their patrician heads turned away from the crumbling neighborhood behind them.

And yet it would be a serious mistake to judge the Center's star tenant by the building's architecture and location: the Continental Broadcasting Network (with its flagship stations, WRAP-TV, WCBN Radio, and W-101-FM) comprised one of the most astonishing success stories in the history of American communications.

The Commerce Center was simply the best accommodation that Eddie Donovan, "The Colonel," could find when he made his daredevil bid in 1952 to launch a fourth network in competition with the established giants.

Now, nearly thirty years later, CBN was both the miracle and the despair of the telecommunications industry. Its total billings for the previous year were $1,007,950,000, fourth place to be sure, but only a shade behind NBC. Two of its prime-time series, *Celebrity Strip Poker* and *The Brawlers* (A Sterling Blade Production) were in the Nielsen Top Ten. The CBN Nightly News, anchored by MacGregor Walterson, reached a respectable seventeen million American households. True, the flagship station's elaborately produced two-hour newscast, *WRAP-Around News* with Lon Stagg, trailed its competitors by a margin not easily smiled away by the public-relations department.

But the Colonel and his lean young lieutenants were determined to do something about that.

In fact, the general atmosphere throughout CBN and its stations was akin to that of combat troops poised for a sneak attack. Talk of "breakthrough" was in the air—breakthrough into ratings parity, once and for all, with the Old Guard. CBN was a hungry network; it already had a reputation as a rogue elephant, dangerous in its impulses, likely to charge in any direction when its competitive blood was up.

As such, CBN reflected the personality of its founder and president. Colonel Eddie Donovan was a magnificent scavenger. He had assembled his empire out of castaway parts in the 1950s, taking shrewd advantage of two seemingly unconnected phenomena: the anti-Communist "Red Scare" of that decade, and a little-understood, mostly ignored tuning knob that was appearing on some of the newer television receivers.

CBN was an all-UHF network.

Every one of its owned and affiliated stations broadcast on the "ultra-high frequency" band—the channels above 13. Donovan and his associates had collected these white-elephant stations at throwaway prices in the 1950s, when no one else had been able to figure out how to make them profitable.

Eddie Donovan knew how. The knack was in the very air around him. Eddie Donovan understood the air.

In retrospect—as *Time* magazine remarked in its cover story on Colonel Donovan in 1963—it was inevitable that the Colonel would fuse patriotism and puttering to promulgate new provinces of public discourse.

Eddie Donovan had emerged from an Easter basket washed up on the shores of the United States from the docks of Dublin. The Easter in question was Easter 1916. Even as British troops were combing Ireland for the remnants of the Sinn Fein Rising, the six-year-old child arrived shivering at Boston harbor in a coal steamer with his ma and his da, the notorious Brian "Red Dog" Donovan, gunrunner for the Irish Republican Brotherhood. The elder Donovan had masterminded and commanded the daring delivery of 1,500 secondhand German Mauser rifles and 49,000 rounds of ammunition to the Irish Volunteers at Howth harbor on Sunday, July 24, 1914. From that day until shortly before Patrick Pearse surrendered his sword at the British barricade in Parnell Street on April 29, 1916, the small boy knew life in the elemental terms of legend.

He knew the dingy shadows of hotel rooms, the eerie silence of journeys by donkey cart through the chill Irish night, the terror of concealment in byres and lofts and strange dark cottages, his pale face pressed deep into the folds of his ma's skirts to muffle his sobs of terror.

He knew the long weeks of waiting in unfamiliar houses in unfamiliar towns, weeks when his da was vanished and his name unspoken; his ma's face sharp and drawn, absorbed in her silent sewing with strange silent women, and no playmates for Eddie, and far from home. In these evenings of agony strange men would come, fierce and gentle like his da, uncles and cousins unknown to him, bringing with them the chill air of danger from the outside, the danger where his da was, and in the firelit evenings one or another of the men would draw a chair away from the rich low circle of adult voices and beckon Eddie, and there would be tales— not of the present, but of the mythic Celtic past: tales of heroes and saints and great battles and the spirits of noble men whose deeds were struck on the night sky; the tales told in the rich and colored imagery of the sanachie, until they took root in the fertile loam of the boy's fantasy, and grew with his own mythic memories, and wound about the awesome and comforting figure that was his own da, until the boy felt that he was living in a world of legend, a world in which good men like his da went out to do battle with disembodied evil spirits that rode on the night air.

The air became a presence in the child Eddie Donovan's personal developing mythos; it became a realm, a palpable if invisible repository where dwelt the forces that absorbed the passions of the strange hurrying adults in his life, and his da and ma. And when his da returned, stepped in off the night air into the welcoming bosom of the strange cottage, red hair flaming in the firelight and thick arms wide, the air filled with the laughter of heroes around him, and the language was the blood language of patriotism, and the child Eddie Donovan came to accept it as his own—the boiling blood-hatred of the unseen despots on the other air that was given articulation by his da and the other strong men long in the blurry evenings of whispers and candlelight, the air heavy and sweet with the breath of poteen.

(Such memories were to be part of the Colonel Eddie Donovan legend. They were, in fact, contained in a singular phonograph album, *The Colonel Recalls,* a series of recorded reminiscences by The Colonel himself, that was distributed to visitors at the Continental Broadcasting Network Library and Museum in Westchester.)

Red Dog Donovan might have fallen before British rifles at the Portobello Barracks—and his wife and child consigned to Kilmainham Prison—had not the Brotherhood itself prevailed on him several days in advance of the Easter Rising, to spirit his considerable salesmanship to Boston in hopes of raising money, and guns, for the Defense of Ireland Fund. Donovan had planned to leave his family in America and return alone to the Rising. Not until the sea-ravaged steamer had docked in Boston harbor did the Donovans learn that the rebellion had failed.

The news broke Red Dog Donovan. The dashing rebel and bold adventurer became a pathetic fixture in the Irish expatriate community of Dorchester Heights, haunting the waterfront speakeasies and retelling the stale legends of Sinn Fein. (When sovereignty did come to the Republic a few years later, Red Dog Donovan was too befuddled by whisky and grief to comprehend.) Out of respect for his past service to Ireland, members of the community saw to it that Eddie and his mother were housed and fed.

Young Eddie witnessed the deterioration of his father. His eyes and ears, sensitized to the slightest nuance through an early childhood in the Irish underground, absorbed the humiliation and rage the elder Donovan felt against the Crown. A resentment of bludgeoning government became forever fixed as the central point of Eddie Donovan's politics. Eddie resented, too, the charity of strangers through which he and his mother survived. His dim infant memories of his father as a grand and honored leader were violated by the sight of the old man now as a virtual beggar. A pride, fueled by anger, began to burn in Eddie Donovan's young heart. What happened to his father would never happen to him.

Eddie Donovan grew up tough and smart among the Irish-Americans of Dorchester Heights. Lambs did not survive long in that gray teeming enclave of longshoremen and their sons, and Eddie learned the ways of an urban wolf. He could take care of himself. His pale, intense face with its soulful blue eyes under sandy curls gave him a poetic aspect that belied the brutality of his fists. Several thin Presbyterian noses were bloodied before the American kids of his acquaintance learned that it was not amusing to repeat their parents' anti-Irish slurs in his presence.

Despite these confrontations, young Eddie was proud to call himself an American. In the curious psychology of many an immigrant child scarred by the bigotry of his adopted country, Eddie developed a fierce patriotism on behalf of the United States.

In 1920—the year in which station KDKA in Pittsburgh pioneered regular broadcasting on the radio airwaves—the ten-year-old Eddie Donovan already had his sights set on the larger world. He was not just another tough, glib, charming Irish kid. He was somebody. He was Gunrunner Red Dog Donovan's son, and in the interconnected enclave of Dorchester Heights, that conferred on him the status of a celebrity: the son of a minor hero of the Republic, although that hero was himself virtually a walking corpse. From his father, Eddie had inherited a silky gunrunner's tongue, a capacity to use the language as an instrument of persuasion. That, and the paternal interest of several Democratic ward-heeler politicians, friends of the slipping elder Donovan, promised to propel Eddie up and out of the immigrant workingman's day-to-day dance with oblivion.

Eddie had inherited one other characteristic from his father: a reverence for apparatus, for things that work, for the inherent divinity of intricate parts. Red Dog's clandestine enterprises had required a certain expertise in such matters: a ship's navigational instruments, the anatomy of firearms, the science of ballistics. At the time he was approached to join the Brotherhood, Red Dog Donovan was not an educated man. He was a simple Wexford fisherman, known for his honesty and stubborn courage, but innocent of the developing complexities of twentieth-century life.

But he was a Republican, an unswerving sympathizer to the cause of Irish severance from the Crown. And if his usefulness to the cause depended on the mastering of new technical skills, there was nothing for it but to master them. It was a remarkable testament to Red Dog Donovan's iron revolutionary discipline that, with the help of his new compatriots in the Brotherhood, he emerged a resourceful jack-of-all-trades in the delicate profession of insurrection: sailor, navigator, ersatz engineer, diplomat, authority on small arms.

And in the dutiful tradition of Irish craftsmen, the elder Donovan endeavored to pass along his new skills to his son.

Of all the instruments and mechanisms in Red Dog Donovan's new arsenal, the jewel was the wireless telegraph machine.

In fact, there were two of them: the Brotherhood had installed one set in the hold of Donovan's coal steamer, the *Curlew*, which, disguised as a Norwegian packet, ran the treacherous course between Lübeck, in Germany, and such Irish ports as Howth and Tralee Bay.

Eddie Donovan never saw this set. He was not allowed near the *Curlew*. But there was a second wireless apparatus, this one in the Donovan's Wexford cottage, in a loft above the living room, concealed in a welter of hay. During the rare times that the Donovans were at home in Wexford between 1914 and 1916, Red Dog would invite his young son to follow him into the loft in the evening, by lantern light, over the protestations of Eddie's anxious ma, and watch as Red Dog's thick fingers twisted the delicate dials and tapped on the clicking key, sending words out on the night air, communing with invisible presences that to young Eddie's mind were no less fabulous than the heroes and spirits in the tales of his strange uncles in the other cottages, when the Celtic night air was sweet with danger.

The wireless set became a powerful force in young Eddie's fantasy. His mind, already overstimulated by the constant intrigue of his own life on the run through the Brotherhood underground and by the fanciful legends of the sanachies, invested the transmitter with an animus of its own. Within its glowing tubes and its arcane dials there resided a living secret, an oracle that spoke the electromagnetic language of the spheres and promised Promethean voyages for those heroes who, like his father, understood the magic of its voice. The transmitter was the child's secret friend. One day he would know its magic as his father did, and together they would ride all the legends of the air.

So it was that Eddie Donovan, the son of a gunrunner, became, in spiritual truth, radio's child. When human voices supplanted the first primitive pips and squeaks of wireless telegraphy in the 1920s, the transplanted Irish youth was awed but not surprised. It was as though a natural promise had been fulfilled. The Promethean voyage was about to begin.

By November of 1920 the ten-year-old Eddie Donovan was a familiar and enterprising figure on the narrow streets and bleak wharves of Dorchester Heights. With the instinct of a born politician (and with the assistance of actual neighborhood politicans, Democratic precinct captains who still venerated the name of Red Dog), the thin, intense child had accumulated something of a power base in the community.

He was out of bed and on the streets at 4 A.M. each day, delivering newspapers to families in the surrounding tenements— papers purchased two for a penny and sold for a penny each; it was arduous work for the boy but it put food on the Donovans' table. With the father a fixture in the speakeasies and the mother taking in consignment sewing, Eddie's contributions helped keep the household together.

The newspaper route gave Eddie a certain visibility among the children of Dorchester Heights. So did his Sunday duties as an altar boy at Saint Michael's Church, a position of some status in the heavily Irish Catholic community. So did his frequent assignments as a door-knocker on behalf of the community's Democratic Club. In business, religion, and politics, young Eddie Donovan was building valuable friendships and earning a respect that had less and less to do with his father's famous name.

(*The Colonel Recalls* album fixed that month, November 1920, as "an autumn of destiny" in Eddie Donovan's life. In that month, the first battery-operated wireless radio receiver arrived in Dorchester Heights, purchased by an order of Jesuit priests at the urging of one of the more socially aware brothers. The Old Man recalls standing in the front rank of the parishioners to gaze at the marvelous instrument, and in his turn, to slip the headset about his ears and listen to the magic sound of disembodied voices on the air.)

What he heard was both historic and prosaic: the returns of the Harding-Cox Presidential elections announced by the voice of H. P. Davis, a vice-president of the newly formed Westinghouse— the first broadcast on the first commercially licensed station in America, KDKA of Pittsburgh.

Whether the small receiver by the Dorchester docks actually picked up that epochal broadcast from far-off Pittsburgh was a matter of some debate by radio historians. But the ensuing months were indelibly inscribed on the record.

Radio swept the national imagination. In two years the number of commercial stations had increased from three to more than five hundred. The sale of radio receivers had become a $136-million business.

The great captains of American industry were indifferent to any question of radio's mission. They did not see the new invention as a lyceum, as a chautauqua, as any kind of theater for ideas or education or enlightenment. The airwaves were another forest to be cleared, another oil well to be dug, another river to be dammed. In due course, they figured, someone would devise a way to turn a profit from the air. For the time being, it sufficed that a new scent of raw power was *in* the air; the air, suddenly, *was* power, and the great brute captains bludgeoned one another to corner the market *on* the air.

Deals were made. Boundaries were drawn. RCA, a cartel of powerful capitalists, snatched up all the patents and assets of American Marconi, a subsidiary company of radio's inventor. RCA entered into cross-licensing agreements with General Electric and Westinghouse. GE and Westinghouse would build the radio sets; RCA would sell them. American Telephone and Telegraph was granted a monopoly to manufacture and distribute broadcast transmitters.

Still, no one had devoted much thought about what to *say* into all of this startling new equipment and technology. It did not seem to matter. Americans were charmed by distant-call letters and sopranos and dance bands. Department stores were setting up radio stations, and newspapers were setting up stations. The bands played on. No one seemed able to think of anything interesting to say.

That aspect of radio broadcasting would have to come from the outside.

In 1924 Eddie Donovan became one of 1,400 Americans to open his own radio station.

The process was not as grandiose as it might seem. Anyone with the few dollars necessary to purchase a tiny five-watt transmitter, and a room in which to put it, was in the radio business. Eddie, who by this time was a bright fourteen-year old student at Boston College High School and the proprietor of a successful string of newspaper routes, had prevailed on the local Democratic Club to advance him the money. The pols had indulged the boy his hobby, and Eddie had set up the transmitter in the attic of the club's headquarters.

For Eddie Donovan, there was never any question as to how the airwaves should be used. The air was for talking, for launching the great tales of heroes into the night, for spinning the ancient legends that electrified and inspired people to become nobler than they were.

At seven o'clock on the night of May 23, 1924, young Eddie turned on his new transmitter and went on the air telling the saga of his father, the gunrunner Red Dog Donovan. There was nothing shrewd or calculating in his choice of subject matter. There was no question of timidity or stage fright; he hadn't given such matters a thought. He had not written out a script in advance, nor even sketched an outline of the story he'd planned to tell. Neither had he attended to such dramatic considerations as elocution, timing, imagery, or the buildup of suspense. Eddie simply sat down in a wooden chair facing the dusty table on which the transmitter rested, turned it on, waited until the tubes warmed up, introduced himself, and in a clear, calm, adolescent's voice, proceeded to recite one of the tales he had heard Red Dog repeat so often along the Dorchester docks.

It was a tale of a moonlit sea chase off the wild Pentland Firth above Scotland in the year 1915, with Red Dog's coal steamer, the *Curlew*, carrying a camouflaged cargo of timber and German

Mauser rifles: pursued by a British patrol boat while twenty-nine British warships were on the lookout; Red Dog's cool navigation through the churning seas of the Pentland Firth; the thump of timber and the cries of sailors; the wash of cold salt sea across the *Curlew*'s bow with the British patrol gaining; Red Dog's daring decision to lead his pursuer between the jagged Scottish coast and the Devil's Finger, a column of rock that stood a half-league off the shore; the British patrol being carried by the waves into the Devil's Finger, and being smashed to pieces under the calm North Atlantic moon.

The story was nearly an hour in the telling—Eddie, without having planned it in advance, assuming the voices of his father and the several sailors as he had heard Red Dog do in the bars. At the end, as though awakening from a dream, he calmly repeated his name, bade all a good night, and turned off his transmitter.

The next morning he awoke to find himself a neighborhood celebrity.

Not many of the immigrant workers in Dorchester could afford radio receivers. But among the ones who could, the household activity centered around the instrument in the evenings—the family arranged in respectful silence on sofas and chairs, while the father attended the ceremony of the dials and knobs and switches.

History did not record which neighboring householder, twisting the dial carefully through the static and the dance music and the ghostly ululation of faraway voices, first happened onto the clear adolescent tenor of young Eddie Donovan recounting, from the Democratic Club attic, the adventure of the *Curlew* off the storm-tossed Pentland Firth. Neighbors later recalled being notified by telephone, by knocks on the door, by invitations shouted across tenement courtyards: put the dial on the young lad tellin' the story of Red Dog. If you haven't a receiver, come join us.

By the end of the hour a strange and wonderful thing had happened along the dockside streets of Dorchester Heights: groups of neighbors clustered in the dozen or so living rooms that had receiver sets. A half-forgotten exhilaration grew in the air, a mischievous sense of festivity that for so many years had been absent from these fugitive families from Ireland's suffering shores. Color returned to drawn cheeks. Women chatted gaily. Men rubbed their hands and cast roguish glances at their wives. In some of the living rooms, accordions were produced and there was dancing.

Friendships that had wilted under the grueling demands of dock-side labor were renewed; old grievances were mended. It was as though young Eddie, in the telling of the saga of Red Dog's daring dash through the Pentland Firth, had told the secret saga of all uprooted Irishmen everywhere; as though the words had somehow entered their veins on the magic of the night air. A great collective truth had been reaffirmed that night within the glowing tubes of Eddie Donovan's five-watt transmitter.

American radio had found something to say.

The rough longshoremen, who always had managed a kind nod for the boy, now rushed to take his hand in theirs. " 'Twas splendid. ' 'Twas a splendid tale, lad. We'll be listenin' for you again this evenin'." Red Dog himself, who had not heard the broadcast, was confounded by a rousing cheer as he shuffled into the Kerry speak-easy. When his companions explained to him what his son had done on the previous night, a long-dead light kindled again in the old gunrunner's eyes. "Surely?" he murmured, looking from face to face.

"Aye. It's a fact."

Red Dog licked his dry lips. For the first time in ten years, he gave his shaggy head a shake and let out a loud roar of laughter.

From that day, Eddie Donovan's rise to the pinnacles of American broadcasting seemed foreordained.

(Vintage photographs on display at the CBN Library and Museum showed a thin, serious-faced young boy in knickers and a starched white shirt, perched formally at a wooden table before an outsized microphone. Next to him, peering solemnly at what obviously was a fake radio script—for the Donovans worked strictly from the heart—was a thick, shaggy-headed bear of an old man, his rampant beard streaked with gray. This was Red Dog, who soon joined Eddie on his nightly broadcasts from the Democratic Club attic.)

As the months went by, Eddie's equipment increased in sophistication and scope—the money being furnished through donations from a grateful community. Soon he was working with a transmitter that beamed his voice throughout Boston. (He had applied for, and received, a license from the Secretary of Commerce, Herbert Hoover.) His free-form reminiscences with his father enthralled families throughout the city; they took on many of the proportions of early soap opera as Red Dog, his life given miraculous new purpose after years of alcoholic despair, proved to be a natural showman and raconteur. A decision by A.T.&T., one month before Eddie's epochal first broadcast, allowed independent stations to solicit sponsors for their programming—and Eddie found the local shopkeepers and merchants more than willing to pay for the honor of being associated with "The Boy Broadcaster." He expanded his station's repertoire to include amateur Irish tenors, folk fiddlers, and Jesuit priests reading community bulletins.

By 1927, Eddie's WIRE was second in popularity only to WNAC—a station operated by the telephone company itself.

By 1931 he was a millionaire.

At precisely 9:30 A.M., Friday, Mark Teller stepped off the elevator at the thirtieth floor of the Commerce Center, the executive office floor of CBN and WRAP, opened a glass door, and strode toward Ed Kurtis's office to face the music.

He was dressed in his normal business ensemble—a tropical worsted suit jacket, dark-blue dress shirt, and orange rep tie over faded dungarees and J.C. Penney sneakers, no socks. Only the top half of Teller's body was visible on camera when he delivered his commentaries, and that half obeyed the dress code. The bottom half expressed Teller's feelings for dress codes in general and for the *WRAP-Around News* team's preoccupation with clothes in particular.

Teller was both fascinated and appalled by his colleagues' notions of couture. When WRAP's motivational research consultants had found that news audiences no longer thrilled to the sight of matching blazers—the galvanic pulse rates were down alarmingly in this area—the anchormen and newsmen had been encouraged to express themselves as individuals. As individuals, they tended to favor a collective look perhaps best described as Upper-East-Side-Brew-Burger-Master-Charge Modern: raffish designer suits, dramatically pinched and flared; great flaps of lapel; billowing silk ties daringly coordinated with the cross-weave of their tapered shirts; calfskin boots shined to Prussian cavalry exactitude.

When fast-breaking news summoned the reporter out on the street, sartorial opulence gave way to tough-minded functionalism. In winter, the reporters peered sternly into their on-location cameras clad in heavy-duty thermal gear that would have served the needs of a ski commando on night patrol near the Laptev Sea: shimmering Abercrombie & Fitch nylon parkas swelling with eiderdown and trussed in place with an intricate assortment of drawstrings and zippers, the fur-lined collars pulled smartly above the ears. (The crewmen aiming the camera and lights at the intrepid correspondent, Teller had observed, were likely to be warmed with surplus navy pea jackets.) The correspondent's circulatory system was further protected by the heated limousine in which he waited until the crew had the cameras and lights arranged just right. On all other occasions short of a heat wave, the reporters' on-location brio was conveyed by majestic trench coats, all epaulets and flaps and slash pockets, the belt-ends tucked back inside the belts just *so*.

No, it could not be said that the *WRAP-Around News* team neglected its appearance. On the contrary, the question of personal choice in dress had become something of a civil-liberties issue at the station. Anchorman Lon Stagg's right to continue wearing his favorite suit, a scarlet denim number set off by navy stitching about the lapels and pockets, was currently a matter of arbitration between Stagg's lawyer and WRAP management.

Only Mark Teller let down the side in the matter of news-team fashion. This fact, coupled with his peculiar squeamishness about the beeper, and his general aura of print-journalism offhandedness, kept Teller outside the *WRAP-Around News* team club.

Teller walked quickly past the main receptionist's desk, where a fat man in a white Stetson and a blue-rhinestone leisure suit was loudly demanding to see whoever ran the station. The receptionist buzzed open a second glass door that led to the carpeted executive-office corridor, and Teller headed for Kurtis's cubicle. He knew that Kurtis would be worrying over the morning papers and sucking at his first cup of coffee. The *WRAP-Around News* department would not organize itself until after ten.

He passed the desk of Charlene, Kurtis's secretary. The nylon cover was still on the typewriter. Good. If Kurtis was going to make noise, Teller would prefer it to be like that of the tree crashing in the empty forest. Executive secretaries knew too much, and knowing, were secret power-brokers. Teller understood that from his own network of sources.

Kurtis's door was ajar and, giving it a ceremonial rap, Teller strode through.

"JESUS H. CRONKITE! LOOK WHO'S HERE! THE PRODIGAL FUCKING SON HAS RETURNED!"

"Good morning, Ed."

"I OUGHTA CAN YOUR ASS, TELLER!"

"Arbitration. My day off."

"FUCK arbitration! You missed the biggest goddamn news story of the year! I'll tell the fuckin' AFTRA to stick arbitration up its ass! What kind of shop do you think we run around here, Teller? This isn't a goddamn newspaper where you can diddle yourself for three hours and then write the story. Somethin' happens, we gotta have it *now*!" Kurtis attempted to bang his fist on his desk, but it sank within a cushion of memos, unanswered letters, newspapers, ratings books, and press releases, and did not produce the emphatic sound Kurtis had intended.

"Ed, listen. I blew it and I'm sorry."

"FUCK SORRY!"

"And if there's any way I can make it up to you, I will. I owe you one. Jesus, you can't have missed me *that* much. One commentary, on deadline?"

Kurtis leaned back in his swivel chair. The tantrum expended itself, and he stared moodily at his belt buckle like a great, simian, crestfallen child.

"Haskell on Seven did a commentary on deadline."

"Haskell on Seven is an idiot."

"No, no shit, Teller. You shoulda seen it. He came on with a stack of his old Bobby Lee Cooper forty-fives, and he broke 'em, one by one. Just snapped 'em in two. It was like a religious ceremony. Like ashes to ashes. Great visual."

Teller stood in front of Ed Kurtis's desk and looked down at the sulking news director. For a wild moment, his entire three months in television news backed up on him like a Rumanian dinner. He wanted to grab Ed Kurtis's shirt and yell into his face, *That is the most disgusting and juvenile stunt I have ever heard, and if that is the kind of material you want out of me, the hell with it, I quit!*

Instead, he placed the heels of his hands on the edge of Kurtis's desk and said softly, "I've got a great one for you tonight. I was up half the night working on it. I promise you, Ed, it'll make everybody forget Haskell's piece."

In fact, Teller had not yet managed to think of anything remotely interesting to say about Bobby Lee Cooper. But he was reasonably sure he could scrape together something.

Kurtis raised his heavy-lidded eyes, while keeping the roll of his chin propped on his chest.

"Really?"

"You're damn right." *Don't ask what it is*, he muttered under his breath.

Instead, Kurtis asked, almost pleaded, "Has it got visuals?"

"It's got visuals. God, does it have visuals."

Kurtis leaned forward and put his hairy arms on his desk. He folded his hands together.

"Teller," he said in a low voice, "my weatherman is pressuring me to let him bring a duck puppet on the air with him. He wants to call his segment the Weather Forequacks. My sportscaster dropped his pants on a film piece Wednesday and when I saw it I threw that chair over there against that wall over there. I would like to suspend the silly bastard except that the backup sportscaster is taking his vacation in the company of the Tornados' number one draft choice. My anchorman is fucking suing me to let him wear his inane suit with the navy stitches. My newsroom is generally speaking New York's most expensive day-care center. We are currently a distant fourth in the New York Nielsens and fourth in the New York ARBs, and I don't have to tell you that the Colonel has been on the telephone reminding me of those statistics."

Kurtis paused to rub his eyes with his knuckles.

"Teller, a lot of people at this station don't like you. I think you know that. There are times when I wish I had never heard of you, times I wish I had hired a commentator from inside our ranks, somebody like Duggan who knows the medium, knows visuals, hasn't got a fucking brain in his head but *looks* as though he is reviewing a movie even when he is talking gibberish and who, I don't need to tell you, would cut your throat if he thought it'd get him your job."

Teller knew what was coming next. They had performed variations on this conversation before.

"But Teller, I am basically glad to have you with us. You write well, you give us a little class, your Q-profile is reasonably high. Plus you have some brains. I feel that I can talk to you as one adult to another."

Kurtis slapped the palms of his hands down onto the paperwork in front of him; they made a flatulent squish.

"Teller, do yourself and me two big favors. Stop dressing like a fucking Scandinavian tennis player. And wear the beeper. You do these two things, your stock will go up around here. And I swear to God, if you ever miss another story like the Bobby Lee Cooper thing, I'll can your ass and I don't care what kind of shit AFTRA throws me."

Teller nodded. He was relieved that the chewing-out had not been worse than it was. And he felt compassion for Ed Kurtis. The man was a borderline incompetent. Whatever perceptions, hopes, sense of mission he may have once possessed were corroded by too many years of trying to maintain a facade of dignity under the drip of small daily humiliations that flow from television's vast lunatic reservoir. It was inevitable that any man, after a given number of years in Kurtis's position, would begin to accept Haskell on 7 as the norm. Perhaps even Haskell had had a brain once.

But whatever Kurtis's professional liabilities, however grotesque his sense of journalistic values, Ed Kurtis in his own strange way cared about the *WRAP-Around News.* Teller understood that. Kurtis wanted to put on a good newscast and perform a public service and win citations from universities and gather big ratings points. He would never do any of those things, but he wanted to. That was more than Teller could say for nearly all of the *WRAP-Around News* team, who wanted mainly to be Lon Stagg, and it was more than he could say for Lon Stagg, who wanted to be either MacGregor Walterson or Monte Hall, depending upon whose position became available first.

In this dewy state of mind Mark Teller impulsively decided to offer the news director a lump of sugar.

"Ed," he said, "I caught a terrific new act last night at Stitch's. It's a place for new comedians. A guy came onstage out of nowhere and brought the house down. Just laid everybody out. I thought if

I could find a spare film crew I might go over and get him to recreate his act this afternoon and I could feature it on my spot tonight. In addition to my Bobby Lee Cooper commentary, of course." A hazy plan was already taking shape in Teller's thoughts.

Kurtis was gazing down at the coffee table to the right of his desk, on which the morning papers were spread out: WORLD MOURNS BOBBY LEE. THRONGS GRIEVE FOR FALLEN IDOL. And, on the front page of *The New York Messenger,* a bizarre photograph with the cryptic caption WASTEBASKET OF DOOM.

"Hell yes," he muttered. "You can do a life goes on type thing. Show must go on sort of approach. Show business, uh, endures. That sort of thing."

"Ed, you read my mind," said Teller, annoyed that his idea was obvious enough to be comprehended by Kurtis. Jesus, maybe Jennifer was right. Maybe he was adapting too quickly.

"I'll get on it," he said, and headed for the door wondering, *what the hell have I gotten myself into this time?*

He was already several steps down the corridor when he heard Kurtis's voice: "Teller?"

Teller retraced his steps and looked warily inside Kurtis's door.

"This comedian. Is he ... visual?"

Teller had to laugh out loud at the absurdity of it all. Months later he was to remember his next words and marvel at the prophecy in them.

"Ed," Mark Teller said, "he is nothing *but* visual."

Teller walked back out through the reception area, where the fat man in the Stetson and rhinestone leisure suit was now plopped on a cushioned sofa, frowning at a copy of *Crawdaddy* magazine. The receptionist (a stunning Asian, her face and lips gleaming with cosmetics) caught Teller's eye and pointed her finger at the man, then at her ear, making a circular motion. As Teller reached the doorway to the elevator bank, the fat man looked up at him.

"Hey, ain't you ... ?"

Teller pretended not to hear and closed the door behind him quickly. He ducked into the stairwell that led down to the twenty-ninth floor of the Commerce Center. This was the floor that contained the separate newsrooms and television studios for the network and the local station. The offices and studios of WRAP Radio, AM and FM, were also on this level, tucked at the end of a bewildering maze of dingy corridors.

Teller stood in front of the glass door leading into the vast television-radio plant. The receptionist on the other side (less cosmeticized than her colleague upstairs, in keeping with the relative status of the floors) smiled, waved, and raised her eyebrows: did Teller want to be buzzed in?

He glanced at his watch. Only 9:36. Nothing doing inside yet. Time for a cup of coffee and the morning papers down on the main floor. He shook his head at the receptionist and hit the elevator button behind him.

Aside from the broadcast colony on its top floors, the Commerce Center was an outpost of wholesale merchants, expatriates from the garment district, and furniture people: ponderous, seamed, anxious men and women who smoked in the elevators and spent a great deal of money on the kind of clothing that was foreordained to look cheap: blazing jackets and color coordinated ties and snappy wing-tip shoes on the men; pantsuits of relentless, paisleyed good cheer stretched across the ballooning buttocks of the women. This ambling herd was invaded by the occasional lean young lioness in jeans, Frye boots, and raw silk tunic striding through the promenade, a buyer en route to account executive. Mostly, the wholesale people were gray and depressing. They seemed wary, yet proud of the television crowd that roosted in the heights above them. The television people were celebrities. The merchants doted on celebrities. There was constant deference and obsequiousness on the elevators; outright glances and stares directed at the on-air people.

Sometimes the fabric merchants and the furniture buyers would try to cultivate the camaraderie of the television crowd by making jovial, ostentatious conversation about news or sporting events. The television crowd always stared straight ahead. Their attention could not be cheaply bought. Not until air time would *they* deign to make jovial, ostentatious conversation about news and sporting events.

Mark Teller disliked the Commerce Center at the teeming height of the business day. The wholesalers, the buyers, the straining entrants in the daily business sweepstakes depressed him. It depressed him to see them hunched, smoking cigarettes, over cold corned beef sandwiches in the deli ('Strami Rama) on the lobby floor, their masticating privacy violated by a plate-glass window. It depressed him to see them standing sullen in line at the Fannie Mae Sweet Shop (what dim romantic notions exercised, what mundane guilts assuaged, with the purchase of a commercially felicitous Fannie Mae gift box?) or furtively scanning the *Messenger* horoscope in the elevator, each exhaled breath enriching the cubicle with the rank aftertaste of fast-food hamburgers. Most of all, it depressed him to hear the occasional reverent hiss: "Aren't you the one on Channel Twenty-six . . . Mark Teller?" Followed by the inevitable: "You're taller than you are . . ."

Teller liked the center most at this hour, before the business rush, or at twilight, when the noisy anxious merchants had emptied out and gone home (to watch television) and he could stand outside the old building and sense some of the intended majesty, the optimism attendant at its birth; the Six Captains, so sinister in the urban glare of noonday, rendered somehow innocent in all their barbaric monstrosity by the setting sun.

He settled into a booth in the lobby cafeteria with a cup of coffee, a Danish, and the morning papers. He opened the pages of the top paper on the pile, and an orgy of morbidity sprang before his eyes. The volume of coverage given to Bobby Lee Cooper's death staggered him. It had shoved most of the national and world news off the first three pages, including a story that Teller, the old sportswriter, had been pursuing with some interest: the intense, competitive bidding-war among the four networks to secure telecast rights for the upcoming Summer Olympic Games from Moscow. The political implications of that bidding war—conservative columnists had already raised the question of Soviet propaganda requirements that might accompany telecast rights—had kept the story on the news pages as well as in the TV columns and sports.

But not today.

As Teller scanned the minutely detailed summaries of Cooper's life, the interviews with distraught fans, the quotes from other giants of show business, the pronouncements of astrologists (I PREDICTED BOBBY'S DEATH, declared the cutline under a photograph of a platinum-haired woman on page 7 of the *Messenger*), a sense of unreality grew in him.

He appreciated the fact that Cooper was a big star, a revolutionary figure in popular music. But not even the political assassinations of the past fifteen years, not even the deaths of venerated artists and statesmen—not even the cumulative deaths in the war in Southeast Asia—had called up the torrents of hysteria and despair that poured out of the newspaper pages.

He pushed his cold coffee cup away, gathered his newspapers, and got up. Time to go to work. If he was lucky, he could reach somebody at Stitch's by phone and track down this Robert Schein character in time to have a film piece on the early-evening newscast. That would make Kurtis happy.

Teller entered the WRAP newsroom and saw that another average workday was unfolding.

Sean Murphy, the star reporter, stood on top of a desk near the Teletype machine. He was staring deadpan across the room, his cold eyes expressionless above the waxed tips of his famous mustache. Every few seconds, Murphy would sail an empty cardboard pizza-carton—from a stack left over by last night's late-news crew —across the room toward the bank of newswriters. This was Murphy's way of showing that in spite of his being a star, he was a crazy, fun-loving guy underneath.

The newswriters, mostly dyspeptic, harried, middle-aged men with pale, anxious faces, were pretending to go along good-naturedly with Murphy's gag. They fended off the empty cartons with raised elbows, crying, "*Hey*, cut that out, Murph!" To a man, the newswriters would have dearly liked to murder Murphy. When they presented him with copy that was not written to his specifications of crisp insouciance, Sean Murphy could be something quite the opposite of fun-loving indeed.

Tony Cazzini stood below Murphy's desk holding an imaginary microphone. "We are unable as yet, ladies and gentlemen, to determine any motive for this seemingly senseless display of violence," he was intoning. "We know only that the man above us has identified himself as 'Son of Pizza,' and has decreed that all rewrite men must vanish from the face of the earth. He has said that he will surrender himself only to an authorized official of Luigi's. Tony Cazzini, *WRAP-Around News.*"

Cazzini was a second-echelon reporter who wanted to be Sean Murphy. He invariably joined Murphy in Murphy's newsroom pranks, trying to create a Butch-Cassidy-and-Sundance aura of boyish camaraderie between the two. As usual, Murphy was ignoring Cazzini. Murphy despised Cazzini. Cazzini despised Murphy.

Several women producers leaned against their desks, arms folded, discussing a new hairdresser that one of them had discovered. "I think he's a fag," one of them was saying, "but he gives good hot comb."

A sandy-haired young man, Lon Stagg's coanchor on the early newscast, sat by himself at a desk near the window, studying a thin yellow sheet of paper. From time to time he would glance up, neck constricting nervously, and announce to the window: "Good evening, I'm Al Adams, welcome to the second hour of *WRAP-Around News*." He reminded Teller of a Styrofoam owl greeting tourists at Disney World. Owl Adams. The young man had been hired recently at the suggestion of WRAP's motivational research team, which had theorized that Stagg's image might improve, and with it his numbers, if he had a "friendly sidekick" as coanchor. Lon Stagg had thrown a tantrum in Kurtis's office when he had learned that he was to have a "friendly sidekick." "In all my years in this business I have worked alone," he raged at Kurtis. "Women eighteen to thirty-nine identify with me as a lone wolf!" He appealed to Kurtis's intellectual side by quoting from the classics: "It's like the Chairman of the Board says, man," he said, spreading his hands. " 'I Do It My Way.' " When that failed to move Kurtis, he kicked a chair. Then he threatened to quit. *Fat chance*, thought Kurtis.

In the end, Stagg accepted his "friendly sidekick" like a gentleman. To show that there were no hard feelings, he threw another tantrum in the presence of Al Adams. Every night following Adams's debut on *WRAP-Around News*, Stagg made sure that Adams saw the telephone clerk's summary of negative telephone calls. The positive ones, Stagg crumbled and threw away. In no time, Adams was terrified of Stagg. It was no wonder that he spent his mornings practicing his own name.

The reporters' desks, the Teletype machines, and the rewrite bank formed the perimeter of the newsroom. In the middle was the communications desk—the nerve center. Here were installed the blaring police and fire department squawk boxes, from which a significant portion of WRAP's daily news agenda originated. Here sat the assignment editor, Morris Kitman, who feasted on the unending alarums of death, destruction, and mayhem. Homicides and four-alarm fires brought a special glitter to Kitman's eye, a spring to his step, a mischievous grin to his Bligh features.

"I've got a double stabbing on Avenue D in East Flatbush," he would announce to the newsroom in the manner of an auctioneer holding up a bottle of Mouton Rothschild '45. "Who wants it?"

The general decor of the newsroom could be classified as somewhere between eclectic and in violation of minimum standards of the Board of Health. A burning candle and a geranium in a tinfoil pot graced the surface of the squawk boxes. In front of Trillin, the dispatcher, were a knife and fork that, according to one office historian, antedated the present management. There was also a box of Kleenex, somebody's color print of a Rocky Mountain photograph, and a newspaper photograph of a monkey bearing the grafted caption, LON STAGG GOES BEHIND THE HEADLINES.

Festooning the walls, desks, chairs, and cabinets about the perimeter of the newsroom there were, variously taped, tacked, hung, stacked, or folded:

—A yellowing full-page newspaper photograph showing the health reporter standing on a bathroom scale, a towel around his middle.

—A montage poster depicting the head of Farrah Fawcett-Majors between the jaws of a shark.

—A chain, Scotch-taped to the wall, made of beer-can tabs.

—Several torn telephone directories with the covers missing.

—An Air Cargo Guide.

—The Detroit telephone directory, its pages and cover intact.

—An American flag on a wooden stick, wedged behind a cork bulletin board.

—A red kite.

—A photostatic copy of the Declaration of Independence.

—Several maps of the United States, and a *National Lampoon* map of the world, showing such cities as Dolores Del Rio, Argentina.

—An organizational poster of the New York State government.

—A cardboard box filled with packets of Hi-Ho soy sauce, drinking straws, plastic spoons, and packets of artificial sweetener.

—The spare green blazer and necktie of a reporter who had left four months ago for Minneapolis.

—The front half of a woman's bicycle.

—A poster of Audie Murphy starring in *Forty Guns to Apache Pass*.

—An autographed group picture of the *Channel 7 Eyewitness News* team.

—A typewriter that looked as though it had been stripped down by car thieves.

—A broken stopwatch.

—A Bible.

One other person stood alone, like Teller, detached from the Murphy-Cazzini horseplay yet taking it in. Teller shifted his gaze to study her across the newsroom.

Elizabeth Scott stood watching with her arms folded, a bemused smile on her face. She was *WRAP-Around*'s weekend anchor-woman. The remaining three days of her work week, she covered odds-and-ends assignments—opera-singing tramps on Upper Broadway, Good Samaritans on the subway, bike-a-thons. The crap file. Murder trials seemed to be her specialty. At least, that's where Morris Kitman liked best to send her.

Although Teller worked on-air with her one night a week—his Sunday commentary fell within her 11 P.M. anchor stint—he did not know her well. (Viewers often assumed that members of a TV news team were in fact the "big happy family" that they appeared to be on the air. In fact, many of the personalities who traded easy gibes with one another during the newscast were virtual strangers outside the studio: nothing personal.)

He felt no desire to know her. She seemed strange and remote—too perfect to be real. Too stylized, with a voice as perfect and soulless as that of an airline stewardess—a porcelain doll, hand-crafted to fit the requirements of the TV camera: tall, willowy, blond (every blond hair sprayed into place), slightly rounded face, saucer-blue eyes; a member of television's Master Race. They came and went. It was hard to know when one Elizabeth Scott had left and another taken her place. He sometimes wondered whether even the Elizabeth Scotts knew. They all saddened him.

He shrugged and turned his attention back to the newsroom scene.

He noticed that the fat man in the white Stetson and the blue-rhinestone leisure suit had somehow made it past the receptionist and into the newsroom. He was bent over the telephone clerk, a practicing yogi, who ignored both him and the bank of ringing telephones as she sat transfixed by a paperback book on levitation.

"Honey, Ah'm the Tennessee Tub-Thumpah an' Ah *got* t' see youah boss on the subject of Bobbah-Lee Coopah," the fat man was saying. Something about the man made Teller's flesh crawl, and he hurried on through the newsroom toward his own cubicle. As a commentator, he was allowed the privilege of a desk, telephone, and typewriter in a smaller, partitioned room away from the hubbub of the reporters' area.

A cardboard pizza-carton zipped by his ear as he stepped into the hallway.

"This is Mark Teller, *WRAP-Around News*. Am I speaking to Robert Schein?"

"Yeah." The voice on the other end was toneless, noncommittal.

"I got your number from the people at Stitch's. Listen, I caught your act last night. I was wondering if I could meet you at Stitch's this afternoon, say about two. I'd like to bring a crew along and film that falling-down act of yours for the news tonight."

A long silence at the other end.

"Hello? You still there?"

"Yeah, I'm still here. Who is this?"

"I told you. Mark Teller, I do a commentary on the Channel Twenty-six news. I saw you last . . ."

"I heard you."

"Well?"

Another long silence.

Finally the toneless voice said:

"This is a joke."

"This is no joke. If you want to check it out, call back the main switchboard number here and ask for me. I'm serious, dammit. You brought down the house last night."

The voice on the other end made a sound that might have been the beginning of the word "shit." Teller was starting to lose patience.

"Look, man, I want to put you on television. If you don't want to cooperate, we'll forget it. Sorry I bothered you."

"What the hell," the voice said. "What time did you say, captain? Two o'clock?"

"Sweetheart," said Lon Stagg, closing the door, "I've told you to never let anyone photograph me before I've licked my lips."

He stood with his back to the makeup-room door, hands behind him, gripping the knob. His head was cocked, so that he looked at the station's public-relations woman out of the corner of his eye, like a mischievous little boy: the Lon Stagg trademark look.

The public-relations woman was trapped. Stagg had beckoned her inside the makeup room as she had passed him in the corridor outside the news set. Now they were alone, and Stagg blocked the only exit from the room.

"Never," said Stagg.

He had on his little-boy half-smile, the ironic pursing of his wide, sensuous lips that brought him an average of seventeen mash notes a week from women in the eighteen-to-thirty-nine age group. Eleven of those seventeen, on the average, came from women ages eighteen to thirty-four, the crème-de-la-crème demographic group. Stagg had it all written down in his desk drawer. Stagg had everything written down.

The public-relations woman made a pitiful gesture with the clipboard in her left hand. Her name was Melinda Wells; she was thirty-four and tried to get interested in Proust once a year during her solo vacation to the Bahamas, and wore festive scarves to camouflage the essential squareness of her body, and she was overworked and didn't need this, and she was having trouble finding her voice and wished to God she was out of the makeup room.

"Never," Stagg said.

Stagg's right hand came out from behind his back and slapped the clipboard away in a clean arc. It clattered against the leg of the green sofa in the corner.

"He was from a high school paper," the public-relations woman managed at last, in a voice that sounded foolishly thin against the bare walls of the makeup room. "I didn't think . . ."

"You didn't think."

Stagg nodded gravely. He appeared to be lost in thought, studying the tops of his brown Botticelli pull-on boots, the pointed toes of which were now crossed as he leaned his weight against the door. With the thumb of his left hand, Lon Stagg slid the drawbolt shut, locking the door. Melinda Wells heard the click.

Behind her was the dressing-room mirror. Stagg could not help looking up past her to regard his image in it, to absorb the little pageant he was enacting. Today he was natty in a conservative Turnbull & Asser two-piece suit, lightweight wool, two-button, blue pinstripes. Four hundred fifty-five at Bonwit. With it he had chosen a cotton voile shirt, white with blue stripes, bunched in threes. Turnbull & Asser. Boots were a nice touch. He made a mental note to call for a full shot this afternoon, a shot of him strolling from the anchor desk over to the sports area so the audience could see the heels of his brown Botticelli boots, see how he could pull together two apparently conflicting fashion statements and make them work, maybe tip off Chapman, the sports announcer, in advance to kid around a little about the boots, the audience liked that. They liked to know a little about the personalities behind the newscast, see that there was some humanity beneath the grim headlines, that sort of thing.

Then Stagg remembered that he couldn't kid around too much on the newscast today; the death of Bobby Lee Cooper was still fresh in the viewers' minds, and Stagg himself was supposed to be almost in mourning. Lon Stagg wanted it clearly established that beneath the serious, impersonal mask that he was forced to wear by virtue of his constraints as the chief news anchorman at the flagship station of a major television network, there flourished the heart and soul of a down-to-earth human being, a guy who had the same tastes and interests as those of the average, workaday people in his viewing audience. It would be an important point to make should he ever be asked to cooperate in a magazine interview; say, the On the Scene section of *Playboy* magazine. Lon Stagg had long since decided that he would set aside his busy work schedule and graciously make himself available should anyone from *Playboy* approach him for an interview. He was right for On the Scene. Not the *Playboy* interview yet, not quite, too premature; but On the Scene would be about right for his image. At forty-two he was still young, still identifiable with the eighteen-to-forty-nine age group. He *was* the chief anchorman for the flagship station of a major television network, and heir apparent for the network anchor slot upon the retirement of MacGregor Walterson. And he had the life-style. The Porsche, and the BMW 733i with the 3.3-liter, electronically fuel-injected engine; the Fifth Avenue penthouse near the art museum just a few doors from Reggie Jackson's; the crushed-velvet furniture; the stainless-steel appointments; the sophisticated sound system and the large-screen videotape unit that allowed privileged friends and special women to view replays of Lon Stagg's most dramatic newscasts.

He had the name: Lon Stagg. A triumph of a name, a media name; short, masculine, predatory but not intimidating, easy to remember, easy to fit into a newspaper or magazine headline. Stagg liked his name; he felt fortunate to have it. It was a far better name than the Clyde Winkleman he had been born with back in La Porte, Indiana. Stagg had not cared so much for La Porte, Indiana, either. His official birthplace was listed in the WRAP biography sheet as Los Angeles, California.

Lon Stagg had the look and the sound of an anchorman.

Which is to say, a look and a sound as manufactured as his name and his place of birth—as disconnected from the traditional fixed points of human perception as a cathode dot.

Viewed in the flesh, he appeared as a creature in chrysalis—the component parts not yet fully formed and blended into a recognizable human being.

His features were too sharp—the dark brows too knotted, the point of the nose too fine, the sculpted circular mop of hair too improbable in its low dramatic swirl over his forehead. The hair was bleached white—a move Stagg had undertaken when the first streaks of gray appeared in his black temples.

But something wonderful happened to Lon Stagg's features when they were reproduced on the cathode tube. The camera—in the vernacular of the business—"loved" Stagg's face, and it worked sorcery on its components as it transferred them to the canvas of the television screen.

The camera took the tortured elements of Stagg's face and arranged them like a bouquet. It smoothed and shaded and polished the lineaments, softening the severity of his brow, rounding out the sharpness of his cheekbones, banishing the dewlaps that were just beginning to form below the corners of his mouth.

His mouth was the crowning ornament in the intaglio that was Lon Stagg's face. In its corporeal state, Stagg's mouth was a cruel and frightening instrument. It was the mouth of Pan: a wide, sensuous, undulating gash that hung low on his face, coiled and pouting. It was the poisoned well from which his anger sprang, his rich corroding anger that withered assistant producers and makeup girls and news directors and anyone else whom Stagg suspected of conspiring against his imperial dignity as anchorman.

But under the healing ministrations of the TV camera, Stagg's mouth was transformed into something delicate and beautiful; a full, curving cupid's bow, the lips shapely as a woman's. Stagg understood the various components of his face and body as objectively as a racing driver understands the valves, pistons, and coils that make up his machine; he understood his body as a competitive instrument that could bring him fortune or ruin him; and he especially understood the fundamental truths that were either revealed, or concealed, by his mouth.

Whether by *The New York Times* or a high school paper.

Stagg pushed himself away from the door and took a step toward the public-relations woman, who didn't know what to do with her hands now that they were shorn of her clipboard.

"Sweetheart," he said, keeping his voice low and casual, "that's a real problem around this candy store, isn't it? People don't *think*. They don't *think* up in Ed Kurtis's office, when they let a bunch of hired pansies tell them how to run the anchor desk. They don't *think* when our resident heavy thinker Mark Teller blows the entire Cooper story and we don't take that opportunity to can his interloping ass.

"And now, sweetheart, you don't think when you bring a high school kid with a camera into my office and let him take a picture of me before I have had an opportunity to moisten my lips."

Stagg reached out and grasped the woman's chin with his right hand. His fingers and thumb dug into the soft flesh of her cheeks, turning her mouth into a ludicrous figure eight. The woman nodded in terror and began making snorting gasps through her nose.

"Maybe you don't see it as important that my lips are wet before a photograph," Stagg said, his voice dropping back down to its menacing casual tone. "Maybe you think it's another one of Lon Stagg's pretty-boy affectations, like everyone else around here."

The public-relations woman struggled to shake her head no. Her face had gone white and her eyes bulged as he lifted her chin higher in his savage grip.

Stagg couldn't help glancing again at his reflection in the dressing-room mirror. He was Harvey Keitel in *Fingers*. Great flick. He didn't see why the critics panned it. Even Teller had found something smart-ass to say about it. Especially Teller. He would never understand critics.

"Well, that's all *right*. Let 'em think whatever they want to. The *point* is, I've been in this business twenty-two years and I understand *detail*, I understand *image*. I understand that a top-rated television newscast starts on the ground floor, with a lot of attention to things that might seem unimportant."

There was a porcelain deep-basin in the left corner of the makeup room, where the WRAP news personalities rinsed their faces after they got off the air, and Stagg began pushing Melinda Wells toward it, still gripping her chin and cheeks with his right hand.

"Like the way the anchorman looks in a news photograph," he said, walking the woman toward the sink. "Like whether his image makes him look like a *winner* or a *loser*." The public-relations woman's gay scarf was all bunched up under his hand, Stagg noticed, and her hair, a lusterless brown, was beginning to come apart from her plastic combs. Jesus, they could find somebody with a little more class, a little more style, to represent the god-damn station to the public.

"If the *anchorman* looks like a winner, then the *station* looks like a winner," he lectured the woman, whose hip was now wedged up against the wash basin. "If the anchorman looks like a *loser*, well, hell . . . now I've been a winner for twenty-two years. I don't like being a loser now. So let's just . . ."

With the open palm of his left hand, he forced the woman's face around and down into the wash basin.

"Let's just have a little object-reminder . . ."

He glanced quickly from the hot-water spigot to the cold-water. Hot water would make her scream.

". . . in the importance . . ."

He loosened his grip on the woman's jaw; the imprints of his fingers left fiery streaks on her cheeks. Deftly, he slid his left hand back to grip the nape of her neck and twist her face around so that it rested under the cold-water spigot.

". . . of moisture . . ."

He turned on the spigot. Melinda Wells jerked as the stream of cold water splashed across her cheek and neck. Harvey Keitel. Helluvan actor. The cold water was splashing on the public-relations woman's festive scarf, darkening the gay colors. She was bawling now, and her nose was running, the snot mixing with the cold water and sloshing down the drain.

". . . on the *face!*"

He turned off the spigot and released the public-relations woman, who fled toward the door, seized the knob, realized it was locked, and fell sobbing on the green sofa, her heaving back to him.

Stagg noticed that the arms of his suit jacket were wrinkled.

Damn.

 At ten minutes past 2 P.M. a cream-and-orange-colored panel truck thrust its nose into half of a parking space in front of a fire hydrant near the entrance to Stitch's. The truck skidded to a halt with an abruptness that left its tailpipe vibrating. The truck's rear end angled carelessly into Second Avenue, blocking a lane of traffic.

Three short, overweight men in identical cream-and-orange T-shirts, Polaroid sunglasses, and poker faces disembarked. The men swaggered to the rear of the truck, flung open the doors, and began unloading long black boxes and coiled black wires.

Not a single motorist hammered on his horn at the sudden obstruction. No curses were bellowed. No fingers were flashed. No mayhem was threatened. On the contrary the oncoming cars, taxis, and delivery trucks changed their course with an alacrity that bordered on genuflection; they cut a respectful arc around the truck, slowing as they went by so their drivers could peer closely at its cream-and-orange-colored crew. The three crewmen, for their part, accepted this homage with indifference. The racy black lettering on their T-shirts, matching that on the sides and back of the panel truck, identified them as crewmen of the WRAP ACTION VAN. They were, in fact, the cameraman, light man, and sound man;

the equipment they were unloading consisted of the station's redoubtable Action Cam, its tripod, lights, microphones, connecting cables, power battery, and videotape cassettes.

The WRAP action van was not just any panel truck. It was a celebrity.

Mark Teller remained slouched inside the truck. He dreaded getting out. He hated location assignments. He hated the rubbernecking attention; the fat women shading their eyes from the sun and pointing; the skinny Hispanic kids dancing in and out, bearing transistor radios the size of suitcases, and mugging at the camera, "Hey, mon, put me on TV!"; everybody with these silly, gum-chewing, respectful grins. He felt like a goddamn orangutan out on a leash.

Only Jennifer Blade managed to perform on location with decorum and crisp modesty, neutralizing the circus instincts of the crowds by remaining aloof from them. Power, for Jennifer Blade, had subtler and richer appeals.

"Hey, Teller. You comin', or you want us to bring him out on the curb for you?"

Teller sighed and slid across the seat to get out nearest the sidewalk. He stood on the hot pavement and squinted at Stitch's. Daylight was not kind to the place. It looked even smaller and shabbier, more desperate, than it had last evening, enhanced by whatever dim phantasmagoria the New York night could still provide. Its torn red canopy hung limp in the afternoon heat, mean as a Forty-second-Street stripper's boa. The imitation Mexican café with its fake-stucco facade crowded in on the left; on the right, there was a shoe-repair shop that might have been closed since the Depression.

The crew couldn't believe it. They stood holding their tripods and lights, staring at the blank windows with their fat lips parted, as though they had just been forced here at gunpoint.

Teller peered inside the window. Darkness. Maybe this Schein hadn't bothered to show up after all. Teller couldn't blame him for not believing it: a network-owned television station coming to cover an unknown comic who had done next to nothing on the stage of a nowhere bar on an undistinguished block of Second Avenue.

The utter self-indulgence of what he was about to do oppressed

Teller. There was no hope in this scheme; he was using the station's expensive equipment and manpower to carry out a childish determination to wipe away his embarrassment at missing the Cooper story.

Somebody behind him on the sidewalk called, "Hey, Mark Teller!" He cringed. He turned back to the crew.

"Come on, guys. I think we're on a wild-goose chase."

The fat little cameraman was looking over Teller's shoulder, into the window. "Hey," he said. "Who's zat? Zat your boy, Teller?"

Teller turned back to the window. A white, skull-like face was staring back at him. The face disappeared, and a moment later the door to Stitch's opened. The skull face was wearing a sharply pressed green leisure suit two sizes too large, over a gaudy floral spread-collar shirt. Teller had a hunch that if he opened the jacket, he would find a price tag.

"You guys are from Channel Twenty-six," the skull face informed them. "I'm Al Gnagy, I run this joint. Come on in and meet my star."

Robert Schein was seated on the same barstool where Teller had first seen him last night: in the corner where the foot of the L-shaped bar joined the wall. His blond hair was illuminated by the same imitation candle above him. Schein did not look up when the five people trooped into the dimness toward him. He slumped like a huge marionette against the wall, his face devoid of expression, the ice-blue eyes fixed on nothing. He was wearing a black T-shirt that revealed muscled arms. Half of a peeled orange rested on the bar by his left elbow.

It occurred to Teller that Schein seemed to absorb light, rather than reflect it. The features, vaguely handsome, were yet indistinct; there was no center to the face, no fixed point that drew the eye. This was the same person who had generated such an astonishing reaction from the crowd last night with his equally astonishing—and brief—appearance onstage. No doubt about that. And yet Teller was not sure he would have recognized Robert Schein had he passed him on the street, in the light of day.

"Bobby," said Al Gnagy, very much the impresario, "these are the boys from the Channel Twenty-six news. Say hello to Mark Teller."

Teller offered his hand. Schein's attention was elsewhere. He gave an absent flick of his left wrist in greeting. Teller wanted very much to take one step forward and smash this insolent bastard in the mouth. Schein's obvious disdain for his incredible stroke of good luck had passed the bounds of simple courtesy.

On the other hand, there was a deadline to be met. *WRAP-Around News* was on the air in less than three hours. In that time there was videotape to be shot and edited, a script to write. Teller checked his anger. He turned to Gnagy, who seemed to have a hand on everyone's shoulder at once.

"How long have you two worked together?"

With a flourish, Gnagy examined a watch on his skinny wrist. "Oh, I'd say right around twenty-two hours now," he said, and flashed a grin. "You can quote me on that. Twenty-two hours." He shot a nervous look at Schein, as though to include him in the hilarity. Schein did not appear to be listening.

Teller was incredulous. "Do you mean that you'd never seen this guy before . . . ?"

Gnagy gave a shake of his head, inviting Teller to marvel at the ironies of show business. "He walked right in off the street about this time yesterday. Asked me if he could be on the program. Now I usually require an audition, but there was something about this kid, something that told me I'd be crazy not to . . ."

"You wanted to throw me out on my ass."

All five heads jerked in the direction of Schein. He still had not moved from his slumped posture against the wall. His eyes were still fixed on nothing. A very distinct silence settled over the room. Even Gnagy was speechless.

"Marvin, why don't you and the guys go and set up through that door," said Teller evenly. "I'll be wanting to shoot Mr. Schein on the stage. We'll be there in a few minutes. Mr. Gnagy, maybe you'd like to show them where the electric outlets are."

When the crew and a highly fearful Gnagy had gone, Teller sat down on the second barstool away from Schein. He ran a hand through his curls, damp with sweat. For the first time, Schein's blue eyes shifted to meet his directly.

"Now look," Teller began. "I could try to sell you a line about how this is going to be a big break in your career, but I get the feeling you don't give a shit about your career. I don't even think you have a career. I don't know who the hell you are or what you thought you were doing up there on that stage last night, and I gather you think it's pretty goddamn absurd to have a television crew here to cover you. Well, believe me, Mr. Schein, I share your feeling. I think it's pretty goddamn absurd myself. But for reasons that are too complicated to explain, and that I doubt you'd be interested to hear anyway, I seem to have gotten my ass in a sling on this little project. If I don't go back to the station with some footage of you doing your pratfall, or whatever you call it, I'm going to be badly screwed this afternoon. My job may be on the line, not that I harbor any illusions that you give a shit about *that.*"

He paused to take a breath.

"Let's just say that instead of pretending to do *you* a favor, I am asking you to do *me* one. Let's just go through with this and make it as painless as possible for everybody concerned, and then we'll forget that it ever happened. We'll tape you doing your fall and be out of here in half an hour. Is that acceptable?"

A smile crossed Schein's face. In the reflected yellow light of the imitation candle on the wall, it gave him the waxy appearance of a male mannequin.

Schein gave a shrug of his muscled shoulders. "No problem. Whatever I can do to make life easy for you."

Teller let out his breath. He glanced through the open door leading to the stage area. The crew had not yet finished setting up the lights.

"How about answering just a few questions. A little information for your many fans." Teller intended it as an irony. He realized he should have known better. Schein's face resumed its glassy, expressionless stare.

"How long have you been doing this . . . act?"

"Last night was the first time."

Jesus, thought Teller. *It gets worse.*

"How, uh . . . what made you decide to try that particular stunt?"

"I was drunk. It just happened."

"Uh . . . *had* you remained standing long enough to go through your routine, what sort of material would we have heard? I mean, how would you characterize your comic style?"

"Don't have one."

"You don't have one."

They regarded each other.

"In other words, I am about to confer celebrity status on a gate-crasher."

Two television arc lights bathed the small stage and the silver floor microphone in a hot white pool of light. Marvin, the cameraman, had the minicam mounted on a tripod, pointing up at the stage from the audience level. Al Gnagy darted importantly from the camera to the lights to the stage, as though he were personally directing the operation.

Teller and Schein stood behind the camera in the darkness, among the tables, looking at the lighted stage.

"All I want you to do," said Teller, "is get up there, pretend you are talking for a few seconds, and then go into your fall. You won't be miked. I just want it to look like you're doing a comic routine in front of an audience. I'll dub in my own voice-over while this part is on the air. Then when I cue you with my hand, you just pitch over, and that's it. Any problems?"

Schein, standing with his big arms folded, gave no sign that he had heard.

Al Gnagy bustled toward them from the stage. He stumbled over a wooden chair in his blustering haste to reach Teller.

"I got it all blocked out," he announced. "Camera opens wide on me, coming out on stage. I introduce Bobby, say a few words about what a sensational . . ."

"That won't be necessary, Mr. Gnagy," Teller said gently. He realized that the little proprietor had bought the green leisure suit specifically for the occasion.

"I'm sorry, we're short on time," Teller added. "We may as well get started."

"You want to run through it once?" Teller called up to Schein. The ice-blue eyes glittered in the arc lights onstage.

"I'm ready."

"We have time to rehearse it if you want to."

"Turn the camera on."

Well, fuck you, buddy, muttered Teller under his breath. *If you look bad, you look bad. I can script it that way, too.*

"Roll the tape, Marvin."

Marvin rolled the tape.

An amazing thing happened.

Robert Schein's face came alive.

He became a nightclub entertainer in pantomime. Like a wax mannequin melting into flesh and blood, Robert Schein, though mute, suddenly took on a live personality. He was wry, he was debonair, he was teasing, he was outrageous. The understated actor's grace that Teller had noticed the night before now informed Schein's every movement. His big hands curled about the microphone stand, the fingers working and reworking the silver level-ring in a professional motion, bringing the mike head within an inch of his lips. The ice-blue eyes were merry now; they twinkled in the hot arc lights' glow, darting here and there as though Schein were looking out over a jam-packed house. He turned this way and that, lips moving wordlessly, sweeping a phantom audience with his soundless ripostes. He shrugged. He scratched his head. He ticked off imaginary points with his fingers. Facing stage left, he shot a glance over his right shoulder and grinned wryly, as though acknowledging an ad-lib from a customer. Now and then he would freeze in mid-gesture, like a comedian pausing a beat to set the crowd up for a punch line—then move his lips briefly and raise both hands, palms upward, nodding at the imaginary guffaws.

Teller stood transfixed, not believing what his eyes told him. It was a masterly performance! In the absolute stillness of the room, he could almost hear the rhythm of the rapid-fire jokes issuing forth from the handsome, friendly, even self-effacing young comic who had the audience in the palm of his hand—could almost fill in the cadences of the familiar, slick, urban comic patter that the gestures evoked. The sound man and light man had glistening half-smiles on their fat lips; *they were enjoying the show!* He rolled his eyes over to the right. Al Gnagy, perched on a tabletop, was nodding his head, the skull face split into a grin.

Jesus! Teller glanced down at his watch. Schein had been up there for nearly three minutes. Teller shot his right hand up and brought it down again. Immediately, Robert Schein crossed his eyes and grasped the microphone stand with both hands. His upper body rotated two, three times around his feet, which seemed to be nailed to the floor.

Then Robert Schein collapsed to the stage like a column of warm putty, taking the microphone down on top of him. Only the soles of his shoes were visible; the left one twitched a couple of times and was still. The crew exploded in loud guffaws; the sound man clapped his meaty hands together several times.

"Cut!" yelled Teller.

"Oh, Jesus H. Christ!" the light man gasped. He had pushed his Polaroid sunglasses back on his head and was dabbing at his eyes with a handkerchief. Al Gnagy had sprinted onstage as soon as Schein hit the floor. "BOBBY SCHEIN, LADIES AND GEN-TLEMEN!" he now crowed into the empty room, his skinny arms stretched above his head, hoping to scavenge the last few seconds of videotape.

Schein was back on his feet, slapping at the dust on his jeans. Despite himself, Teller was still caught up in the pantomime persona that the man had created onstage. He stepped up onto the small raised platform and offered his hand.

"That was tremendous," Teller said.

A stranger's face looked back at him. Two ice-blue eyes, cold, impersonal, somehow mocking. Teller dropped his hand.

"I don't get you."

"Nothing to get."

"I mean, who are you? Where do you come from, what do you do, what do you *want* to do?"

"That's my business."

"Yeah. Okay."

"Ciao," Schein said and ambled toward the door.

"Wait a minute, Bobby," yelled Al Gnagy, running after him. "You're coming back tonight, ain't ya? You're the fuckin' star of the show!"

 Teller returned to the Commerce Center with the crew. The crew was in a considerably better mood after having witnessed Robert Schein's "performance"; they chattered on about what a tremendous comic he was. Teller was mystified to observe that the men were describing Schein's routine as though Schein had actually spoken, had actually delivered jokes and impressions. Teller almost pointed out this curious fact to the crew, but thought better of it.

When he stepped from the elevator on the twenty-ninth floor, Teller heard the shrieking.

It came from the inside corridor leading to the newsroom: a man's voice, shrieking with pitiful intensity.

"Aaaaaaaaiiiiiiiiieeeeeeeooooooo," wailed the voice. It was a sound wrenched from the depths of terror.

Someone was being mugged in the corridor!

He raced past the receptionist and burst into the darkened corridor.

"Aaaaaaaaiiiiiiiiieeeeeeeooooooo."

The shrieking seemed to come from behind a closed orange

door twenty feet away from Teller on the right. He dashed for it and seized the knob.

As he did, realization dawned. He released his grip on the doorknob.

Teller always forgot.

Friday was the day for the voice coach.

Her name was Edith Trilling. She was a retired Method actress. Ms. Trilling "aided" soap opera actresses, news anchormen, retired defensive tackles seeking to become color commentators, weatherpersons, politicians, aspiring talk show guests, TV commercial pitchmen, and disc jockeys in "communicative skills."

Teller recognized the shrieking voice as belonging to Al Adams, Lon Stagg's "friendly sidekick" at anchor on the early newscast. No doubt Adams was undergoing "assertiveness reclamation," or whatever the expert jargon was for getting his balls back. Adams's particular impediment to "optimum vocal potentialities" was a voice that sometimes quavered on the air, under the manifestly unfriendly glare of Lon Stagg.

Edith Trilling was just one of several consulting services the WRAP chain of command had hired in the past year in its drive for ratings respectability.

Another service was the Hawthorne Collective.

The Hawthorne Collective was a group of six earnest young Bostonians—four men and two women—who had rudimentary training in Gestalt psychology. (Two members were psychologists, one had run a day-care center, another had lived on a macrobiotic farm in Vermont, and the remaining two were former advertising people who had read the works of Wilhelm Reich.)

The Hawthorne Collective promised to improve a station's competitive performance by instilling what it called "productive management modes." This, in turn, would be accomplished through a sort of on-the-spot healing of management-employee psychic ills.

The Collective had an impressive title for its methodology: Psychodynamic Interpersonal Intervention.

This meant that the six members of the Hawthorne Collective flew in from Boston one day a week, usually Mondays, to roam about the WRAP newsroom circulating questionnaires and asking the various staff members how they felt.

"You," a member of the Hawthorne Collective told Sean Murphy one morning in a "confrontational exercise," "are a Rebellious Child."

"And you," replied Murphy, "are a Son of a Bitch. Get out of my way before I bust your stupid mouth open."

"I hear that," said the Collective member. "I really hear that."

Mark Teller walked away from the orange door and the wailing of Al Adams behind it.

As he turned left off the corridor and hurried into the newsroom, Teller glanced at his watch. It was 3:47. The newscast started in one hour and thirteen minutes, but Teller's commentary did not air until 5:45. Two hours to bang out a script and supervise the editing of the videotape that would accompany it: he wanted some stock footage of Bobby Lee Cooper in performance, to be followed by the fresh footage of Schein.

It would be a tight squeeze pulling it all together.

He dashed the length of the newsroom, past the desks of newswriters and reporters working furiously on copy. Jennifer Blade was at her typewriter, and Teller felt the inevitable rush of admiration and desire as he glanced at her. Even slouched in her chair, a telephone cradled in the hollow of her neck, a cigarette jammed squarely in the center of her deep and sensuous mouth, and scowling, Jennifer Blade was an elegant woman.

A note on his typewriter informed him that his producer had pulled forty-five seconds' worth of Bobby Lee Cooper tape from the files, and was awaiting instructions. Teller picked up his phone, dialed the videotape editing department, and alerted them that the Schein footage was on its way; he would be there in twenty minutes to supervise the editing.

Then he rolled a book of copy paper, with carbons attached, into his typewriter and began banging out a script that he had been roughly blocking out in his head.

Fifteen minutes later he cranked out a draft that read:

Teller/live on cam   He was more than a rock'n'roll
                                      hillbilly, more than the fleshy carica-
                                      ture of himself that later haunted the
                                      Las Vegas clubs. At his greatest, Bobby
                                      Lee Cooper was a democratizing force

—not only in American popular music, but perhaps on the social stage as well.

cut to tape roll/Bobby Lee Cooper, sound low

More than any of the other pop figures of the 1950s, this Tennessee potato farmer's son opened the nation's gates to admit black styles and sensibilities into the American mainstream.

He was the first singer to blend the guitar—a white, country instrument—with black rhythms and the blatant sexuality that was missing from the urban Italian crooners whose era he forever closed.

Yes, the television cameras could cut Bobby Lee off at the waist during his first great assault on the Eisenhower middle class—but they could never cut off the liberating influence of his insistent working-class passion—a passion that made Bobby Lee Cooper the greatest celebrity that America ever knew.

cross-roll to tape of Robert Schein, w.o. sound

Now Cooper is dead. But his spirit lives on in the hopes and dreams of a new generation of American entertainers, both inside and outside the sphere of music. It is a tribute to his legacy that on the day of his passing, entertainers like this man—Robert Schein, a promising young comedian appearing at Stitch's Comedy Workshop on Second Avenue—continued to please audiences in the great tradition of Cooper himself.

Schein collapse here

The show must go on. And perhaps America's next great superstar will be a young man like Robert Schein, literally *knocking himself out* in obscurity here on the stage to build his following—just as Bobby Lee Cooper did in Tennessee nearly twenty-five years ago.

Farewell, Bobby. And hello, Robert.

Teller gagged as he read the copy. The transition from Cooper to Schein—spurious beyond the limits of decency! Beyond the worst excesses of Haskell on Channel 7! He took a stopwatch out of his middle desk drawer and read through the copy aloud, wincing again as he reached the part where Cooper's spirit "lives on in the hopes and dreams," etc. It didn't even make sense! Assuming the unassumable—that Robert Schein *was* any sort of legitimate entertainer, instead of an innocent bystander in Teller's idiotic scheme—the linkage between him and Bobby Lee Cooper still screamed out for clarification. Clearly, this commentary would stand the test of time as one of the more foolish pieces ever to air on a New York television station.

But there was one thing, Teller knew, that the piece had going for it—one thing that would endear it to the hearts of the executive producer, the technical director, and everyone else associated with running the early evening newscast.

It ran one minute forty-five seconds—fifteen seconds under Teller's allotted two-minute time.

Judged by the criterion of the stopwatch, the commentary was practically eligible for an Emmy.

No time to rewrite. Teller made a few penciled corrections on his copy, took it into the newsroom, and handed the original to a desk assistant for retyping onto TelePrompTer paper. Clutching the carbons, he headed for the videotape editing room, breaking into a loping run when he reached the corridor.

In the videotape room an editor already had the Robert Schein cassette cued up and was looking at it when Teller walked in.

"Hey, this guy's *great*," she exclaimed, glancing up at Teller. "Where'd you discover him?"

Teller gazed at Robert Schein's image on the screen. It was eerie. Schein, his blond hair highlighted by the full lights, his blue eyes twinkling in apparent mirth, looked for all the world like a polished nightclub performer in control of a responsive audience.

"The bastard *is* good," Teller murmured under his breath.

"Huh?" said the videotape editor. "Hey, Teller, I asked you— where'd you *find* him?"

"Stitch's," Teller said, switching his gaze to the woman at the controls of the videotape-editing console. Now his astonishment was focused on her. It had dawned on him that she, like the

WRAP ACTION VAN crew, was reacting to "material" that she could not hear—could not hear because it didn't exist.

What was it about Robert Schein that made people supply their own reasons for loving him?

The videotape editor clapped a hand to her mouth and gave a little shriek of delight. Teller glanced back at the screen in time to see the camera's pan down to Schein's inert body on the stage floor. As the left foot twitched once, twice, the editor giggled again.

"All right," Teller said. "That's the crucial segment. I want that pratfall edited in . . . here," pointing with his thumb to the appropriate place in the script. "Up until that point . . . from here to here, about twenty-eight seconds, I want closeup footage of Schein."

"His name is Schein? What's his first name?"

Teller ignored the question. "The out-cue for the closeup footage—it's marked here on the copy—is, ' . . . tradition of Cooper himself.' Then I want a cross-roll to Schein's pratfall; the voice-over that segment will take, uh, eighteen seconds. Any questions?"

"What's his first name?" asked the editor.

Teller's Cooper-Schein commentary aired, as scheduled, at 5:45 P.M. The fifteen seconds he had saved the station with his abbreviated copy were immediately consumed by Lon Stagg. Leading into Teller's segment, Stagg ad-libbed a few extra thoughts that were not on his TelePrompTer copy. When Lon Stagg ad-libbed, the entire WRAP news department froze in its tracks. Listening to Lon Stagg ad-lib held the same fascination as watching a drunk climb onto a balcony railing at a penthouse cocktail party. The sense of impending disaster was overpowering, but there was absolutely nothing to be done except let it happen.

Coming out of a commercial break, Stagg leaned over the anchor desk and peered soulfully at Camera One over his right shoulder. His white-ringleted head was cocked to one side and his brows were knotted quizzically—Stagg's well-known Sincere posture.

"Anybody who saw this program last night knows that I was kinda *torn up* by Bobby Lee Cooper's tragic death . . . " Stagg began.

In the control room, Ed Kurtis flung his clipboard to the floor. "What the fuck is he doin' *now*?" he screamed.

". . . seems like I knew Bobby Lee all my life," Stagg went on. He pursed his sybaritic lips as he paused to study his clasped fingertips. "Seems like we kinda . . . *grew up* together . . ."

"GIVE THAT IDIOT A WRAP-UP SIGN," Kurtis yelled at the executive producer, who relayed the order through his headset mike to an assistant director on the studio floor.

"Should I cue 'Happy Trails to You'?" cracked the technical director, pushing back his swivel chair.

" . . . and his music, in many ways, was *my* music," Stagg concluded finally, with a glance at the pistoning fist of the A.D. "Here with more on that is Mark Teller."

Camera Two came up on Teller, catching him—as it did with so many WRAP reporters—staring incredulously at Stagg. The anchorman had managed to read not a single word of the lead-in that had been written for him—a lead-in, Teller had hoped, that would lend some coherence to what he was about to say.

Teller faced the camera. "Thank you, Lon. . . . He was more than a rock'n'roll hillbilly . . ."

When it was finished, Teller waited in his seat until Stagg had introduced the sports segment. When the first piece of sports-tape footage began to roll, he undid his lavaliere mike and stood up to leave the set.

"Hey, man."

It was Stagg, who usually ignored him.

Stagg placed his index finger against his thumb, forming a circle, and shot Teller a wink.

"Heavy piece, big fella."

That ices it, thought Teller. It *was* a piece of shit.

On his way through the newsroom to lock his desk drawer before leaving, Teller was hailed by the telephone clerk.

"Phone's ringin' off the hook, man. Which one do you want first?"

"What do they want?"

"Most of 'em want to know where they can go to see that comedian you reviewed just now, Schein."

I didn't review the bastard, thought Teller.

"Tell 'em I've gone home."

"There's one guy says he knows you."

"What's his name?"

"Uh, Gnagy. Said he runs the nightclub where Schein works at."

So now it's a nightclub. He was tempted to stiff Gnagy and put the whole misbegotten episode behind him once and for all.

He remembered the new leisure suit.

"Which line is he on?"

"Oh-three."

Teller punched the button and picked up the receiver. "Hello, Al."

"Mark! Hey, that was a helluva plug you put in for us, my friend!"

"It wasn't a . . ."

"Mark, I want you to know that you and a friend of your choosing can be the guests of Stitch's *any time* . . ."

"Can't accept freebies, Al. Hey, thanks for the call."

"Mark . . ." the old man's voice had a sudden note of panic in it. Teller thought he knew what was coming. Again, he was tempted to drop the receiver.

"Yessir."

"Mark, I got a problem here. How should I put it, uh . . ."

"You expect a big crowd to see Schein tonight and the son of a bitch doesn't even have an act to give 'em."

Gnagy's voice was soft with embarrassment. "That's about the way it is."

"I'd say you had an interesting problem." Not *my* problem, Teller thought. He was anxious to get Gnagy off the line. Jennifer had tickets to Solti and the Chicago Symphony at Carnegie Hall. He was to meet her there. It would be the last time he'd see her for a week—she had been assigned to travel to Chattanooga with a camera crew to do a "reaction" piece in the wake of Cooper's death.

But in a way, it *was* Teller's problem. Or at least, his responsibility. After all, he had, in effect, dropped Robert Schein in Al Gnagy's lap.

He thought hard for a moment.

"If I were you," he said, "I'd go right to the front door this minute and put a SOLD OUT sign in the window. Send your other comics home when they show up. Now, there's one guy who might be able to do something with Schein, in the unlikely event that Schein will sit still for it. He's an older comic who was on your bill last night. Name's . . ." Teller rummaged in his mind. The name had already escaped him.

"You mean Wyler?"

"Yeah, that's it. Wyler. You know him? You ought to put him together with Schein; if you'll pardon my candor, he was the only guy I saw up there who knew his ass from third base. Maybe he can drum some funny lines into your man's skull by tomorrow night, but I imagine he'll expect a pretty fancy bundle in return. Hell, I don't even know if Wyler'd be willing to part with his material. Not many comics would."

When Gnagy spoke again, the note of panic was gone from his voice. It was replaced by something cold and hard.

"We'll see about that."

"Good-bye, Al." Teller dropped the phone. The End, he thought, to all that.

"When are you going to take me to California? Meet your dad?"

They were lying in Teller's bed. The sheets were soaked with the perspiration of their lovemaking. Jennifer made love like an athlete; her thrusting was almost competitive, her muscles taut and straining. She always wanted him almost as soon as they were naked. "Come into me," she would hiss between clenched teeth, her head dropping backwards off the side of the bed, cords in her long neck taut, hair splayed out behind her to the floor. It was only afterwards that her body would relax into the softness that thrilled him, that compelled his hands and mouth; only then that her breasts, which had been drawn tight against her rib cage as her arms flailed above her head, resumed their natural lushness—only then that her superb thighs softened about the secret rain forest. Teller had learned to reverse his sexual routine with Jennifer. With her, it was orgasm first, foreplay second. Afterplay. They seldom kissed, although her mouth was lovely and warmly wet. It didn't matter. The first sight of her nude body, pale in the windowlight; the first electric touch of his hand on her flesh, drove Teller into a frenzy of need. Their coupling was swift, silent, and intense; the release—dizzying, suctioning—left him gasping for breath. He had dreamed of her as a vampire, sucking his semen with vaginal teeth.

Now they lay quietly, her right leg resting atop his left, nearly as long as his. Teller's left hand traced feather strokes along the hollow of her damp thigh, that perfect inward curve. The acrid smoke of Jennifer's inevitable postcoital cigarette drifted across his nostrils.

"Huh?" He jostled her thigh. "When you gonna show me around L.A., lady?"

He felt her body stiffen in the darkness. He knew, without seeing it, that her jawline was hardening.

"Mark . . ."

He waited quietly. The sickening sensation, the unfailing response to that quiet, iron tone, was beginning to spread through his stomach.

"We can't do what we did tonight again."

The ceiling fell on his stomach. His body went cold. He sat up in bed, flinging the sheet aside. He tried to read her face in the windowlight. Her eyes were fixed on the darkness above her.

"What do you mean," he began numbly, searching for the right words. Had he heard her right? Why did she always time these conversations to occur just after sex?

"Are you saying you don't want to, uh, see me any more?"

She exhaled cigarette smoke, long and thoughtfully, before she answered him.

"No. I'm saying we can't do anything like go to a concert together." A slim arm came up, the knuckles of her hand rubbing his chest.

He had a wild impulse to seize her by the throat. Her games drove him to a frenzy at times. He held himself still instead, and waited.

After a minute, she said:

"I care about you, Mark. But I can't let us be seen together in public too much. I don't want people printing stuff about us. I don't want to cause gossip at the office."

She had a point. He didn't want to be in the gossip columns either. But it was a blow to his pride to know that if his name did appear, it would be as Jennifer Blade's love interest—not the other way around. She was assuredly the star in this affair.

Trying to make it sound offhand, which it was not, he muttered: "If your dad were making a TV movie out of this scene, it'd be the man saying your lines and the woman saying mine."

He could feel her shrug in the darkness. Most women of Teller's acquaintance would have taken that remark as an opening for a lecture on sexism. Such admonitions were beneath Jennifer, immaterial to her.

"Look," he said, serious now, to the beautiful shadowed face below him, "if you think I'm going to be some kind of . . ."

"Sex object?" Her thin fingers were fluttering at his groin.

He didn't finish the thought. Already, he was trembling again with need.

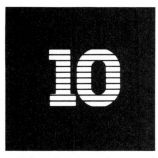
10

"Saw your man on the tube last night." Sean Murphy poked his head into Teller's cubicle.

"Hah?"

"That guy you did your piece on Friday, what's his name? Schein?"

Teller's pleasant midday fog evaporated. "What do you mean, you saw him on the tube?"

Murphy was drumming out his usual nervous energy with his fingertips on the doorjamb. "Bob-bop-a-wop," he said. "Haskell. Haskell did a big king-hell takeout on him. Took a crew down there and filmed his act."

"You are kidding me." Teller's leg dropped heavily to the floor.

"No, man. Big king-hell takeout. They got the crowd laughin', cutaways of Haskell laughin' his ass off, Haskell interviewin' his manager . . ."

"His *manager*?"

" . . . did a little interview jobby with Schein, the total shot, man. Haskell kinda gave himself credit for discovering a hot new talent. Maybe you wanta call him up and tell him to go hustle his own. Huh?" Murphy snapped his fingers and shot his cuffs.

Teller leaned back in his chair and dug the heels of his hands into his eyes. "Some other time. If Haskell needs an exclusive that bad, I'll gladly give him this one."

Haskell's "exclusive" discovery lasted exactly one day.

"Watch Cynthia tonight," advised the telephone voice of a Channel 2 producer, a woman friend of Teller's from his days at *The New York Messenger.*

"Why?"

"Just watch. You'll love it."

It was Thursday afternoon—Teller's other day off besides Saturday. The call had reached him at his apartment, on one of his two unlisted telephones.

At six o'clock he put aside his notes and flipped on Channel 2 to catch the second half of its newscast. The agenda was not inspiring. The top-of-the-hour story was a live report from Chattanooga on the state of the city "one week later."

"It is safe to say," summed up the Channel 2 correspondent, standing inexplicably before the city's famed Confederama at the foot of Lookout Mountain, "that the immortal Bobby Lee Cooper did for Chattanooga what Jesus Christ did for Bethlehem."

"Oh, God, Benson," Teller roared at the figure on the television screen. "You didn't really say that. Say you didn't say that, Benson!"

Jennifer Blade was also in Chattanooga. She had filed a brilliant report the previous day—an analysis of Bobby Lee's sensual persona as an expression of prevailing gospel styles in his homeland. Using film footage from country churches around Chattanooga, Jennifer established a subtle link between Tennessee church congregations and Las Vegas cabaret crowds.

Teller had to hand it to her. The woman had a way of turning the trashiest of assignments into first-class news reports. She had certainly spun circles around the Channel 2 collar-ad. Teller wondered whether the two of them . . . he made himself focus on the newscast.

There were a number of Cooper-related items from the local anchor desk. One of them was a brief interview with the curious fat man in the blue-rhinestone leisure suit Teller had seen lurking about the WRAP studios. The "Tennessee Tub-Thumper." He was, according to the report, an ex-porn king, a born-again Christian, and self-appointed "custodian of Bobby Lee Cooper's legacy." That meant he was hustling souvenirs. What was a major TV station doing giving air time to this clown?

It was time for Cynthia Carter's "Lively Arts" feature.

Cynthia Carter, a sallow woman with a Swarthmore accent, solemnly informed her audience that her "network of talent tipsters" had led her to "a remarkable new interpreter of the minimalist school of comedic expression."

Robert Schein's face appeared on screen. Without sound.

In an instant, Teller was out of his sofa chair and across the living room savagely punching out the Channel 2 producer's direct-line number.

Behind him, he heard the voice of Cynthia Carter proclaim: "Robert Schein's *pièce de résistance* is that sadly overlooked *pas* of the physical comedian's ballet, the pratfall. In this sense, Stitch's new star may be paying a neo-Keatonesque *hommage* to the pristine era of nonverbal comedic dialogue."

"NETWORK OF TALENT TIPSTERS?" Teller screamed at the producer as soon as she answered her phone.

"Oh. Mark. It's you. How sweet of you to call." The producer's voice was playful. "Didn't you love 'neo-Keatonesque *hommage*'?"

"Sally, for Christ's sake. Can't you people dig up your own story ideas? Do you always have to feast on everybody else's leavings?"

"*Mark.*" Sally sounded genuinely shocked. "I'll thank you to keep civil. Look, I called you up because I thought you might get a hoot out of Cynthia's rhetoric. Where do you get off telling *us* who to *cover*? You had Schein. Haskell had him. God, Mark, that's the way the game's played in this town. You put somebody on your television station, it doesn't mean you have them for always."

"I understand that. But this guy's a no-talent, Sally. Cynthia made him sound like Chevy Chase."

"That's Cynthia. She thinks she's the Critic Princess. Come off it, Mark. If you kept everybody off the air who's a no-talent, New York would be without television news service. Excepting your scrumptious self, of course. And your friend Jennifer Blade. By the way, I heard you two were an item. Confirm? Deny? No comment?"

"No, I mean it, Sally." Teller ignored the reference to Jennifer. "Cynthia was puffing up a nobody, and even Cynthia must have realized it. Robert Schein is a cipher. An empty suit. Goddammit, he's *not even a real comedian!*" Teller was astonished at his own vehemence. It was not like him to belittle anyone, especially behind their back. It was not like him to have a temper. Was the television news business making him crazy?

Sally asked quietly:

"Then why did you have him on?"

Teller was unprepared for that.

"Touché," he conceded. "I guess I was feeling jealous. Look, can we have a bit of lunch next week? Or is it a capital offense for anyone in your shop to consort with the enemy?"

"The reclusive Mark Teller emerges for lunch. I should feed that item to Liz Smith. Maybe we should invite Thomas Pynchon and J.D. Salinger to join us?"

"Don't forget Garbo. How about Tuesday? I'll call you."

"Hey. You didn't answer me about you and La Blade."

"Jennifer Blade and I enjoy a mutually satisfying and ongoing friendship."

"You could run for senator from New York on that statement. See you Tuesday."

He awoke in the night. Down on the street a car was honking. His head throbbed. For a minute he thought it was the honking car that had awakened him.

Then he realized that his doorbell was ringing.

It was Jennifer Blade.

"I'm back," she said. There was a suitcase in her hand.

She was wearing white slacks and a blue silk blouse, knotted at the waist to show a few inches of her elongated tanned torso. Just off the plane from Chattanooga.

Backlighted from the hall, she stood like a proud and graceful huntress. The clean energy, the latent motion of her shoulders and thighs, were visible even in silhouette. Teller could see the soft hairs of her bare right arm, taut and corded and lovely with the weight of the suitcase.

For a wild instant he thought of the Six Captains, and then of warriors impaled on stakes.

"May I come in?"

He was naked and on the bed before she was. He lay on his back with his arms clasped behind his head and watched as she stood folding her white slacks onto a holder, one knee bent forward, the other back, the shadows of her deep breasts dancing on her skin in candlelight. Her delaying, toying with her clothes, was a slow tease, a game that excited them both. Her eyes avoided his, kept lowered, attentive to her business with the slacks and the hanger. It was important that the game not be acknowledged. She turned to the closet, and the mature, unutterably adult swell of her buttocks sent waves pounding through his skull.

He wondered, even through the urgency of his desire, about Jennifer's sense of her own body. He thought of her in the fast press of a business day, intent on assignment sheets and telephones, the penetrating mind working fast and impersonal, thinking fast at press conferences, competitive with the straining men around her, improvising a fast and dirty question to get the subject to look *her* way, talk into *her* microphone. In that hellish cacophony, the antipode of sensuality, where legs are utilitarian, breasts invisible and forgotten, balls shriveled and morose, on the line and vulnerable to a fast knee in the joint; in that fast, vast desert of synthetic urgency, of counterfeit tumescence where all erect microphones are offered up to an official mouth in a grotesque oral parody (Was *this* the subliminal appeal of the five o'clock news? To see a great elected public official give head to CBS?); in that crazed democracy of gender where sweaty cosmeticized women jostled shoulders with tense, hair-sprayed men, where *Quote Scoop Angle Hot Stop Cut* were the words of passion; was there, in spite of all of this, a corner of Jennifer Blade's mind that retained an awareness of her essential erotic force?

Then she came to him, strode to the bed in two lanky steps and was on him, under him, insistent, "Come into me," and Mark Teller was cursed with a sudden paradoxical thought:

Was Jennifer Blade *ever* aware of her essential erotic force?

It didn't matter. She had come to him. She was back, in his arms, cool and warm at the same time, she needed him. He took satisfaction in that.

His orgasm with her left him dazed as usual, and then the euphoria overtook him, put him on a trajectory down all the hollows of the night, hurtling him down through spiraling space; and he dreamed the underground dream, the recurring dream he had of a cool, damp city beneath a city, a secret city in the earth, a city of labyrinths and tunnels, a city of intimate cafés chiseled into the clay, a dark, cool city like an enormous cave, a city of flickering candles and quiet and comrades, and long subterranean afternoons of quiet talk and wine and candles; and a calm woman, austere and dark and cool and remote, like the city itself, the city beneath the city, but welcoming, judicious, and intimate, and sharing its secret; it was a dream that smelled of damp clay, and candle-smell, and comforting dark, and a woman's hair, and home.

By 1931 Eddie Donovan was a millionaire. He was twenty-one years old. He owned a Pierce-Arrow and twenty-five silk suits and a radio station that was, depending on one's point of view, an American success story or a damned nuisance: WIRE, "A Touch of Ireland on the Air."

After the names of Mayor Curley, the Lodges, and Sacco and Vanzetti, Eddie Donovan's was the most instantly recognizable in Boston. "The Boy Broadcaster." He was one of the rare romantic success symbols of the Depression: an immigrant kid who beat the odds through personal charm and shrewd business instincts. He had mastered a revolutionary new tool of commerce—radio—before most of his elders in the business world had noticed it under their noses.

His original advertising base of local shopkeepers had expanded throughout South Boston to include department stores, automobile dealers, newspapers, and dairy companies. In 1929 he had triumphantly moved his transmitting equipment out of the Democratic Club attic and into a prestigious storefront.

Soon he discarded his original 500-watt transmitter for a 10,000-watt marvel. With it, he beamed an eighteen-hour-a-day diet of eclectic programming throughout Boston, but tailored specifically for the massive Irish-American communities of Charleston, East Boston, and Southie.

Eddie Donovan flourished in the Depression. Radio was one of the few capitalist enterprises that proved Depression-proof (baseball and the movies being the others) as America eased its terrible anxieties through cheap entertainment.

Even in those early days, Eddie Donovan was as beloved for his personality as he was admired for his business success. In the pretelevision decades of radio, listeners constructed mental images to fit the voices they heard on their receivers. The mental images nearly always erred on the side of glamor and beauty—but in Eddie Donovan's case, the collective image fit the man.

His voice came across as that of a vibrant, intelligent, dashing young rakehell. It betrayed more than a hint of his Irish roots, but the brogue was tempered by a crisp urban-American clarity. Eddie Donovan's radio voice bespoke a sandy-haired, green-eyed youth, firm of jaw, scrubbed and trim and full of flash and mirth—a "gogetter," as the new business slang had it.

That was Eddie Donovan, all right. But there was more.

What the radio voice concealed was the cold will of the ideologue.

Eddie Donovan had been weaned on a fierce hatred of oppressive government and a fervor for self-determination that bordered on religious worship—the legacy of his I.R.A. father. He came to believe that all institutions were corrupt, that nobility resided not in collective benevolence but in the individual soul. He was fascinated by the unexplainable power that seemed to grow out of his own voice—a power that made him a personage among the anonymous cadres of his fellow immigrants, the longshoremen, the shipbuilders, the strugglers in a world he found ripe with opportunity.

He was a celebrity. The realization boggled him—but at the same time, it inspired unsentimental dreams indeed.

Why could Eddie Donovan not combine his personal force—his talent for making people love him—with his political beliefs, and establish a new order of enlightenment on the airwaves? The airwaves were his—no one could harvest magic from them the way he could. The route was open to him.

He made it his life's commitment—his life's obsession.

Thus, in those early days of outward merriment and adventure, the first hazy outlines of the Phaëthon Society were forming in Eddie Donovan's mind.

He never married. As the 1930s, the Depression years, wore on, he shaped and honed his vision for a broadcast empire.

Gradually, so that his loyal core-audience of Irish working-class families would hardly notice the change, he pared away the more amateurish elements of his daily broadcast agenda. In place of *The O'Dwyer Family Singers* and *Breeda Cassida, Harpist,* WIRE listeners began to be exposed to programming of a more substantive and politically grounded nature: *The New Deal vs. the New Party,* for instance, and, *A Plain Fellow Looks at the Supreme Court*—both symposiums by conservative Massachusetts state senators.

Donovan could not equal the resources of the emerging radio networks. Thus he could not compete for prestigious commentators such as H. V. Kaltenborn, Lowell Thomas, and Boake Carter—men who, by the very magnetism of their voices, were exciting a new American interest in political thought.

It didn't matter. Eddie Donovan became his own commentator. The same voice that had carved spiraling cathedrals of fantasy with his father, that had stopped children's breath with its intimations of witches and goblins, that had tugged smiles from drawn faces with its playful Celtic wit—now stirred deeper passions with its ringing exhortations for patriotism, sternness of purpose, resistance to the corrupting embrace of the Roosevelt dole.

Along with Lindbergh, who appeared in his Boston studio many times, Eddie Donovan emerged as one of the country's leading advocates of isolationism in the months leading up to Pearl Harbor. His stand was not popular among his listeners; many of his devoted followers were shocked and saddened at this extreme (and to many, unpatriotic) position. But once the United States entered World War II, Eddie Donovan adjusted quickly to reality. He strung together a loose affiliation of about a dozen radio stations on the Eastern Seaboard (among them a New York station), appointed himself war correspondent for the group, and dashed off to the European Theater to deliver florid, imaginative accounts of the Allied Campaign. His style of war coverage ranked with Murrow's and Elmer Davis's in its imagistic sweep. He described battles with the zest and glee that sportscasters would later employ for professional football games. He became a sort of surrogate hero, an armed-forces advocate beloved by troops and listeners back home alike. His earlier isolationism was quickly forgotten (a fact that was not lost, but catalogued, somewhere in Donovan's developing mental library of broadcast wisdom).

As for the owners of the stations that joined Donovan's war-coverage alliance, they remained close and trusted colleagues, partners in Eddie Donovan's postwar broadcast empire.

They also comprised the inner circle of the Phaëthon Society.

After the war, Eddie Donovan lost no time in joining the right-wing militarists in warning that Russia was the United States' inevitable next enemy. His radio commentaries rang with the message. (His honorific "Colonel" was bestowed on him then by a grateful American Legion, "for contributing to Americanism on the airwaves.")

The loose association of stations evolved into a network—the Continental Radio Network—president, Colonel Eddie Donovan. By 1950 Donovan was a broadcast baron—embarrassingly rich, bored, bursting with his ever-expanding dream to create a national lyceum on the air, a lyceum of enlightened political thought—a wakeup system that would keep right-thinking Americans ever-vigilant against the slide into collectivist ruin.

Television was the coming thing—the big, warm dish of American apple pie, just now emerging from the oven, that some day would spread its luscious, smothering crust across the nation, from sea to shining sea—its viscid juices sluicing into every household.

Donovan knew that. He could see it as plainly as he had seen radio's first potential more than twenty-five years before in Boston.

The trouble was, the pie had already been carved up.

Corporations with more millions than Donovan dreamed of controlled the prosperous stations in the big cities. The networks ruled.

How to dig one's fingers into the pie?

Colonel Eddie Donovan studied the situation.

There was one way.

One piece of the pie cooling all by itself, virtually unnoticed by everyone else.

A piece of the pie called UHF.

Ultrahigh frequency. The first UHF stations appeared on the American airwaves in 1952.

UHF was envisioned as television's equivalent of FM radio—a band of channels for small, selective audiences that would offer the "quality" and "educational" programming that the VHF (very-high frequency) stations already were consigning to the fringe hours, if not dropping altogether.

The UHF stations fulfilled part of that promise.

They drew small audiences. Small to the point of invisible.

Few Americans even knew about UHF. Few purchasers of new sets bothered with the extra knob that was required to tune them in—a knob that didn't make the reassuring, purposeful "click" of the VHF channel switch, but which required something of the art of the safecracker, a precision dialing and spinning that seemed to yield nothing but static.

America gave UHF a cursory look-see, burped, and went back to Uncle Miltie.

But Colonel Eddie Donovan took the long view. He knew that public tastes were not changed overnight. He also recognized that there were certain advantages to operating in a relative vacuum of massive public scrutiny. Certain things might be said, certain chances taken, a certain type of audience cultivated.

He mobilized his business associates, the station owners in the Continental Radio Network. A corporation was formed. Calling upon the esteem of certain influential Congressmen in Washington, Donovan and his associates had no trouble in convincing the members of the Federal Communications Commission that it would be in the public interest, convenience, and necessity to grant a license for the operation of a UHF channel in New York— Channel 26.

Office and studio space was secured on the twenty-ninth floor of the Commerce Center, a fine old mercantile bastion in the West 60s that had lately experienced trouble attracting tenants.

A news announcer was hired—a man with the unlikely name of MacGregor Walterson. A puppeteer and ventriloquist with a string tie were given retainers, as were a three-piece "studio orchestra," a four-member Irish glee club, a Polish polka band, and a woman who demonstrated recipes on a working gas range.

Colonel Eddie Donovan, at age forty, had himself a television station.

Channel 26 made its debut on Christmas Eve, 1952. In honor of the timing, the publicity announcements had noted that "A Christmas Present to New York Will Be Unwrapped."

To coordinate with that campaign, Colonel Eddie Donovan had requested—and been granted—the call letters WRAP.

Not very many people witnessed those first awkward stirrings of the Continental Broadcasting Network television empire—the Hooper ratings had the number down below five thousand. But Colonel Donovan and his people were patient. They knew that over the haul, the picture was bound to change in UHF television.

As the fifties wore on, Colonel Donovan's station slowly took hold in the consciousness of New York. One strong factor was Colonel Donovan.

Each weekday night at 7:30 the colonel appeared on the air live, to deliver a half-hour television version of his popular old stem-winding radio commentaries.

Thousands of his former radio admirers from the war years went to the bother of grappling with that unfamiliar knob on their new television sets, just to see whether the face that accompanied that thrilling voice matched their fantasies.

What they saw was a visage seemingly designed by God and Norman Rockwell.

Eddie Donovan sat ramrod-stiff, facing the camera straight on, looking very much like a bona fide colonel indeed in his light business suit (the padded jacket squared off at the shoulders like a giant pack of Lucky Strikes), holding a sheaf of notes at which he glanced from time to time.

Fluttering kinescopes from those days, stored in the CBN archives, showed a stern young martinet with a high, glossy forehead, curly hair brushed up flat against the crown. His pale eyes, set wide apart, blinked rapidly as he spoke—his only sign of nervousness. The jaw was long and hard; it was a Smilin' Jack jaw, a jaw that clearly brooked no interference from those who would destroy the fabric of American society. Donovan's one serious flaw in his on-air delivery style was a tendency to screw his mouth slightly toward one side of his face—an old radioman's tic—but this only evoked subconscious comparisons with Dwight Eisenhower, and so it became a beloved mannerism, an affectionately lampooned trait, like Liberace's smile or Bishop Sheen's brogue.

For a half hour, five nights a week, Colonel Eddie Donovan barked his jingo sermons to the God-fearing, UHF-loving super-patriots of New York—with only two interruptions, from the makers of Mother's bread (a farsighted company that, thanks to its early association with Colonel Donovan, was able to diversify into presweetened breakfast cereals in 1962).

There was plenty to talk about—the heroism of Senator Mc-Carthy, Korea, the evil of the Rosenbergs, the Communist infil-tration of the State Department, atheism in the public schools, swing music (later, rock'n'roll), the Hollywood radicals, the Com-munist master plan to spread its influence across Europe (Colonel Donovan pointing to maps and charts).

Colonel Eddie Donovan did not exactly become the toast of New York City overnight. But he gained a solid word-of-mouth vogue, a respectable slice of the viewer-pie. (Children who sat gaping dully at him would later tune in his station out of loyalty as fathers and mothers themselves.) He gained enough of a follow-ing to save WRAP-TV, Channel 26, from the living-dead status of most UHF outlets.

Colonel Donovan was one of television's early curiosities—a name, a draw, a celebrity. A pleaser of crowds. On the strength of that appeal, his station survived.

And prospered. Over a period of eight years, Donovan Enter-prises, Inc., began to collect bargain-basement properties around the country: failing UHF stations that seemed at the time to be foolhardy investments. Tiny, overlooked FM radio outlets in medium-sized cities. An occasional AM radio property.

By 1961, Donovan Enterprises owned five UHF stations—the legal limit—and claimed affiliations with twenty-three more.

The Continental Broadcasting Network was born.

One of the five stations owned was a Los Angeles outlet. Eddie Donovan made his first trip west to consolidate the deal in 1959. The experience proved to be one of the most important in his life.

The pale, intense Irish Catholic from the East had his first ex-posure to Hollywood and its sunny pleasures, its sense of easy voluptuous power, its guiltless embrace of the cult of celebrity. There, he met men who created and tore down human personalities as easily as they changed movie sets. There, he realized for the first time (forgetting himself) that the public persona might have nothing to do with the private one. (He was shocked and delighted.) There, he witnessed firsthand the raw equation between personality and power.

There, he met the young pioneer in television series creation, Sterling Blade—then a lowly executive producer—and signed him to supervise an "adult western" for the network-to-be. (Donovan's early discovery of Blade was to yield high dividends over the years for them both.)

There, he danced long into a Hollywood evening amid the impossible, flowing fountains at a famous producer's mansion. There, he had sex for the first time in his life—with a golden goddess who had turned his heart in the movies back on Broadway.

It was a strong and combustive welding of forces, Colonel Donovan's first Hollywood odyssey. The disciplined, repressed, ascetic political ideologue confronting the intoxicating knowledge that personality and power are interwoven—and that where one is created, the other will spring naturally.

It was a lesson he never forgot. Decades ahead of his time among major television executives, Colonel Eddie Donovan nurtured and expanded his Hollywood ties.

And to the ones he felt he could trust—the shrewdest, most visionary, most politically "enlightened"—Colonel Donovan offered membership in the Phaëthon Society.

The Society itself was never revealed to the American public. Its name never appeared in the newspapers; it was never invoked in the halls of Congress nor even in the confidential records of the FBI. Officially, it did not exist. And yet, the Phaëthon Society influenced the texture of American life in the 1950s and '6os, in the spheres of broadcasting and of government.

In broadcasting, Society members—acting publicly as interested individuals, station owners, programming executives—helped persuade the major networks to seed their prime-time entertainment programs with highly doctrinaire themes and values: action series that glorified the exploits of G-men and anti-Communist spies, comedies that celebrated the starchy pieties of home and church. (Sterling Blade was a principal supplier of the early superpatriotic cop shows.)

But if the Society was effective in the nature of the programming it steered onto the airwaves, it created a far greater influence through the kind of material it kept off the air.

Society members kept a meticulous checklist of American playwrights, novelists, and humorists whose work it considered too "radical" or "freethinking" for the respectable mass—a list that differed from the Hollywood Blacklist only in that it was more thorough. Artists whose work threatened to venture beyond certain tacit limits of social thought never saw their plays performed on the prestigious, live-drama showcases of the fifties. Thus did the Phaëthon Society wield a subtle cudgel over the First Amendment.

(In the sixties, as the radical style took hold in America despite the best efforts of TV sitcom daddies and iron-jawed secret agents, Society members acquired a certain sophistication: they encouraged action series whose heroes had the look and the rhetoric of disaffected youth—who seemed in a vague way to defy the "Establishment"—but who, in the end, upheld the values of white, consumerist, militaristic America.)

In politics the Society was effective in placing a number of handpicked candidates in state and local offices—chiefly through its members' ability to bestow or withhold favorable television coverage. But the equal-time provision of the Communications Act made such maneuvering risky and difficult.

Colonel Eddie Donovan and his fellow members of the Phaëthon Society knew that in order to achieve meaningful power in America—to fulfill their vision of a national ideology—they would have to break through the electoral process. They would have to place one of their own in a position of unassailable power.

As the years went by, the Phaëthon Society waited for its chance.

L. Malcolm Bass summoned a meeting in the executive conference room.

It was a glorious Monday morning in mid-October. Autumn drifted down the Hudson into Manhattan on a blue haze from the hills and hollows upstate. Maples flared red in Central Park; on Fifth Avenue the chestnut vendors were out again, the smoke from their rusted pots touching the nostrils like a sudden memory. There were high white clouds against the blue sky, moving fast; a cold swirling wind had knifed in off the Atlantic to blow the thick, stale summer air out of Manhattan.

None of this was evident in the executive conference room of station WRAP. In the executive conference room, the seasons did not change. The executive conference room was brown, dry winter, a winter of darkness and shadows, and no cold. No temperature at all, that anyone was aware of.

The WRAP brain trust trooped in: the program director; Kurtis, the news director; the director of advertising and public relations; the executive producer for newscasts; the head of public-affairs programming; the station's editorial director; the station's legal counsel; the head of sales.

There was little conversation. Everyone sensed that this was not going to be a pleasant meeting.

The summer-ratings books had not been a disaster for WRAP, but they had not shown any dramatic improvement either, and that, in the eyes of L. Malcolm Bass, WRAP's station manager and chief executive officer, amounted to disaster. His mandate from the Colonel had been simple and direct: get the goddamn station up there in the pack with the others. If he did, Bass knew, he would have an excellent shot at a network title. But first there was the matter of the flagship station, WRAP, as a proving-ground . . .

A white-uniformed maid entered the conference room and began setting coffee cups in front of the assembled executives. Most of them were already smoking. All of them were nervous. They had expected L. Malcolm Bass to be there at the appointed hour, 9 A.M., but it was now almost 9:20 and the station manager had not made his appearance. Except for the public-relations director with her *Running Woman* magazine, no one had brought anything to read, not even a morning paper.

Especially a morning paper.

It had been a hellishly uncomfortable twenty minutes.

"You're all probably wondering why I called you here," Kurtis ventured, to break the tense silence.

Nobody laughed.

L. Malcolm Bass strode noiselessly into the conference room, his rimless glasses flashing. Under one arm he carried a stack of bound loose-leaf volumes.

Bass made his way to the head of the conference table. He nodded or spoke to no one.

Bass stood in front of his chair, arranging the loose-leaf binders on the table. His movements had a damp remoteness about them. He was a tall, thin man, almost six feet four, big-boned but with the sallow executive's color and the rings of flesh about his middle and on his neck. His sandy hair had thinned away off the crown, leaving a freckled tundra. No glorious autumn mornings for L. Malcolm Bass.

His voice was deep and rumbling, like a broadcaster's, although Bass's background was not in broadcasting. He had gained his stripes in one of the city's most aggressive and influential market-research firms.

Without looking up from his papers, and still on his feet, Bass used his deep rumble to clear his throat. The people around the table glanced at him expectantly.

"Griffin, you are finished here," Bass remarked, eyes still lowered, so casually that most of the executives thought they had misunderstood him.

"Sir?" whispered Archibald Griffin helplessly. He had spent twenty-five years at WRAP, the last fifteen as head of public-affairs programming. The walls of his small office were covered with framed citations, broadcast society awards, certificates of appreciation from churches, service organizations, and ethnic groups whom he had featured on his good, gray, Sunday-midnight round-table discussion show, *Let's WRAP About It*.

"We had a little summit talk, Griffin, didn't we, when I came here three months ago. I put you on notice then, didn't I. I told you your programs were very good television—for the nineteen-fifties.

"You haven't budged off dead center, Griff! Talking heads don't cut it in the nineteen-seventies. I am not going to sit still for three bald-headed Latino priests sitting around a goddamned coffee table and pulling up their Supp-hose for an hour on my station, I don't give a good goddamn whether it's a public service or not."

Griffin's hands were trembling. He was a dignified, soft, silver-haired man, a decent and comfortable old-school broadcaster. Nothing like this had ever happened to him. He decided to make a stand. His voice was shaking as he half rose from his chair.

"You can't do this, Malcolm. Those shows aren't meant to be, uh, zingy. Our license agreement with the FCC stipulates a minimal amount of programming for minority . . ."

Bass's booming baritone cut the old man off.

"I've read the license agreement, Griff, thank you. Nowhere in it could I find a clause stipulating that we have to be dull."

"My rep—"

"Furthermore, as you know, we've just had our license renewed. We're good for three more years. If at the end of that time, in my judgment, we have not represented religious and other special-interest groups across the broad spectrum of our programming, I am sure we can find a way to reinstate—"

Bass couldn't bring himself to pronounce the words, *"Let's WRAP About It."* Griffin, in a rare display of contemporary awareness, had affixed that title in 1968. The previous title had been *Dialogue*.

"—uh, your program in some form that will be mutually acceptable to both the station and its viewers."

Griffin was standing erect now, like a prisoner hearing his sentence. Now the full impact of what Bass had done was sinking in. Not only was his own career being terminated. Equally as painful, the show that had occupied the last fifteen years of his life, the show that had won him and the station so much praise, so many awards—"The award-winning *Let's WRAP About It*," was the way the lead-in announcer described it—was being abruptly scrapped.

Archibald Griffin stood stiffly at his chair, his fingertips touching the edge of the table. Tears were running down his cheeks.

"You'd better go now, Griff," said Bass, his tone gentle in a metallic sort of way. "You are welcome here, to finish up whatever business you may have, and to collect your personal belongings, until six P.M. today."

Griffin's place had been only two places away from the head of the table where L. Malcolm Bass stood. Now he began the longest and most humiliating walk of his life, down the row of his silent former colleagues, around the far end of the conference table, past the unused platter of Danish, toward the door.

No one looked at him. No one spoke.

As Griffin put his hand on the doorknob, his beeper went off.

Someone was paging Archibald Griffin. Someone at the station required his presence. His decision on some programming question was needed, his advice sought. *"Pip-pip-pip-pip-pip,"* went Griffin's beeper.

Andy Gimble, the executive producer for newscasts, burst out laughing. He couldn't help it. It was the sort of high-pitched, uncontrollable laughter heard at the scene of automobile accidents, or among soldiers after a firefight.

With Andy Gimble's hysterical laughter in his ears, the closing fanfare of a quarter-century in broadcasting, Archibald Griffin walked out of the WRAP executive conference room. Three weeks later he would be dead of a massive coronary.

The door swung shut.

Gimble brought his laughter under control; his face was shot with a painful crimson flush.

For the first time, L. Malcolm Bass looked up from the pages of the loose-leaf notes spread before him and appeared to notice the group.

He smiled briefly at the stricken faces. His glasses glinted in the reflected glare of the table.

"Now that I have your attention," he remarked pleasantly, "let's get down to business. We have a lot of ground to cover."

Twenty-five minutes later, the WRAP brain trust appreciated how much ground, indeed, L. Malcolm Bass had intended to cover.

The entire CBN network was retooling, Bass explained to the group, most of whom were eyeing him as though he held a smoking revolver in one hand.

"Colonel Donovan is no longer content to have his network regarded as the miracle of UHF television," Bass announced. "He is not pleased, to name but one example, with the fact that most observers do not take the Continental Broadcasting Network seriously as a competitive bidder for telecast rights to the Summer Olympics in Moscow.

"The Colonel's thinking is that with the advent of digital UHF tuning devices as standard equipment on television sets, the distinction between UHF and VHF broadcasting is obsolete. And that the time has come to impress upon the American viewing public once and for all that we are an entity on equal footing with CBS, NBC, and ABC. And I agree.

"From now on," he continued, "CBN will cease to regard itself as the first UHF network. CBN is one of *four major* networks, competing in a very tough neighborhood for the same cookies as the other kids. Realistically, we don't expect to become number one overnight, nor in the next six months to a year. After that, it is an open question as to how high we can reposition ourselves. In the meantime, the thinking is that neither the network itself nor any of its owned or affiliated stations can accept *last* place as a viable position. What that means, ladies and gentlemen, is that as of today, we are going to commence, as the saying goes, to kick ass and take names. What happened to Mr. Griffin could happen to any one of you sitting here, I assure you." His eyes met Kurtis's, and his gaze locked for several seconds.

After a long moment Bass continued his lecture.

"With WRAP as the flagship station, each of your heads—as well as mine—will be on the block, perhaps more so than anywhere up and down the line. How well this station performs in the critical months to come will have a large bearing on how the network performs."

The new strategy for CBN centered around one word.

"Personalities," Bass said. "Write that word down in your little memory books and keep it under your pillow. 'Personalities' is going to be the operative phrase at the Continental Broadcasting Network from here on in. The American people are in love with personalities. With celebrities. And we are going to give them personalities. We are going to condition the American public to the fact that when they tune in a CBN station, such as WRAP, they can expect to *wallow* in personalities. Henceforth, we are going to be selling celebrityhood. *Not* programming. *Not* genre this or genre that. *Not* tits 'n' ass. *Not* sports. *Not* news. *Not* public affairs."

He paused, and pounded his fist softly three times on the table.

"Personalities," he whispered. He looked around the room again, his glasses flashing.

"When we are through," he went on, "our viewers are going to feel as though they *live* with the stars of CBN programs: eat, sleep, go to the goddamned *toilet* with them. Our stars' lives are going to be open books. There will be no secrets. There will be no aspect of a star's private existence so personal that it will be withheld from our publicity department's bio sheets or from the newspaper columnists."

"You mean make CBN a sort of national *Tattler* of the airwaves," Ed Kurtis blurted out before he could stop himself. The thought was a sarcasm, and for a moment he had the wild fear that he might just have ended his own career at WRAP. But L. Malcolm Bass merely smiled at him; looked pleased, in fact.

"Yes, that's it, Ed, you're getting the idea," he said. "In a way it's ironic. Television created the superstar system in this country, but having done so, we needed the magazines like *Tattler* and *People* to show us what we'd done. They exploited our concept, so what CBN is doing now is exploiting their refinement of it.

"Of course," said Bass, adopting a "reasonable" tone of voice, "we must cover the important news stories of the day, whatever they may be. I yield to no one in my devotion to aggressive, serious journalism. *However!*"

Here it comes, thought Kurtis.

"We have to deal within the realities of the time-frame we live in. Here is the way I want to see it played from now on. These are your marching orders, Ed."

Kurtis made a show of opening a felt-tip pen and holding it over his yellow legal pad. He knew that everyone in the room was waiting to see how far Bass would push him; it was no secret that Bass regarded Kurtis as "old regime." How he reacted to the upcoming "marching orders" would be the decisive test of his subservience to the new regime. Kurtis had a brief flash of himself applying for a job in a public-relations company.

"Every news story on the air, insofar as possible, will be filtered through the prism of celebrityhood."

Kurtis's pen was on the paper but he was having trouble making it move.

"What this means is this: I want a celebrity angle to *every story,* if you can get it. By celebrity I don't mean just show business. I mean any name that's fixed in the public mind. I want to see famous faces on the screen reacting to any political news item. If there's a big murder, get file footage on the air of big-name killers from the past. Compare it to scenes from *The Godfather* if you have to. Are you with me so far, Ed?"

Kurtis's mind raced. He had played the company game so long, made so many compromises, had so often done on his own what Bass was nakedly announcing as policy, that in a way it didn't seem to matter any more. But the old newsman deep inside Ed Kurtis wasn't entirely lobotomized yet.

He knew there would be literally dozens of stories a week that had not the remotest possibilities of a celebrity tie-in. He groped for an example—one that would not make him sound unnecessarily provocative.

"What about something like a flash flood, Malcolm? I wouldn't see any tie-ins there . . ."

Bass flashed him a deceptively disarming grin. "Interview Esther Williams. How the hell do I know? That's your department, Ed. I'm giving you policy. I would say one thing. Maybe some of those stories *don't absolutely have to be on the air.*"

Bass paused, smiling, as though welcoming further debate. Kurtis kept his mouth shut, hating himself for it.

"All right," said Bass. "That leads us right into Rule Number

Two. We are going to have to change our definition, to some extent, of what is news and what isn't. We are not *The New York Times*. We are not a newscast of record. We have the latitude—some would call it the *obligation*—of grabbing people where they're involved. And the American people these days are involved in a wide spectrum of interests that do not affect just their pocketbooks and their sense of justice. They are involved in a *vicarious* world—a world that we in television have created for them. I am suggesting to you that it is our duty to cover that vicarious world as diligently as we cover the city courts and the mayor's office.

"Our own market research shows that only fifty-four percent of our viewing audience knows for sure who their goddamn U.S. senators are—but eighty-seven percent correctly identified Brooke Shields. What that tells me, and should tell you, Ed, is that Brooke Shields is a legitimate news item.

"On that subject, I want to see Jennifer Blade doing more celebrity-oriented coverage. We're wasting her talents on hard news. She's sort of a celebrity in her own right, famous father and all, plus she's a helluva looker herself. Melinda, I'd like to see more in the columns about Jennifer. And Ed, I want you to reshuffle Jennifer out of the news deck and into the personality-oriented deck. She's our hole card. But we have to market her in the right way."

Even Bass seemed taken aback somewhat by the stricken look on Kurtis's face.

He opted for flattery—an infrequent tactic with Bass.

"Look, Ed. I know you can do it. I saw it in your coverage of the Bobby Lee Cooper thing. You loaded up the show with Cooper bullshit for a week. Our ratings went through the roof. I was damned proud of the team that week; meant to send you all a memo. But you let the story die! Cooper stuff is still hot, believe me. Ride that story, Ed. That's the sort of thing I want."

Bass plunged his hands into one of the loose-leaf binders and came up clutching a folded copy of *The Village Voice*. Bass held the paper out away from him, as though it were wrapped around a decaying fish.

"Here's an example of what I mean," he said, opening it to a folded-back page. "I was reading *The Village Voice* just this morning and came across this."

Sure you were, thought Kurtis. *You probably bought it while you were making the scene on Christopher Street.*

"This guy Schein, this new comedian," said Bass. "He's been getting a lot of ink around town. Here's a review of him in the *Voice*, with a photograph."

Andy Gimble spoke up for the first time in the meeting. His voice betrayed a slight tremble, fear, or anger, Kurtis wasn't sure which.

"I read that review," Gimble said. "They mopped up the floor with Schein."

BANG! Bass's fist slammed down on the table. "BUT THEY RAN HIS GODDAMNED PHOTOGRAPH!" he roared at Gimble. "Don't you see that's what I'm driving at! People don't read the fucking reviews! They look at the pictures! That's where you people are living in a different world! I don't give a shit whether Robert Schein is the next Steve Martin or a stiff. *Point* is, he's been getting publicity all over town. Everywhere but WRAP! I haven't seen one mention of Robert Schein on our station. There's a new star being created in New York and we haven't had a thing on him. This is what I mean, gentlemen, when I say give me personalities!"

Ed Kurtis was secretly gloating. He couldn't wait until Bass was finished. Here was his chance to one-up the bastard.

"Our staff can take credit for Robert Schein, Malcolm," he said. "Mark Teller, our pop-culture critic, was the guy who discovered him. We had him on the night after Cooper died."

Bass cursed silently. He'd missed that. To cover his embarrassment, he roared, "ALL RIGHT. Then let's *remind* everybody we discovered him. I want a five-minute session with him live next week; I want Teller to interview him, update his career so far. Understood, Ed?"

"Yes, sir."

"All right. I think now we're all on the same wavelength."

13

"Mr. Kurtis would like to see you in his office right away, Mark."

"Thanks, Charlene. Be right up."

"Oh, Mark." The secretary's voice was singsong.

"Yeah?"

"We tried paging you on your beeper. No luck."

"Gee, I must have forgotten to wear it today. Yep. That's it, Charlene, that's exactly what happened. I must have left the damned thing at home."

"I'll tell Mr. Kurtis. He'll be so relieved to know it was just an oversight."

It was a little game they played.

Kurtis's door was ajar, as usual, and Teller walked through without knocking. Although it was two hours until lunch, Kurtis's office already smelled of brine and coleslaw. Kurtis lifted his heavy, pugnacious face from the customary pile of memos, unanswered letters, newspapers, ratings books, and press releases on the desk in front of him. He looked even more fatigued and lumpy than usual.

"Ed, if it's about the beeper thing again . . ."

Kurtis dismissed the remark with a violent shake of his head and motioned Teller to the sofa beside his desk.

"You want coffee?" he asked in a flat voice. "How do you take it?"

So this was going to be a ceremonial visit, a diplomatic occasion. "Cream."

"Charlene?" Kurtis craned his head to see out the door. "One cream, one black." He pushed his heavy torso back in his chair and rubbed his eyes with hairy knuckles.

"What's up, Ed?"

Kurtis turned his pale, simian face toward the window to his right and scowled through it at the seasonless New York skyline view.

"Lovely day," he growled. "Great football weather."

"Yeah. So what is it, Ed? Did I libel somebody again?"

"Jesus, Teller, you're more morbid than I am. No, I wish it was as simple as that. I think it's worse."

"Worse?"

"I'll tell you in a minute. Helluva fine day out there." He indicated the window again, as though he were contemplating an exit through it. Teller realized he was stalling until Charlene brought the coffee.

"Set 'em down there, Charlene. And close the door, will ya?"

They sipped their coffee.

"Mark, I just got out of a bloodbath you wouldn't believe. Malcolm Bass just put the newscast in the toilet and he's got his hand on the plunger."

"You called the wrong guy. Sounds like a case for the Ty-D-Bol man."

"None of your wise-ass. This is serious. Mark, you gotta promise me. Nothing you hear me say goes past that door."

Teller nodded.

"Bass is gonna take this newscast and turn it into the biggest three-ring circus this town has ever seen."

"Nothing personal, Ed, but he doesn't have that much turning to do."

Kurtis glared at him. Teller could see that the man was under an intense strain. He was instantly sorry for his remark.

"Just kidding, Ed. Go on."

"No you weren't. And if I didn't think you were right I'd personally throw your ass out of here. You're honest, Teller. That's one reason I talk to you more than I should."

"So what else?"

Kurtis picked up a yellow legal tablet in front of him and scowled at it. He shook his head slowly.

"So CBN is going to turn into the Personality Network, or some such shit, and we're privileged to be a part of the scheme. All the news we do has to have a personality tie-in, or a celebrity tie-in."

Teller gaped at him. "So Bass is getting involved in news content."

"You might say. Here's another one. He wants Jennifer Blade off the serious stuff; he wants us to remarket her as a kind of celebrity specialist."

Teller made himself keep his voice detached. "Jennifer Blade's a helluva news reporter."

"You think you're telling me anything? It breaks my heart to do that to that kid."

"By the way, I thought you already had a celebrity reporter. Me."

"I'm coming to that. Anyway you're a commentator. Before Bass is through, everybody on the goddamn *staff* is going to be a celebrity reporter. So you better get used to the company."

"All right. Where do I fit into all this?"

"Not in any way that I think you'll like. That's the main reason I'm spilling all this stuff to you. Mark, I've said it before. You dress like Fidel Castro's gardener and the staff thinks you're a prima donna, but you're a fine reporter. You take your beat seriously. Too seriously for Bass's taste, I'm pretty sure. He's going to want you to stop shoveling shit in everybody's face and start coming in your pants over every new movie and fag musical that hits town. And I fuckin' *know* you're gonna have to lay off the media-criticism pieces."

"Bass is the station manager. *You're* the news director."

"Yeah. And Elizabeth Regina runs England."

"Okay. I'll fight my battle with Bass if and when the time comes. What about you, Ed? What are you going to do?"

"Me?" Kurtis raised his bushy eyebrows. "I got a kid halfway through Williams College, studying to become an English teacher. I'm payin' alimony on one marriage and keeping my present wife happy in fine stores everywhere. Plus a twenty-year mortgage out in Westchester. You think maybe I should quit and write a column for *The Village Voice?*"

"Just curious. Frankly I think you ought to stay around. If Bass gets his way with these changes, we're going to need you to give the news any dignity at all."

Kurtis blinked at Teller. Then his voice dropped to a husky pitch Teller had never heard before.

"Thanks, Mark. I appreciate hearin' that." Kurtis made himself chuckle. "Even if it is bullshit. Oh, by the way. You just said if and when the time comes. It may come sooner than you think. Remember that guy Robert Schein?"

Schein. Was there a day in the last two months when Teller hadn't heard the name? Schein was the monkey on his back, the private thorn that reminded him he had already done, in microcosm, all that L. Malcolm Bass had set out to do.

"Yes," he said evenly. "I remember him. What about him?"

"He's an example of the kind of coverage Bass wants us to emphasize. He's-a-new-celebrity-on-the-way-up type of thing."

That much was true. In the past six weeks Robert Schein—with behind-the-scenes tutoring from Bill Wyler, Teller was certain—had, insanely, become the hottest "in" act on the East Side-Village circuit. He had become a weekend headliner at Stitch's, which, Teller understood, was now beginning to attract the cognoscenti, the thin, sharp-faced leisure-time shock troops who took their pleasure in deadly earnest and who consulted (as nearly as Teller could make out) chicken entrails before deciding which establishment to grace with the benediction of their sanctioning presence.

The cognoscenti had observed Robert Schein—and decreed him a hit.

Not just a hit, exactly:

An Important New Interpreter of the New Comic Minimalism

A Comedic Anarchist—His New Silence Subverts the Tyranny of Oververbalist Overkill

The Ultimate in Neolaconic Wit

A New Voicelessness for the New Deaf Ear of the Late Seventies

The reviews—appearing mostly in the small, smart, neighborhood weeklies—had made Teller's stomach turn.

He had not been able to hear the name "Schein" without wanting to drive his fist through a wall.

"Bass wants you to interview him," Kurtis said. "Live, on the news."

"*Oh*, no." Teller jumped up off the sofa. "Absolutely not." He leveled a finger at Kurtis. "Nothing doing, Ed. No way. Not me. Get somebody else. I'm not gonna do it."

Kurtis sat squinting up at Teller with his mouth open. He slapped a heavy palm down on his desk top. It sank within the paper rubble.

"WHY THE HELL NOT?" he bellowed. "Goddammit, Teller, siddown! Now what's wrong with that? It's a reasonable request, the guy's hot around town. Jeezuz, Bass said he wants you to *interview* the guy, not marry him."

Teller put his hands on his hips and gazed down at his sneakers.

"Look. Ed. I found out a lot about Schein the day we went over to film his act. He's a nobody, Ed. He doesn't *have* an act. At least he didn't have one then. He's a total fluke; he's got some has-been comic propping him up, writing his stuff for him, and he'll blow over, I guarantee you."

"He's pretty goddamn hot right now."

"He's hot because he's different and because a bunch of TV stations put him on the air. I had him so Haskell had to have him; Haskell and I had him so Cynthia Carter had to have him. Then the *Voice* did him; then the weeklies. I think his name turned up in Earl Wilson, maybe a couple of other places. Jesus, Ed, you know how the business works. For two weeks the media in this town could make a pop superstar out of the guy who cells cigars in the lobby."

"I remember that piece you did on him," mused Kurtis. "Great visuals."

"Yeah, well," said Teller. He was still on his feet, pacing, looking for a way out. "I guarantee you, Ed, by Christmas nobody'll remember ever hearing about Robert Schein. He's peaked already. He can't last. My information is, he gets up there, he stares at the audience, he tells a few jokes, he stands there staring some more, and he falls down. The critics call that 'comic minimalism,' or something. Point is they love him because they're afraid not to. Everybody's scared they'll be *missing* something if they don't. As soon as they find out there isn't anything to miss, they'll drop him like a leper for the next stiff."

"We got a lot of mail on that piece, I remember."

There was one last position for Teller to take. He knew that if he held to it, it could cost him his job. He thought about Robert Schein's vacant, contemptuous face, and decided that losing his job was a chance he would have to take.

"Robert Schein doesn't merit any further coverage by *WRAP-Around News*. That is my professional judgment. I'm your critic and I've just given you my critical opinion. I've got a reputation to think about, Ed. I won't do the Schein interview."

Ed Kurtis folded his hairy knuckles under his chin and stared up at Teller for a long time. His eyes looked tired, but a cloud of anger had come over his face.

Teller wondered how it was going to feel, finally, to hear the words "You're fired." He thought, for one panicky instant, of modifying his stand. But there was no way.

When Kurtis spoke, his voice was soft.

"I ought to can your ass, Teller. Maybe I'll have to before this mess lets up. I'll tell you one thing. You're taking your stand too early. You're fighting the wrong battle. Bass is going to want stuff from you that will make Robert Schein seem like Alistair Cooke. I'll tell you another thing. If his scheme works on this station, there won't be anywhere else for you to go in New York, because everybody else'll be doing the same shit by Easter, you can bet on it. And something tells me it's going to work.

"I tell you what, Mark. Your contract doesn't call for a vacation till you've been here a year. Bass doesn't know that, no reason he has to. Take a week, get out of town, think it over, decide whether you really want to keep the job you have. Think it over, whether television news is the right place for you.

"When you come back you can quit and I'll hate to lose you. Or you can stay, and I don't have to tell you there'll never be another scene like this one when I give you an assignment or I *will* can your ass and fix it so you won't ever work in television again this side of Moline. Now, do you understand me?"

"I hear you, Ed."

"I'll get Jennifer Blade to interview Schein. I guess that'll be as good a way as any to get her feet wet in Bass's new game plan. By the way, this is none of my business, but are you two, uh—?"

"Are we what, Ed?"

"Uh—you know—"

Why was it, Teller wondered, *that profane men could never ask a simple, direct question about women?*

"I heard that rumor, too, Ed. She's a little out of my league."

"Great ass on that broad," mused Kurtis.

"About that vacation, Ed. I'll take you up on it. Starting next Monday."

Instead of returning to his cubicle downstairs, Teller wandered aimlessly for a while through the unfamiliar corridor of the thirtieth floor—the very power center of the Continental Broadcasting Network. The thirtieth floor was a culture apart from the grasping, overcrowded, chaotic level below, with its cavernous sound stages and their separate control rooms for both network and local news broadcasts, its smaller auxiliary studios, its separate newsrooms for CBN and for WRAP staff, its cacophonous communal cafeteria, and its beehive of ancillary cubicles, cubbyholes, and laboratories. The noise level on the twenty-ninth floor of the Commerce Center was a wondrous phenomenon that Teller had never become accustomed to; not even a newspaper city room, with its fish-market vulgarity, approached the steaming hysteria of a television station. Walking through the corridors of the twenty-ninth floor was like walking through New York City itself, in microcosm.

Upstairs it was different.

Here was a lyceum built of eggshells. Here was a discreet and correct universe of marble walls and carpeting, a world in which no footstep clattered, no telephone rang, no voice was lifted against the stately stillness. A world of clocks and mirrors. Of tasteful waiting rooms and pleasant waxen receptionists; of frosted-glass doors and stenciled titles:

OFFICE OF THE PRESIDENT

Of air-conditioned airwaves unmolested by the primitive expressionism below; of iridiscent corridor walls tapering to a vortex far away, the journey rendered painless, timeless, by tasteful displays of modern art.

Here, Teller thought, was an echelon of broadcast aristocracy that sought to disassociate itself from the implications of its existence, as surely as did the cadre of industrialists memorialized thirty stories below as the noble Six Captains—an aristocracy that pretended no responsibility for the seething enclave beneath its carpeted floors, even as it plotted to manipulate the enclave, and thereby a city.

For profit. For the bottom line. Why was the bottom line, Teller wondered, so often on the top floor?

Here was the frosted door leading to Colonel Eddie Donovan's suite of offices. To one side was the elegant trophy case filled with CBN mementos: the Emmys, the Peabodys, the plaques and certificates and commemorative microphones, the yellowing black-and-white photographs of company luncheons, the silver gavels, all the silently screaming evidence of legitimacy.

Teller tried to recollect his impressions of Colonel Eddie Donovan. He had met him only once, shortly after he joined the station; the Old Man had knocked on the jamb of his cubicle in the ostentatious show of democracy that the most imperious executives can affect at times. Teller recalled little of the man: white hair brushed back, eyes that tended to stare a little too nakedly, the faint, fanatic's glitter there—some murmured pleasantries.

He wondered whether the Colonel was indeed mad.

He wandered a little farther down the corridor. Past the frosted-glass door marked:

OFFICE OF ADVERTISING
PRESS, PROMOTION, AND CORPORATE COMMUNICATIONS

The public-relations department. From here, couched in the noncommittal phraseology of Corpspeak, would issue forth the high-minded justification for CBN's all-out assault on the public's most infantile impulses.

He wandered farther. Past the frosted-glass doors marked SALES, past CORPORATE COUNSEL. Past other executive offices—past Bass's, past the vice-president in charge of owned-and-operated stations, past the network vice-president for programming, past the network vice-president for news and public affairs, past other, equally authoritative titles on equally imperious frosted-glass doors.

He had reached the end of the second corridor now. He stood before a heavy wooden door marked PRIVATE—AUTHORIZED PERSONNEL ONLY.

He had a master key. He used it.

The corridor on the other side of the wooden door was darker, danker, somehow more metallic. He saw a series of large glass windows affording visibility into control rooms. The control room walls were stacked with computer equipment. He saw red ON THE AIR lights winking above closed doors. He saw studios with rows upon rows of cartridge tapes stacked on revolving shelves.

Still, he saw no other people.

Teller realized that he was inside the radio arm of the CBN communications combine: the CBN radio network and its New York stations, WCBN and W-101-FM.

This, he surmised from the computers in the control rooms, was W-101-FM.

W-101-FM broadcast a twenty-four-hour soft-rock format. It advertised itself as "Your Personality Rock Station." Its advertising—tending heavily to splashy posters in subway stations and on buses—emphasized the glamor, looks, sex appeal, and likability of its disc jockeys.

W-101-FM was a fully automated station.

This fact was not advertised on the subway-station posters.

The disc jockeys were not "live" on the air, listening to and reacting to the "sounds" they played, as the W-101-FM computers artfully made it seem. They recorded their lead-ins, lead-outs, patter, and commercials in one continuous session, reading the song titles from a master list, without waiting for the album cuts to be played.

"Sound like you're really into the music," the W-101-FM station manager had instructed his deejays. "Project intimacy. In fact, project as though you've just smoked a couple of joints."

After the jocks had recorded their continuous tape, a computer mixed the voice tape with a music tape. The transistor-radio crowd was never the wiser.

"Your Personality Rock Station," the advertisements said. "People like you . . . playing the hits you like."

Sometimes the machine made a mistake. Sometimes it ran out of sync, and would mix the prerecorded jock's lead-in with the wrong song.

Far from betraying the mechanistic nature of "Your Personality Station," these occasional slips enhanced it.

"Far out," the telephone callers to W-101-FM would say. "Your man, he's so stoned, he don't even know what song he's playin'."

W-101-FM was the top-rated rock radio station in New York.

Teller stood looking at the gray equipment, the bobbing needles, the shifting, spinning tape cartridges, for several minutes.

Outside, it was rich autumn. You'd never know that in here.

The changing seasons in here were charted in ARB and Nielsen ratings.

Teller decided he needed a vacation.

A chauffeured silver-gray Cadillac Seville carried Jennifer Blade uptown on Broadway, toward a preliminary interview with Robert Schein.

The Seville was a CBN car. WRAP staffers normally took taxis to their assignments, or hitched rides in the Action Van. L. Malcolm Bass was giving Jennifer Blade the star treatment. She understood corporate symbolic language well enough to grasp the implication: if she handled her new role to Bass's and Colonel Donovan's satisfaction, there would be chauffeured Cadillac Sevilles for her every day.

Because she would be a CBN correspondent.

Jennifer smiled at the thought as she gazed out the window. The limousine was dashing across 71st Street, and the driver swung right onto Amsterdam. Jennifer gazed at the Ansonia Hotel, its granite curves visible through the coppery leaves of Verdi Square, the little arrowhead of a park that formed the wedge between Broadway and Amsterdam. On the street people were looking back at her. Tall, glistening black dudes in tank tops and sunglasses, pasty women in ridiculous print dresses, swarthy, mustached Greek merchants—everybody was leaning down and trying to peer into the Seville and see what celebrity was inside.

Jennifer liked that. She never betrayed an awareness of it at the
scene of a story, but she liked it. Loved it. She could get into the
chauffeured Seville scene, she decided. Her daddy used to drive
her around in his. Now she was getting close to having one of her
own.

She lighted her third cigarette of the trip and almost giggled out
loud. They had all been so sublimely *ginger* about breaking the
news to her, like they'd been worried she'd lock herself up in the
women's room and take pills or something. If it'd been a man they
were reassigning, they'd have said, here's your new job, go do it or
turn in your little laminated I.D. photo. With her they did everything but buy her a new hat. That was all right, too. It kept clear
the notion of who was important to whom.

Ed Kurtis had called her into his pitiful little office that smelled
like a delicatessen and outlined the plan. He made it sound like
one of her relatives had died. At first the idea shocked her a little.
It didn't make sense that she would no longer be covering the hard-
news beats that had earned her such quick popular and critical
prestige in New York. Kurtis had told her he hated to lose her
"investigative talent," and she could believe that. Everybody else
on the staff thought "investigative" work meant reading *all* the
newspaper clippings on a story, instead of just the *Times.*

Then Bass had talked with her, had actually taken her out to
lunch at Café des Artistes—she was petrified the creep would try to
order yogurt flambé—and impressed upon her how much "the
management level" had "its eye on her."

She could believe that, too. Down the front of her shirt, if Bass
was any evidence.

But it was Bass's conversation that wiped away any serious
doubts Jennifer Blade might have had about accepting the reas-
signment to celebrity gossip—or "news about the 'now' people, the
'involved' people," as Bass had actually put it.

She instantly discerned that this shift of emphasis would affect
not just her, but WRAP and probably the network as well. Shop-
talk on the street, among her competitors, had convinced her the
other stations were unfolding similar strategies, softening up their
news agendas, emphasizing personality features. Fluff. Everybody
had the same market research; there were no real secrets; fads and
themes moved through the New York stations like summer wind
in a wheat field.

If hard news on TV was going to become obsolete, it suited her just fine to move with the tide, or a step ahead of it. It wasn't that she disliked sending two-bit crooked pols up to Albany or exposing gambling rings behind Hadassah fronts. If that was her job, she'd do it better than anybody else around her; she'd give more than a day's work for a day's pay. Nobody could say she rode Daddy's coattails. Or any man's.

It was just that she wasn't *wedded* to investigative journalism. She had her career goals, and her timetable. How she achieved those goals was immaterial to her. If Bass and Donovan wanted fluff, she would give them the best damn fluff anybody had ever seen on television. She'd become the standard by which quality fluff would be judged. She had done it in Chattanooga and she'd do it with this guy Schein that Mark had so effortlessly catapulted into stardom.

She took a long drag on her cigarette. She'd do it all, whatever the client wanted. And leave them wanting more.

She could have been a very good hooker, she told herself, neither particularly amused nor scandalized by the thought.

It would have scandalized Teller. She chuckled at that. Poor Teller. Nice guy. Dear, really. She should tell him that sometimes. No, she shouldn't. He *was*, as she'd suspected right from the first, a little out of his element in this league. A little over his head. Talented. Articulate. But lacking. Guts? No. Killer instinct maybe. And he let it all get to him. Too sensitive. Too emotional. Heart on his sleeve.

And too easy to manipulate. Like all the men she'd ever known, even the self-styled bastards, except her father, who was a serious bastard, who'd made a life study of it, and was therefore fascinating. Nice in bed, Teller. But the firecrackers were not popping quite as loud anymore. Maybe she'd dump him soon. Maybe not.

The Cadillac Seville's tires screeched as the driver executed an insolent right turn onto 82nd Street, scattering pedestrians—and immediately lurched to a stop behind a double-parked U-Haul truck. From behind her sunglasses Jennifer Blade peered out at the neighborhood, which, with the cessation of the car's velocity, suddenly closed down upon her.

They were within two blocks of the address Schein had given her (a bit brusquely, it had seemed to her) by telephone. She couldn't believe it. Why anyone would want to live on the Upper

West Side of New York was beyond her. World's biggest outside fruit stand. Teller lived on Riverside; that was different. Slightly. This neighborhood, heavy with humanity and cheap gaudy colors, depressed her.

The CBN chauffeur tried a couple of blasts on the horn, cursed, threw his right arm over the seat, and backed the Seville up a few feet to get around the U-Haul. Jennifer was annoyed. Her jawline hardened. The area was claustrophobic. Her entire morning would be shot, and her mood for the rest of the day along with it. What the hell was a "preliminary interview" anyway? Didn't they assign producers or researchers to do those things? They damn well would when she got to the network, she would make sure of that. Barbara Walters didn't waste her time on "preliminary interviews," Jennifer was reasonably certain.

The chauffeur inched the Seville east on 82nd Street, as though he were afraid he would scrape it on an unwashed fender and contract a dread disease. Barbara Walters. The name did not improve Jennifer's darkening disposition. Already she was being compared to Barbara Walters. Every new woman reporter, at some point, underwent the ritual of being compared to Barbara Walters. "It's not so bad, Jenny," a WCBS woman had told her on the day the initial comparison appeared in the *Daily News*. "We all go through it. It's like getting your first period."

One columnist had even dared suggest that Jennifer was "tailoring" her voice to imitate the voice of Barbara Walters. That would be the day. A cello imitating a trip-hammer. Jennifer had toyed briefly with the fantasy of having her father get the bastard fired. She'd have done it in a minute, but she had made a pledge to herself, upon coming to New York, never to rely on Sterling Blade for one more favor in her life. It was a pledge she took seriously. Yes, she had been spoiled by Blade, especially after her mother died when Jennifer was four. Sleeping pills. The fashionable suicide, in those days. And for the fashionable reasons: starlets. After that, the flamboyant Blade had lavished on Jennifer the affection he had withheld from her mother. Television producers were still parvenus in the Hollywood of the late 1950s—the movie colony hadn't yet surrendered the last of its dignity—but Sterling Blade was one of the barbarians who were changing all that. He spoiled his daughter by rubbing her in their faces: the right neighborhood in Beverly Hills, the right childhood friends, the right prep school, the right clothes.

Even the right lovers. Old Sterling, nothing if not thorough, had been thoughtful enough to provide Jennifer with just the right stud to correct the matter of her virginity, at age sixteen—a courtly, aging film star, a former leading man by then reduced to attempting a comeback in an absurd Sterling Blade series about police medics, or medical policemen, she couldn't remember which. The actor had been sweet, and tender, and thoughtful, and she had eagerly absorbed everything he had to teach her—Jennifer was an avaricious consumer of information on all things—and it had been, all in all, an extremely considerate gesture on Daddy's part.

Of course the man had fallen in love with Jennifer, and when she took up with a rock star's agent—at age seventeen—he had gone on an alcoholic binge that terminated his career and his sanity; the last she'd heard, he was vegetating in a home for Luded-out actors, or something. It was too bad, but it was not Jennifer's fault, actually.

The Seville was idling at 82nd and Columbus, waiting for a light. Violent traffic thundered past them. Schein lived not far from here. Jennifer rolled down her window and let the smells and the foreign noises of the neighborhood flood the car's interior.

Open fire hydrants spewed dark water down the gutters, water that carried with it the residue of most of the crap that was advertised on television, including an inordinate amount of literal crap; the harvest of God-only-knew-how-many tail-wagging dog food commercials. They always show them lapping it up, Jennifer mused. They never show them hunkering down in the middle of the street to plop it back out again.

She looked again at the neighborhood; the lopsided storefronts on Columbus with their drooping canopies and their gaudy splotches of turquoise and orange and yellow. The bored knots of people perched on parked cars like flies, drinking from bottles wrapped in bags, eating from tinfoil containers; the men dark and muscular in their white undershirts, the girls thin and coquettish, their black hair piled on the sides of their heads in the Hispanic style. Did they watch the news? Did they watch her on the news? Did any of them give a good goddamn about revenue sharing or the Dow Jones average?

The light changed and the Seville ventured across Columbus like a banker entering a bordello. Now Jennifer was aware of boarded-up windows, a spidering of fire escapes above her, of faces boldly thrust up almost inside the window. "Hey, girl, take me fo' *ride!*" She shrank back. Sorry, she thought, but you don't come from Beverly Hills into this and not feel it stick to your skin. She knew that certain young actors lived in these neighborhoods, and that was fine. For them. She would take the East 70s, thank you. Did, in fact. But what kind of beggar was this Robert Schein that he would live here? Was he slumming?

"This is it, Bernie." She had her head down almost between her knees so she could see up at the addresses atop the stairways. She checked to see that her notepad and her cigarettes were in her shoulder bag. Behind them, a pickup truck honked. She took a deep breath.

"Wait for me," she instructed. And got out.

Jennifer felt that the hot eyes of the neighborhood itself were on her as she picked her way across the street and onto a sidewalk littered with scraps of dusty scaffolding and smashed bricks. She could hear disco music from at least three radios blaring out of open windows. She squinted up at the building that bore the address in her notebook. Three stories of brick, the first story coated with green paint. She could see workmen in yellow hard hats through the windows of the first floor. No, this couldn't be Schein's address.

Two muscular Hispanic toughs, each with a dog leash in one hand and a transistor in the other, stopped boldly in front of Jennifer and looked her up and down. For one of the few times in her life, she was intimidated. She dashed up the twelve concrete stairs leading to the building's foyer. There was a rusting intercom system, half torn from its fixture in the wall. She pushed a brown button the size of a pencil eraser. She waited.

At the foot of the concrete stairs she could see the two Hispanics looking up at her. Whistling at her. That, combined with the irregular thumping of the workmen's hammers through the open door beside her, set her nerves on edge. She thought about bolting down the stairs, past the toughs, and into the Cadillac Seville. If she did that, she knew, it would be the last ride in a Cadillac Seville she ever took.

Still it was tempting. The situation was absurd. A wild-goose chase. Why the hell couldn't this guy come down to the station . . . ?

"Hey."

The voice floated down from above her. She noticed that the door to the stairway gaped open. She leaned into the stairwell and looked up the stairs. Her eyes, behind the sunglasses, had not adjusted to the dimness, but she could make out the shadowy form of a man at the top of the stairs.

"Is this . . . are you Robert Schein?"

"Yeah."

She waited, reflexively, for an invitation to come in. Come up. Something. Apparently there would be none. Her edginess turned to a more familiar mood—fury.

"Well, I'm Jennifer Blade! Shall I come up or do we stand here yelling at each other?" Her voice was strident through the strident hammer-blows.

The dark figure at the top of the stairs was silent for a long minute. Jennifer sensed that he might simply fade back into the shadows. Dust particles gleamed in a shaft of sunlight. She was perspiring. The detached voice said:

"Help self."

The most fashionable young news personality in New York adjusted her shoulder bag and climbed the shadowy stairs.

A door was ajar on the right. She pushed it open with her left hand and stepped through, pulling her sunglasses away with her right hand.

She found herself standing in a drab room. Sunlight poured in from the far windows. The sunlight nearly silhouetted a figure standing motionless near the center of the room. Jennifer had an impression of gleaming gold hair, crescent of light defining large shoulders, glowing needles of body hair on the forearms and strong legs.

For a moment she thought the man was naked. Then, as her eyes adjusted to the harsh light, she saw that he was wearing a pair of cutoff jeans.

The man said nothing and did not move.

To recover her self-possession, Jennifer took three long steps into the room, so that she was looking at the man at right angles to the strong window light. Two ice-blue eyes stared back at her, blank of expression. The silence between them grew. Seldom had Jennifer Blade ever felt so absurdly at a loss to control a situation.

"I am Jennifer Blade," she told the man. She realized she had just said that, in a much more assertive voice, at the foot of the stairs. Saying it again sounded foolish. But the silence had to be broken.

"I know," said Robert Schein tonelessly. "I saw you that night."

Despite herself, Jennifer was flattered. She knew he meant the night she had come to see him at Stitch's, with Mark. She relaxed a little. But still Schein made no attempt to further the conversation. He seemed to be waiting for her to take the initiative.

Jennifer felt her confidence returning. She was used to that sort of hesitation from men.

"And you are the famous comedian," she said, with something of the old mockery in her voice. "Make me laugh."

The bland face hardened, the ice-blue eyes narrowed a little. Jennifer sensed a temperament similar to her own. The awareness frightened her; it carried the suggestion of an electromagnetic shock.

She began again. Start with the obvious, she told herself.

"We talked on the phone. I'm here to gather some background material for your interview on *WRAP-Around News.* You agreed."

The direct stating of business seemed to animate Robert Schein. For the first time since Jennifer had entered the room, he moved— to gesture vaguely toward a chair.

"Have a seat," he said.

Jennifer became aware of the rest of the room. It was simply furnished—clean, functional. A few plants, a small breakfast table, sofa, chairs. It occurred to her there was a strange absence— bookcases. This was one of the few apartments she had seen without a visible book.

The most important item in the room—judging from its central position facing the most comfortable chair—was a large, expensive color television set. A picture was on, but there was no sound.

Schein had taken a seat on the sofa, at right angles to Jennifer's chair. He rested an ankle on a sinewy knee and picked up a peeled orange from the card table. He hefted it in the palm of his hand and gazed away from her, toward the television set, while Jennifer completed her fast survey of the room.

"What I am here to do, Mr. Schein—is it *Mister* Schein—?"
Silence.

"—Mr. Schein, is to collect some background information on
you so that I will appear to know what I'm talking about when I
interview you on the air tomorrow. You may or may not know
that the station is running some heavy newspaper ads to promote
this interview, so we hope to have a big audience."

It irritated Jennifer to realize she had said all this *brightly*, like
some goddamn rent-a-car clerk trying to hype a customer. She was
straining already to produce some kind of reaction from this
zombie—*ingratiating* herself to him.

And for nothing. He gave no sign of having heard any of it.

She studied him as he gazed indifferently toward the television
set. Even without the glare to blur his features, the man appeared indistinct—hazy, undefined, like a TV picture on a dim
tube. Only the eyes seemed hard and real—and they did not invite
intimate scrutiny.

"So I guess we may as well begin." Jennifer rummaged in her
shoulder bag for her notepad and pen. Her face was burning.
Virtually without saying a word, Robert Schein had managed to
make her feel like a high school senior sent out to interview a
Famous Personality. How she would love to smack the insolent
bastard's face. The downstairs hammering alone was making her
crazy. But it was far too late to back out of it now.

"I guess everybody is familiar with your professional rise," she
began, sounding to herself ridiculously formal, for all the world
like Irma Interview. "But I don't recall hearing much about your
personal background. I wonder if you'd mind telling me something about where you come from, about your family."

"I mind."

Jennifer sat blinking at him. Trying to make some sense out of
what she had just heard. Trying to believe she had heard it. No
one. Had ever. Spoken. To her. Like that.

She almost said: "Well then, I wonder if you'd mind very much
rotting in hell, maggot." She came very close to saying that. But
instead, Jennifer Blade, with visions of L. Malcolm Bass and the
Continental Broadcasting Network dancing in her head, heard a
voice very much like her own, only more unctuous, saying:

"Well then, Mr. Schein, perhaps we can talk about your remarkable recent impact on the New York comedy scene."

It was one of the most patently phony sentences she had ever uttered in her life. She nearly laughed out loud at the sound of it.

His body seemed to relax on the sofa. For the first time, he turned to face her directly. His face came into focus. The eyes lost some of their hardness.

"I guess you'd have to say I was lucky," Schein said. "I was in the right place, right time . . . that night . . . I didn't expect it . . ."

The gruff facade had vanished. Speaking seemed to pain him. He looked away, his eyes darting as if by habit to the TV screen.

"Robert," she coaxed gently, "it's easy. Just think of all the interviews you've ever seen on television. Just talk like they talk. It's no big problem."

"Yes . . ." he looked back at her. An almost childlike cunning had spread across his face, knowing and innocent at once.

The hammer blows continued from below, like a metronome. There were dust particles in the air. The setting was unreal, hypnotic.

"*Impact . . .*" Jennifer prodded.

Schein glanced quickly toward the silent TV screen, as if for support, then back to Jennifer. When he spoke again, his voice had a new authority.

"You asked me about my impact. Really, I can't take any credit for that . . . I owe a debt to Al Gnagy—he's the owner of Stitch's . . . he let me get up there onstage . . . no prior experience . . . and prove I could make people laugh." He paused, a pupil seeking approval after reciting.

Better . . . at least he's talking in sentences now . . . but hardly the stuff of a TV interview.

Playing a hunch she did not fully understand, Jennifer said:

"Pretend you're on Dinah Shore. You're a guest on Dinah Shore. You've seen Dinah Shore, haven't you?"

Schein gave a slight trancelike nod. He resumed talking as if there had been no interruption.

". . . and finally, I'd have to give credit to a very gifted and totally wacked-out guy, a veteran comedian in his own right—a guy named Billy Wyler, a guy who has taught me so much about comedy in such a short time. Without these two people, Jennifer, not to mention the terrific audiences who came to see me, I wouldn't be here talking to you today."

It was incredible—he was heating up as he went along, trans-forming himself. Coming into focus. A current of power seemed to be flowing through him, changing him, brightening him; a power she felt she had somehow activated.

She didn't understand what was going on. But she was drawn by it—hypnotized, as the man before her seemed to crystallize with each hammer blow from downstairs.

Power—of any kind—fascinated Jennifer Blade.

She wanted to see how far open she could throw the switch.

"How would you categorize your comic style?" she asked, in the too-cordial voice of the TV interviewer.

"Well, now, that's hard. That's like asking Woody Shaw to define a C-note, you know?" He gave a slight, self-deprecating, boyish smile, just a twitch at the corners of his lips; Jennifer imag-ined a fast-reacting studio director catching it in closeup. "I guess the best way that I could approach that question is to tell you . . ."

The new voice continued, its tones unctuous, almost hypnotic in their preestablished rhythms and patterns. But something else was now happening, something else that had no continuity, no relationship with all that had gone before. As he talked, his ice-blue eyes fastened on hers, Robert Schein's hand had reached out to the top button of Jennifer Blade's silk Giorgio shirt. Jennifer watched it as though she herself were disinvolved; as though both the hand and the bosom belonged to other people.

". . . 'minimalist humor' is the phrase most often used by critics, I guess, but I'm not sure that adequately defines what I'm trying to . . ."

The fingers of Schein's hand unbuttoned the top button of Jennifer's silk shirt.

". . . audiences today are less politically involved than they were, oh, even five . . ."

Schein's fingers reached the second button.

His eyes, the eyes of a talk show guest, never left hers. The voice continued its polite Muzak rhythms. The essence of Robert Schein had shifted now to the hand. The reality of the man, or the curi-ous collection of absences that amounted to his reality, was now concentrated below her throat.

The hammering continued from the room below them. Jenni-fer could hear radio music in the street.

She was thrilled. And aroused. Intrigued. And yet—detached. It was not clear to her whether Robert Schein's invasion of her breasts was an erotic advance—or whether it had to do in a strange way with the power she had activated in him. Were the fingers trying to stimulate her—or seek her milk, her own nourishing strength?

". . . can learn a lot from the other young comedians working with me . . ."

She decided to keep the switch open; let the scene play to its natural consequences.

"What did you do before you broke into comedy?" Jennifer's voice was disinterested, professional. Below his twisting fingers, she rested her pen lightly on her notepad.

"I was an actor. Off-Off-Broadway. If you consider Connecticut Off-Off-Broadway." They both laughed lightly, two amused and amusing professionals sharing a little joke with an unseen audience. His fingers had found the front clasp of her bra. "I studied originally at the Neighborhood Playhouse School of the Theater," he said. "Improv stuff, mostly." The fingers were pushing at the clasp. Jennifer could feel it start to give.

The ice-blue eyes held her gaze as the clasp burst free. "That was a lot of years ago," the pleasant voice said. "I didn't stay with it very long. Got my Equity card. Did this and that. Summer stock in Connecticut. Some stuff in the neighborhoods. Nothing you've heard about, I'm sure."

He had pushed both halves of Jennifer's bra aside. A slight breeze was playing through the open windows, and she felt it touch the moisture on her chest. Schein's eyes did not leave hers. She could feel that her nipples had hardened; she waited for the shock of his fingertips on them. She glanced down to her notepad to complete the phrase "Summer stock in Conn." and saw that his hand had dropped away.

"Why did you quit?" she asked. "The Neighborhood Playhouse, I mean," she added instantly.

"Because I value my privacy," he said. Something of the earlier tonelessness was back in his voice now. "They try to make you get into your past."

Jennifer recalled his unexpected response to her first attempt to probe his personal background: *"I mind."*

"Yes," she said. "Well, what do you do to sustain yourself while you're not working in theater?"

"Wait tables." Schein said. "Drive a cab. This and that."

She sensed that the interview was over. A flow of tacit energy had peaked between them; a barrier to intimacy had opened, then closed again. But not before an understanding had been reached. She had felt *herself* in his fingers. And by allowing him to explore her, she had communicated that to him. She was not sure how explicitly he understood it. But the ice-blue eyes held some measure of new understanding.

She folded her notepad shut in her lap and ran the pen through its wire spiral. She dropped her eyes frankly to his naked torso. It was hard and muscular. His chest was covered with fine blond hairs. The scent of him carried to her on the thin breeze.

"Are you going to finish what you started?" Jennifer Blade asked him. She felt an urgent stinging desire for him, she wanted him to take her with her hands on the windowsill, looking down at the Cadillac Seville and the Hispanic toughs, and with the television set turned up loud to muffle her screams, her famous screams. But she sensed that if either of them admitted lust, it would violate the secret understanding, the unspoken rules of the game, the mutual narcissism.

Schein's face had resumed its impassive mask. The convivial talk show guest of a moment ago was nowhere to be seen. The features had again become guarded, somehow indistinct.

The game was over. For today.

They both stood.

"Thank you for the interview, Mr. Schein." Jennifer bent down to rest her notepad on the chair, then clasped the front of her bra. "I'm sure we'll have an excellent show tomorrow. Be at the studio at four thirty if you can. Do you know where it is?"

Silence.

She extended her hand.

"See you then."

The game was not quite over.

Robert Schein lifted his other hand. The one holding the peeled orange.

He held it over Jennifer Blade's bosom, at the point of the first button of her newly buttoned Giorgio shirt.

He squeezed.

Pulp and juice flooded onto her chest, staining the shirt beyond recovery.

Her deep-brown eyes were wide as she raised them to his. But he was between her and the windowlight, and she could not discern his expression.

She wondered whether he was aware of the violent shudder that coursed through her, or noticed the change in her breathing. It was several seconds before she felt able to move.

Her breathing had returned to normal by the time she reached the Cadillac Seville and slid into the backseat.

She lighted a cigarette. Her hands were calm again.

"We have to make a detour by my apartment on the way back, Bernie," she instructed the chauffeur. "I've somehow managed to spill gunk all over my shirt."

Jennifer Blade's on-air interview with Robert Schein was a huge success. WRAP viewers—their numbers bolstered by the promotional ads—saw a new comedian who was handsome, boyish, thoughtful, modest, and eager to praise the many people in his life who had contributed to his success.

They also discovered an entirely new side of Jennifer Blade, whom they had known until now as a beautiful but somehow serious and detached news reporter. The audience was surprised and delighted to find that Jennifer was a "nice woman" as well as a stern journalist. Instead of sitting formally in one of WRAP's militaristic swivel chairs, where she normally was seen when in the studio, Jennifer perched on the edge of anchorman Lon Stagg's anchor desk and swung her leg playfully while she chatted with Robert Schein, who sat cross-legged in Jennifer's swivel chair. The audience loved the switch; they were as enthralled as kindergarten pupils watching one of their own sitting in the teacher's chair.

Jennifer's questions to Schein were posed in her familiar crisp, professional style, but it was her reactions that brought out the "real person" in her: she laughed out loud, smacked her hands in glee, wrinkled her nose, and several times faced the camera to include the audience, conspiratorially, in her mirth.

She even coaxed Schein into doing the centerpiece of his act, his famous comic collapse. Using the swivel chair as a prop, Schein weaved and staggered humorously for several seconds before finally pitching over the back of the chair onto the floor. In the background, members of the *WRAP-Around News* team could be heard applauding and roaring with laughter.

At the end of the interview Lon Stagg himself got up from his anchor seat and ambled across the set, his hand outstretched to Robert Schein. To the audience it was obvious that Stagg was having trouble controlling a case of the giggles.

"Man, I've got to hand it to you," said Stagg, getting serious as he took one of Schein's hands in both his own. "You are *some kind* of new talent. And you're a heckuva nice guy to boot."

"Hey, speaking of boots," cracked Robert Schein, pointing down at Stagg's feet, "what is this, anyway—the news or *Frontier Anchorman?*"

Stagg slapped a hand to the side of his face in mock dismay at this teasing. Jennifer seized the moment. "Hey," she called merrily to the director, "can we get a shot of this?"

A closeup of Lon Stagg's Botticelli boots immediately appeared on the home screens. Viewers could hear Stagg's good-natured voice saying, "Aw, you guys . . ." while the crew hooted.

The director came back for a long shot of the three of them, laughing and shaking their heads, before dissolving to a commercial.

Jennifer was enormously pleased with herself. She had choreographed every detail of the Schein interview. Even the "spontaneous" reaction by Lon Stagg, and Schein's "spontaneous" kidding of Stagg about his boots. Jennifer had alerted the floor director beforehand that she would call for a closeup of Stagg's boots. Everyone had done as they were told, and the segment worked to perfection.

The next day, the following item appeared in the *Daily News* TV column:

> Don't look now, but ace WRAP newsgal Jenny Blade may soon blossom forth as top personality in her own right. Dau'ter of West Coast made-for-TV'er Sterling Blade ("Cop Medic," "Celebrity Striptease") revealed showbiz in blood during yesterday's interview segment with upcoming comic Bob Schein. Move over Babs! Jenny sizzled screen. Confident'l to WRAP boss Mal Bass: we all know this gal's got brains and nose for news. But don't hide her other talents under bush'l.

The *Daily News* columnist, of course, had been tipped off about the plans for Jennifer by none other than L. Malcolm Bass himself.

The segment yielded quick dividends for Schein, too. New York's major morning talk shows, tracking him down desperately through Jennifer, booked him for appearances, with the stipulation that he perform his complete comedy routine.

A network morning show called to express interest.

Cue magazine telephoned, asking whether Jennifer knew Schein's agent. They wanted to do a cover.

A Lutheran youth magazine called, wondering whether by chance Schein was a member of that religion and whether he could consent to an interview on how to be a comedian while retaining Christian values.

Jennifer said she didn't know, but she'd surely try to find out.

"He'll be a snake-handling Baptist if that's what you want him to be," she thought as she hung up the phone.

That night, Al Gnagy changed his billing. He had replaced the elegantly lettered sign in his window that read:

STITCH'S COMEDY SHOWCASE
FEATURING
ROBERT SCHEIN, ETC.

The new sign, just back from the printers, read:

THE ROBERT SCHEIN SHOW

When Schein returned to his apartment following his performance that night, he encountered a dark figure waiting for him on the staircase.

"Hello, Robert."

It was Jennifer Blade.

They walked silently to his apartment.

By lamplight he saw that she was wearing jeans, a striped halter top, and white sweat socks. She carried an overnight bag in her hand.

Later that night, she screamed and dug her nails deeply into him. His face, in the darkness, was inches from her. But even in her ecstasy, Jennifer Blade knew that Robert Schein's eyes were focused on nothing, nothing at all.

Teller slept on the back porch. Beside his arm on a serving tray, a glass of iced tea warmed in the Ozark sun.

From time to time his mother came to the back door and looked at him asleep on the wicker sofa. She was making fried chicken soaked in buttermilk, his favorite meal as a boy. She was a thin woman with frosted hair, and she was wearing her best pink polyester pantsuit, and she didn't know anything to say to her son, who had so unexpectedly come home. She didn't know what to do for him. So she was making fried chicken soaked in buttermilk. Usually Mark came home at Christmas and Easter; other times, when he took his vacation, they'd get postcards from places like Athens, Greece, and Paris, France. Mark's mother kept the postcards in the middle desk drawer in the living room. Now here he was spending a week's vacation with them. Oh, she was pleased as could be to have her boy at home, but she was troubled by it, too.

She went back inside the kitchen, where her own mother sat dozing at the table. There was a *Dick Van Dyke Show* rerun on the portable TV set by her mother's wrinkled elbow. Her mother was nearly blind, but she enjoyed Dick Van Dyke and Johnny Carson and the colored comedy on CBS. Mark Teller's mother reached over and switched off the set. Then she went to the cupboard and unplugged the electric percolator from the wall socket and poured herself a cup of coffee.

"Is Matthew still out there on the what-you-call-it?" asked her mother, awakening from ancient dreams. Matthew was the name of Mark's brother, who was a physical-education coach in Oklahoma City.

"You mean Mark, Mother. Mark's the one who's home." Their thin, melodic voices hung in the still afternoon air; Teller was vaguely conscious of the voices as he dozed. They mingled with the past, with all the things that didn't change, like the wicker sofa and the low willow tree on the corner of the house, brushing the porch screens; like the Ozark autumn itself, quick with scarlet sumac over the warm soil, then slowing to deep pools of blue haze on the ridges; the Ozark autumn, warm and eternal and smelling of burst crab apples and brittle cornsilk.

The Ozark autumn was drawing the poison of New York out of his pores. He had surprised his father and mother by announcing his trip home just two days in advance of his arrival and he had landed at the little airport (two flight changes from LaGuardia) a celebrity of sorts, handshake with the ticket agent, smile and a wave to this and that couple from the town ("Why, I do believe that's Cecil Teller's boy. Howdy-do, Mark, hear you got a TV show in New York now"); Teller all hale and grinning and slapping his bandy-legged father on the back, the thin back, father's glasses glinting, old go-to-hell felt hat slipping forward when he bent to pick up Mark's suitcase ("Lemme get this one, Mark"), betraying the pink, untanned crown of the suntanned skull; Mark full of fun and tall tales to tell from the big city; New York far away now, the madness receding, his problems at WRAP disarmed now, somehow comic and glamorous, good talk for the dinner table. The clean remote Ozark town would restore him.

The restoration had begun in Saint Louis, at Lambert-Saint Louis field: Mark had disembarked from his TWA flight into a sudden sea of his countrymen: red-faced, open-faced men strutting in cranberry blazers and white belts and white shoes; tall, broad-shouldered salesmen with slicked-back hair, wearing honest leisure suits with western stitching; the women ample and proud in their festive print dresses. None of the dark arrogance, the furtive, sharkskin knowledgeability, of the scuttling LaGuardia mobs.

He knew as he stepped into the main terminal building, with its kitschy, full-size replica of Charles Lindbergh's *Spirit of St. Louis* suspended by wires from the ceiling, that he could easily carry the romanticizing of these people too far. These wide, open, generous faces had stood foursquare behind Nixon and sent their sons proudly to die in Vietnam. They had paid the price but were oblivious to it; God help the Nixon-baiter in an Ozark café. There were dark tribal passions in the Ozarks, camouflaged by double-knit, but there; dark suspicions, iron-bound ways. He knew he could never again be rooted to the soil of this region; he knew too much and had forgotten too much, and this saddened him.

But for now it didn't matter. For now he just wanted to be in a place where the seasons changed; to be away from the artificial cathode glare of the Commerce Center and its sterile intrigues, away from the soilless world of clocks and mirrors, where a man's worth was measured in lines of newsprint or flickering dots on a screen; back among the plain melodic people of his youth, back with his father, whom he had ceased to know well in the years of his adulthood.

He had boarded the second of his three connecting flights to the small Ozark town full of relief and optimism, full of an inchoate, urgent love.

And for a brief while it worked. He took the wheel of his father's dusty station wagon and they sped away from the small airport in its meadow, heading for town through an arcade of golden maples. Father and son. Pals always. They had told each other they were looking good. They had vigorously sworn their common determination to go fishing on Osage Creek. Drink beer. *Damn* those Cardinals all to hell anyhow. Past the white Community Baptist church on the edge of town. Big new shopping center going in over there. Hurt your bait-and-tackle business you think? Don't reckon it will.

Then Mark had made a mistake. He had tried to express to his father his feelings upon seeing the white belts and the white shoes at Lambert-Saint Louis. Instantly he could feel his father drawing in. Hell, white belts and white shoes were what people *wore*. They were what Cecil Teller wore behind the counter at the bait-and-tackle shop. Mark couldn't make clear the essential gratitude he had felt toward the white belts and white shoes; he stumbled, hesitated, made it come out condescending. It was like a dream he'd had in which, struggling to free himself from quicksand, he had only sunk deeper into the mire. By the time they'd reached the house, the old dread silence between them had returned.

Still, he was home. Out of New York's gravitational belt. In a small Ozark town as far removed from the colonizing imperatives of television as one could likely get in America.

For a chance to think about reality and illusion.

He started the week by running each day on the track at the consolidated high school where he had set a state record in the two-mile so many years ago. His stride was still good and he liked the October sun on his bare shoulders. A cyclone fence ran the length of the athletic field. Beyond it, facing the high school, was a perfect small gem of a neighborhood street, poplars and elm shielding white gabled houses built in the 1920s. The street had not changed since he was a boy; he could remember the year in which TV antennas began appearing on the rooftops, forever blunting the castlelike illusion of their turrets against the sky.

The honest houses as illusion and the TV antennas as corrective reality. He would have to think about that. Funny how the antennas were now a quaint link with old days, a reminder of innocence.

He enjoyed looking at the neighborhood street as he loped out of the south turn on the track; enjoyed the coppery glint of the poplars in his eye. But by the third day of his running, word had circulated through the consolidated high school that a famous guy was out there running on the track, a guy who was on television in New York. Horsefaced teens had gathered between classes and at lunch hour to stare at him; dark appraising stares, nothing of the open recognizing glances that accepted him as a townsman returned. The teens wore Fonz T-shirts and Travolta T-shirts on their rawboned, farm-strong chests. When one of them asked him for his autograph, Teller stopped coming to the track.

He strolled along the main street of the small town. The IGA grocery store where he had shoplifted a Hershey bar as a kid was still in business but a McDonald's occupied what had once been an open swell of ground opposite the courthouse square; a small preserve of trees that had balanced the composition of the courthouse and its statuary against the longer rectangle of the town. Children were clustered around a man dressed in a red wig, a clown's makeup, and oversize shoes near the red-and-white building's entrance. The man was dispensing small black objects from a bag. Christmas in October. At what age were the children told there was no Ronald McDonald?

Teller noticed that most of the children, like the high school students at the track, were wearing T-shirts that identified them with a television character. Some of the fathers sported short-sleeved shirts designed to look like a field of beer labels—another current TV promotion. Everyone seemed to be wearing plastic caps.

Bumper stickers on cars proclaimed loyalty not to the U.S.A. or God but to radio and TV stations. AMERICA—LOVE IT OR LEAVE IT and REGISTER COMMUNISTS NOT GUNS had given way to I'M A KLTZ since the last time Teller had taken a good look at his hometown.

He examined the small business storefronts along the streets that ringed the courthouse square. No proprietor was visible through the windowglass. The merchants—the connecting fibers of the community's life—had, it seemed, subordinated their own identities to the cardboard personas of TV stars, who served as surrogate salesmen. Cardboard eyes and cardboard smiles followed him down the sidewalk. Ed McMahon offered him some dog food. Tom Seaver recommended a pair of double-knit slacks. At the drugstore Sammy Davis, Jr., held out a fizzing glass of Alka-Seltzer.

It was a town of phantoms, of cardboard celebrities more real, more expressive, more vital, than the besloganed citizenoids moving through the streets. The Arch-Phantom was Bobby Lee Cooper. His ghostly presence dominated the town. His sneering plump face, big as a Presidential candidate's, occupied the entire front window of Sound Investments (formerly the D&W Record and Phonograph Shop). The legend under the poster-photo read: "Bobby Lee Live as You Remember Him!" It was part of a national television promotion-campaign.

As Teller approached the window, the door to the record shop swung open and two adolescent girls hurried out, each clutching a white vinyl album bag. A Bobby Lee Cooper face, a duplicate of the giant face in the window, undulated between each pair of blossoming Ozark bosoms.

After that, Teller stayed away from the center of town.

He spent the latter days of the week hanging around the house, reading and sleeping on the back porch and making halfhearted conversation with his mother. Trying to tell the jaunty stories

about his adventures in New York, stories that did not seem worth
the telling anymore.

Waiting—as he had waited in boyhood—for his father to come
home.

To sit with him and talk, tell the old baseball stories, compare
notes, drink beer; to tell the old man how it was in New York—
he'd understand. Maybe the ribald outrageous humor of it would
all occur to Teller again in the telling, maybe he'd remember the
enormous joke he had set out to play on New York, maybe he
would discover in the old man what it was he was missing in
himself, now that the white glare of the cathode tube was paralyz-
ing him, now that the airwaves were turning him into something
he had not intended to be.

But they sat in silence through most of the meals.

Teller knew that he terrified his parents.

He was an alien to them now, like the cardboard people in the
store windows. He was one of the things the town worshiped. That
his parents worshiped.

And therefore an awesome thing.

On his last day the dinner-table silence was broken by the clink
of his blind grandmother's spoon against the lid of the jar of
watermelon preserves. In the living room, out of sight but present
in the household like a benevolent spirit, the disembodied voice of
Walter Cronkite gave the news.

"I wanted that Creamette," said his grandmother.

And then, blind, oblivious, sounding like a cheery note out of
an ancient memory:

"*We* know what's good, don't we, Matthew?"

"Mark, Mother," said Mark's mother.

His father said abruptly:

"Does that *Washington Post* circulate in New York?"

It was a bid for conversation. Teller knew it. His father's choices
of topics became less predictable with his rising desperation.

"Uh, yes, yes, it does," remarked Teller conversationally. "You
can get it on the newsstands," he added. "But I don't read it too
much," he added again.

His father considered this. Then:

"Have you ever been to the Carolinas . . . uh, North and South?"

They watched television together in the darkened living room
after the others had gone to bed.

Teller was struck by the intensity of his father's face as it reflected the white glare of the screen. There was a childlike pleasure in the features. The lips were slightly parted, the glasses glinting. The pain had dropped away from his father's face—the pain Teller had brought with him into the household. For the first time in his visit, Mark saw his father fully concentrating, fully at peace.

"Boy, that's something, ain't it?" his father murmured.

The next morning Teller left for New York.

By Christmas, Robert Schein was one of the two hottest celebrities in New York. The other was the late Bobby Lee Cooper.

Harwell had stopped in at Stitch's one Thursday night in November to catch Schein's act. Harwell, the famous Pop Art painter of the sixties, who had established an international following on the strength of his ability to capture the essence of crossword puzzles and sacks of brown sugar in shockingly realistic detail. He appeared at the club incognito, wearing a floppy black hat and smoked glasses; his cover was blown only because someone noticed the New York Yankees jersey over velvet leotards which he happened to be wearing.

"He's the Mount Rushmore of comedy," pronounced Harwell when asked (by his personal publicist) what he thought of Schein.

The remark, taken to be a compliment, appeared the next morning in Liz Smith's column. "'Monumental' Praise," ran the subhead.

"And this place," Harwell had added, looking around at Stitch's purple decor, with its accent of red lips, "is just the place where I'd send a murder suspect if I wanted him to sign a confession."

It was duly recorded. Along with a photograph. Of Harwell.

"Jesus Christ, I'll remodel the damn place!" blurted Al Gnagy when he read the item.

"Don't do it, ya monkey," growled Bill Wyler, already on his third Bloody Mary of the morning. "He likes it the way it is. He'll bring his pals here. You make it look like Baskin-Robbins, I promise you it'll go down the tubes."

"Maybe if I knock out the wall and add a few tables," said Gnagy, doing a quick calculation of the number of Harwell's pals.

"Don' lay a finger on it, Al. You're sittin' on a goddamn gold mine. The idea is to keep it lookin' as cheap and tacky as you have all these years because you were too goddamn *tight* to fix it up."

"Yeah. Well, you just stay fuckin' sober enough to write Bobby's material, my friend. I'll take care of runnin' the place."

Wyler had long since abandoned his own comedy act to devote full time to creating Robert Schein's performances. To creating Robert *Schein*, as far as that went. It was an odious task for Wyler in many ways, not the least of which was Schein's personality. Or lack of one. The bastard was as cold as any Outfit enforcer Wyler had ever run into on the Coast or in Vegas. Never a word of thanks. Or greeting. Or kiss-my-ass. "Fucker'd eat your eyeballs for grapes," he remarked to Gnagy once. Gnagy, something of an eyeball-eater himself, was not noticeably moved by the lament.

Cold fish was Number One. Number Two was that Robert Schein was no natural comedian. Oh, he had an uncanny knack for adapting to any kind of suggestion, Wyler had to hand him that. Bastard was unreal in that respect. See him onstage, you'd want to introduce your daughter to him. Laid back, good eye contact, good presence, good charm. Run into him backstage, he'd look at you like you was a side dish he hadn't ordered. (Ring Lardner had said that.)

Wyler suspected it was only a matter of time before Schein's basic antisocial personality showed through the material, and that would be the end of Robert Sonuvabitch Schein. And the end of a good gig for Bill Wyler. He missed being up there performing his own stuff, but this was the best-paying gig he'd had in years. Gnagy had put him on a straight retainer, ten percent of the house, off the top. Place held seventy-five customers, five-dollars-a-head cover. Since Gnagy had trimmed back the acts and gone to two sets a night, five nights a week (Wednesday–Sunday), that was a $375-a-week paycheck for Bill Wyler.

Not Caesar's Palace. But then not the Salvation Army. Enough to keep busting his ass keeping the slimy bastard propped up.

When Schein did come back to earth, Wyler would miss the money. But he wouldn't be sorry either. He only hoped he'd be there the night they turned on the toad and hissed him back into oblivion.

Wyler's intuition was that the more lines Robert Schein had to say onstage, the higher the risk of exposing his serpent personality. The trick for Wyler was to build an act that was long on stage business and short on one-liners. Since Schein had somehow managed to get a big laugh that first night just by walking out there and falling down, Wyler had played on his man's knack for creating audience suspense merely by standing still and examining the house with those scary blue eyes of his. All that crap in the papers about "neo-minimalist humor" or whatever—it was nothing but stalling! If the suckers thought it was a riot, well, it was their money. "Evocative of Benny," somebody had written. Jesus.

If the truth were known, Wyler thought he had detected a slacking off in the audience response to Schein in the last few weeks. They weren't automatically laughing their asses off at every gag, every moment. Some customers were actually giving evidence of their confusion as to just what all the critics and TV people had seen in Schein's act.

But now that Harwell had showed up and put his imprimatur on Schein—and Wyler was by no means certain that Harwell's remark was meant to be taken as a rave—the bastard had a new life. Now all the pseudo-intellectual jerks who owned a pair of French jeans and had pretended to be moved by THIRTY-TWO ACROSS in the sixties would be stiffing one another to get in.

That was the way it turned out. The next night, half of the spillover from Studio 54 was lined up in the cold along Second Avenue.

"What do we do now?" Gnagy asked Wyler, peering out the window at the undulating belt of leather that stretched down the sidewalk. Behind him, a barful of trendy customers kept up a raucous din.

"Stick your head out the door and tell 'em to get the hell out of here," advised Wyler.

Gnagy spun his skull head around and glared incredulously at Wyler.

"What the *hell* kind of business is that?"

"Go on, do it. They'll be back tomorrow night. They love that kind of treatment."

And that was the way it turned out.

Gnagy increased the cover charge to fifteen dollars, told most of the young comedians—who had supplied him with almost free talent when the place was just another East Side hole in the wall—to get lost, and began building a "quality" review around Robert Schein.

The "quality" review included one of the more successful of the new wave of Bobby Lee Cooper impersonators.

Liza showed up. And Truman. And Bianca. Rex attended and wrote a full-page paean to Schein, calling him "a comedic feast for sore ears, a Robert Redford with punchlines and no facial lines. There's gold in them there hair, sapphire in them there eyes, and diamonds in the pearls of wit that issue from his lips. Here's one comedian who knows what Frank Lloyd Wright (sic) meant when he said, 'Less is More.' Go see Robert Schein. And I *do* mean Schein."

The Harwell crowd squashed the original clientele at Stitch's like bugs. The young college and working-class kids that had formed the core of Schein's following the past summer were given to understand, by an unsubtle system of snubs, frozen stares, and outright insults, that they were trespassing. Harwell had claimed Stitch's as official celebrity and protocelebrity turf.

"They wanted to make this an 'in' spot," thought Wyler ruefully, watching a red-faced kid guide his trembling date toward the door through a pitiless gamut of stares and stony grins. "God, I guess they succeeded." His comic's mind toyed with the thought. "Reminds me of Bethlehem. No room at the 'in.' "

"Hey, this place reminds me of Bethlehem," Robert Schein shouted to the faithful as he strutted onstage the next night. "No room at the 'in'!"

The faithful loved it.

Al Gnagy hired a bouncer to make sure that the wrong people got in and the right people stayed out.

In January he upped the cover to twenty dollars a head. Drinks, five dollars each, on a three-drink minimum. Two shows, five nights a week, Mondays and Tuesdays dark.

He squeezed four more wooden tables, each with four chairs,

onto the already crowded floor, making it nearly impossible for any customer to move without affecting the rest of the room like a molecule in a chain. The lack of ventilation and disreputable plumbing added to an overwhelming discomfort.

The beautiful people loved it.

"You need something fresh," Wyler told Schein late in January. "You need something to replace that pratfall; it's getting old. You need some kind of tag line, something the audience'll always know is coming."

"Give me one."

Wyler went to work on it.

An old expression had been rattling around in his mind. A phrase from his grammar school days. A line that kids had used to sum up those obligatory "theme" essays with titles like, "My Most Embarrassing Moment."

The line was unbearably cloying, simplistic, and childish.

It went:

"Boy, was my face red."

Wyler worked out a couple of anecdotes for Schein to use as lead-ins to the tag line.

"Don't use it more than once a set," he said. "We'll see whether they pick up on it."

Two weeks after Schein began using the line, the audiences were gleefully chorusing along with him:

"BOOOOOOOOOYYYYYYYY, WAS MYYYYYYYYYY FAA-AAAAAACE RED!"

Schein used it on a television appearance. Lon Stagg, who had made it a point to be seen at a Schein performance, picked up the line to cover an on-air fluff.

Within days, people throughout New York were telling one another:

"Booooooyyyyy, was myyyyyyyy faaaaaaaaace *red*!"

Gnagy ordered a supply of white T-shirts decorated with a red cartoon face and the gold rhinestone initials:

BWMFR

They quickly became collector's items. Aretha was photographed wearing one to a reception for the Soviet ambassador.

"You need a manager," Jennifer whispered to Schein as they lay in her bed. It was 2:15 in the morning. Schein had returned from

Stitch's a half-hour ago. As happened always when Schein elected to spend the night at her apartment—she could never be sure which nights he would appear—they had made love swiftly and silently upon his arrival.

"Manager," Schein belched. He was eating a peeled orange, section by section, in the darkness, while Jennifer smoked. "What for."

Jennifer exhaled smoke through her nostrils.

"Because you are not earning a hundredth—maybe not a thousandth—of what you are worth. Do you realize you are one of *the* names in this city? You could be merchandising yourself into a national superstar. Gnagy's paying you chicken feed. It really is time for you to make a move, Robert."

Schein was quiet for a long time. Jennifer thought for a moment that he had drifted off to sleep. It would not be unlike him.

Then he said:

"I'm happy where I am."

In Jennifer Blade's world, hustle was a given. She had grown up assuming that everyone was like her father, his friends, the people who worked for him, her friends, and herself: driven by the compulsion to succeed and ruthless in the way they achieved success.

She did not understand weakness. Weak people were crushed—usually by strong people like her father. Teller, for example. Teller was not weak. Not exactly. But he was not ruthless either, which in the end amounted to the same thing. Teller was letting the competitive realities of television crush his spirit. He couldn't shrug it off, roll with it, use it, manipulate it, as she could. He had been in a deepening funk since his return from his vacation in October. He'd muttered to her about resigning. But in the end he had plunged back into his work, redoubling his attacks on the celebrity pop-culture with an almost suicidal disregard for Bass's policies. Weakness.

Schein did not fit into that category. He was not a weak man. Passive, definitely. Enigmatic in the extreme. But not weak. It was as though his very passivity were a valve on the enormous violent strength that he kept suppressed inside him, which flashed horrifically into his uncanny penchant for aping the extroversive style of others, then retreating abruptly into his own mysterious shell.

Jennifer knew that she could not argue Robert Schein into becoming ambitious. But she had learned that arguing with him was not necessary. She had learned how to manipulate his passivity.

"How would you like it if I found a manager?" she whispered to him.

"Suit yourself," he said.

She had not told Mark about Robert Schein. She knew that it would devastate him. She was aware of the horror and revulsion with which Teller had observed Schein's ascent into stardom. She had heard him rage and fulminate against the grotesque absurdity of it all, and about his own blunder that had set it all in motion.

Eventually, he would have to find out. It was not her problem, actually.

She had continued to see Teller, even though her involvement with Schein was deepening. Despite her contempt for emotionalism, another form of weakness in her estimation, something about Teller's vulnerability touched her. She enjoyed the conversations with him; he was, at his best, a truly original character. And conversation was not among the highlights of her affair with Schein.

Then, too, Jennifer admitted to herself, there was her slightly perverse enjoyment of Teller's fascination for her. Even more than the other lovers she'd had, some of them famous for their sensual artistry, Mark Teller was enraptured with her body. His kisses and caresses sometimes lasted for hours—even *after* the act of coitus itself, which she insisted on early. There was an almost childlike fascination that Teller had for her flesh, a fascination that seemed to go beyond sexual fulfillment and into some secret realm of Teller's mind, filling wells of need left empty by God knew what deprivations. It was curious that frequently, after an intense intertwining with her on his bed, Teller would talk about his father.

With Schein it was different. Schein's hands never explored her body. Except for that first day at his apartment, when he had half undressed her, he seemed indifferent to the aesthetics of her breasts or belly or thighs. He expected her to be naked when he came to her, or, if she were not, to undress herself quickly for him. He came into her with brutal, impersonal thrusts—another surfacing aspect of his violence. His eyes never met hers during the taking. After a while, she stopped looking at him, and closed her eyes, sinking into her own fantasies. It was fine, it was the way she liked it. She did not love Robert Schein. She did not like him very much. She knew no more about his background or his wishes in life than she had on the first day.

All she knew was that he represented the sheerest force of potential power she had ever experienced—a potential power that, androgynously, needed her own fertilization in order to gestate.

That, and the fact that making love to him was like making love to herself.

"You're not cutting it, Mark," said Ed Kurtis.

"Bullshit, Ed. My stuff has never been stronger. Goddammit, the *newspapers* picked up my exclusive on the drug busts at Madison Square Garden. They even had to give us credit. They couldn't develop their own sources."

"You know that isn't what I mean. Look, this isn't me talkin' to you. This is L. Malcolm Bass talkin'. You know the rules. He doesn't want crusades. He wants more pieces on celebrities."

"He's getting them. Day before yesterday. I pointed out how Sandy Meadows has patterned her entire acting style after Doris Day."

Ed Kurtis blew his nose on a piece of carbon paper.

"Mark. That's the point. You made Sandy Meadows out to be a laughingstock. She was America's sweetheart when she had her TV series about the nun on roller skates. Now she's come out with her first big movie and you stick a stiletto in her ribs."

"Ed, the movie is a goddamn obscenity. Have you seen it? It's supposed to be about a Vietnam veteran adjusting to civilian life. Bobby Dooley plays the vet. Remember Bobby Dooley? Gino Ginarelli on *Real Gone Bygones*? He plays the vet like one of the Bobbsey Twins. At the end of the movie he had an adorable nervous breakdown. Meadows spends the entire time blowing air up at the spit curl on her forehead. How'd you expect me to review her? Like she was Anne Bancroft?"

"Mark, America doesn't want—" Kurtis broke off and started again. "Let me put it this way. Malcolm Bass's research shows that America doesn't want to be confronted with negative ideas about its stars. Now listen to me, boy. You've been on a rampage ever since you came back from your little sabbatical in the Everglades, or wherever the hell it is you come from. You've been sticking your head in the noose since before Christmas. I mean, how the *hell* can you go on the air poking fun at Robert Schein knowing he's Bass's baby, that he's *our* fuckin' house celebrity, and that *you* are the guy who discovered him?"

"Easy. Want to see it again?"

"Mark, this is no joke. I've stood up for you to Bass. Told him we gotta have one segment of the show that *looks* like it's got some bite in it. He seems to understand that. But you see, he doesn't really give a damn about it. He's not going to tolerate much more of your insolence. I can't shield you forever. My ass is on the line same as yours. Now I've done what I've been told to do. You are officially on notice, Mark."

"Thanks for the warning, Ed. Hey—didn't you use to be in television news?"

"Coming up in the next half hour," Lon Stagg said, leaning his left shoulder into *WRAP-Around News*'s Camera One, "our medical unit will have a report on kitty cancer—the growing problem of leukemia in felines. Sandy Dennis's cat was one of those afflicted. Carlos Arroz will examine a new phenomenon that's sweeping Manhattan: Rent-a-Bobby Lee. Professional imitators of the late great recording star, depicting the various stages of his life. Our commentator Mark Teller will fill us in on the latest controversy surrounding television rights to the upcoming Summer Olympics in Moscow. All that and more when *WRAP-Around News* continues."

Camera One pulled back to show Lon Stagg rising from his seat behind WRAP's mahogany anchor desk, vaulting lightly over the top onto the floor near a marble-topped table, giving a jaunty wave to coanchorman Al Adams (who could be seen gathering up his papers preparatory to taking Stagg's place) and sauntering the length of the set. That stroll was the highlight of Lon Stagg's day. In many ways, it was what he lived for. It was the one moment in the newscast that showed him as the king of his domain, the man in charge, the star.

Stagg milked that stroll for every second before the fade to commercial. He walked the same way he gave the news—left shoulder thrust forward, head cocked whimsically to one side, a swirl of unruly white hair falling boyishly over his forehead. Stagg's gait had been likened to that of a football player getting ready for an onside kick. WRAP staffers privately debated whether his Porsche was outfitted with a special bucket seat pointed at a forty-five-degree angle to the right, allowing Stagg to peer over his left shoulder as he drove to work.

"I hear he even screws over his left shoulder," the weekend weathergirl remarked once. "I guess it's all right if you don't mind getting a blister."

Stagg kept walking off the set and through the sound-stage door. There would be five minutes of commercials, then Al Adams, the little creep, would open the next half-hour by reading the headlines.

Time for Stagg to check his makeup. And maybe take a quick nip.

Mark Teller was in the dressing room when Stagg entered. Stagg grimaced. Stagg did not like Mark Teller. Critics of any kind made him uneasy. And this one especially. This one was like a goddamn subversive. Maybe a hippie. Didn't know how to dress. Didn't wear a beeper. Knocked television—although there'd been less of that lately, Stagg had noticed. Worst of all, he refused to banter with Stagg at the close of a commentary. Kick it around a little. Let the audience see the human side of Stagg, the side that was vitally interested in what Teller had to say. Maybe a laugh or two.

Not a team player.

"Hello, Lon," said Mark, looking up from a copy of his script.

Stagg, as usual, was a model of tact.

"Guess you're going to rip into the hand that feeds you again, huh," he said.

"What?"

Stagg had his face screwed into the ironic half-smile that suggested this might be nothing more than a little harmless bantering. Among Stagg's many lesser talents was the ability to insult people while making them feel churlish for replying in kind.

"Guess you're going to go out there and give us all an uplifting sermon on why the television networks ought to stay out of the Summer Olympics. Something about the purity of the sport, uh, sullied by the crass commercialism of TV? Is that about the way you'd put it, Teller?" Stagg put his fingertips on his waist, flipping back his suit jacket—a Ralph Lauren, today—to reveal the beeper clipped to his belt. He stared down at his boots, then back up to Teller for a reaction. Teller had put aside his script and was listening, expressionless.

"Guess you think anybody who wants to watch the games ought to *go* to Russia. That be about it, Teller?" Stagg was pleased with this thrust. It had a goddamn double meaning. "Yeah, go to Russia," he said, rubbing his hands together, unable to resist appraising his face in the mirror. "Maybe we should send all the *critics* in this country to Russia, to *watch* the games—" Stagg was pacing now, enjoying his irony—"*they* know what we've seen anyway, better than we do, with our own eyes—send the *critics* to Russia, let 'em cover the games . . . *and see how many of 'em come back!*" Stagg spun and pointed at Teller, a little flourish to the punch line. Then his face cracked into its most likable boyish grin; his own cleverness had dissipated his distaste for Teller; he was inviting Teller to be a sport and share in the joke at Teller's expense. No hard feelings.

"I have a better idea, Lon," said Teller pleasantly. "Let's keep the critics here and send the anchormen. And see how many of them can find their *way* back. We'll have somebody here squirt a can of hair spray into the air every few days so you can pick up the scent."

"What the hell is that supposed to mean?"

". . . a string of dental floss across the Bering Strait . . ."

"Keep it up, Teller." Stagg shot his cuff as he pointed at Mark. His voice was suddenly nasty. "You go right ahead and put me down. I know how you feel about me. I see it on your face every time you come on the goddamn set."

"Just kidding around, Lon. No hard feelings."

"No hard feelings my *ass!*" Stagg was ranting now; the sybaritic mouth was savage. "I've put up with your condescending attitude ever since you came on this newscast, and I've swallowed it because you're a stiff and I'm a goddamn professional and I get paid good money for sitting out there and making you look good on the air! I could cut your throat out a hundred different ways if I wanted to, Teller, because I understand this goddamn medium, and if I raised my eyebrow the right way after one of your smart-ass little sermons, half the people out there would fall on their asses laughing at you.

"But goddammit, I prop you *up*, because that's my job. I say,

'Thanks, Mark,' like you've just said something that ordinary people out there can relate to. And I'm sick of it. You don't do what everybody here has asked you to do. You don't do the personality pieces. You're not playing on the team, you're in your own goddamn ivory tower, man, and pretty soon I'm not going to have to puke every time you come on the set because you're going to be *gone*! I know for a fact that management has had a bellyful of you, the viewers have had a bellyful of you. Have you looked at the phone-message chart lately? Goddamn, Teller, I hope you *haven't* looked at the phone-message chart, because the phone-message chart will tell you what you're doing wrong, and I'd personally just as soon you didn't find out until Mal Bass hands you your pink slip. *Now put that in one of your artsy-fartsy commentaries!"*

"Lon, something's bothering you," said Teller. "I can sense it. You have something you want to get off your chest. Why don't you just come right out with it?"

Stagg's eyes were hard with hatred. "You are going to crawl out of here some day soon, Teller."

Teller stood up slowly, offhandedly, not making the move seem too direct. When he was at his full height, he folded his script and put it in his jacket pocket. Then he looked down at Lon Stagg.

"You think today'll be the day, Lon? You think today I might crawl out of here?"

Stagg glared at him for a long moment. He declined the tacit invitation. "Your time is coming, slugger," he said through clenched teeth, and stalked out of the dressing room, slamming the door.

Teller sank back heavily in the chair. The defiance he had marshaled for Stagg's benefit was bogus. In his own malevolent way, Stagg had been right, of course. Teller was an interloper, an outsider who had no business being a part of *WRAP-Around News*. Worse, he was a hypocrite. One thing he'd have to give Stagg: the guy made no attempt to be something he wasn't. Stagg had never claimed to be a newsman; he was a highly specialized performer, an actor, really, doing well what he was paid well to do. He belonged. Teller didn't.

It had been rough since October. He hadn't found what he'd been looking for back home in the Ozarks. What he'd been looking for was a strong reason to quit, a sense of contrasts, something to return to. But what he had found in his hometown was the outer perimeter of New York-Los Angeles; the deadening ring of sameness, the colonizing culture of the airwaves that he'd tried to leave behind. Bobby Lee Cooper's ghost had already tainted the town.

After that, there wasn't much reason for quitting his job. But there was no great reason for staying, either. Maybe the answer was to let the system eject him when it found him too much of an irritant.

Thirteen minutes to air time.

It would all be easier, more bearable, if things were going better with Jennifer. But in the late fall and winter, they had quarreled, split up, reconciled, made love ferociously, quarreled again in an ever-widening circle. There were still moments in which the splendor of her beauty took his breath away; moments in which her intelligence, her unexpected rich humor, her flashes of empathy, touched the old chord of deep, loving comradeship between them, and for a little while it was inexpressibly good. Then, he loved her.

But mostly, the relationship was strained. Jennifer was driving hard for a network assignment. There were times when he didn't see her for weeks on end, except fleetingly, at the office.

And she continued to insist that they keep the remnants of their affair secret. No more public occasions together.

Maybe it would be better if he broke off the affair cleanly and eliminated that source of anguish from his mind. There were times when he groped for his love feelings toward Jennifer and felt only dead indifference. Hatred, sometimes. Deep anger.

He would have to think about ending it.

But not yet. Not for a while.

He turned on the portable TV set in the dressing room and let his attention drift into the newscast. On the air, Lon Stagg and Al Adams were both roaring with laughter over some joke, boon comrades of years' standing.

"Well, all I can do, Al," Stagg finally gasped, recovering, "is echo the immortal words of Robert Schein: 'Booooooyyyyy, is myyyyyyy faaaaaaaaace *reeed*!"

Al adams giggled.

"Back after this with Mark Teller," said Stagg into the camera. "Don't go 'way."

The dressing-room door opened. An assistant director, earphones on his head, looked in.

"You're in the next segment, Mark."

"Right. Thanks."

Maybe after this one, Lon, he thought, pushing open the door to the Studio 2 sound stage, you'll get your wish.

Teller took a seat in one of the wire-backed chairs around the small marble-top table that served as the commentary- and special-report area. Stagg was seated at the table with him. There was a bouquet of fresh flowers on the table, and there were coffee cups in front of Stagg and Teller. The intent—as the research people had explained to L. Malcolm Bass—was to create a subliminal atmosphere of warm cordiality, a fantasy of a couple of likable guys kicking an idea back and forth.

The problem was that when the two people at the table despised one another, the illusion was hard to sustain. Teller and Stagg had covered up their mutual detestation for the good of the show. So far.

A technician clipped Teller's lavaliere mike to the lapel of his jacket. The hot arc lights brought up every detail, every color on the set to an unnatural pitch of intensity.

"Let's have a level, Mark."

"Mark's level is *always* above everybody else's," said Stagg in a loud falsetto, loud enough for the crew to hear. He was staring at Teller like a heavyweight fighter in the center of the ring. Stagg's eyes glittered in the unnatural light.

"Level level level level level," said Teller, ignoring Stagg. He looked into the TelePrompTer.

"One minute," called the floor director.

"Can you move Camera One?" Teller called out to the director. "I'm getting a reflection in the 'PrompTer screen."

"Critic's getting a reflection!" repeated Stagg in mock alarm. "Stop the show! Cut to black! Somebody call an ambulance!"

He looked around the set with his only-joking grin spread across the face. Several floor technicians laughed dutifully.

The cameraman shifted a foot to his left.

"How's that, Mark?"

"Better." Teller began to mouth the first few lines of his script to himself, a routine drill.

"Thirty seconds."

"I think I know one reason you don't have anything good to say about Bob Schein." Stagg's voice was low now, just loud enough for Teller to hear. And the control room, if Stagg's mike happened to be live.

"Twenty seconds."

Teller looked sharply at Stagg.

"Maybe you're jealous of Schein because he's screwing our star reporter. I understand you had the hots for Jenny."

A white light formed itself in Mark Teller's brain and exploded. The light inside his head was so intense that he could see the veins in his own eyelids when they fluttered shut. It was as though all the lights on all the ceilings of all the television studios of the world had coalesced into a hard little nova that now seared inside his skull.

The hot light slowed time down, made it crawl through a molten sea of sick particles, thoughts, images; and Teller's mind flashed ahead down along all the images: the mundane Tele-PrompTer; Robert Schein humping Jennifer Blade; the glazed indifferent faces of the technicians staring at him; a black assistant director at the point of paring a fingernail with a key on a ring; Jennifer's legs open to Schein's thrusts; blazing reflector glass; the sportscaster at the far end of the set, off-camera, his fingers at the knot of his tie; Jennifer, the secret rain forest violated, invaded; Stagg's glittering eyes searching Teller's to gauge how well the blow had struck; everything bathed in the hot, merciless, unnatural lights of television. Teller's mind hopped crazily among the paralyzed particles of time and thought and image—could he read the TelePrompTer?—Stagg was bluffing, continuing the war begun inside the dressing room, detonating just one of the media tricks, the hundred ways he could cut Teller's throat on the air.

And Teller knew—

"Ten seconds."

—that Stagg was not bluffing, he wasn't smart enough to cut that close to the jugular, his anchorman's mind couldn't comprehend the totality of the macabre joke that was contained in the truth of it: that Teller had created his own betrayal out of something as thin as the airwaves, the airwaves that within seconds were to carry his image out across New York, to the very television set, perhaps, that was nearest the point of Jennifer's and Schein's copulation, the set that had perhaps been carrying his own image as they made love, Teller's unseeing, airwave image a blind witness to his own mockery, his own betrayal . . .

"Five seconds."

If he was a victim, Teller thought, he was at least victim of a national disease.

The whole country was getting screwed by celebrityhood.

The words on the TelePrompTer swam into focus.

The director's hand went down.

"There's been much controversy over the upcoming Summer Olympics in Moscow," Lon Stagg read from his own TelePrompTer screen, "and the cultural role that television's coverage of the games will play in our lives. Mark Teller has been following that controversy, and today he's back with—" here Stagg departed from the 'PrompTer copy to ad-lib his own twist "—another in what seems to be an *endless* series of looks at the negative side of television. Mark?"

Teller fought back a sudden impulse to seize Stagg and beat him bloody in full view of WRAP's viewing audience. Instead he forced himself to favor the anchorman with a crisp professional smile.

"Thank you, Lon," he said. He drew a deep breath.

He turned to face his camera. In a steady voice, he read:

"We're all familiar with the growing tide of sentiment being launched by American conservatives against any kind of network participation in the Summer Olympics in Moscow. With the games more than a year away and the networks still battling for coverage rights, certain influential columnists have already warned that the 'winning' network could turn out a big 'loser'—that is, it could unavoidably lend itself to Soviet propaganda and manipulation.

"But what about another kind of 'propaganda' and 'manipulation'—the winning network's own voluntary and deliberate manipulation of American values and behavior patterns? I'd like to read to you an excerpt of a memo that I have obtained. This memo was sent from the director of sports publicity to the public-relations vice-president . . . at the network that currently seems most likely to win the telecast rights."

Teller pulled a copy of the memo from his jacket pocket—a slight concession to theatrics, as the memo's contents were included in his TelePrompTer copy. He read:

" 'Successful coverage of the Summer Olympics could give our network momentum that would carry us into overall ratings dominance for years to come. Therefore, it is essential that we plan and execute a public-relations campaign that would turn the population of America into *Summer Olympics junkies*. It must be our objective to condition the public, in advance, to regard each and every event in the Summer Olympics as having *intrinsic nationalistic importance*. If we do our job right, our network will be hailed for a public-service contribution comparable to that of the BBC during the bombing of Britain.' "

Teller folded the memo and put it back into his pocket. He looked into the camera silently for a moment.

" 'Summer Olympics junkies,' " he repeated. " 'Condition the public, in advance.' With language like this, you have to wonder who the real enemy is—Russia, or the American system of broadcasting, which hands us prepackaged celebrities and social values with equal indifference.

"Lon?"

Upstairs, in the cool silence of the thirtieth floor of the Commerce Center, a white telephone rang on the desk of L. Malcolm Bass. Bass was watching four screens simultaneously—each of New York's network-owned stations—but he had the volume up on Channel 26, WRAP.

A copy of Teller's script was spread out on the desk in front of him.

Bass knew who was on the other end of the phone. The Colonel. It was his hot-line phone. He also thought he knew what was on Donovan's mind. He'd seen Teller's commentary, and this was Teller's execution order.

Bass picked up the phone. He couldn't blame the Colonel. Teller was off the deep end; he'd been warned, and he hadn't come around. The hell with prestige, no reason to keep a wild-eyed insurgent on the air, flagellating the system that pays his salary, especially in a crucial ratings-sweep period—perhaps the most crucial period in WRAP's history.

"Yes, Colonel?"

Bass listened for a moment. Then his eyebrows came together in concentration. He shifted the receiver to his left hand, picked up a silver ballpoint pen, and made some notations on a memo pad. "Yes, Colonel."

Bass put down the phone. He folded his hands under his fleshy chin and stared for a long moment at the tidy desk surface before him. Then he gave a slight shrug of his shoulders. He was a company man. His was not to question why.

He picked up a black telephone receiver and punched his secretary's extension.

"Get Mark Teller on the line right away. You better page him, he's probably on his way out of the building."

Teller heard the page as he ambled down the corridor, away from the studio and toward the WRAP newsroom. The image of Jennifer Blade coupled with Robert Schein had invaded every crevice of his consciousness. The thought of it set his temples to pounding. He was consumed by a combination of helpless rage, despair, and a persistent lacing of dark, evil humor. The cumulative effect was nausea. He didn't yet know for a fact that it was true. But every instinct told him it was.

"Mark Teller. Mark Teller, please call the operator."

He continued his dazed, ambling stride into the newsroom. He would call from the phone in his cubicle. He had the vague assumption that he was being fired. He could not deal with that situation now. He had to resolve the question of Jennifer Blade.

He felt a mixture of frustration and relief that she was not at her desk in the newsroom. He walked through it.

"Hey, Teller," called Sean Murphy. "I got a memo you might be interested in. It says we're supposed to condition New York City into believing Lon Stagg is from the planet Earth."

Teller gave no evidence of having heard.

"Don't waste your breath," said Cazzini, who was standing nearby. "Fucker's in another world."

Teller entered his cubicle. There was a copy of the *Messenger* tucked under his typewriter bar. He hadn't read it yet. He pulled it out absently and tossed it on his desk. He picked up the phone and dialed Bass's extension.

"Mark! Mal Bass here. Hiya, chum. Say, the Colonel just called and asked me to tell you he thought your piece on the Summer Olympics was right on the money."

"What?" Teller was only half-listening to Bass, but he couldn't believe what he had heard.

"Yeah. He said he'd like to see you return to that theme from time to time. Go get 'em, Tiger. Ciao."

Teller hung up the phone and shook his head, as though to clear it. Plenty of surprises in the last half hour. Somehow, the notion that the Colonel liked his piece was even more disturbing than it would have been had the Colonel disapproved. In some mysterious and probably distasteful way, Teller had managed to serve the interests of CBN, of the corporation.

The corporation, he sensed—as he had sensed before—was moving toward something big and decisive, employing some arcane strategy Teller couldn't even begin to fathom.

Whatever it was, it had probably saved him his job for the moment.

That wasn't important now. All that mattered was the truth about Jennifer Blade.

He tried her home number. No answer. He decided to wait a while and try again. He didn't feel like leaving the station and going home to his apartment. The anxiety had to be laid to rest, one way or another.

He put his feet up on his desk and opened the *Messenger*. He skimmed it idly.

The Summer Olympics was still a hot issue, all right. There was a story on page 3. But it didn't have the network memo. That was his exclusive.

He read through an article quoting a woman psychic as saying she had received instructions from Bobby Lee Cooper, "beyond the grave," asking tourists to stop trampling the grass at his Chattanooga estate. The article was four times longer than a piece next to it, about a Justice Department investigation into corruption in the longshoremen unions.

He flipped to page 6—the gossip-and-celebrity page.

He saw the photograph first, but the faces in it didn't register. It was a typically fuzzy, overly harsh newspaper snapshot. He glanced at the caption beneath it:

SHE'S THE 'SHINE' IN COMIC'S EYE

He started to turn the page again, to check out the movie reviews. But something in the phrasing of the caption triggered an alarm in his brain.

He scanned the two vertical columns of *Messenger* gossip,

searching for the boldface names that he knew would be in there.

He found them right under an item about BOBBY LEE COOPER's divorced father, GENE, announcing his engagement to a Nashville nurse:

> NEW PROOF THAT NEWS, COMEDY MIX: Dancing up a storm at Studio 54 last night were two of New York's most glittering new personalities. Rave comic BOB SCHEIN boogie'd with no one but hot young newsprincess JENNY BLADE, the latter heir apparent to BABS' throne. Pair say sparks flew when Jenny interviewed Bob on the set of "WRAP-Around News." WRAP's on the rise, so is Schein. Jenny denied hot romance, but friends say it's no "news" to them.

Teller folded the paper and placed it carefully on his desk. He got up from his desk and walked back into the newsroom, which by now was nearly deserted, the day shift having left and the night shift just wandering in.

He strolled past the desk of Cyrilee Chassen, a reporter who came as close as anyone to being Jennifer Blade's intimate friend. Cyrilee was cramming scraps of paper into her purse, preparatory to leaving for the day.

"Where's Jennifer?" Teller tried to make it sound offhand. "I haven't seen her around today."

Cyrilee shot him a look that told him how little he had managed to fool anyone—her, at any rate.

She smiled an overly cordial smile.

"I thought you might have heard, Mark. She got her stripes this afternoon."

"Stripes?"

"That's right. She's been promoted to weekend anchorwoman. I think I heard her say she was going to take off a couple of weeks and go home to Los Angeles."

Part Two

Oh, God. This was it. Like being back in Los Angeles already. Out of a cold April New York rain into the temperatureless TWA departure lounge at Kennedy Airport. This is where Los Angeles begins, Jennifer Blade decided, in the TWA departure lounge at Kennedy Airport. All those deep-scarlet seats, winding around in circles against the blank cream-colored departure-lounge walls. They reminded her of the poinsettia gardens swirling against the blank stucco walls of Beverly Hills palaces. Maybe Beverly Hills was the world's biggest departure lounge, and this was *it*, this was really *it*.

She loved it. She giggled at the thought. She had been drinking a little vermouth cassis, and she loved it, and she wished she had someone to share the joke with.

Then she remembered that she was with Robert Schein.

Robert Schein, and two first-class tickets to L.A. International. Robert Schein, and two first-class tickets to L.A. International, and a new title, her new stripes, weekend anchorwoman, *WRAP Around News*. And two first-class tickets to L.A. International. And Robert Schein.

And no one to share her little joke with.

It didn't matter. She was going home in triumph. Back to the

Coast, a Somebody in her own right. Not just Sterling Blade's daughter, child of Hollywood, doomed to some horrid success as a model or a minor actress, to marry a John Wayne or a John Dean, write a best-seller some day about how sordid it all was, fade into the talk shows, the softening benediction of Merv Griffin.

But as a Somebody. A professional. A newswoman. Better than her face and her body and the privilege her family name demanded. Hired as a curio, a promotable commodity, on the authority of her father's decree, she had required herself to learn the infinitely subtle craft of journalism, as well as television's added image of it. She had succeeded. People were on their way to prison because of her. She had power. Now she had position: weekend anchorwoman. The assignment was a springboard. If she handled it, she knew, her next promotion would be to the CBN Network.

She had mastered Sterling Blade's medium, television, but not in the way either of them had ever expected. And now she was a star. But not, perhaps, in a way he would understand.

She was going home to erase all possibility of misunderstanding.

With her trophies. Including the one sitting next to her.

Jennifer looked around the lounge. It really was an L.A. colony, she told herself (she had grown used to having silent conversations with herself when in the company of Robert Schein). Opposite her—opposite them—was a murmuring group of soft young men with soft beards and soft jeans, square silver cases at their feet, the cases bearing the name of a rock band in red sticker-stencil. To their left, an elderly couple that would answer cheerfully to the description, "Angelenos." The man in a western straw hat and a string tie, the woman leathery and square-faced, in a sensible denim skirt. The lounge was filling up with returning refugees, Californians on the way home. The thought excited her. She wanted to tell it to someone.

To Schein? He sat impassively beside her: a piece of hand luggage she had grabbed that afternoon, on impulse, after it had all happened. She had made him wear sunglasses; they *both* had on oversize sunglasses so that nobody would recognize them. She had worn her tightest, most scandalous pair of faded California jeans, her most bitchy high-heeled calfskin boots, a sensational rust-colored mosquito-cloth tunic, tied up at the midriff to show a little skin. Festive. Her hair was piled high on her head.

She could be anything, anyone she wanted on this day, she had decided; create any identity she chose for this celebration of a flight home: Career Woman. High Chic. Laid-back Student. Transcontinental Whore. Why not? It was all pretend (she had told herself back in her apartment, sipping the third of several vermouth cassis, cassises, cassissi?), all dress-up. After all, she had created her own identity in New York. Invented herself. Reversed the usual procedure, west to east. She had chosen Stars Incognito for herself and Robert Schein, because that is what they were. And why, now, in the TWA departure lounge at Kennedy Airport, high on stripes and vermouth cassis and homecoming, was she close to tears?

She looked sideways at Schein. Goddammit, they were stars. It was just that in the sunglasses, Schein didn't look like a star. That was okay, that was the point. Not to be hassled by celebrity-seekers. But somehow with the sunglasses over his ice-blue eyes, sitting there in his usual fog of silence, Robert Schein did not seem to be anyone at all. It was as though the sunglasses covered two pits of emptiness, the sockets of a blind man. Give the bastard a tin cup . . . Oh, God. It wasn't supposed to be this way. Robert Schein was a Somebody. There were the press notices and the television appearances to prove it. And it was all comic. This whole scene was comic, the two of them sitting here in their over-size sunglasses, incognito. See, the comedy of it all was that every-body in the damned *lounge* had on oversize sunglasses. Even the Angelenos. *Nobody* was into being recognized. Everybody was a heavy. It was going to be, like, a heavy trip.

Jennifer wanted to say it aloud, to whisper it to somebody. She was in rare form. She checked the impulse automatically, made it not matter. The comic sitting to her left would not understand the comedy of it.

Teller would have understood; Teller would have thought it was a stitch; Teller and she would have laughed like . . .

"Do you have a cigarette?" she whispered to Schein, out of the sudden urgency to say *something* to *someone*.

Two opaque Polaroid disks, like empty TV screens, turned toward her; she saw her own face in them, her own eyeless face. It was not the first time she had seen herself reflected in Robert Schein.

"Tryin' to quit."

The bastard. Even looking right at him, you couldn't remember what he was wearing. Some tweed sport coat, some tie. Something he'd probably had on this afternoon before he even knew he was going to sleep that night on the other side of the continent.

A stitch. Stitch's. He'd been wearing that tweed coat the night he performed at Stitch's, the night she and Teller had first seen him, and now Teller was unavoidably back on her mind, and she knew that at least part of the reason for this sudden festive celebration of a flight home was so that she would not have to face Mark Teller and explain to him about the picture and the item in the *Messenger*.

Which was absurd. Not only did he not own her—no man ever did or would—but she was phasing him out of her life. He was an inconvenience, a mistake, a toy, an amusement. He would never be a star, never be a high-roller, never be any of the strong, vain, well connected, moneyed, male faces who had passed in and out of her life like butlers, some of whose balls she had broken, some of whose balls had refused to break. He was not one of the jocks who had used her as an ornament; not one of the silky New York pols who had introduced her around; not one of the coarse, florid gin-drinkers on the circuit from the Hamptons to the Bahamas; not one of the money men, the power men who draped arms around her shoulders and put hands up her dress, who always started out calling her "sweetheart" without bothering to look her way, and always ended up calling her at four o'clock in the morning until she unplugged the cord from the phone. No sobbing senator, no imploring linebacker, no French rock impresario calling from Marseilles to see whether she had changed her mind. Just another second-rater, out of his depth, interesting, promising at first, the illusion of a potential star, now inconvenient, and if he had more humanity, more gentleness, more humor than the men she was used to knowing, well, she would just have to get used to doing without it again. It was beginning to look like she'd have to do without a smoke for a while, too.

But he would have loved all the sunglasses . . .

She glanced at her wristwatch. Ten minutes until boarding time. Oh, God. She would kill for a glass of champagne. For celebrating.

Goddamn *The New York Messenger* anyway.

She would call Mark from California. She owed him that courtesy.

Speaking of calling:

"Have you called Al Gnagy at Stitch's?" she asked Schein, who had apparently lapsed into a catatonic trance.

"No."

"Please do it. I think we at least owe him that courtesy."

The most celebrated young comedian in New York held out his hand for a dime.

She watched him saunter away. A sickening wash of panic suddenly consumed her. What had she done? What had she set in motion? Why, in the very flush of her most unexpected career coup, had she elected to place Schein's career and her own in jeopardy?

She could understand her impulse to fly back to California and flaunt her little triumph before her father. But taking Schein along—it was a foolish risk. Walking out on Gnagy without advance warning could send Schein back to oblivion as abruptly as he had been yanked out of it. As for her, she had just been burned by one gossip item in the *Messenger*. A cross-country fling with a recent interview subject could invite the sort of lip-smacking coverage that would mock her credentials as an anchorwoman, embarrass the station during a key ratings struggle, and send her back to covering parades and Soap Box Derbies.

And yet the impulse to take Schein with her had seemed as natural as breathing. It was Schein, after all, who was indirectly responsible for her promotion.

Donovan had notified her of the promotion at 10 A.M. that morning.

"We've had you penciled in for this ever since the Schein interview," Bass had told her. "That showed us you're a versatile gal, and naturally we want to showcase you as much as we can."

"What happens to Elizabeth?" Jennifer asked of the quiet blond woman who presently held the weekend anchor spot.

"Elizabeth was the reason it took us so long to get you into harness. We had to hold her feet to the fire a bit to resolve certain contractual difficulties." Bass smiled. Just like that, Jennifer thought. Anchorwoman to nonperson. It won't happen to me.

"Speaking of contracts," Bass continued briskly, "we assume

you'll be wanting to renegotiate yours. Don't take all the Colonel's cigarette money, for Chrissakes. Leave some for the rest of us. Now make yourself scarce around here for a few days so you can hit the ground running. We'll rehearse you a week from Friday and you go to work the following day."

Bass did not mention the *Messenger* item linking Jennifer and Schein—thank God. Jennifer had to assume, against all probability, that he had not seen it.

Jennifer passed Teller on her way back to her office. Although she was bursting with excitement, she chatted gaily with Teller for several minutes, even tentatively accepted a dinner date for the evening, without once mentioning the news.

Not until she was in her office and had Robert Schein on the line did she have any notice of what she was about to do.

"Get some stuff together. I'm taking you to California with me tonight! We're celebrating. I'm the new weekend anchorwoman!"

Silence at the other end of the line.

"Schein! Did you hear me?"

"Yeah. I gotta work Stitch's tonight."

Thanks for the congratulations, you bastard, she thought. Aloud, she said: "Never mind Stitch's. You don't have a contract there, do you?"

"No."

"Ever been to California before?"

"No."

She asked the next question without quite intending to:

"Have you ever been on a plane before?"

"No."

A shudder ran through her. Was she dealing with a genuine zombie? She shrugged it off.

"Well, here's your chance. You deserve a vacation. Look. Meet me at the TWA ticket counter at JFK in an hour and a half. I'll reimburse your cab fare. Don't bother packing a lot of stuff. We'll buy you some clothes when we get out there. I'll take care of the tickets."

Silence.

"Robert? Is that all right with you?"

Is that all right with you???

"Suit yourself." He hung up.

She let out a shriek of frustration into the dead phone line.
Then she called her father.
Then she began drinking vermouth cassis.

"Good evening, ladies and gentlemen, thank you for waiting. In just a few moments we will be boarding TWA Flight Nine, nonstop Seven Forty-seven service to Los Angeles International Airport. For the convenience of passengers . . ."

She wondered how Gnagy had taken the news. Would he fire Schein on the spot? Perhaps not. Stitch's without Robert Schein would be like Michael's Pub without Woody Allen. Worse. The place would go straight down the tubes. Gnagy had tooled his entire act around Schein, while exercising the inexplicable judgment not to sign him to a contract. Maybe Gnagy assumed Schein would just keep coming around, like the hapless nontalents whom Gnagy had so summarily torpedoed when Schein began laying the golden eggs. Well, Mr. Gnagy was about to receive a free lesson in sound business management. Screw him anyway.

Jennifer admitted to herself now that she would not have left Schein behind in New York even if it had meant breaking a contract with Gnagy. He was the key to her impromptu California pilgrimage. Yes, it was a risk, unplugging him from the only source of his power—a calculated risk. The strange, artificial light that was Robert Schein would go out temporarily. But Jennifer understood now what it was she had set out to do. She was going to take Schein west, plug him into other, more powerful energy sources. He would return to New York more incandescent than ever. And so would she. In a way she could not define, her own brilliance depended on his.

She had to find out something about Robert Schein. She had to find out what he was. *Who* he was did not seem to matter anymore; in any case, it was a futile question. (Sometimes she had the feeling that he was everyone who used him.) But *what* he was: that was the question that intrigued her. She had come to think of him as a mechanism that had been triggered inadvertently and that now fed off the energy of other people's desires, and she had been present at the triggering, and her desires had fed the mechanism, and now she wanted to follow it to its ultimate consequences. She wanted to test the nature of her own attraction to him, a powerful, even an irresistible attraction that was yet neither love nor friendship, but something more compelling still, like the attraction to oneself.

In order to do this, she knew that she had to take Robert Schein to Hollywood, to make the connections that could keep the string of energies alive, the chain reaction of energies that worked almost like the airwaves themselves.

She knew that she could not pull it off on her own. She needed help. In order to keep making the connections that would keep Robert Schein alive by redefining him—reinventing him, as she continually reinvented herself—she would have to break a cherished resolution.

She would have to ask Sterling Blade for help one more time.

She had made the decision to do so without even thinking consciously about it.

". . . *Passengers holding first-class boarding passes rows one through six . . .*"

"Champagne," Jennifer Blade instructed the stewardess who was passing down the aisle, checking seat belts. A Bobby Lee Cooper tune, "Heartbreak Flight Now Boarding," was on the intercom.

"I'm sorry, miss, FAA regulations require that we refrain from serving alcoholic beverages until . . ."

Jennifer whipped off her sunglasses.

"Fuck FAA regulations. Bring me the champagne. I am Jennifer Blade."

Al Gnagy replaced the telephone on the wall beside the cash register at Stitch's. His skull face was ashen white as he turned to face Bill Wyler, who was nursing a Bloody Mary at the bar.

"That was Schein."

"So?"

"He's not comin' in tonight."

Wyler looked up. Gnagy's eyes were bulging. He looked as though he might be having a heart attack.

Wyler shrugged. "So maybe he's got laryngitis or the flu. Take it easy."

Gnagy shook his skull head violently. "He ain't got no fuckin' laryngitis. The son of a bitch is leavin' for Los Angeles."

Wyler spat out a mouthful of Bloody Mary. Some of it got on

the cream-colored Qiana shirt he had taken to wearing these days, along with flared hip-huggers, in place of the western denim suit.

When he recovered, he said:

"He's pulling your leg."

Gnagy gave a humorless snort. "Have you ever seen Robert Schein pull anybody's leg?"

"How long's he going for?"

"Didn't say."

"Been nice workin' for you, pal."

That night, the Beautiful People booed the master of ceremonies when he announced that Robert Schein was ill and would not perform.

Wyler, the seasoned pro, attempted to stand in for the man whose material he created. The Beautiful People never gave him a chance. He was hissed off the stage before he could get a line out.

Hissed into oblivion.

Someone lobbed a wooden chair onto the stage as Wyler, woozy with Bloody Marys, turned away from the microphone. Wyler tripped over the chair and went sprawling.

There was scattered applause and laughter from the audience. Someone yelled out:

"Nice try, buddy, but you'll never be another Bob Schein!"

Someone else yelled:

"BOOOOOOOYYYYYYYY, WAAAAAAAS MYYYYYYY FA-AAAAACE REEEED!"

Sterling Blade's driver met them at the airport. He was in the black Mercedes 450 SLC. The warm dark-green California night air told Jennifer Blade she was home, home after a year of enduring the heavy, blatant, alien eastern air of another civilization. The California air nuzzled her skin like an old conspirator, it floated on her neck and teased her with intimations of palm trees and drinks in the afternoon and jewelry, of all the lean brown bodies she had left behind for her year in New York. And now she was coming home in triumph. To celebrate. The air seemed to know that, and the driver: he gave a ceremonial click of his heels and said, "It is an honor to have you back with us, Miss Blade!"

They drove north on 405 at seventy-five miles an hour, and

Jennifer kept the window down to let the dark-green California night air stream in on her neck and shoulders. It restored her sense of adventure and festivity. Five hours on an airplane with Robert Schein was not an experience to be recalled lightly. She had made convivial conversation almost by the force of her will. They had drunk champagne, and she had told him all about her father, the baron of action-adventure TV series and made-for-TV movies. Schein had listened with more attentiveness than usual. From his occasional monosyllabic comment, Jennifer gathered that Schein was familiar with most of her father's product—even the early stuff, the fifties Westerns and the sixties West-Coast-private-eye shows.

His awareness reinforced her notion that Schein had accumulated a great deal of his worldly knowledge by watching television.

Aside from her brush with the stewardess, neither of them had removed their sunglasses during the flight.

Now they were hurtling north on 405, and she was pointing out landmarks to Schein: Venice Boulevard, where the darkened M-G-M studios lay off to the right; the first distant glimpse of the glow that was Century City.

Schein took it all in silently. But Jennifer could sense by his stiffened posture, the intensity of his gaze out the window, that already Robert Schein was beginning to absorb Hollywood—Television Heaven—in the way that he must have absorbed television itself.

The thought filled her with an almost erotic glee. She did not understand why.

Sterling Blade was in the doorway to greet them when they arrived at the estate after a tire-screeching dash up Canyon Drive: a flourish, Jennifer was sure, that Sterling had stipulated for Schein's benefit. The screeching tire, after all, was a Sterling Blade TV-movie trademark.

Backlighted by the living-room glow behind him, Blade in silhouette projected an elemental image, power incarnate. (The lighting was no accident, Jennifer knew.) He looked every inch the conqueror he was, the conqueror of an old and decaying empire, the movies. Sterling Blade had shouldered his way into Beverly Hills and into the movie-rich society that Beverly Hills represented. He had converted the motion picture technology into a tool of television in the days before it was fashionable to do so, and no one associated with him was ever allowed to forget it.

He stood tall in the doorway, long legs planted apart. He was wearing his fringed buckskin jacket—a touch that would have looked ludicrous on any other man, but one that subordinated itself to Sterling Blade's style. The wisps of silver hair, fanning out over his ears, shimmered in the light behind him. Seeing him in this costume—tight jeans and calfskin boots completed it—one gossip columnist had compared his machismo to that of John Wayne in *Red River*. The image inspired in Jennifer a different thought: the Arnold Toynbee adage that "time is on the side of the barbarians."

"Son of a bitch," came his low, rumbling whisky baritone across the warm, thrilling night air. "I said go to New York and try to get a job. I didn't say go to New York and take the goddamn place over."

The two tall, lean figures embraced in the doorway.

"And this is the Wonder Boy, the new Bob Hope of Broadway." Sterling Blade brought a ham-hand down on Robert Schein's shoulder with a force that would have staggered a lesser man. Schein did not flinch. Sterling Blade marked it, and was pleased.

Suddenly Blade took a step backward and spread his arms. His lips arranged themselves into a figure eight.

"Booooy," he bellowed, "waaaas myyyyyyyyy faaaaace reeeed!"

Jennifer was impressed, as she always was with the old man. He had done his research.

As for Schein, he was suddenly the picture of flattered surprise. A boyish grin creased his features; he smacked his hands together in helpless disbelief. It was all too much for him.

"I can't *believe* it, Jenny," said a voice that indisputably came from Schein's throat. "This man is one of my all-time idols, and the first time I meet him, he does *me*!"

They were in Sterling Blade's living room drinking Wild Turkey, the three of them: Sterling Blade, Jennifer Blade, and Robert Schein. There was a fourth person in the living room, curled very close to Sterling Blade on the sofa, but she was not drinking Wild Turkey. Her name was Cassidy—her first name, apparently—and she was about Jennifer's age, and she was having something green and lumpy from a small silver Thermos.

It was after midnight. They had been in Los Angeles two hours now.

"Two helicopters," Sterling Blade was saying to Robert Schein, in the man-to-man voice that Jennifer knew he used when playing the Great Producer Just Being Himself. "I mean I was actually selling the two helicopters as *leads* in the goddamn series. You've got to remember, this was before the whole *Star Wars* thing. The whole *Close Encounters* number. With the Mother Ship and all. This was still back during the Vietnam thing, and nobody had run any research on the public identifying with *machines*, for Christ's sake, but I had a *gut feeling* that the helicopter, qua *helicopter*, had a built-in recognition factor with the American public. Hell, it was on the six o'clock news every night. Excuse me one moment."

Sterling Blade reached across Cassidy's lap and punched the blinking button of a white telephone that was resting on a stand fashioned out of petrified wood. The petrified log was in harmony with the low-slung, western-style decor of Sterling Blade's living room.

"Sterling has a wonderful karma with the American public," said Cassidy in a tiny voice. "He doesn't even need market research." She favored both of them with a beatific smile.

Jennifer regarded Cassidy from her Leatherette easy chair across the alpaca rug. "Sterling is my father," she said pleasantly to the young woman. "I think I know as much about his karma as you know about flavored vaginal douches."

Cassidy's smile froze into something grotesque, and she turned cow-eyes on Jennifer, hoping to find evidence that it was a joke. Jennifer continued to stare disinterestedly at the woman until Cassidy dropped her gaze to the silver Thermos in her hands.

"What the hell are you doing in Tahiti, Frankie," Sterling Blade said softly into the telephone.

Jennifer continued to study the girl's face as though it were a poster. Schein was up and moving around the room now, looking at the plaques and signed glossy photographs that occupied the entire south wall of the living room.

Jennifer had been trying to place the girl's face ever since she arrived—her father had been typically noncommittal in the introductions. Now she had it. Cassidy was a starlet in a syndicated TV series, a country-and-western variety show. She appeared in the background in a polka-dot Daisy Mae blouse and cutoff shorts and smiled and wiggled her hips while big-name country stars sang their hits. Two weeks ago Jennifer had seen Cassidy's face on the cover of a national tabloid weekly in a grocery store. She was the second in a series of three starlets who "confessed" to having had affairs with Bobby Lee Cooper. Good career move.

Her hair had been black in the photograph. Now it was platinum. That was why recognition had come so slowly.

"Number one, Frankie, my gut feeling is he was drunk when he told you he'd do a television series," Sterling Blade was saying quietly into the phone. "Number two, he's too goddamn fat to do a television series. We'd have to stuff him in a wheelchair like Raymond Burr and wheelchairs are not big this season. Number three, you have broken a rule by telephoning my home after midnight. You don't work for me anymore, Frankie. Enjoy the rest of your stay in Tahiti."

Sterling Blade reached across Cassidy's lap to replace the white telephone on its cradle. "So anyway," he said, resuming his conversational voice, ". . . where'd Bobby go?"

"Over here, Mr. Blade." The voice came from Robert Schein, but it was not Robert Schein. It was an actor portraying Robert Schein, the promising young New York comedian and attentive Beverly Hills houseguest. Jennifer scarcely marked the monstrosity of it; she was used to it by now. Her father got up to join Schein at his trophies. Jennifer remained in her seat, loggy with booze and the fatigue of five hours in the air, alone with her thoughts, and the effort required to avoid the notion that it couldn't work, none of it. She concentrated on staring at Cassidy, who was trying not to look anywhere.

"So tell me," Jennifer said in a low throaty voice, as if conversation alone would restore a sense of reality to this invented evening. "I didn't get all the way through the piece in the *Intelligencer*. Was Bobby Lee a good lay, or what?"

Sterling Blade had put them in the room that had been Jennifer's. It was a strange and terrible thing, at first, making love in a room where she had slept as a girl, a room that had been hers growing up, a room that she associated with innocence. But halfway through it, she accepted the realization that she had never been innocent, and let herself move willingly to Robert Schein's savage impersonal thrusts. She abandoned herself to the eroticism of defilement, it was the room itself she was defiling, with its left-over hopes of childhood, its naive promises of romance.

Her orgasm was so intense she cried out, for the first time ever in Schein's arms, but it was not Schein she was thinking about, nor anyone else. It was the room.

After Schein fell asleep, she slipped out of bed and went out into the hallway, where she knew there was a telephone on a nightstand, and called Mark Teller's number in New York. She felt that she wanted to tell him something reassuring, possibly even that she loved him, in a way, although she was by no means sure of that. But although it was three hours later in New York, Teller's number rang and rang and Teller did not answer. After a long while, Jennifer gave up, and placed the telephone back in its cradle, and went to bed, to sleep alone with Robert Schein.

Teller did not return to his apartment after the news that night. He left the Commerce Center and walked into midtown, his tall body slouched inside a nylon parka jacket against the March rain. He walked to 58th Street, then east on 58th to Seventh Avenue. Around him, gray-faced people were pouring out of office buildings like rainwater, trickles joining rivulets joining streams, emptying into subway holes, a great gray wash of humanity sluicing home. Home to watch television. Action, suspense, and, of course, laughs galore. Heartwarming comedy. Network-quality news with a local touch . . .

He felt that he was being encircled and suffocated by celebrities, by hosts and cohosts and guests and guest-hosts. Famous, luminous faces hissed past him on the wet streets, fastened atop taxicabs, emblazoned on the sides of buses.

A white-faced woman in Polaroid sunglasses pushed her face in front of his. "You're Mark Teller," she shrieked at him, and disappeared into the crowd. He put his hand out to buy a final edition of the *New York Post*. His glance fell on a photograph on the front page, above the fold. It was of the daughter of a former president of the United States. She was visiting New York to help promote a new movie about killer porpoises. Teller drew back his hand. He decided that he needed a drink.

There was a Palmerton-Westex nearby, the flagship of a nationwide, computerized chain of cubicles for businessmen.

The lobby bar was mobbed. Elbowing his way inside the mock-Old Western swinging doors, Teller saw the reason why: On a small raised platform, under a blue spotlight, a man in a pink-sequined jump suit was lip-snyching a Bobby Lee Cooper song. The man sneered down at his pelvis and gave it a bump-and-grind, then threw his black-pompadoured head back to the squeals of the crowd.

A fortyish woman in an expensive, tailored business suit, sitting below Teller's elbow, said in an earnest, low voice to her male companion:

"He's good, but I think I like the one who was at the Palladium better. This one is a Bobby Lee in his thirties. I like the Bobby Lees in their twenties. They make me cry more."

Teller did not exactly remember leaving the lobby bar of the Palmerton-Westex. He did not recall coming to lean against this wall in the lobby, beside the cigarette machine, or how long he had been trying to clear his head, to make the thoughts come one at a time. He did not know how long he had been staring at the kiosk in front of him before he became aware that it contained a message board, and that there was a framed message inside a glass case on the message board, on stationery bearing the Palmerton-Westex logotype. The message was printed beneath a photograph of a young man, a young man who was smiling heroically. The young man had the soft, full black hair and flowing mustache of a television news star, an ethnic reporter, maybe.

The message read:

> The Palmerton-Westex is proud to announce the winner of our Employee-of-the-Month program for February, Mr. Duane Ontiveros. Duane will receive a $25 cash award and dinner for two at the Branding Iron. His name will be displayed on a permanent gold plaque to be displayed at the Front Desk in the Lobby.
> Congratulations Duane!

Teller realized that he was reading a blurb for a celebrity bellhop.

"Excuse me. Are you Mark Teller?"

The voice came from somewhere off to his right, somewhat behind him, out of his vision, and it was a woman's. A woman's clear, precise voice. He turned and tried to focus his eyes in its direction.

The woman who had spoken had dark hair, and was wearing some sort of tweed coat, and she was standing with her feet very close together and she was holding her purse in front of her with the fingers of both hands. He could not make out her expression, but he assumed it was stricken.

"I am indeed Mark Teller. *WRAP-Around News.* And you, I take it, are a celebrity."

There was a moment's pause. When the woman spoke again, the clear voice was more measured, guarded. But the quality was wonderfully clear.

"I just wanted to tell you," the clear voice said, "that I saw your commentary tonight on the Summer Olympics and the television networks. I thought it was very courageous of you to speak out the way you did. I think your commentaries are quite good generally." There was an uncertain pause. "That's all."

Teller considered this for a moment. "Are you a celebrity?" he repeated. "I do not speak to anyone below the rank of celebrity." He fired off a crisp salute.

The woman was silent for what seemed a long time. He tried to get her in focus. He became vaguely aware of blazing eyes. The clear voice spoke again, and now it had contempt in it.

"You're drunk, aren't you, Mr. Teller? I'm sorry to have disturbed you."

After a moment, he was aware that the woman had gone.

He did not want to go home. He registered for a room at the Palmerton-Westex. "No luggage," he told the scowling desk clerk, but the clerk assigned him a bellhop anyway.

"Your name wouldn't be Duane Ontiveros, would it?" Teller asked the bellhop on the way up the elevator.

The kid gave a nervous smile and stepped back into the elevator's farthest corner.

"No, sir. This your first trip to New York?"

Teller eyed the bellhop, or what seemed to be the bellhop.

"You know," he said, "right people to handle you, you be a big star in this game. Bigger than Ontiveros. My name's Teller, I guess you've heard of me. . . ."

"Here's your floor, sir. Down that corridor, make a left, third door." The bellhop handed Teller his key, gave him a discreet shove, and disappeared without waiting for a tip.

The next morning Jennifer Blade handed Robert Schein one thousand five hundred dollars in cash. "Raoul will drive you down to Rodeo," she told him. "Buy yourself some clothes. If anything needs to be altered, tell them to have it for you by tomorrow. Mention my name. I've got some errands to do. Use the pool when you get back if you want to. I'll see you this evening."

Schein accepted the stack of thirty fifties as though they were a piece of mail addressed to "Occupant." He slipped them indifferently into the rear pocket of a pair of faded jeans he was wearing. Jennifer felt certain it was the largest sum of money Robert Schein had ever held in his life.

"You are welcome," she said after a moment.

"Thank you," he muttered through slitted lips, and went off to find the driver.

It was the nicest thing he had ever said to her.

Jennifer took the Jaguar. She gunned it down Santa Monica Boulevard toward the Highway 101 interchange. Although she had not been behind the wheel for a year, she knifed the superbly responsive machine in and out of traffic lanes with a violent skill, like a man, cutting off the lumbering trucks, flashing through stoplights, slipping around cars in the left-turn lane, at the last possible instant before impact. She wore no makeup. With her outsize sunglasses and a cigarette planted squarely in the middle of her mouth, she looked the way she felt—a tough, beautiful, Beverly Hills bitch on her way to do something nasty and necessary.

She drove the Jaguar onto the Hollywood Freeway where it passed over Santa Monica, with scarcely a backward glance into the traffic lane. The Hollywood Bowl flashed by, and Lake Hollywood off to the right; beyond it, Griffith Park. She could see the brown buildings of Universal Studios, and then they were behind her, and she was crossing the Ventura Freeway interchange, heading into the valley floor with Burbank on the right. Her jawline was hard, and her third cigarette was little more than a glowing bullet between her teeth. She was headed for Blade City, to ask the favor of her father she had promised herself she would never ask.

"What the hell did you say to Cassidy last night? She came to bed with a burr up her ass. I had to give her a Darvon to make her quit mewing, and then it was fade to credits. I doubt if she's woke up yet. Goddamn, Jennifer, first thing you do when you get back in town is you screw up my sex life. Excuse me a minute."

Sterling Blade mashed a gigantic index finger down on one of the fifteen plastic buttons on his telephone bank. From the sofa opposite his desk, Jennifer inspected her surroundings. The office was the same as she always had seen it—a mausoleum dedicated to the living memory of Sterling Blade. The light came from behind him, as it always did when Sterling Blade could control the situation. An opaque window above his shoulders showered his silver head with shards of highlight. Jennifer thought of the Six Captains in front of the Commerce Center, and then of Teller. She brought her attention back to the office.

"Well, then, goddammit, *cut* the blowtorch murder scene. But hold the line of the simulated sodomy," Blade was barking into the telephone. "Ask Freddie does he want reality drama or does he want lofty, dimensional shit."

The miniature bar was still in the corner, with the Beefeater and the J&B bottles in full display. The ceramic horse was still there, and the imitation cactus arrangement artfully displayed, and the bookcase—Sterling Blade's last literary purchase, judging by appearances, was Milton Gross's *Nize Baby*. The gloriously inappropriate Chippendale shelves still stood, bearing the testimonials to the vision and artistry of Sterling Blade: the twelve Emmys and the framed certificates of appreciation, the signed photographs of Presidents, the commemorative ribbons and ashtrays and gavels, the Indian beads and the California Angels baseball cap.

And there was the dart board. The inevitable dart board. Jennifer could not remember having seen an office in all Hollywood—and she had been in a lot of them, records, movies, television, creative management—that did not have a dart board. The aggressive energy released on dart boards from Sunset Boulevard to the San Fernando Valley each day could fuel a medium-sized tribal war in the Brazilian jungles, she imagined.

"Because if Freddie wants lofty dimensional shit he can bring back *Star Trek*," Sterling Blade was saying into the phone. "He can bring back the fucking Longine Symphonettes. Tell Freddie I remember him from the days he was hustling three broads with no bras on the other network. Tell him to cut the respectable crap or Sterling Blade's got three other networks to sell product to." Blade slammed the phone down and glanced up at his daughter.

"Salem atmosphere," he grunted. "Liberals and the news media have the networks on the rack again. TV violence. Networks scared shitless as usual. Now they're telling *me* I should limit my product to three, uh, acts of aggression per episode. You know how they define 'acts of aggression'? Everything from cutting a guy's throat to throwing a fork down on the floor. Shit, the next thing, they'll have the National Football League playing touch tackle. I wonder what these lily-livers'd do if they had—"

"Shakespeare writing for them," Jennifer finished with him. It was an old and familiar chorus.

"Yeah, that's right," said Sterling Blade. He licked the end of a cheroot and held a match to the opposite end. When he had a blue cloud of smoke going around his head, he appraised his daughter through crafty, half-slit eyes.

"Now what do you want to see me about, sweetheart?" he asked. "Want to land a job for your boyfriend?"

Jennifer flushed. She hadn't wanted it to be this obvious. She hated it when her father saw through her. But her father saw through everyone.

She decided not to be coy.

"What can you do for him?" she asked.

Sterling Blade hadn't extinguished his match, and now he sat looking at its dwindling flame.

"I don't know if I can do anything for him," he said. "I've kept up on him through the trades. He's had a helluva press back east. Including a socko interview on *WRAP-Around News* conducted by Jennifer Blade, says in *Variety*." He snapped the match out and glanced sideways at his daughter. Jennifer kept her face impassive and held his gaze. The bastard saw everything.

"Anyway," Sterling Blade said after a minute, "I'm sure the boy's got talent. Great looks—looks a little bit like the young Redford. He certainly has the personality . . ."

He hasn't seen through Schein, Jennifer thought.

". . . But talent, looks, and personality aren't exactly unknown commodities in this town, as you are well aware. Besides, Jenny, you know the kind of product I do. I don't do comedy."

"Maybe Robert does more than comedy."

"Maybe so, maybe not. That puts him one of about thirty thousand guys in this town who'd *maybe* pass a screen test for an action series. *Maybe*. Let's say he passes. Let's say he looks good on camera. Now he's up against let's say five hundred guys, all of whom have something your sweetie *doesn't* have, and that's national name value."

Blade exhaled a stream of blue cheroot smoke between his teeth.

"Nobody had ever heard of Jim Arness before *Gunsmoke*."

"Yes, but now you're talking about a guy who's six-seven and has a chin you could churn butter with. Besides, those were the old days when he was hired. Business has changed. You come to me with an actor for a Sterling Blade series, a Sterling Blade TV movie, and the first thing I ask is, how many people've heard of him?"

"*Charlie's Angels?*" said Jennifer, a bit desperately.

"You trying to say nobody had heard of *them*? You forget about Farrah. She'd made it in the ads first. She had the recognition factor, and she carried the others along with her. Now look, sweetheart," said Blade, lapsing into the paternal tone that made Jennifer wish to God she hadn't come to him, "I'm not sayin' your friend Bobby *doesn't* have a good shot at makin' it. He's got a helluva name factor in New York, and sooner or later a New York name's gonna translate to national. I'm sayin' he's a year away."

Sterling Blade spread his hands. Jennifer remained silent.

"I run a precision instrument," he said to his daughter in a quiet, firm voice. "I invented a formula and I made it work like a Swiss watch. Now I got the liberals and the goddamn do-good media all over my ass, tryin' to run me out of business. I can't afford to mess with the formula, Jenny. I can't take an unknown and stick him in a production, even if he's the boyfriend of my daughter."

"You can't help me, then."

Sterling Blade considered his cheroot for a long moment.

"I didn't say I couldn't help you," he said finally.

"You just said you wouldn't use Robert in a series."

"I said I couldn't afford to do it the way things are now. Jenny,

the way I see it you have two choices. You can take your friend
back to New York, see that he gets a good agent to manage him, let
his career develop the way it develops. If he's as good as I think he
is, you'll be back here in a year with a nationally known personality. Maybe then we could talk realistically."

"What's the other choice?"

Sterling Blade nodded. "I thought you'd ask that. All right.
Here's how I can help you." He held up a business card between
two fingers.

"He's expecting you in his office tomorrow afternoon at two.
Bring Bobby with you. He knows all about him. He owes me a
couple of favors. It is possible, although I am not in a position to
promise you anything, that he will take Bobby on as a client."

Jennifer examined the name on the business card. She looked
back at her father.

"You're kidding." Her grin betrayed a little too much glee.

Blade gave a rueful shake of his head. "No, I'm not kidding,"
he said. "But you and Bobby Schein may wish I was kidding before it's over. This man is the best there is, Jennifer. I've known
him for twenty years, and I swear to God I don't know how he
does what he does. He's one savage son of a bitch, he's a killer, and
I'm not sure that's just a figure of speech where he's concerned. If
he takes Bobby on, you might just as well forget you ever knew
him, because his life is not going to be his to control anymore. If I
was any kind of father, I wouldn't let you get near this shark or
any of his buddies. But I guess you know what you want, and if I
read the trades right, you've learned how to take care of yourself
when I'm not around. Now," Sterling Blade said, waving Jennifer
to the door, "get your ass out of here and let me get some work
done. Your friend want to see a little of the town tonight? I've got
us a table at Chasen's. Dean Martin said he might drop by."

Just like her father, Jennifer thought with a wry smile as she left
the executive office building at Blade City and waited for the
Jaguar to be brought around. Dinner at Chasen's with Dean
Martin is a big deal to him. It was funny. In her childhood, the
press had painted Sterling Blade as a bold young usurper, one of
the New Breed that was snatching Hollywood away from the old
bulls. Now, less that twenty years later, she was a young woman
and Sterling Blade was an old bull. He probably still didn't know
who Thom Mount was, or Clair Townsend, or Paula Weinstein,

didn't know any of the kids who were running the big old studios. Probably never heard of Lucy's El Abode.

Didn't matter. What mattered was that Sterling Blade was a powerful old bull. Power was still a hip commodity in this town.

And speaking of power . . .

She settled herself behind the wheel of the Jaguar and placed her shoulder bag on the seat next to her. She reached inside it and withdrew the white business card and looked at the name on it once again—the name printed in small, unadorned black type:

MAL BOOKMASTER

"Hello, Doctor Grant? This is Michael and I'm twenty-nine."

"Hi, Michael. And what seems to be your problem today?"

"Well, Doctor Grant, I suffer from periods of intense depression in which I fantasize strangling myself with the extension cord on my telephone. I have one of those cords that reach all the way across the room, you know? So you can talk while you're either in the kitchen or in the bedroom? And I think that sometime I might do it. And I was wondering whether you might be able to suggest any kind of, you know, anything that might keep me from actually acting out this fantasy."

"Well, Michael, I think that first you should tell me a little bit more about the nature *of these depressions . . ."*

The afternoons floated by, the afternoons on the freeways that crisscrossed Los Angeles like roller-coaster tracks. Robert Schein sat in the back of Sterling Blade's black 450 Mercedes SLC, and Blade's driver, Raoul, whipped the heavy machine in and out of traffic lanes at seventy-five miles an hour, except when jam-ups forced them to a crawl.

Schein wore clothes from the wardrobe he had bought with Jennifer's money: cream-colored shirts with military epaulets that stretched tightly across his muscular torso; French jeans with elaborate stitching, European loafers with heels as hard as diamonds, no sox. He wore bracelets of gold and heavy chains about his neck, and polarized sunglasses with gold rims, the lenses a fine pearl-gray.

He changed into a fresh set of clothing each day, although never before had he given much thought to what he wore or how long he wore it. He dressed in the manner that he surmised men in Los Angeles dressed, based on the styles he had seen on the television talk shows.

He looked as though he had lived in Los Angeles all his life.

They were going nowhere. Some days Raoul would head the Mercedes due south on 11, the Harbor Freeway, and they would race savagely for Long Beach Harbor as though military security hung upon their swift arrival—turning, instead, west onto the Pacific Coast Highway, then back north on Hawthorne until it joined 405. Other days, they would wander northeast through Glendale and into the dry, bleached hills of Angeles National Forest, tires screeching along the winding ribbon of macadam that took them among the mesquite and the cinders of burnt trees and the lizards and the diamondback rattlers.

Always, the radio was on. There was no conversation between Schein and Raoul. Schein sat in the backseat and listened to the radio and looked out the window at Los Angeles and Beverly Hills and Torrance and Inglewood and Burbank and Alhambra and Santa Monica and the ocean and the Palisades. Some days Raoul stayed off the freeways and drove instead the great boulevards, Sunset and Santa Monica and Wilshire and Olympic. Robert Schein listened to the radio and studied the artifacts of the new civilization around him, the voluptuous celebrity billboards towering above Sunset Strip and the cool disowning lawns and palm-shrouded mansions farther west; the brittle, stylish, elderly shoppers on Wilshire and the barefoot bronze-legged waifs at Hollywood and Vine; the synthetic restaurant facades along Santa Monica and the beautiful serious runners on the swards of San Vicente. He felt no desire to have Raoul stop the car, to get out, to look inside the restaurants or the bars or the mansions or the Polo Lounge of the Beverly Hills Hotel. The view from the window of the Mercedes was his television screen; he was learning about L.A. by watching it on television in person; and the radio was his sound track.

At a stoplight on Sunset, a beautiful girl had suddenly run up to the Mercedes, thrust a pen and notepad through the open window, and begged Schein for his autograph. Without changing expression, Schein had taken the pen and solemnly written his name on the pad. The girl studied the signature.

"Oh, God, *Robert Schein!* Oh, God, I adore all your movies!"

The woman psychiatrist who had been dispensing advice to her suicidal caller a moment ago was now reading a commercial, reading it in the same crisp, professional, *polite* voice with which she diagnosed the most intimate compulsions of her unseen callers.

Robert Schein slid back into the cushioning of the 450 Mercedes SLC and gazed at the ceiling, gazed at nothing. He liked California.

Jennifer was gone. She had left several days ago. He didn't remember how many. He scarcely thought about Jennifer. There were times when he realized he had forgotten, temporarily, that Jennifer existed. The past was not particularly real to Schein, not even the recent past. That was another reason he liked California. Despite its showy penchant for memorializing its history—the Hollywood Wax Museum, the movie-studio back lots, the preserved Art Deco statues and buildings and monuments—California was a land without a past, without shadows. There was no sense of loss when Jennifer left, no vacuum, no pleasant anticipation that he might soon see her again, no imagining of her back in New York, no imagining of New York. He lived now like a goldfish in the inverted blue-domed bowl that was Los Angeles, in the eternal present as memoryless as a television screen.

Twice a week he went to see the man with the reptile eyes, Bookmaster.

"Hello, Mal."

"Jennifer! Absolutely delighted to see you. My God, don't move. Stand there. I don't think I've set eyes on you since you were twelve or something. Am I right? My God, Sterling told me you were a woman now, but I mean, my God! And, uh, now you're a very successful magazine writer in New York, I've been keeping up with your career."

"Television journalist."

"Television journalist, of course. And this must be the man of the hour, Robert Schein." The hard, reptile eyes had already moved from a quick study of Jennifer to a cold, appraising analysis of Schein's face.

"Mal Bookmaster, meet Robert Schein."

"The man who's breaking them up in the Apple, the man with all the, uh, funny lines. 'Booooy, was my faaaaace red.' Am I right?"

"It's a great pleasure to meet you, Mr. Bookmaster."

"Well." Bookmaster folded his white hands like a mortician. Brass-tacks time already, Jennifer sensed. "Robert, why don't you make yourself comfortable out here while a couple of old friends take a few minutes to get reacquainted?"

Mal Bookmaster Associates commandeered the top five stories of a high rise on Sunset Boulevard a few blocks west of Laurel Canyon Drive. The building contained the offices of some of Hollywood's most powerful performers' agents, and one network had a few of its executive offices there. But Mal Bookmaster's office was not a Hollywood office. It had none of the self-congratulatory totems of Sterling Blade's hunkered-down digs; none of the flattering, trick light-sources, the amiable, shelftop kitsch.

There was a chilling, understated tastefulness about Bookmaster's choice of decor. Everything that Jennifer had heard about Mal Bookmaster seemed to be confirmed by this oppressive correctness. She studied one of his touches—an artistic display of shaped canvases on the far wall (the work, Jennifer knew, of a young German immigrant woman just beginning to establish an important reputation among the New York collectors) from one of the Eames chairs upon which they now sat, a silver tray of Brie and chilled grapes on the coffee table between them.

But none of his affectations quite matched his central statement: The Desk.   •

It commanded the center of the room, a huge, black, angry slab of polished ebony—that seemed to predate the building itself; seemed perhaps to have hung in the ether for ages until civilization built up around it. It was less a desk than a massive, primitive force, brutal and dangerous-looking in its placid, correct surroundings. A Tiffany lamp somewhere on its surface was almost lost to the eye, like the pilot house of a supertanker. Jennifer tried to imagine Bookmaster seated behind the desk—how its scale would seem to place him at the far end of a great forbidding steppe, impossibly distant from his visitor, small, yet somehow dominant, menacing.

It was a desk to break down wills, to test the spirit, to remind one and all of Mal Bookmaster's primacy.

"Champagne?" asked Bookmaster.

He arose and strode across the room to the bar. She watched him move with the exaggerated strut of the small man. She had seen his physical type a thousand times in New York: slight of build, pale skin, the hair almost gone at the crown but still black and shiny on the edges, bloodless mouth, sharp cheekbones—the successful junior partner, tailored within an inch of his life (black three-piece suit, white shirt, and orange silk tie) aggressive, cocky, full of surefire money-talk and quick macho.

The difference was that not one of them could go up against Mal Bookmaster and emerge without a thin red crescent extending from earlobe to earlobe.

As Jennifer watched Bookmaster trim the tinfoil from the champagne bottle, she tried quickly to recall some of his more famous clients. They included:

—An Italian-American crooner, a bobby-socks idol of the 1940s whose popularity had faded for several years until he signed a long-term contract with the young Mal Bookmaster in the early sixties. Today, the crooner was one of the elite superstars of American show business.

—An aging, beefy, homosexual actor whom Bookmaster had transformed into a macho TV cop-hero, and whose clothing styles were being imitated by middle-aged businessmen throughout the country.

—A "wholesome" brother-sister singing duo, whose plastic good looks and inane personalities Bookmaster had packaged into a long-running prime-time variety series. (The sister half of the act was now outgrowing her childlike, innocent image, and the trade press was reporting "on good authority" that Bookmaster planned to "repackage" her in a new hairdo, sophisticated makeup, and body-revealing gowns—television's first teen-aged "jiggly" heroine.

—A husband-wife rock'n'roll team that reached an early peak of fame in the sixties, then fell into oblivion. An inside Hollywood legend had it that when the couple signed with Bookmaster, his first move was to order the woman into a public affair with a younger rock singer. Bookmaster then orchestrated a highly publicized divorce—it was good for two *Faces* covers and countless columns of gossip and TV-column copy. He then decreed that the divorced couple reach a "professional reconciliation" and appear as cohosts of a TV comedy-variety series. Their premiere performance broke all existing Nielsen records for single-program viewership.

—A dissident folksinger of the sixties whose lyrics bitterly mocked the Establishment and helped create the dialectic of student protest in America. Upon signing the folksinger, Bookmaster withheld him from public interviews for three years, carefully leaking bits of gossip about him to selected columnists and rock-oriented newspapers. When the singer finally reemerged, Bookmaster authorized a series of "exclusive" interviews with various magazines and weekly papers, stipulating in return the right to make "corrections" in the final galley proofs, and that each of the interviews be used as the magazine's cover story. In the space of six weeks, the singer appeared on the covers of seventeen major publications trumpeting "exclusive" interviews. His subsequent concert tour made him a millionaire independent of previous wealth.

—An obscure model from a medium-sized city in Texas, whom Bookmaster happened to meet during a luncheon involving several high-ranking TV executives and salesmen. The woman had spent the last eight years of her life in a Mediterranean country, consorting with wealthy European businessmen. Sixteen months after the luncheon, the model was an anchorwoman for a major station in New York. Aside from Jennifer Blade, she was the city's best-known local TV newswoman.

There was another important personality who owed his public life to Bookmaster's genius. His name was one that Jennifer heard nearly every day of her life, yet for the moment she could not recall it. She searched the wall for the man's photograph, but it was not there. No matter. It would come to her.

Bookmaster was returning with the champagne. She shook out her honey-blond hair, feeling it spill over her bare shoulders. Could she handle Bookmaster? She thought so.

Bookmaster sat down opposite her and filled two crystal goblets with champagne.

"Since when do television newswomen hustle show-biz gigs for amateur comics? Here's to your good health, Jennifer." Mal Bookmaster inclined his head and raised the glass.

Jennifer Blade gaped at him. The booming affability he had affected in the outer office was gone. Bookmaster's voice was quiet, almost inaudible, now that they were alone.

"I think I've just been insulted," she said.

"Bullshit." The voice was still unnaturally quiet; the epithet passed through immobile bloodless lips curved in the semblance of a genial smile. Bookmaster sat on the low Eames chair opposite her with his legs crossed at the knees. His posture drew his trouser legs up over skinny shins, revealing tightly drawn silk stretch-hose. With his black-polished shoes, black socks, black suit, black hair at the fringes, and his darting, narrow-set black eyes, Mal Bookmaster looked like an urbane vampire.

"I don't insult people, Jennifer. I break them in half. A lot of nice people have had their lives altered right where you're sitting."

"I have no intention of listening—"

"Now, let's get one thing straight, Jennifer," Bookmaster cut her off without raising his voice a decibel. "If anything is insulting anyone, you are insulting me by walking into my office and trying to enlist my services in representing your boyfriend who is a no-where comedian from some dive on Second Avenue. You really should try your champagne, Jennifer. It's a difficult *cuvée* to obtain in this country."

Jennifer's jawline hardened.

"Do you have any idea who you're talking about? You are talking about the hottest act in New York City."

"Schein is a stiff. My people have seen his act." Bookmaster looked directly into Jennifer's eyes and gave a small shrug.

"And if I needed proof," he continued, "I got it when I laid eyes on the guy. He got off at Chicago, Jennifer. There's nobody in there."

"The reviews," Jennifer said.

"The reviews," said Bookmaster. "Don't tell me about the *reviews*. The *reviews* are written by monkeys, Jennifer. Tourists. Economy section. Do you *know* anybody who actually does *reviews* for a living?"

Teller, thought Jennifer.

"They are not among the enlightened, Jennifer. Am I right?

Burt Reynolds gets good *reviews*. Olivia Newton-John. Barry
Manilow. Those people get good *reviews*. Look at Bobby Lee
Cooper. He's dead. He still gets good *reviews*. I mean, am I right?
Can I fill your glass?"

Reflexively, Jennifer held out her champagne goblet.

"I guarantee you, Jennifer, that your man will be an unknown
in six months. Among the missing. Dropped off the edge of the
earth. Sad but true. Bottom line."

"So you—"

"So I sit in this office, behind that desk you see over there, I sit
there maybe fourteen, fifteen hours a day, Jennifer, trying to
represent my clients in a manner that is commensurate with the
considerable fees that I am obliged to charge. And I am getting
telephone calls from people who are known throughout the *world*,
Jennifer, asking me to represent them. And so I am at times inclined to feel insulted when the latest Beverly Hills brat comes
strolling into this office and flashes me a little tit—"

"You bastard."

Faster than Jennifer Blade could follow the motion, Mal Bookmaster cocked his right arm and hurled his crystal champagne
goblet toward her. It whistled past her ear and smashed against the
wall behind her.

"That will leave a nasty stain," Bookmaster said thoughtfully.
"Never call me a bastard, Jennifer. As I was saying, it can be
insulting when the latest Beverly Hills brat comes strolling into
this office and flashes me a little tit and expects me to make a
superstar out of her particular stud of the moment."

Jennifer dug her fingernails into the arms of the chair for self-
control.

"You agreed to see me. You knew what I was here for." She
forced herself to make the next sentence come out. If he hit her,
she'd claw his eyes.

"Is this part of your scene, Mr. Bookmaster? Are you the kind of
man who gets his kicks browbeating women?"

The eyes brightened; the pale nostrils flared. Other than that,
Mal Bookmaster remained exactly frozen for a very long moment
—legs crossed, fingers locked, a faint ironic half-smile on his face.
She braced herself to lash back. Something throbbed in her
stomach.

"No, Jennifer. I wanted to see whether you had a spine or

whether you're jelly, like most of them. You passed. No, the fact is
I may be able to use your friend Robert Schein."

Bookmaster abruptly arose, and strode to the far side of his
desk.

"Come over here, Jennifer. There are some things I'm sure
you'd be interested to see."

Jennifer hesitated, then followed.

Bookmaster opened a drawer of the desk and pulled out a sheaf
of photographs. He dropped the stack on the desk top.

"My God."

The photographs were of Robert Schein.

She picked up the stack and began to sort through them. They
were high-quality, black-and-white photographs, obviously taken
by a professional. Many of them showed Schein in performance at
Stitch's. These amounted to a catalog of Schein's most characteristic gestures, postures, and facial expressions. None had been taken
with a flash.

But the photographs that truly unnerved Jennifer were the ones
not taken at Stitch's. These showed an unsuspecting Robert
Schein as he walked the streets of New York. Waited at an intersection. Emerged from a Laundromat. Dined at a luncheonette on
Amsterdam. There was one of Schein in a waiter's tunic at a fashionable restaurant near Lincoln Center. Another showed him
squinting from the driver's seat of a taxicab.

There were even six photographs of Schein being interviewed
on the *WRAP-Around News* set by Jennifer Blade.

Many of the candid photos of Schein had been cropped and
enlarged to concentrate on some specific detail—his eyes, the part
in his hair, his teeth, the musculature of his arms and torso. A
highly efficient and complete portfolio of her lover, turning up in
a desk drawer three thousand miles from home.

Jennifer dropped the sheaf of photos on the desk and turned to
face Mal Bookmaster. Her heart was beating hard.

Bookmaster was smiling at her.

"There's no mystery, really, Jennifer. We've known about
Robert for quite some time. I keep an information file on all the
important new talent around the country."

Jennifer put a fist to her forehead and tried to think straight.

"I thought you told me that Robert Schein was a stiff. 'Utterly hopeless' was the way you described him, I believe. If he is a stiff, if he is hopeless, why have you kept a dossier on him? Who the hell gave you the right to . . . ?"

"Utterly hopeless *as a comedian.* I dislike having to repeat my-self. 'Dossier' . . . Jennifer, you have a tendency toward the bathetic. My people have *observed* him as a prospective client. In many respects, we like what we see."

"What, for instance, if I may ask?"

"Face. Good television face. Versatile face. Could do a lot of things with it."

"Tell me some of the things you could do with Robert Schein's face."

Bookmaster spun around and regarded Jennifer Blade care-fully.

"I will assume you're not being insolent. You have made me lose my temper once today already, Jennifer. Don't do it again. Now I will answer your question in the manner I trust it was asked. Your boyfriend, should he have the minimal brains neces-sary to perform simple motor tasks, might fit in very well with a certain television pilot project which I understand is in develop-ment now. It's a dramatic role. That's all I can tell you now. *If* I accept Robert as a client I will receive twenty percent of his total earnings, and I will demand the contractual right to approve every career decision he makes for the duration of our relationship. And by 'career decision,' I mean how long he wears his hair, what brand of ketchup he puts on his cheeseburgers, and how many times a week he has it off with you. Now you can march out there and fetch me your boyfriend, Jennifer, and then you will get out of my sight. I think I have had my fill of Beverly Hills brats for one . . ."

The slap of Jennifer Blade's right hand across Mal Bookmaster's cheek brought up the blood on the left side of his face. Jennifer could see the red outlines of her long fingers in his white skin.

"That will leave a nasty stain," she heard herself say.

Bookmaster fumbled a white pocket handkerchief out of his suit pocket and held it to the side of his face. His shoulders were heaving. Jennifer knew that she had just performed one of the most dangerous acts of her life. It flashed in her mind that one of America's best-known magazine writers was taking an extended

vacation in Europe following publication of an article mildly critical of Bookmaster's style. She knew that most men would not have
dared what she had done.

"Some ground rules," she said. "Your fee for handling Robert
Schein will be fifteen percent. What you normally charge. Not
twenty. Number two: never call me a Beverly Hills brat again.
Number three: never again make mention of my sex life or the
parts of my body. Number four: if you want Robert Schein, you
can fucking well go fetch him yourself."

She dug a hand into her shoulder bag and held out a silver case
to him.

"Cigarette?"

Jennifer took a seat in the receptionist's anteroom as Robert
Schein disappeared into Bookmaster's office. After a moment, she
arose and smiled politely at the woman at the switchboard.

"Excuse me. Could you tell me the way to the ladies' room?"

"Down that corridor, second door on the right, honey. You'll
need this key."

Jennifer took the key and walked slowly to the rest-room door.
She unlocked it, stepped inside, checked to see that no one else was
there. She opened the door of a toilet stall. She gazed for a moment at the cool-looking, white oval of the toilet bowl. Then she
raised the lid, braced herself against the sides of the stall with her
hands, leaned down close, and began to vomit.

When it was over, she flushed the toilet, sobbed for several
minutes, cleaned her face and lips with soft tissue paper from the
dispenser in the stall, rinsed her mouth with water, and put two
breath mints on her tongue.

She returned to the receptionist's anteroom, handed the elegant
matron the key with a silent smile of thanks, sat down on a sofa,
and opened a magazine.

Jennifer was not concentrating on the magazine. She was thinking about the man whom she had just slapped and the extent of
his power to take revenge, should he choose.

She had finally managed to recall the other famous client of Mal
Bookmaster's, the one whose photograph did not hang in Bookmaster's office, the one who had not, for some reason, been publicly linked to Bookmaster by the press.

The client was the young Governor of California.

 Robert Schein lived at Sterling Blade's Beverly Hills estate. He seldom saw the elder Blade. He slept in a little-used wing of the great house, and when he came down to breakfast mornings, Sterling Blade had left for his office. At those times, Sterling Blade did not exist in Schein's mind.

Sometimes the two of them had dinner together. Schein would make conversation in the manner that he knew people in the world of television and show business conversed, based on his years of carefully watching television and seeing movies. His conversation seemed to please the elder Blade.

"Bookmaster treating you right?" Blade would ask.

"Beautiful. Really a superbeautiful human being. Good chemistry between us. I think we're moving toward some very exciting concepts in terms of my career."

The remark was a verbatim recreation of a response Schein had heard that afternoon, in the Mercedes radio, from a celebrity guest on a radio call-in show.

"That's mighty fine, Robert. How about those damn Angels, anyway?"

"Well, Mr. Blade, I think that any championship ball club has to start with good pitching . . ."

A sports call-in show had followed the celebrity interview.

"Robert, I'd like you to meet my assistant, Marvin Reed. Marvin will be your liaison here on those days when I am unable to be in touch with you personally."

"Mr. Reed, it's a pleasure indeed."

"Hey. That rhymes. He's quick, Mal. Hey, I just love your ass, Bobby Schein. I've been your admirer from afar. 'Booooy, was myyyy faaaaaaace red.' Am I right?" The fat little man with the fish lips and the blue-tinted glasses bared two rows of capped teeth.

"Marvin reports directly to me, so you can assume that his thinking is my thinking."

"Welcome to the firm, Bobby. You just sit back and leave the driving to us. Just love your ass."

Mark Teller ran into Jennifer Blade in the corridor the second day of her return from California.

"Congratulations," he said to her.

"Mark, it's not a big deal with Schein. That thing in the paper was just absolute, irresponsible . . . *that's* why I say we can't appear in public . . ." Her voice trailed off lamely. Teller waited with stony politeness for her to continue.

"I was referring to your promotion to the anchor desk," he said after a moment, and walked away.

She felt a pang. Then she realized an old movie line, a favorite of her father's. John Wayne had said it several times in *She Wore a Yellow Ribbon*:

"Never apologize. It's a sign of weakness."

Her jawline hardened. *So be it,* she thought.

The WRAP publicity department sent out a jubilant press release: "For the first time in its 27-year history, *WRAP-Around News* has surpassed a so-called 'Big Three' flagship station in average weekly audience share, 18 to 35. Latest A. C. Nielsen figures show that *WRAP-Around*'s 5 to 7 P.M. edition, coanchored by the popular Lon Stagg and Al Adams, has achieved a scintillating 9.7 weekly share, placing it ahead of WNBC's *NewsCenter 4*, which has a 9.2. Station manager L. Malcolm Bass attributed the breakthrough to "our firm dedication and commitment to providing the hard-nosed, digging journalism that New Yorkers demand."

At a staff celebration at "21," anchorman Stagg was photographed good-naturedly holding coanchorman Al Adams's head inside a bowl of punch. The photograph made all four New York papers, and Al Adams agreed that it was a great gag.

Double-page ads promoting the WRAP newscast began to appear in the New York dailies. One ad showed the face of the WNBC anchorman superimposed on the body of a man reading a large sheet bearing the word, NIELSENS. The ad was captioned:

BOOOOOOOY, WAS MYYYYYYYY FAAAAAAAAACE REEEEEEED.

Ed Kurtis and L. Malcolm Bass found themselves on the same elevator heading to the twenty-ninth floor of the Commerce Center.

"You're finding the strike zone, Ed," said Bass, standing as far from the pudgy, aromatic news director as the elevator space would allow. "Really humming the high hard one."

"You must be quite a baseball fan," said Kurtis politely.

"I'm a winner, Ed. So are you, big guy. I thought that three-part series Sean Murphy did last week on celebrity muggings was right over the heart of the plate. I thought it brought home the whole crime problem in this city with great impact."

"Yeah, well," mumbled Kurtis. Before he could stop himself, he had added, "but Jesus, Mr. Bass, if we do any more celebrity stuff, we're going to have 'em *reading* the goddamn news." He winced at his gaffe and studied his shoes.

L. Malcolm Bass gazed at Ed Kurtis for a long moment, a deep reflective scowl on his face.

"That is a *very* innovative concept, Ed," he said finally.

"Robert, for the time being we are going to continue to project your comedic image. I have booked you into the Group Comedy Session in two weeks. It's a showcase similar to Stitch's, except that I think you'll find the level of talent a good deal more professional. But don't worry about it, you'll do fine. Here is your material. I want you to know it in a week; you'll start rehearsal a week from today. Marvin will assist you."

"I'll get right on it, Mr. Bookmaster."

Marvin Reed watched Schein leave Bookmaster's office through his gleaming blue-tinted glasses, his fish lips still spread in an ingratiating grin. When the door had closed, Reed turned to his boss.

"Mal, for God's sakes, throw me a line. Get me out of this. I'll sign the goddamn confession. Anything. Mercy!"

"What's the problem, Marvin."

"It's *him. It!*" Reed pointed a stubby finger at the door. "Three days and I am a screaming wreck. Darlene says I talk in my sleep. Hey, Mal, I'd walk over hot coals for you, baby, but *that*—" again, Reed waved a finger at the door—"*that* is a creature from another solar system!"

"You're not getting along with Schein?"

"*Getting along?*" Reed half rose from his chair. "Mal, excuse me for having a fatal heart attack right here on your expensive carpet. It isn't a question of *getting along. It isn't alive, Mal.* It's made out of transistors. Around *you*, it behaves like it's almost human. When we're alone, for Christ's sake, when it's just the two of us, it sort of sits there and hums. My electric typewriter has given me more intellectual enrichment. I mean, I'm doing *Invasion of the Body Snatchers* numbers after the second martini at the Polo. Seriously, Mal, I don't think he's wrapped all that tight."

"Marvin, what would you say if I told you that Robert Schein is the top-priority client of Mal Bookmaster Associates?"

Marvin Reed pulled off his blue-tinted glasses and peered at Bookmaster with rabbit-pink eyes. "I respectfully refuse to answer that question," he said after a minute, "on the grounds that it might tend to incriminate me."

"I'm serious, Marvin. Now listen to me. I don't want to hear any more whining crap about Schein's lack of brotherhood. I am not paying you to be entertained by the people you work with. He doesn't have a personality? Good. Fine. So much the better. One less set of headaches, Marvin. Christ, it's an *asset*. Would you prefer that he had the strong, interesting personality of our teen-age rock'n'roll queen? Or her transvestite brother?"

"Jesus. I'm beginning to hear you, Mal."

"Think of him as a blank slate, Marvin. Pure potential. The important thing is, he's an incredible mimic. He absorbs things.

My hunch is that he's learned to be a comedian *strictly by watching other comedians on television*. Think of it. A guy who's essentially without a sense of humor becoming the top comic in New York City."

"The Apple. Jee Cry, Mal—" a sly grin creased Reed's face; Bookmaster knew a gag was coming—"think where he'd be if he had somebody to manage him?"

"You're hearing me, Marvin. Think of him as an instrument. A secret weapon. Now do you want to back out? Or do you want to help me install the warhead?"

Reed slapped his Foster Grants back over his eyes and fired off a salute.

"Christ, I hear the 'Marine Corps Hymn,' Mal. I see Old Glory snapping in the breeze. I wanna reenlist. Give me an order, Captain."

"All right. He's been out of circulation in New York for several days now. He won't have a long shelf-life, Marvin. I want his picture in every paper in the country by the end of the week. I want him on the network news. Think you can handle it?"

"You got it, Mal. Old Glory."

Alone in his office, Mal Bookmaster picked up his telephone and put through a call to the publisher of *Faces* magazine in New York. The publisher, a socialite and sportsman, had found that it increased his personal mystique, and that of his magazine, to be notoriously inaccessible. There were practical reasons for this as well: every performer, athlete, businessman, and politician in the country wanted to be in *Faces* magazine. Faces was the ultimate arbiter of American celebrityhood. An article in *Faces*—more important, a photograph—could literally be worth a fortune.

"I'm terribly sorry, Mr. Bookmaster," said the voice of the publisher's private secretary. "I know that Mr. Swallows would be very eager to speak with you. Unfortunately, he is sailing off Martha's Vineyard this week and is totally incomm—"

"I know the party line, Barbara," interrupted Bookmaster in his mildest and quietest of tones. When he was certain that he had the uneasy attention of the private secretary, he mentioned the last name of the Italian-American crooner who was his most celebrated client. He waited a moment to let that sink in. Then he said:

"Tell Bob he has exactly twenty minutes to call me back."

Eight minutes later, the number one button on Bookmaster's telephone panel lit up. Bob Swallows's voice, crackling with short-wave static, was on the line.

"Mal! You old sonuvagun! Great to hear your voice, fella!"

"You haven't heard it yet, Bob. Don't shoot your load till the foreplay's over."

"I heard a *name*," crackled Bob Swallows's voice—Bookmaster noticed he chose to ignore the insult, a fatal sign of weakness. "Barbara quoted me a *name*. Is this about what I hope it's about?"

"You've got him," said Bookmaster. "Cover. We retain manuscript approval. May seventh issue."

"*Hot damn*," bellowed the publisher. "How the hell'd you do it, Mal? I thought the bastard was never gonna do another magazine interview?"

"I finally got it into his head how important your magazine was to his career, Bob," said Bookmaster, tossing Swallows a crumb. As a matter of fact, he had not yet mentioned the matter to the singer.

"Wait a minute!" Swallows's high-pitched voice was suddenly tense. *It finally sunk in*, thought Bookmaster. "I'm having trouble hearing you, Mal. I thought I heard you say May seventh issue."

"That's right."

"Jesus, Mal, you know that's impossible. We've already got the May seventh cover at the printers."

"Guess you'll have to tear it up and start again, Bob."

"Holy God, Mal, do you have any idea what that'll cost me? That's never been done before."

"His Nibs has never done a cover before in your magazine . . . or any of your competitors'," Bookmaster added, using the singer's media nickname. Swallows got the point.

"Oh, Christ, all right, it's gonna blow my budget all to shit . . . who do you want to do the piece, Mal?"

Bookmaster named one of the country's most famous feminist novelists.

"Holy Gee, Mal, do you know what you're sayin'? She'll tear the guy to shreds. She hates His Nibs and the whole macho trip he stands for . . . Jesus," said Swallows after a moment's reflection, "it's a helluvan idea. Yeah, it'll work. I'm for it if you're for it if he's for it if she's for it."

"It'll be arranged," said Bookmaster. "I want one other little cookie."

There was a pause, a beat, before Swallows's voice piped back, with forced bonhomie, "Name it!"

"I want a major takeout on another of my clients in the same issue."

"I kind of thought that was comin'. So now we rip the whole issue apart. Holy God. Who is it, Mal?"

"Guy named Robert Schein."

"Never heard of him. Oh, wait a minute. Isn't he that comic in town?"

"That's right."

"He's a name in New York, Mal, but around the country he's a nobody. Nobody's ever heard of him."

"They will have by May seventh. You have my word on it."

Five P.M. in New York.

Time for Oz.

Mark Teller switched on the small TV set in his office cubicle.

Oz was the unofficial nickname, in New York television circles, for *WRAP-Around News*. In the months following L. Malcolm Bass's now-historic staff meeting, WRAP had become the barbarian inside the gates of "respectable" TV journalism. Its newscasts had taken on an almost surrealistic quality. *WRAP-Around News* no longer even pretended to depict life as it was lived in the city of New York. Reality, as now represented on *WRAP-Around News*, was the reality of television's own stylized universe: the lurid pseudocrises of prime-time escape shows and the equally lurid pseudojoy of TV commercials.

The good deacons were properly shocked. Newsmen from competing stations—custodians of the Journalistic Grail, every one—clucked with horror at WRAP's brazen exploits.

Their bosses delivered high-sounding exprobrations to the newspaper critics.

And plotted strategies to imitate the winning formula.

In midtown Manhattan's media watering holes, a popular pastime was the WRAP-Crap of the Week: a poll to decide which of the station's stories or gimmicks qualified as worthy of special recognition.

Sometimes the winners were clear-cut.

One week, it was WRAP's live coverage of a pop singer giving birth—part of Dr. Loren Bannister's "Here's Your Health" reports.

Another was the hiring of a former Miss America, presently dying of cancer, to do a weekly commentary on the various aspects of preparing oneself for death.

One of the most popular winning entries was WRAP's coverage of a terrorist takeover of the World Trade Center. After holding thirteen maintenance employees hostage for nineteen hours, and wounding two with a machete, the terrorist announced that he wished to surrender—not to the police but to a newly hired reporter named Shawnee Dawn (who had attracted Bass's attention as a Penthouse Pet of the Month "interested in Scorpios and journalism"). Interviewed herself by Sean Murphy after she emerged from the terrorist's barricade—with the smiling, waving terrorist in tow—Ms. Dawn remarked that she'd had trepidations about going in, but wasn't too worried "because he had gentle eyes—like Omar Sharif."

For three days after that, WRAP promoted the incident with double-page ads in the New York papers. The ads showed a photograph of Ms. Dawn, looking dazed but dazzling, surrounded by police and microphones. Emblazoned over the photo was another of her quotes, in 18-point type:

IF IT WORKS, I COME OUT A WINNER. IF IT DOESN'T, I COME OUT FEET FIRST.

In the ensuing six weeks, five other terrorists insisted on surrendering to TV journalists—three of them to Ms. Dawn.

Teller watched moodily as his small set flickered to life. When he had joined the station a year ago, this time of day had been the least tolerable for him: that lull of two hours or more when he had finished writing his commentary, finished the telephone calls that were the groundwork for the next one, and had nothing to do but wait to go on the air. Boredom, Sean Murphy had once remarked, was the Black Lung Disease of television news. Cute. But it had its kernel of truth. Hurry up and wait—true of the army, true of the television journalist. All those expensive gorgeous faces, so animated and engaging on the air. Waiting for that moment of incandescence, slouched and slumped, they looked like huge waxen dolls in their torpor, a warehouse of Pinocchios awaiting their Geppetto.

Teller had been affected by the boredom at first. No longer. Now he awaited 5 P.M. and the onset of Oz with a certain morbid relish. What new atrocities today, what new perversions of information, had been dreamed up by Bass, or Kurtis, or the Hawthorne Collective, or whatever unspeakable cabal was now in control of the newscast?

It was fascinating to sit there and watch Oz unfold, in the grubby, mundane surroundings of his cubicle—amid the wastepaper baskets, the telephone, the effluvia of uncounted cubicles in uncounted American office buildings—with the knowledge that shortly he would walk down a long dark corridor, turn a corner, open a door, and enter Oz himself.

Lon Stagg's slanting visage filled the screen. His mouth was twisted into its usual puckish smirk. "I'm Lon Stagg and this is *WRAP-Around News*," Stagg said. "Our headlines in a moment. But first—" he glanced off-camera to his left and the smirk widened into a grin.

"If you'll recall, Friday night we promised you a special surprise on *WRAP-Around News*. Remember? Well—" he glanced off-camera again, and his shoulder shook in barely suppressed merriment. "Al Adams, our coanchorman, is on vacation this week. And we think we've found a replacement who just *might* put Al out of a job. Ladies and gentlemen, meet our guest coanchorman for the week!"

The camera pulled back to reveal the person sitting next to Lon Stagg at the anchor desk.

"What are the top stories tonight, Liza?"

Robert Schein lay naked on the bed in the guest room of Sterling Blade's estate. The script for his comedy debut at the Group Comedy Session was scattered about him. He was eating an orange. His telephone rang.

He turned down the volume on his television set, which was tuned to Mike Douglas, and lifted the receiver.

"Is this the party to whom I am speaking, the funniest goddamn comedian to hit Tinseltown since the late great Chuck Chaplin, the man whose face is red, Bobby Schein?"

Schein held the receiver to his ear and said nothing. After a moment the voice of Marvin Reed continued, in a slightly altered tone.

"I hope you enjoy the great American sport of baseball, amigo, because tomorrow night you and I are going to take in the Angels' Opening Night tussle against the Bronx Bombers, the feared Yankees, who have been your favorite team since boyhood, in case you should happen to be interested. Dress is casual and sincere. Plaid short-sleeved shirt and suntans. Get 'em if you haven't got 'em. No jewelry, no bracelets. Doctor's orders. Pick you up at six P.M. on the dot."

The Governor of California was finishing up a working lunch at his Malibu beach house with a delegation from the Sierra Club. The Governor was in rare form. With his robin's-egg-blue work shirt rolled up on his tan, freckled arms, his thin, bronzed face crowned with a tousle of red curls, he looked more the naturalist than any of the business-suited Sierra delegation.

Which was a good thing, because the Governor was in the midst of pushing through an industrial development bill while making it seem that he was a friend of the preservationists.

The leader of the Sierra delegation was a ponderous young man in horn-rims who perspired as he dabbled at his alfalfa sprouts. Clearly, he was awed at the experience of sitting on the Governor's fabled beach-house floor, in perhaps the very spot where the Governor had copulated with the beautiful celebrity poetess and rock singer. Nevertheless, he pursued his main theme with dogged determination.

"I hate to sound like a broken record, Governor," he was saying now, "but we're committed to the issue of saving the Eel River from pollution—" he felt the floor beside him with one flabby hand for his sheaf of notes and statistics.

"Pollution," the Governor echoed, rocking lithely on his haunches. "Buzz word!" He flashed a brilliant grin at the delegation leader, as if to confirm that the two of them shared an equal contempt for buzz words.

"What would you fellas say if I proved to you that my bill would not only provide forty thousand new jobs for Californians, but pump *one billion dollars* into the economy in the area of municipal sewage projects? Isn't sewage a form of pollution? Can the Sierra Club afford to take a public stand against a project that would flush out waterways amounting to . . ." he pretended to calculate silently . . . "*ten times* the volume of the Eel River?"

"Well . . ."

The billion dollars had nothing to do with projections based on the Governor's industrial expansion bill. It was an educated estimate of impounded funds that might be released by the Supreme Court within the next two years. The Sierra Club didn't have to know that. Nobody was taking notes. *Effects, not causes.* A line from the blueprint. The Governor was in rare form indeed, pretending everything, promising nothing, charming the Sierra Clubbers with the geometaphysical cant that some experts were predicting would float him all the way to the White House . . .

The Governor's secretary poked her head through a doorway leading into a small room where the Governor reportedly slept on a mattress made of dried kelp. She held up a white telephone receiver until she caught the Governor's eye. The Governor, annoyed, scowled and shook his head.

The secretary mouthed the word: "Bookmaster."

"Excuse me, guys." The Governor did a quick backward somersault, landing on his feet. "Gotta transfer some experience into linear language." He bounded into the bedroom. The Sierra Clubbers exchanged triumphant glances, pleased to be in on the Governor's famed hip media jargon.

"Hey, Mal." The Governor strained hard to keep his voice casual, under control.

"Don't 'Hey-Mal' me, you little bastard. I have your San Diego speech in front of me."

The voice was so quiet that the Governor could barely make out the words, "bastard" and "San Diego." Yet he did not ask Bookmaster to speak more distinctly.

"Covered all the points you, uh, suggested, Mal."

". . . know . . . talking about."

The Governor plugged his left ear with a finger. "Look, Mal. I *can't* go on record against the U.S. networks covering the Olympics from Moscow. The people of this state are sportsoids. They don't connect the Red menace with . . ."

"We've been . . . before . . . last chance . . . disobey orders."

The Governor took a deep breath. It was time to say the little speech he knew he would have to say sooner or later.

"Look, Mal. With all due respect. I appreciate the tremendous job your organization has done for me. I know I owe my political life to you. But I can read the polls just as well as you, Mal. The people of this state are *into my karma*, Mal. *I know the goddamn blueprint backwards and forwards.* Anyway, I have my own media staff. And I regret to say to you that 'following orders' is no longer a relevant part of my dialogue with you."

There was something on the other end of the line that might have been a laugh. Then:

". . . think . . . it alone?"

The Governor's little tirade had set his adrenaline flowing. More sure of himself than he had ever been with Bookmaster—the man had frankly terrified him for the past two years of their relationship—he could not resist scorching Bookmaster with a final, severing boast:

"I won't be exactly alone, Mal. Remember you introduced me to Mary Ellen Olds? Well, it worked. She has agreed to become the First Lady of this state. Just in time for the next elections. I think she's worth about as many votes as your admittedly sage advice."

The name of the daughter of the former President hung in the sudden silence.

The Governor felt a rush of exhilaration. He had done it! He had freed himself from Bookmaster's smothering grip. Some inner voice cautioned him that he had gone too far already, to let it go and hang up. But it was irresistible to drive one more stake into the cold bastard, for all the private humiliation the Governor had endured at his hands the last two years.

"And *fuck* your Senate blueprint, Mal. Come visit me at the goddamn *White House!*"

In his office, Bookmaster punched a button that disconnected the Governor and got his own private secretary on the line.

He ordered a call to New York.

"Colonel? Mal. Bit of bad news. We just lost Gareth."

There was a gasp on the other end, and a shocked pause.

"Jesus, Mary, and Joseph! Assassinated?"

Bookmaster chuckled inaudibly. "Self-inflicted," he murmured. Then, louder. "No, Colonel. I mean he's cutting the umbilical.

He's decided he doesn't need us. The polls have revealed to him that he is Moses."

"Oh, that is very bad news indeed, Mal. Very bad."

"It was inevitable. You know that, Colonel. We've all seen it coming. He challenged us on the one issue we had to have total concurrence on."

"He was the only young politician we had with a national profile."

"He was dangerous to us. Headstrong and stupid. Stupid, I can forgive. Headstrong might have killed us down at the wire. I can't say I'm sorry about this, Colonel."

"The elections are coming up this autumn." The Colonel's voice turned ugly. "By Christ, Mr. Bookmaster! Three years of planning wiped out in one stroke and you can't say you're sorry. WE DON'T HAVE A CANDIDATE!" The trembling voice dropped to a whisper. "If for some reason you are attempting to destroy us, rest assured, Mr. Bookmaster, that we will destroy you as well."

Bookmaster's tone betrayed no hint that he had just been threatened. "Politics is a form of adaptation, Colonel. You'll be happy to know that I've been adapting for just this contingency. You'll have your candidate. And he'll be better suited to your purposes than the Governor."

"Who?"

"If I told you his name, I doubt that you'd recognize it."

"Then it's damned certain that the rest of the country won't either."

"They will by tomorrow."

"Mr. Bookmaster, as much as I dislike the ultimatum as a form of . . ."

"Colonel." Bookmaster's voice was soothing, assured. "Let's talk again tomorrow. I assure you your disposition will have improved. Look. I know you're a great baseball fan. Let me recommend that you watch the Yankees and the Angels game tonight. It's opening night. I believe that's Channel Eleven in New York."

"What in the name of all the saints . . . ?"

"*Channel Eleven, Colonel.*"

Bookmaster replaced the telephone on its cradle. In the privacy of his office, behind his thrusting fortress of a desk, the slim, dapper executive closed his eyes and pushed the knuckles of each hand deep into his temples.

For the first time in his life, Mal Bookmaster realized that he was dependent on another human being.

Fitting, at least, that the other human being should have a minimum of observable humanity.

Robert Schein, he muttered into the heels of his hands. It didn't sound, somehow, like a household name.

Neither did "Percy Faith," he imagined, before he got to be *Percy Faith*.

Robert Schein, he muttered some more. *Robert Schein, Robert Schein, Robert Schein.*

Teller saw the footage on the *Today* show.

"In Anaheim last night," Floyd Kalber intoned, "a popular young New York comedian demonstrated that he didn't think that desecrating the American flag was a *laughing matter*."

Teller lifted his sleepy eyes from his bowl of cereal to the portable TV screen on his breakfast table. A familiar knot of tension was already forming in his stomach.

"It happened in the seventh inning of the Yankees opening-night game against the California Angels," Kalber's voice continued as the screen showed a panorama shot of a baseball stadium. "When these two men, carrying an American flag, raced out of the stands and into right-center field."

The camera zoomed in on two scruffy figures running across a field of green, in the semicomic bandy-legged trot that seemed to mark the running style of demonstrators everywhere.

"They knelt in the outfield," said Kalber's voice, "and proceeded to soak the flag in kerosene. Their intent, apparently, was to light it. Now watch carefully the upper right-hand corner of your screen."

Teller's teeth were clenched. *It can't be*, he heard himself muttering. *It can't be. . . .*

So quickly that the motion was a blur, a figure streaked into view. It hesitated between the two men, then disappeared off-screen to the bottom left.

"Who was that masked man?" Kalber's voice was saying. "Well, his name is Robert Schein . . ."

Teller's forehead thudded against the table top.

". . . and by trade, he is a comedian. One of the top young names currently in New York City. He was in California to open his act at a Los Angeles nightclub . . ."

Teller lifted one eye to behold a shaky closeup of Schein, the rescued American flag billowing from his upraised fist, trotting past the pitcher's mound. He closed the eye and resumed butting his head softly on the table.

". . . and attended the game, he said, because he was a lifelong Yankee fan. But afterward, Schein told reporters that he did not consider the incident a *joke*."

"Maybe I've been in too many veterans' hospitals in the course of my work," came a voice that was familiar, yet somehow alien to Teller's ears. "But I can't sit back and watch when people try to violate a symbol that meant so much to our fighting men in Vietnam. And I think it's time that the *decent* people of this country . . ."

Teller's left hand groped blindly for the "off" switch.

"Linda Ellerbee of our KNBC station got out to the stadium in time to talk with Robert Schein," Kalber's voice continued, "and we'll have a tape of that interview a bit later on in . . ."

Teller's left hand sent the TV set crashing to the kitchen floor.

COMIC IN HERO DASH,
bannered the *Daily News*

NY FUNNYMAN FOILS
FLAG-RANT FIENDS,
announced the *Post*

Even the *Times* remarked demurely, in a box below the fold:
NEW YORK COMEDIAN, IN L.A.,
RESCUES FLAG FROM VANDALS

But the *Messenger* topped them all:
BOOOOOOOY,
WAS HIS FACE
RED, WHITE, AND BLUE

Newspapers around the country splashed the story, and Schein's photograph, across page one. Few editors were motivated by either news judgment or patriotism. But they correctly saw the piece as an ideal example of the "good news" that their readers eternally demanded—as though the "news" in the Style, Home, Food, Leisure, Sports, Entertainment, and Weekend sections were too oppressive for the human spirit.

A good many of the editors scented a publicity stunt. But it didn't matter. Real or fake, this guy Schein had suited their needs.

At noon, the Mayor of Los Angeles called a special press conference to present Schein with the Key to the City. Network crews recorded the event for the evening news shows, complete with fresh interviews with the bashful-but-accessible Schein.

The Los Angeles Civic Club scheduled a luncheon in Schein's honor.

The Veterans of Foreign Wars and the American Legion sent urgent requests for speaking commitments.

Bob Swallows, the publisher of *Faces* magazine, heard the news on the radio as he sailed off Martha's Vineyard. He contacted his secretary immediately.

"Get somebody on him right away, Barbara," Swallows commanded in his excited, high-pitched voice. "I want him in our— let's see, July would be the soonest available—"

"You're forgetting, Mr. Swallows. You already have him. In the May seventh issue."

"What? That's 'm—Holy Christ, you're right."

Swallows handed his telephone receiver to a crewman.

"Bookmaster . . ." he muttered, shaking his head. ". . . Holy Gee . . ."

Marvin Reed was at Schein's side to orchestrate the interviews, accept and reject the personal-appearance requests, and deflect questions as to where Schein was staying in Los Angeles.

"Nobody has to know you're staying at Blade's place," he confided to Schein. "Doctor's orders."

Ed Kurtis summoned Mark Teller to his office. When Teller arrived, he found L. Malcolm Bass there as well—perched with stiff amiability on the edge of Kurtis's desk.

"Hiya, Big Boomer," said Bass in his robust baritone.

Big Boomer . . . ? thought Teller.

Kurtis cleared his throat. "Uh—Mark, Malcolm has some good news for you." A glance at Kurtis's knotted eyebrows told Teller the news was not, in fact, wonderful.

"Mark, fact is you're the Man of the Hour around here," thundered Bass. "You're just about the mule's eyebrows. Ed, are we paying this lad enough loot around here?" Bass jerked his head back to face Kurtis, his features contorted into a mask of humorous helplessness—the good-natured executive turning his pockets inside out.

"Mark, America has a new hero today." Bass snatched up a copy of the *Messenger* and thumped the front page with the knuckles of one hand. "Bobby Schein is on every front page in the country. And we at *WRAP-Around News* can take a special pride in that fact, can't we? Because *WRAP-Around News discovered* Bobby Schein. In the person of one perceptive pop-culture commentator, *Mark Teller*. Ace stargazer!"

Teller fought back an impulse to laugh in Bass's face.

"Well, I can't take credit for Schein's heroics. Seems to me this adventure is pretty incidental to his comic talents," he said carefully.

For just a fraction of a second Bass's eyes narrowed. Then he grinned at Teller. But his eyes were cold.

"Ed, our man is not only discerning and farsighted, he's *modest*," said Bass through teeth that were clenched in his grin. Then his face went slack.

"Surely you're kidding, Mark. You must realize what this coverage can do to a person's career. There's a little bird in my head that tells me Bob Schein's on the verge of national stardom, Mark. And I think it's in our interest to promote the fact that we spotted him first among every news shop in this city."

"He's a fluke . . ." began Teller. But Bass held up the palm of his hand immediately, talking over the last word.

"Now, I know what you're thinking, Mark, and I want to assure you I'm totally in line with you. The ratings book is *off limits* in the newsroom of this television station. *Quarantined.* I'm a numbers man, yes. But when it comes to the news, I don't even want to know what's inside the damn books, and I can speak for the Colonel and Ed Kurtis and everyone else in management in that regard."

Kurtis gave a pious nod.

Bass clasped his long fingers and puffed his cheeks.

"Nevertheless," he said. "It's no secret that there has been some very encouraging movement on the part of this station in, uh, that area, in recent weeks. I think it's reflective of the fact that we're giving the people of this city the kind of news they want. *Your discovery of Robert Schein is at the heart of that kind of news, Mark.* I think it's safe to say that that piece of commentary could well be a turning point in your career."

Bass paused as if to let the meaning of that remark sink in.

Teller remained silent.

"I like to reward my people for work well done," Bass continued. "I have a reward for you, Mark. I'm sending you to California. With film crew. Your assignment is Robert Schein. I want you with him every waking moment. I want you to put together a five-part mini-doc on the flowering of a new American star."

Teller stood gazing at Bass like a man in a trance. His mouth hung open. He was conscious of attempting to speak, but failing. He felt a kind of paralysis; it was like living out a nightmare in which one is unable to lift a hand to forestall calamity.

After a long moment he was able to wrench his eyes from Bass. He stared at Kurtis. Kurtis looked away.

Bass apparently mistook Teller's horror for fascination. He warmed to his subject.

"Think of it, Mark. It is the dream of every television reporter to be present at the *first cause*, the *decisive moment*. And it is the central bane of our industry, the central *curse*, if you will, that we cannot achieve it. We cover *climaxes*. *Aftermaths*. We arrive on the scene *after* the fire, *after* the crash, *after* the murder has occurred. What do we show our audiences night after night? Fireman poring through the wreckage. Ambulances and stretchers. The cop guarding the door. Now *imagine*, Mark—imagine how exciting it could be if we could have our cameras there *at the moment the fire is lit . . .*"

Even Bass himself seemed aware of what he had just said.

". . . not that I would for a moment *wish* for such a, uh . . ."

Teller continued to gaze in silence at the station manager.

"The *point* is that here we have a chance in a lifetime. A chance to be in on a *genesis*. A chance to be there at the source of the

Nile. To show our viewers history *as it's being originated*. And why? *Because we're making it*, Mark. *Not* Schein. *We* are. The others have done it. Cronkite corners Sadat and Begin . . . CBS makes history. Walters corners Castro . . . ABC makes history. Now we have our *own* name, and what's more, we've *incubated* him. We have *quality control*. We can make Robert Schein a bigger name in America than Begin, Sadat, and Castro put together! And Ronald McDonald and R2D2! And now's the time! I understand that our man Schein is opening a comedy revue in Los Angeles next week. *You'll be there, Mark!* Right there in the manger, so to speak. *A Star Is Born* . . . real life . . . that'll be an ideal promo slogan; Ed, scribble that down . . ."

"Gee, Mr. Bass. That really is a fantastic concept. Absolute dynamite."

"I was pretty sure you'd be excited by it, Mark."

Behind Bass, Ed Kurtis snapped to attention. He peered at Teller with an incredulous scowl.

"I think your idea of guaranteeing news by creating it is—well, historical. People talk about 'media events.' The Yippie marches. Rigged press conferences. Phony demonstrations. They all pale alongside this concept."

"I knew you'd relate to it."

"Cradle-to-the-grave coverage, as it were. There's no reason we couldn't extend your vision, Mr. Bass. To its natural conclusion, I mean. We could make Robert Schein an ongoing news story. Make his career a WRAP exclusive. Ram his life down our viewers' throats every week. His ups, downs, triumphs, failures. News as soap opera. Remember the Loud family? All their private laundry, washed on public television for thirteen weeks? Why not make Robert Schein an extension of the Loud family? An American Celebrity."

Bass was on his feet. "An American Celebrity," he repeated. "Jesus Christ, Mark, that is a brilliant idea. Absolutely brilliant!"

"It's your idea, Mr. Bass. I just polished the edges a little bit."

"Well, yes. But you are grasping the concept brilliantly. Hell, that's why we call him our *media commentator*, isn't it, Ed?"

Kurtis was still studying Teller's face in disbelief.

"What? Oh, you bet your ass, Mr. Bass. Uh—your life . . . uh . . ."

"When can you leave for California, Mark?"

"I can't. That's the sad part."

Bass had been gazing out Kurtis's window. Now he turned to look at Teller like a sheep dog looking up from a lamb's throat.

"You *can't?*" the baritone was soft and deadly.

"Not next week anyway. I thought maybe Ed had told you. It's my 'Sex in Baseball' series."

"Your 'Sex in Baseball' series." Bass's face was hard as an inquisitor's, but Teller thought he detected the faintest tremor of prurient interest. He plowed ahead quickly.

"Yes. I'm doing an in-depth probe of how sex affects the careers of top major-league baseball stars. The most famous ones. Who's getting it and who's not, and from whom. We've already spent about a hundred man-hours; we must have three—four thousand feet of film in the can. Some really explosive interviews."

"With the, uh—ballplayers?" Bass was intrigued now.

Teller nodded. "*And* their women. You'd be shocked, Mr. Bass. Some really high-quality women are available to these guys. Some real beauties. Educated women. Well, anyway, I know you'd hate to lose the production we've put into this report already. I've timed it to coincide with the Yankees' home opener a week from Wednesday . . ."

"*Educated* women," Bass murmured.

"Yes. Some of them with masters' degrees. It's an important piece of journalism, Mr. Bass. I think it gets right to the heart of the crisis of the family in this country, the pressures and temptations that the average working-man must face every day. I know your commitment to news. I don't see you wanting this piece of investigation spiked."

"You have *interviews* with women with masters' degrees who . . . ?"

"I'm ashamed to say it. But yes."

Bass put his hands into his pants pockets, jiggled some change, and took them out again. He rubbed his chin.

Kurtis spoke up.

"It's a dynamite series, Malcolm."

"Still, we absolutely must be in on the ground floor with the Schein thing . . ."

Kurtis rummaged his disheveled desk for an assignment sheet. He flipped through a couple of pages.

"Jennifer Blade's back from vacation. I can spare her, Malcolm."

Bass poked his head down toward the assignment sheet as though it contained the secrets of the universe.

"That might solve it. Still, Mark is the guy who discovered him . . ."

He looked up at Teller again. His expression was probing, skeptical. Teller stiffened, waited for the worst.

"Cinematography?" Bass whispered. "What kind of footage do you . . . ?"

"I can only leave that to your imagination," said Teller. He forced himself to wiggle his eyebrows.

"Jesus," breathed Bass. He straightened up and shoved his hands into his pockets again. "Well." His deep voice was decisive, businesslike. "I suppose our only choice is to send Jennifer. She does have some claim to promoting Schein . . . that sensational interview . . ."

"I was wondering," said Kurtis slowly, as though choosing his words with care, "whether her, uh—her reported, uh—*association* with Schein might not, uh—"

"Association? What association?" Bass had his back to Kurtis.

"You didn't see it, Malcolm? It was in the *Messenger* a week ago. I'll have a clipping sent over to your office." Bass was scarcely listening to Kurtis. He was still looking intently at Teller.

"One other thing, Mark. We're leading with the Schein story tonight. Now, this is a little unusual, but I'd like you to be on the set live with Lon after the footage from California. Sort of toss it back and forth for a few seconds. He'll remark how you were the first to spot Schein. You'll remark what a star he's become. Just a little transitional by-play. Remind our viewers of *WRAP-Around*'s special role in this big story. Okay?"

Teller opened his mouth to improvise another wild excuse, any excuse. From the corner of his eye he saw Kurtis shaking his head violently. He knew he could expect no further support from his immediate superior.

He sighed.

"Sure, Mr. Bass. Glad to."

"Good. Sorry about the California thing. I know you'll hate to miss it. But I appreciate your honesty in mentioning your other obligations. Say, uh—" Bass jiggled change in his pants pockets. "Any chance I might stroll back and preview a little of that, uh, cinematography on the 'Sex in Baseball' piece?"

"Well, you know how film editors are, Mr. Bass. One of those idiots might just file a grievance. Management interference."

Bass's face darkened.

"Tell you what. I'll save you some of the outtakes. Some of the good ones."

Bass was suddenly all business again. He buttoned his coat and strode for the door.

"Carry on, Big Boomer. An American Celebrity. Helluva concept."

When he was gone, Kurtis slammed his fist down on his desk. It disappeared inside his usual pile of debris with a soft *thwump*.

"I don't know why in hell I always put my ass on the line for you, Teller," he growled.

"Forget me, Ed. How much more of this shit can you stand to take?"

"Me? I take no shit. I'm just a news director doin' my job."

"You know the Schein stunt with the flag is a phony. If you don't, I'm telling you now. I *know* the guy, Ed. Believe me. He isn't capable of an act like that on his own. He's a zombie. Somebody put him up to it, Ed."

"That's not my concern. As the lawyers say, that's conjectural. All I know is, it's a helluva story. People want upbeat news. Good news. What the hell's the harm?"

"The harm is that it's corroding you, Ed. You used to be a pretty damned good news director. Now you're letting these guys walk all over you without a whimper. Are you turning into a Good German, Ed?"

The pudgy news director stood up behind his desk. "Don't talk to me about Good German, Teller. You're gonna march into that studio at five o'clock today and tell Lon Stagg what a *phenom* Bob Schein is, and you're gonna do it for the same reason I play ball with these clowns: You want your job. You got it cushy and you make more money'n you ever did on a newspaper or shoveling shit wherever it was you came from in the Ozarks. Your ass is tied to Bob Schein same as mine is. Now who was it was tellin' Bass he oughta make Schein into some kind of daily soap opera?"

"I was steamed. It was sarcastic. You know that. I was astounded that he took it seriously. I'm sure he'll forget about it."

Kurtis thought back to his chance remark to Bass in the elevator.

"Don't be sure about anything concerning L. Malcolm Bass or any of those guys," he said. "Up to and including the Colonel. He ain't the same guy he was five years ago. Now I'm telling you seriously, Mark. I'll never cover for you again the way I did just now. Some time soon you're gonna have to either make your peace with the way this station handles the news, or clear out."

"Yeah. Well, thanks again for the support, Ed."

Teller turned to leave.

"Oh, Mark. One more thing."

"Yeah?"

Kurtis was leaning forward, knuckles on his littered desk, staring up at Teller through his knitted black eyebrows.

"You'd better get your beloved ass on the stick right away and come up with one king-hell three-part series on sex in baseball."

"Mr. Bass will see you now, Jennifer."

"Hello, Jennifer. Have a seat."

Jennifer sat. L. Malcolm Bass turned his attention back to a piece of paper in his hands. He read it with his eyebrows raised, his glasses pushed down on his nose.

The office rang with unnatural stillness. Jennifer was uneasy. She wondered what Bass was reading. She felt like a ridiculous schoolgirl summoned before the principal.

At length Bass looked up at her. He turned the piece of paper toward her.

"You're aware of this, Jenny, I assume?"

She looked at the newspaper clipping pasted onto the sheet of paper. Although the type was too small to read from that distance, she instantly recognized the item by its very shape and size.

Her heart exploded in her. She fought panic. It was the *Messenger* gossip item linking her and Robert Schein.

"Jenny, I've reconsidered assigning you to the weekend anchor desk."

She bit down hard on her lower lip. Her hands were tight fists in her lap. For an instant Bass and his office and his damned piece of paper swam before her.

There it went, the anchor assignment, the network chance, the career, the life . . . she sat very still, fighting for control. She was

goddamned if the bastard was going to see what he'd done to
her . . .

Bass's voice was droning on.

". . . like to reward my people for work well done," he was
saying. "I have a reward for you, Jennifer. I'm sending you to
California. With film crew. Your assignment is Robert Schein . . ."

Robert Schein's West Coast debut at the Group Comedy Session had all the trappings of an "A"-list celebrity event. The obscure cabaret on Sunset Boulevard was bathed in unaccustomed glitter. Where Pintos and Camaros normally parked on that stretch of the boulevard, chauffeured Mercedes, Jaguars, and El Dorados now jockeyed for spaces. A searchlight swept the heavens. Television crews from rival networks fought subtle, vicious battles for prime turf near the entrance.

The New York gossip press had landed en masse, and was working the celebrity crowd for tidbits like thieves at a hanging. Chicago's legendary Kupcinet had lent his stately presence, preceded by his smoked glasses and cigar—he could be glimpsed on the sidewalk, bathed in a hand-held fill light, being interviewed by Geraldo Rivera for part of a *Good Morning, America* package. Amid the cluster of people watching that event unfold stood an elderly columnist for the *San Mateo Times*, notebook in his hands. He was waiting to interview Rivera.

Few of the Hollywood luminaries emerging from the luxury automobiles into the flash of paparazzi cameras had ever heard of Robert Schein's name before it was emblazoned in the previous week's headlines. Few of them had heard of the Group Comedy Session, for that matter.

That wasn't the point. All of them had heard about a thing called media exposure. On the quasipsychic grapevine that trailed through the Hollywood Hills had flashed the message that Robert Schein was a hot property. It couldn't hurt anyone to be seen at his opening—especially since the name "Bookmaster" had flashed out on the grapevine in connection with Schein's.

Inside the cabaret, photographers illuminated the faces, the jewelry, the tans, and the capped teeth of the famous. No one seemed to notice that the room was small and hot, the chairs were hard, and the red flock on the walls was faded and soiled. This was a certified Media Event. Everything was lovely.

Among all the beautiful and celebrated women in the audience, none drew quite so much spellbound attention as the goddess who dominated the first row of the press section.

Jennifer Blade, representing the Continental Broadcasting Network and New York station WRAP, had nearly stolen Schein's show before it began.

She was stunning in a black, silk, off-the-shoulder pantsuit, which billowed about her but tended to cling to the curves of hip, thigh, breast. The dark honey-blond hair trailed down her bare back. She wore no jewelry. Her generous lips glistened. Her dark eyes blazed with excitement. A single ribbon of black satin, fastened at her neck, completed her image of a beautiful, sophisticated voluptuary.

A perspiring woman from the *Hollywood Reporter* knelt on one porcine knee beside Jennifer's chair, attempting to interview Jennifer simultaneously on the subjects of her couture designer and the rumor that Robert Schein was her lover. Jennifer was ignoring the woman, chatting instead—for the benefit of the audience—with CBS's most dashing network reporting star.

She had truly come home this time. In a way that Hollywood understood, the Hollywood of her father and the Hollywood of Mal Bookmaster. They hated her and loved her, and that was the way she wanted it: hated for her success, loved for her scandal, her delicious decadent scandal of being sexually involved with the man she was covering as a network television reporter. Hollywood could relate to that.

At Bookmaster's instruction the Group Comedy Session would go through the pretense of business as usual on this night: Robert Schein's debut was to be just one of several comic acts. Most of the other comedians on the bill were unknowns—talented unknowns. Serious, gifted, on the verge of stardom, they were razor-sharp in their timing, suavely topical in their subject matter.

"Jee Cry, Mal, they'll murder the guy. He can't stand up to this kind of comparison." Marvin Reed licked his lips and fidgeted with his blue-tinted glasses as a plump Chicano comic left the stage to an ovation.

"Relax, Marvin, and enjoy the show. Julie, darling, let me pour you a little more champagne. It goes beautifully with what you're sniffing." Bookmaster's gaze trailed away from the stupefied movie star who was his date; it swept the room and lingered on the tanned bare shoulders of Jennifer Blade.

The warm-up comedians kept their acts brief, put their blandest material forward, and worked Robert Schein's name into their routines as the target of good-natured "roast"-type gags. They knew which of their lines, if any, had a chance to get spliced into the Schein coverage.

"And now, ladies and gentlemen, please join me in welcoming a newcomer to the Group Comedy Session. The man who in *one night* captured more *flags* in Anaheim Stadium than the *Angels* have in *twenty years* . . . direct from Stitch's in New York . . . ROBERT SCHEIN!"

The crowd gave Schein a standard Hollywood ovation as he stepped from behind the curtain into the spotlight. His gold hair gleamed like a surfer king's. His glittering ice-blue eyes darted about the glamorous maw of faces. The band struck up a few rousing bars from "Stars and Stripes Forever."

As the network TV lights and cameras panned the crowd, the assembled celebrities held up small American flags and waved them gaily. Some celebrities continued to wave their flags over the faces of adjacent celebrities.

"Nice, Mal. Just very nice," purred Marvin Reed.

Robert Schein waited until the applause had died down. He stood for a moment with his hands clasped, his head cocked slightly to one side, a whimsical half-smile on his face—a trim, attractive figure in his tailored tux and blue ruffled shirt.

The crowd fell silent, expectant.

Oh, God, thought Jennifer Blade. *Let him be good.*

Her heart was beating hard. In the brief silence before Robert Schein opened his mouth to speak, she comprehended the full weight of the peril he faced—the foolhardy recklessness of Book-master's gamble.

This audience was not the crowd at Stitch's—not even the Harwell crowd of bored dilettantes. The people behind her, the people staring up at Robert Schein, comprised perhaps the most demanding comic audience in America. They were used to the likes of Rickles, Steve Martin, Johnny Carson. These people *ate gags for breakfast!* And no matter how persuasively the New York media—including herself—had painted Robert Schein as a natural comic genius, Jennifer knew the reality: he was some kid from nowhere who had walked in off the street one night and cashed in on a million-to-one shot. *If he's ever going to come down, it's going to be right now,* Jennifer realized with anguish.

In that split second she came as close as she ever would to feeling sorry for Robert Schein.

And, in the next instant, for herself. If Schein died up there, she would no longer be the glamorous reporter-consort.

She would be ridiculous. In her saucy silk pantsuit.

She tried to think of a prayer.

Oh, God, was all that came.

"WELCOME TO IWO JIMA EAST!" roared Robert Schein.

In the split-second after that, in the flash of lightning before the thunderclap, Jennifer's mind raced madly again.

Not that funny it's quiet it's quiet it's quiet it's quiet it's . . .

Like a roll of thunder came the laughter.

It exploded out of the split-second of silence with percussive force. It welled out of the celebrity throats and rained on her back, sending vibrations up her bare shoulders. Laughter, deep thrilling laughter, mysterious and terrible as water, as rainwater, life-giving laughter you could drown in, she wanted to drown in it, to throw back her head and open her jaws to it, let it trickle down the sides of her cheeks, wet animal laughter, ugly and beautiful. Her back was a field of gooseflesh under the laughter-shower; she was swept in an erotic tide. It was as though Hollywood's most beautiful people had conspired to arouse her in a most inventive way, to caress her flesh with their laughter. Laughter, powerful laughter—laughter *was* power, power was erotic, and she was aware that her eyes were shut and her hands were at her breasts.

As quickly as the laughter died away, she heard Schein's voice again, or a voice that came from Schein—relaxed, alert, seemingly spontaneous:

"This is a *very patriotic crowd*! Over in the corner I just saw three Marines trying to plant their flags in *Ann-Margret's cleavage!*"

The flood of laughter came down again. Through it, through the storm, Jennifer could just barely make out Schein's voice, shouting at top volume into the microphone:

"BOOOOOOOY, WAAAAAAS MYYYYYYY FAAAAAACE REEEEEED!"

The laughter rolled down once more, sprinkled now with applause, and Jennifer swayed to it, abandoned herself to it. She was aware that she was laughing, too, her head back, mouth open in rapture, there was a wetness on the sides of her cheeks, tears of laughter.

Not funny! She kept thinking, *not funny*! The truth of it seared into her, and made her laugh some more. For now she saw the whole of it. Saw the depths of truth beneath the surface appearance of peril. Saw Bookmaster's genius for what it was. *There was no gamble*! Robert Schein was as safe on the Group Comedy Session stage as in his own bed! *They needed him*! The assembled celebrities, Hollywood's most dazzling icons, were no different from those first grubby crowds of hangers-on at Stitch's! The stars needed to be certified through Schein's success, just as the nobodies had! In that blazing moment, it was clear to Jennifer that Robert Schein's genius was in his nothingness. Just because he had no discernible traits of his own, he was the mirror of everyone else's needs, wishes, fantasies . . .

"The ultimate celebrity," she breathed, just as the flood of laughter died down.

"What did you say?" The dashing CBS reporter was peering at her with a quizzical expression.

She turned to face him, tossing her honey-blond hair.

"I said that everybody in the United States needs Robert Schein," she hissed, and showed him a flash of her tongue.

"It was a 'banner evening' in more ways than one here at a place called the Group Comedy Session on L.A.'s famed Sunset Boulevard!" Jennifer Blade was fairly shouting into her hand-held microphone. A few feet in front of her, a CBN crewman steadied a minicam on his shoulder, while another aimed a fill light on her face. The celebrities, press, and photographers streaming out of the cabaret had no choice but to pass directly behind Jennifer, who had taken up a position just outside the entrance door.

"Robert Schein, the New York comic sensation, took on the West Coast celebrity crowd here tonight—and he captured their hearts and minds with the same élan he used to capture the American flag from vandals last week in Anaheim Stadium."

Famous faces flashed in and out of the fill light's glare behind Jennifer. Because of her obstructive position near the door, it was inevitable that both she and the cameraman would be jostled from time to time, causing the TV screen image to jump and blur. Fine. Exactly what she wanted. That, plus the tight camera angle, plus the extra shotgun microphone aimed toward the crowd, would combine to give the impression of an event two to three times as large as it actually was.

"That incident," shouted Jennifer, "served in a freakish sort of way to herald a new phase in this young comedian's astonishing career. Robert Schein laced his monologue tonight with some scathing social jabs that had the star-filled audience reflecting as well as laughing. His favorite target was the controversy over whether American television should cover the upcoming Summer Olympics in Moscow. Schein at one point quipped, 'The Russians are pinning all their hopes on one event—the two-hundred-twenty-million brainwash.' A reference to the propaganda obligations that many feel would accompany American broadcasting rights."

A male shoulder brushed against her. A voice off-camera mumbled, "Sorry, Jenny."

"That's all right, Warren." Jennifer flashed a smile, then—back to business—consulted a small pad of notes in her hand.

"All in all, Robert Schein's topical harpoons were as sharp as anything since Mort Sahl's political barbs of the late 1950s—with one important distinction. Sahl spoke for a new generation of liberalism. Robert Schein seems to be leading his audiences in the opposite direction—wrapping itself, as it were, in the American flag."

Jennifer paused a beat, then gave the familiar slight nod of her head which signaled to TV audiences everywhere that the reporter was coming to the wrap-up.

"Why are we here covering a comedian's debut? Well, if the

polls are correct—if Americans are now receiving most of their social and political opinions from spokesmen within the pop culture—then Robert Schein could well be an important new voice on the American horizon." Jennifer flicked the corner of her mouth in the hint of a wry smile. "Let's just hope he doesn't put people like me out of a job. For the Continental Broadcasting Network in Los Angeles—I'm Jennifer Blade."

She did one more take of the closing, identifying herself as "Jennifer Blade—*WRAP-Around News*." That would be spliced into the piece for the local-station package. The minicam transmitted it all to the CBN-owned station in Los Angeles, where it was recorded on videotape for distribution to the network the following day.

The technician switched the fill light off. "Minute-fifty," called her producer, checking his stopwatch. Jennifer ran a hand through her hair. It was damp. She released a long sigh. The night air felt cool and conspiratorial on her bare shoulders.

"I liked that spot a lot, Jenny. Very impressive indeed."

She turned around. Mal Bookmaster stood on the edge of the thinning crowd, dapper in his black tuxedo, a champagne glass in one hand. His dark, reptile eyes bore into her. On his other arm leaned an actress that Jennifer recognized from half a dozen landmark movies of the early seventies. The actress's eyes were bright, unfocused.

"I was especially impressed by your analysis of his political content," said Bookmaster. "I owe you an apology, Jennifer. I've seriously underestimated you. You're not a Hollywood brat at all."

He took a thoughtful sip of the champagne and dropped his gaze boldly to her breasts. And offered her what she knew was the highest compliment in his arsenal.

"You are potentially a very important property."

Teller flicked on his TV set, as usual, to catch the top of the *WRAP-Around* newscast.

The celebrity coanchor today was Bette Midler. Al Adams, the "friendly sidekick," never had returned from his "vacation." Teller suspected he never would.

At least, Teller noted grimly, the Robert Schein opening was not the lead story today.

The lead story was the funeral of a cat that had starred in cat-food commercials. Sean Murphy, in black waistcoat, reported it deadpan. With footage.

"And so ends the saga of a stray feline, a drifter, who ended up better known to the people of America than most of their own senators and governors," he intoned from the graveside. He looked at the camera solemnly for a beat.

Now the zinger, murmured Teller.

"Gives a fellow . . . *paws.*"

Another beat. *Straight face,* murmured Teller. Murphy faked an attempt to keep a straight face.

"For *WRAP-Around News* . . . Sean Murphhhhhhhh-he-he-he . . ."

The camera came back on Lon Stagg at the anchor desk. He was looking off-camera, grinning at the monitor screen. He swung around to face the camera over his left shoulder, the grin still plastered on his face.

"*Paws,*" he repeated. He shook his head. "That shows you what happens when Sean Murphy *undertakes* to be funny. 'Go *West*'—" Stagg interrupted himself with a fresh fit of giggles, sharing the off-camera mirth of the production crew—'Go *West*, young comedian, go West.' Big yoks last night in the Golden State. Our Jennifer Blade was there."

This was the spot Teller was waiting for. He slouched down in his chair and pressed his fingertips to his temples. It would be painful.

"Robert Schein, the New York comic sensation, took on the West Coast celebrity crowd here tonight . . ."

Jennifer's voice came up under cover footage of Schein onstage. The bastard looked like a pro. He had to admit that.

". . . whether American television should cover the upcoming Summer Olympics in Moscow." At that point, the shot switched to Jennifer outside the cabaret. Despite himself, Teller sucked in his breath. God, she had never looked more beautiful. The longing, still acute, stirred in his groin. It mixed with a stab of sadness and a deep fury.

He tried to force Jennifer from his mind and concentrate on just what in the hell was happening with Robert Schein on the West Coast.

A woman's voice behind him said, "Mark . . ."

He half turned, glimpsed a tall shape, and turned immediately back to the set.

"I just stopped by to say good-bye . . ."

Distracted, he held up a hand for silence.

". . . seems to be leading his audiences in the opposite direction —wrapping himself, as it were, in the American flag."

Realizing his rudeness, Teller whipped around to see who his visitor was.

It was Elizabeth Scott. The weekend anchorwoman.

"One second," he said. He turned back to the set.

". . . receiving most of their social and political opinions from spokesmen within the pop culture . . ."

"Jesus," Teller breathed. "This is the most *insane* goddamn . . ."

". . . like me out of a job. Jennifer Blade—*WRAP-Around News.*"

Teller reached out and flicked the set off. Then he leaned back in his chair, brooding, for several seconds.

"Ahem."

"Oh, God, I'm sorry, Elizabeth . . . had my mind on that idiotic . . ." he stood up, gestured toward the set.

Elizabeth Scott smiled. There was a blue cashmere sweater around her shoulders and she drew it close around her. "No problem. I know that's a toughie situation for you, Mark."

"Wait a minute. Did I just hear you say something about leaving the station?"

Teller was surprised. He didn't think people like Elizabeth Scott ever left stations of their own accord.

"Gee, I thought when they reassigned Jennifer to the West Coast, they'd offer you the weekend gig back."

"They did. I'm not taking it."

Teller raised his eyebrows. He dug his fingertips into his jean pockets. "Where you going?"

"Nowhere. I mean, I don't know. I have some money saved— well, that's not your kettle of fish, is it?" she turned on her perky TV smile. "Well, so long, Mark. Sorry we didn't get acquainted very well. I like your commentaries." She stuck out a hand from inside the cashmere sweater.

Teller stood looking at her. He didn't take the hand.

"Just walking away from it, huh?"

"Wouldn't you? In my position?"

Without exactly meaning to, he said: "That's a good question."

". . . *like me out of a job,*" echoed Jennifer's voice inside his head. For the first time, oddly, he was able to think of the woman without longing—with no emotion to dilute the hatred and contempt.

He studied Elizabeth's face. He had never happened to be near her apart from their once-a-week encounter on the *WRAP-Around* set—and her face was coated with the heavy makeup that accented her aura of superficiality. Without it, some of the porcelain-doll aspect was gone: he could see the hard little crease just beginning to form under the chin, the small lines denting the flesh at the corners of her mouth and eyes. She had turned thirty, he guessed—quicksand decade for a woman in this business. But he was intrigued with the intelligence he now found in her features, a weary intelligence that was infinitely more compelling than the porcelain-doll image . . .

"Well, you don't have to come up with the answer *right now.*" She was making a light joke of his silence.

"So long, Mark. Don't let this insane asylum get you down."

"Wait a minute. Uh—Jesus, Elizabeth, I'm sorry to see you go. Will you have dinner with me?" He hastened to keep it on a professional plane. "I'd like to compare a few notes about the way they're running this place."

She shot him a sharp and thoughtful look. "I don't know . . ."

Teller was used to automatic acceptances from women to his invitations. Elizabeth's hesitation astonished him.

She brought her shoulder bag up and rummaged through it until she came up with a dog-eared red calendar book. She flipped through the pages, frowning.

"I think I have something for tonight . . . I'm sorry, Mark. I do have something."

"Well, look. Why don't you scribble down your number? Maybe we can get together sometime."

Again, she gave him the thoughtful look. He sensed reluctance. He held her gaze.

"All right . . . I'm not always in . . ."

He took the piece of folded paper and slipped it inside his billfold.

"Well—good-bye, Mark. It's been nice working with you."

"Hey. I'll give you a call. Remember?"

She disappeared through the door of his cubicle.

Most WRAP staffers who left the station were given send-off parties: somebody took up a collection and there was cake and a few bottles of white wine.

Elizabeth Scott, the weekend anchorwoman, just walked out the door. Nobody noticed her leaving.

"Good afternoon, Mal."

"Colonel! Good to hear you."

"Was that our candidate on the network news, Mal? A night-club clown?"

"It's a long way to the primary, Colonel. A lot of time to do a lot of things."

"I hope for the sake of a lot of people, not excluding your own self, Mal, that you know what you're doin'."

"Ding-a-ling! Good Humor Man here with the happy returns!"

Marvin Reed swept across Bookmaster's office, his little potbelly rolling under an outrageous body shirt. He deposited a bound sheaf of papers on Bookmaster's jagged desk with a flourish: a digest of the major reviews of Schein's opening.

"Thank you, Marvin. By the way, get Schein out of Sterling Blade's place. I don't want his ties with the Blades to be all that cozy. Book him in at one of the hotels."

"The Beverly Hills?"

"Come on, Marvin. Can't you just see some of the bright guys going at him in the Polo Lounge? They'd take his personality apart in ten minutes. He needs privacy. Book him a suite at the Beverly Wilshire. And make sure they understand we want complete discretion. Do you have a bio yet?"

"Mal, I'm tellin' ya. The guy is from Venus. He won't talk to me about what happened to him yesterday, much less the story of his life. I think he was cloned. From Bjorn Borg."

"Your sense of humor is a constant refreshment, Marvin. Well, we're going to need something for the newsmagazines. I'll try to pull some stuff out of him sometime this week."

"Oh, Jesus, almost forgot the big news, Mal. Carson show called. They want a preliminary interview with our man."

"Tell them Robert Schein doesn't do preliminary interviews. If they want him they'll book him cold."

"That's impossible. They pre-interview everybody. Ironclad policy. Even Orson Welles."

"Tell them to take it or leave it."

"Jee Cry, Mal, you know I hate to be a squeaky wheel, but we *need* Carson. That's our biggest . . ."

"Marvin." Bookmaster's voice was so low that Reed's blood turned to ice.

"I want you to remember something that will be invaluable to you should I manage to restrain myself from sending you and your flapping fish-mouth as far from here as the science of aviation will allow. The only *policy* you are to be concerned with in the matter of Robert Schein is *our* policy. And *our* ironclad policy is that Robert Schein needs *no one*. As time goes on, people will understand that they need *Robert Schein*. Is this all clear so far?"

"Yes, sir."

"Then get your ass out of here."

When Reed had scurried out of his office, Bookmaster picked up the sheaf of digested reviews and skimmed the important ones:

From the *Los Angeles Times:* ". . . What's amazing is the instant authority of the comedic voice. Schein sounds as if it's taken him years to understand all his material had to say, as if he's daring the triviality surrounding his act's composition to enter his performance . . ."

What blather, thought Bookmaster. He knew the reviewer: A frustrated rock critic.

From the *Examiner:* ". . . Some of the sharpest political barbs these ears have beheld since the days of Mort Sahl . . ."

That reviewer had been standing next to Jennifer Blade during her stand-up, he knew. Barely standing.

From the *San Francisco Chronicle:* ". . . Unlike Steve Martin, he looks for spaces in his phrasing . . ."

A recent graduate of Werner Erhard.

From the *Chicago Sun-Times:* ". . . breaking them up with one-liners a la Old Ski-Nose himself . . . leading the applause at ringside was his heart, CBN newsgal JENNY BLADE . . ."

From *The New York Messenger:* ". . . almost frightening sincerity . . . I found it impossible to do anything but listen . . ."

The only disquieting review was a thoughtful column that appeared in the *Chicago Tribune:* ". . . I sat there amid the famed, the famous, and the fame-est, wanting to join in the jollity but not quite able to . . . I had never seen this Robert Schein before, but I had the impression I'd heard all his lines, somewhere, somehow, out of all my old memories of television gags, maybe . . . and why did I feel there were invisible wires holding him up? And where does a comedian get off anyway, telling us how to feel about politics? And *who is* this person . . . ?"

Bookmaster grimaced. He'd read her stuff. Glib goddamn yenta troublemaker. Prided herself on not being bought. He knew how to get under her skin. He'd send her a case of champagne and a thank-you note.

But her review turned his satisfaction sour, left him unable to relish his general triumph over the small media bandwagon he'd orchestrated. She had seized on a few items that Bookmaster would prefer not to have seen in print. Not to worry. No such thing as bad publicity. All right, granted: he did not—as yet—have total control over the press. But his every instinct, built on twenty-five years of brokering personalities in Hollywood show business, assured him he had total control of something even more important:

A commodity called Robert Schein.

He flicked the intercom switch to his secretary.

"Send in Miss Blade and her crew."

23

Jennifer Blade's five-part mini-documentary on Robert Schein gave the nation its first detailed glimpse of the entertainer it had until then only read about.

Not incidentally, it showcased Jennifer Blade to the nation as well.

Originally assigned to WRAP in New York, it was elevated to network status at Colonel Eddie Donovan's personal instruction. It ran for two minutes on each of five nights in June, as part of *The CBN Evening News with MacGregor Walterson.*

In deference to the network news's image of journalistic sobriety, the working title, *An American Celebrity,* was discarded. National newspaper ads promoting the mini-documentary billed it only as *A Critical Examination of the Anatomy of Packaging a Pop Idol.*

Robert Schein's status as an "idol" was somewhat questionable at that point—as John J. O'Connor, alone among the nation's TV critics, grumbled in *The New York Times.*

O'Connor went on to grouse that the "Critical Examination" hardly lived up to the no-nonsense of its title. "It amounted," he wrote,

> to part of the packaging process itself—a full-scale sneak preview of a personality who reeks of being as pre-engineered

for stardom as did the rock singer Bruce Springsteen a few years back, when he burst full-blown onto the covers of *Time* and *Newsweek* simultaneously.

The series purported to dissect the elaborate media machinery through which modern popular-cultural stars are stamped out and peddled to the public irrespective of their talent or inherent appeal. And indeed there were cursory glimpses of Schein's entourage . . .

The rest of it was a pastiche of highlights in Schein's almost providential rise to ersatz fame: clips from his successful stint at Stitch's in New York, a videotape replay—perhaps the eleven thousandth, by now—of his propitious rescue of the American flag in Anaheim Stadium, still more clips from his ballyhooed opening in L.A., and clips from the more endearing interviews which the great talent has bestowed thus far. One had the feeling that had this putative documentary aired during football season, it would have been penalized for clipping.

Correspondent Jennifer Blade, who had built a legitimate reputation for toughness as the top reporter for CBN-owned WRAP in New York, seemingly forgot everything she had learned in her first network outing. Her idea of 'Critical Examination,' it appeared, was to interview a selection of the nation's gossip and television columnists on the subject of Robert Schein. The newspaper corps thus emerged not only as advocates for the comedian in question, but as celebrities in their own right . . .

"GODDAMN HIM!" Jennifer Blade raged about Bookmaster's office, swinging the crumpled column in her fist. "Oh, *damn* him! Who the hell does he think he is!"

"Relax." Bookmaster touched a match to a cigar. "Even O'Connor is allowed a miss once in a while."

"No, goddammit, he's *right*!" Jennifer's jaw was iron-hard, her eyes were blazing. "Oh, God, every word of it is *right*. It was a piece of shit, Mal, it was the shabbiest, most despicable piece of crap I've ever done!"

"Look at it this way. Who reads John J. O'Connor? Other John J. O'Connors. The pinstripe leading the pinstripe. I'd think you would be crowing about the rave you got in the *Messenger*."

The *Messenger* gossip columnist was among those interviewed by Jennifer Blade on the "Critical Examination." The *Messenger* columnist had cooed.

"That doesn't change the truth of it. I feel like a whore."

"Now there is a packaging concept with real possibilities."

"Watch it, you son of a bitch . . ."

The two had become better acquainted during Jennifer's work on the Schein documentary.

"Here's a review you might enjoy a little better." Bookmaster stretched his arm across the width of his massive desk. "This one's by the A.C. Nielsen Company. Legally, I'm not supposed to have access to their service. But I do."

"Read it to me."

Bookmaster shot her a glacial glance. Then he withdrew his arm.

"Overnights. The gist of them is that *The CBN Evening News with MacGregor Walterson* drew an average thirty-five share during the week of the Robert Schein mini-doc. That is *fourteen points better* than anything Walterson has ever done before on the best day of his life."

Jennifer stopped her random stalking and stared at Bookmaster.

"Fourteen ratings points is ten million households in America," he went on. "That's twenty-five million adults eighteen to thirty-four who wouldn't have been watching CBN except for your piece of crap on Robert Schein. Well, *five* pieces of crap; let's be precise. What that means is that you can go back to New York and hold a gun to Colonel Eddie Donovan's head. Do you want to talk to me some more about shabby and despicable?"

"No," whispered Jennifer. She had come to rest on the edge of Bookmaster's desk, lighted a cigarette, and was staring into space.

"Talk to me about Frankenstein."

The June ratings coup by *The CBN Evening News* fueled the growing prosperity of the "Cinderella" network throughout the country. Viewers were streaming to the five CBN-owned stations. In New York, WRAP was solidly ahead of WNBC's *NewsCenter 4* and breathing down the neck of WABC. The owned stations in Chicago, Los Angeles, Boston, and Pittsburgh all had adopted the "celebrity coanchor" concept—to the hand-wringing distress of the critics, but to the ring of cash-register bells. Industry analysts were already beginning to speculate that CBN and its stations were on the verge of a golden age that would beggar ABC's sudden rise from poverty to domination in the early 1970s.

L. Malcolm Bass, his horse face gleaming with pancake makeup, sat stiffly on the edge of news director Ed Kurtis's desk. Kurtis, equally smeared with makeup, sat miserably in his chair.

They were taping a promotional spot for *WRAP-Around News*. Camera, cables, and lights added to the normal chaos of Kurtis's office.

"Jeezuz, if we could somehow transmit the smell in here," muttered a technician, "we'd have five thousand new viewers automatic—every deli owner in the city."

"Roll tape," said the director in the control room.

The assistant director pointed his finger at Bass.

"America has a new hero these days," L. Malcolm Bass's baritone droned as he peered at the camera. He snatched up a copy of the *Messenger* and thumped the front page with the knuckles of one hand. "Bobby Schein has been on every front page in the country. And we at *WRAP-Around News* can take a special pride in that fact. Because *WRAP-Around News discovered* Bobby Schein. In the person of one perceptive pop-culture critic, Mark Teller. *Ace stargazer!*"

"Heh-heh," croaked Kurtis, on cue.

"Let's talk bluntly," Bass went on. "The definitive news story of the nineteen-seventies *isn't* the economy . . ."

On May 7 *Faces* magazine hit the American newsstands with the Italian-American crooner's face on the cover—his first interview to the press in more than six years.

That issue broke all records of single-issue distribution of a weekly magazine. There were three extra press runs—also a record. Nearly six million Americans paid one-fifty each to read the thoughts, astrological sign, favorite recipe, and future plans of the famous crooner—and to ponder black-and-white photographs of him "scuffling" with his "beloved" terrier.

A terrier that Marvin Reed had snatched up from a Beverly Hills kennel on the day of the shooting. It was later put to sleep.

On page 12 of the same issue, *Faces* fans got an unexpected bonus: a two-page takeout, with a sexy, closeup face shot, of Robert Schein, AMERICA'S HOT YOUNG COMIC—WITH A CONSCIENCE.

The copy (which had been delivered to *Faces* the day before the Anaheim incident) recounted Schein's impromptu heroism at the ballpark. It quoted him as "laughing off" a question about his "reported" romantic interest in "stunning New York TV news-lovely Jennifer Blade." It portrayed him generally as "an easy-going kind of guy who takes his country more seriously than he takes success."

It confided that Schein had flashed his "puckish" wit frequently during the interview—as when he snatched up a dog-eared back issue of *Faces* magazine and "joshed" to the interviewer: "Booooy, is myyyyy *Faces read!*"

As for his comic point of view? " 'I guess I just came by it naturally,' " Schein "shrugged."

Scanning *The New York Messenger* two days after the *Faces* issue appeared, Mark Teller's eye came to rest on a one-paragraph item on page 37. A suicide. The man had jumped from the fourteenth-floor window of his room at the 34th Street YMCA.

The name was somehow familiar to Teller: William Wyler. But he couldn't think from where.

CBN announced to the press that it had completed a deal with Malcolm Bookmaster Associates to air Robert Schein's prime-time television debut July Fourth: An hour-long special of skits and songs, *The Many (Red) Faces of Robert Schein.* Special guest-stars were announced. Among the special guest-stars were a country singer currently appearing in Las Vegas, an ex-pro football quarterback who had taken up country singing, and—extra special, to give the program a dash of patriotic glamor—the popular ex-President of the United States, V. W. Olds.

"Carson's people on the phone. They want him."

"For when?"

"June twentieth. They wanna steal CBN's thunder."

"No pre-interview?"

"They say no pre-interview."

"Tell them there are ground rules. We want a monologue. We want the first half hour of the show. We want him to come up and talk to Johnny. We want him to last through one station break, minimum. No questions about his family. No questions about

Jennifer Blade. He has a deep interest in American social affairs; we guarantee it doesn't get heavy, they guarantee one question on the political scene, minimum. Am I clear to you, Marvin?"

Mark Teller pulled the scrap of paper with Elizabeth Scott's telephone number from his billfold and smoothed it out on his desk. It was hard to find enough space there even for that. An avalanche of letters smothered the surface, as it had every day since Jennifer's mini-doc. At first, he had opened a few of them. Then he stopped bothering. All of them wanted information on Robert Schein. Phone number. Address. Was he married? Was he really that cute? What was his sign? When was he coming back to town? Would Teller please forward . . .

He hadn't seen anything like it since Bobby Lee Cooper died.

It made him nauseated.

He studied Elizabeth Scott's telephone number.

It had been a little more than a month since their brief conversation in his cubicle, on the day she left the station. He wasn't sure why he had not telephoned her. He recalled very well the attraction to her on that day.

It had been a rare surge of emotion. He wasn't responding to much of anything lately. The hideous ascension of Robert Schein, that shadowy stranger he had pressed into service to save his own tail that August afternoon; the loss of Jennifer Blade; the lacerating union of the two of them—it had the dimensions of a Biblical judgment on his soul. (There was enough Ozarker in him at least to reflect on that.)

It had paralyzed his spirit. There were days when he thought he could feel the very life-force, the very personality, draining from the pores of his skin. Robert Schein and his grotesque expansion filled the limits of Teller's vision, obsessed him.

There were times when he found himself fantasizing—half-believing—that he had created Robert Schein. Created him not just as a media entity but as an essential, corporeal form. Discharged him, yes, that was it, (in that August occasion of inadvertent necessity) *farted* him from the bowels of his libido, in the form of some foul, psychic gas—*farted* Robert Schein into the ether, where he grew, an infinitely expanding combustion of Teller's own secret perverse appetites, vanities, guilts, and cancerous covetings that coated the underside of his own character.

But the fart had grown too large, the gas wouldn't stop expanding; it accreted and absorbed all the fetid multiplicity of delusions, lusts, and megalomanias, the morbid fastening on the infantile self that rotted in the collective bowels of the country. The fart had coated itself on the airwaves; it had sucked the good vapors out of everything, out of Teller, out of Jennifer, out of the station he worked for; it sucked and absorbed and devoured the good and the bad indifferently; and the stench was on them all, and the fingers were pointed at Mark Teller—*he did it, he let the fart!* But they weren't accusing him; no, they loved him for it. They thanked him for letting the fart that was Robert Schein: *hey, thanks, buddy, that was just the right kind of fart you let, that one hit the spot . . .*

The fantasy aside, he knew that his future was perversely lashed to Robert Schein; the thing he hated, the thing that had robbed him of so much, yet gave him something as well, and that fact fueled the hatred even more. He knew that his career was in a sense insured by virtue of his having discovered Robert Schein. He couldn't rise above it, and he seemed immune from his own wish for destruction; he couldn't pull it all down around him no matter how hard he tried.

And so he existed in a torpor. His work was flat. He knew that. The station was indifferent. Management didn't seem to notice that his pieces had grown less incisive, less angry; that they relied less on first-hand reporting and more on a rehash of the daily celebrity stew that bubbled from two dozen magazines and newspapers. There was a murderous rage below the torpor, but he didn't dare release it—didn't know how. He existed in an eternity of days, passing in and out of the lurid Oz, indifferent to ideas, as dull and indestructible as one of the Six Captains, twenty-nine stories below . . .

Today was especially gruesome. He had just read CBN's press release on the Robert Schein July Fourth special. With the former President as a guest, no less. No end to the nightmare.

But it wasn't just the indignity of seeing Schein on a network special that weighed on Teller. The event would force a confrontation which, he now admitted to himself, he had been avoiding for months: a confrontation between himself and Schein, or with the gaseous chimera that stood for Schein.

So far, he had managed to finesse his way around the personal humiliation of genuflecting to Robert Schein on the air. That fact was the one shred of self-respect he still clung to. It hadn't been easy. He had done it by dodging, by scampering; a squirrel in a maze, avoiding the trap by dumb cunning. And with Ed Kurtis as a grudging accomplice.

This time there would be no way out. Bass would want a review of the program. There would be no point in even discussing the *content* of the review. Bass was not even aware of Teller's true feelings toward Schein, Mark was certain—so adroit had been his shameful dancing!

This one called for a decision. He could do one of two things: he could sit back, let the gaseous cloud wash over him totally, absorb him as it had absorbed Jennifer, absorbed the station; do the damn puff review, haul in his comfortable salary, make a reasonable concession to the inevitable forces.

Or he could resist—refuse to do the piece. And expose himself to instant dismissal.

If that happened, there was nothing for him to fall back on. He couldn't expect support from the staff. He was even more isolated than ever at the station; his brooding preoccupation with Schein had set him apart almost totally from the rest of his *WRAP-Around* colleagues. Even easygoing Sean Murphy avoided him.

There was no woman. Jennifer had left a large void. No family; all back in the Ozarks that were no different now from New York anyway.

Interesting problem.

He realized that he did not feel an overwhelming urge to sit back and let the gaseous cloud take him. Not yet anyway.

He looked again at Elizabeth Scott's telephone number on the smudged scrap of paper.

And swept away a fluttering pile of Schein fan mail.

And lifted the phone.

"Robert, I want you to take these and study them each night before you go to bed." Mal Bookmaster indicated a pile of videotape cassettes on the edge of his desk. "We're going to install a playback system in your bedroom at the Wilshire. We've cleared it with the management. Marvin will show you how it works. Just look at the tapes. Don't feel you have to memorize anything, don't spend a lot of time with them, just run one or two through every night before you drop off. Am I making myself clear on this?"

"You certainly are, Mr. Bookmaster. Check. I'll play the tapes every night."

"I guess you're wondering why we're laying the tapes on you, Bobby," chimed in Marvin Reed, pushing his blue-tinted glasses up on his nose. "I guarantee ya, we're not trying to start up Watergate again." Reed spread his fish lips in a grin, pleased with his topical humor, and waited for Schein to acknowledge his curiosity.

Two opaque ice-blue eyes stared back at him.

There was an awkward moment of silence.

Bookmaster shot Reed a glance that made the fat little assistant's face go white. Then he looked at Schein with a faint smile.

"Marvin has brought up a valid point, Robert," he said in his unnaturally quiet voice. "I mentioned a moment ago that we are going to project your comic talents for the time being. However, I feel that in the long run, you have a very exciting potential in the dramatic metier as well. One of the scenes in your CBN special is going to involve you and President Olds. It's going to be a complete change of pace from the rest of the show. In fact it's the centerpiece of the program. You're going to step out of your comic persona and demonstrate to the country that you can handle a sensitive, serious role as well as you can handle comedy.

"Mr. Olds will play himself—or a fatherly, American president very much like he was. You are going to play a young senator faced with your first crucial vote, a test of your conscience. Details don't matter right now. The point is, I want you to *convince* the viewing audience that you are a senator, an idealistic, deeply concerned, and courageous young senator. Now the skit won't be long, but it may be the most important three to four minutes you ever do."

"I understand, Mr. Bookmaster."

"Good. Rehearsals start a week from today. I'll have the scripts over to you by Friday. For now, get into these tapes. They are news clips of various politicians. Just look them over. Mannerisms, gestures, style. That sort of thing.

"Any questions?"

"No, sir. I'm very flattered to be considered for such an interesting challenge."

Mal Bookmaster arose and thrust a comradely hand across his massive desk surface to Schein. "Don't be flattered. Be ready when the tape rolls. See you next week."

They met at a small trattoria in Little Italy, one tucked away from the tourists and the rubbernecking New York celebrity-spotters.

"Hi! Gosh, you've looked *terrible* lately!"

Her smile was so engaging, her eyes so merry, that at first he didn't pick up on the admonition in her remark.

He would not have recognized her. The lacquered TV coif was gone. She wore a simple cotton scarf over her hair, which was drawn back. There was no makeup on her face. He noticed again the incipient lines about the chin, eyes, and mouth—but despite that, she looked beautiful. It was the unassisted beauty of a fresh, vigorous woman, not the glazed confection he remembered.

"I wish I could say the same for you. Unemployment seems to agree with you, Elizabeth."

He winced. "I didn't mean it—"

She waved him silent. "No, no. You don't know how right you are, Mark. That place was getting to me. Every day I felt like I was some kind of giant wedding cake in a window. Nothing but frosting." She made a comic face.

He hadn't figured her for a sense of humor.

"Uh, let's get back to me looking terrible. You don't mean to tell me you've been watching the station, now that you've escaped?"

"Criminal returns to the scene of the crime. Sure I have. I want to keep up with my old friends." She shot him a glance that underlined the irony of that statement. Teller recalled once again just how alone Elizabeth Scott had been at WRAP—not ostracized, really, as much as taken for granted, in the way of anyone who did not tap-dance constantly for inclusion in the inner circle.

"Been job-hunting? You shouldn't have trouble catching on at one of the other shops in town. I hear WABC is looking—"

"Good God, *no*. I've been taking a vacation. Enjoying life a little. Running in the park. Seeing some of the museums." She plucked a bread stick from its basket and shook it at him in mock sternness. "Mark Teller, do you know how many anchorpeople in this town couldn't even find their way to the Whitney without a roadmap? The Guggenheim? I think it's a scandal. I was one of 'em. We come into town and we're supposed to be telling New Yorkers about the city they live in, and we don't even know which side of the city the ocean's on." She folded her hands under her chin. "Most of us just care which side of our head the part's on. *Gets* to you. Yecccch!"

"You mean you're not from New York?" Teller just wanted her to keep talking. He was growing more charmed by the minute.

A waiter handed them menus. "Nice to have you with us, Mr. Teller."

They both ignored that. "Why?" Elizabeth Scott probed him playfully. "Because I showed up every day in my Cinandre 'do' and my Estée Lauder eyeshadow and my chic little Bonwit gowns, you thought I was some Park Avenue dollie on her way up?" He laughed out loud. That was *exactly* what he'd thought.

She was from Pittsburgh. Teller was surprised to learn she had not been in the business long—a little over two years. Before that, schoolteaching. A marriage that didn't take. No children.

"You wouldn't believe how I got into this racket," she said, as they lightly clinked glasses of Bardolino.

It was Teller's turn to score a surprise.

"Let me guess. It was at some restaurant. Dinner. No, lunch. Friend of your husband's—guy in the business. Sales end, probably. He'd been giving you these looks all through the meal. These long, lingering looks. Finally, meal's over now. The guy has a nice buzz on. He says—just before your husband gets up to go over and pop him one—he says, 'You know, Elizabeth, you oughta be on TV. With your looks . . .' Am I right?"

She nodded her deference to his acumen.

"You're close, chum. It was dinner, and I was already divorced. But *danged* if the guy wasn't a salesman. He said I had the look. I guess I did. One year in Pittsburgh, then on to the Big Time. How'd you know? You peek?"

"That's just the way most women seem to get started. You overcame it though. Went on to become a helluva trial reporter in spite of your enormous physical handicap of being beautiful. Now tell me. Why would anyone want to become a specialist in murder trials?"

"You know Morris Kitman?" They both laughed at the image of the assignment editor. "He had a crush on me. Murder trials were his idea of a good time."

An hour later they were sipping espresso.

"It's good to see you laugh, Mark. You're not laughing so much on your commentaries. The old zingers aren't there." She looked at him with an eyebrow raised.

"Is 'Elizabeth Scott' your real name? I always had the idea that 'Scott'—"

"Don't avoid the subject, Mark Teller. The Robert Schein business is eating you alive, isn't it?"

Once again, he was amazed at her sharp perception.

"How did you get it together enough to walk away from the place?" he asked her, in lieu of an answer.

She shrugged. "Wasn't a matter of getting it together. I think it was already together. I'm not a person who goes looking for trouble, Mark. And I'm no prima donna. But what Ed Kurtis did to me—well, it was Bass, really—was something you just don't ignore. That place is bad medicine, Mark. Pardon me for butting in, but I think you've got something on the ball. How much longer are *you* going to be able to stand it?"

Her compliment stirred him more deeply than anything had in a long time. But again, he chose not to answer the question. He turned the subject back on her.

"No, but really, Elizabeth—and this is none of *my* business— what's next for you? How long can you stay on vacation?" He reached for her hand. Casually, as though not noticing his, she drew hers away to her napkin.

"A while. I'm careful with my money. I've got enough saved to keep me going a couple of years—*hey*, I'm not a charity case. I'm a happy lady. Free at last. I can always teach school again. I just might knock off a year and see this country I've been telling everybody about on television. You know—beat-up old car, pair of jeans, jelly sandwiches. Seriously. I've wanted to do that."

Teller realized that he did not want her to do that. He wanted her around. Goddammit, infatuation was a messy, childish business. But it was the first emotion he had felt toward anything for months. He decided to indulge it.

He signed his name to the check. As they strolled to the door of the restaurant, he glanced at his watch.

"You don't have to be up bright and early for the office tomorrow," he said, making it sound offhand. "Care to come up for a nightcap?"

They were outside now, on the sidewalk. Elizabeth Scott turned to face him directly.

"If you're asking me whether I'll go to bed with you, Mark, the answer is no." Her voice was gentle but firm.

They walked along the crowded sidewalk in silence.

"I'm a tough nut on that score. My divorce wasn't easy for me. And you media types . . ."

She put a hand on his shoulder to soften what was coming next.

"I think Jennifer Blade kind of had a hand in rearranging both our lives."

"It was that obvious, huh?" He had never met a woman as direct as Elizabeth Scott.

"Written all over you. Point is, I don't like rebounds."

They had come to the corner of Canal and Broadway.

"I'll hop a cab," she said. "I'm actually not too far from here and you go uptown." She took his hand between hers. "It was a terrific dinner, Mark. It was really nice getting to know you finally. I'm glad we did it."

"I'm going to call you again, Elizabeth."

A taxi had slowed.

"I'm not always in . . ."

The cotton scarf fluttered.

"I'll call you again."

Bob Swallows pushed his blue skipper's cap back on his head and ran a hand through his thinning, sandy hair. Holy Gee! His last attempt at seclusion had been blasted to hell by that rascal Bookmaster . . . good for the magazine, though, dammit. Issue lost money but it was a collector's item; they'd been able to jack the ad-lineage rate up twenty-five percent . . . wanted to get some serious sailing done, though . . . maybe he ought to listen to the man, though . . . Holy Gee. . . .

"All right, Barbara, put him through."

"Hello, skipper. Just wanted to phone up and offer my congratulations."

"On what? What congratulations?"

"On your forthcoming debut as a major prime-time television producer."

"My *what?*" Swallows wished the man would speak up; that low-key voice was maddening, especially on a short-wave connection.

"I said . . ." A miracle: Bookmaster actually raised his voice—a subtle deference, Swallows was pleased to think, to Swallows's importance—"congratulations *on your new prime-time television program!*"

"That's what I thought—Holy Christ, Mal, what are you—"

"*Face to Face!* TV version of your magazine . . ." Bookmaster's voice faded . . . "My client Jennifer Blade . . . tell you the details at Ma Maison, Thursday, my table, one thirty P.M. . . ."

"Ma Maison! Do you realize who the hell you're asking to fly all the way across . . ." Bob Swallows realized he was sputtering into a dead line.

Well, the hell with *him. Nobody* summoned the publisher of *Faces* magazine across the country to discuss *anything.* If Bookmaster wanted Bob Swallows, he could goddamn well come hat in hand. . . . Holy Christ, did he mention Jennifer Blade? Swallows could count; he had read the numbers on her CBN mini-doc on Schein . . . TV version of his magazine . . .

He snatched off his skipper's cap and skimmed it across the cabin.

"Barbara? I'll be taking the Lear jet to L.A. International the day after tomorrow; get it all set up . . ."

The call came through to Colonel Eddie Donovan in his limousine as it inched crosstown on 59th toward the Sherry-Netherland. The Colonel was en route to deliver the welcoming speech to the National Association of Broadcasting News Directors. It was to be a corker, an Eddie Donovan bell-ringer in the old man's flashiest TV-commentary style: a counterattack on the latest groundswell of criticism on the irresponsibility of television programming.

It pleased the Colonel enormously that the rival networks, as well as his own, would be there to record his speech—gnashing their teeth all the way, he knew, but with the videotape rolling. When it came to smacking down the self-appointed guardians of broadcast virtue, making them all seem like sniveling, unpatriotic ingrates, no network chieftain did it better than the Colonel.

"Hands Off the Airwaves"—that was the title. The Colonel

leafed through his copy of the speech, typed in the large Tele-PrompTer lettering that was easy to read from the lectern, and silently rehearsed some of the phrases that would bring the assembled news directors to their feet.

"Are we professionals," he would shout at them, "or are we a bunch of self-apologetic little clerks, tending this mighty nation's airwaves at the whim of the federal government and all who presume to speak for it?

"Have we truly—as our critics never *tire* of whining—allowed profit to cloud our eyes to the public-service responsibilities that are the cornerstones of broadcasting? I won't stoop to answering hysterical charges with equally anguished denials. A cold look at the record of *all four networks* for prime-time public-affairs programming should silence . . ."

The first button on his silver telephone glowed. Sighing, he interrupted his mental rehearsal of grandeur and lifted the receiver.

Mal Bookmaster's tone was uncharacteristically lighthearted.

"What congratulations are you talking about, Mal? I haven't announced any schedule changes on this network."

"Details, Colonel. Seriously, I'd like to discuss with you a proposal for a unique programming concept for your network this fall. A video version of *Faces* magazine . . ."

"*This fall?* The fall season's less than three months away. We're locked in." The Colonel's tone turned sharp. "Mr. Bookmaster, it's rather acutely obvious that you have your hands full performing the task for which we've retained you. Dreaming up programming ideas is not your responsibility."

"Looking after the interests of my clients is. I believe you are acquainted with my client in this matter, Colonel Donovan. Her name is Jennifer Blade."

Rage welled up inside Colonel Eddie Donovan; he was at the point of handing this impudent West Coast hustler a tongue-lashing. The naked gall of the man! Daring to represent one of Donovan's employees while under contract to Donovan himself! And now dictating a program idea—it was grounds for dismissal on the spot.

But the Colonel held his tongue. Above all, he was a realist. He knew that Jennifer Blade's value to the network had skyrocketed on the strength of the Schein mini-doc. He wasn't surprised that she had obtained herself a manager; he felt a bit let down that it had been Bookmaster—but then, of course, how was she to know . . .

He decided to suspend his chagrin for the moment.

"Jennifer Blade, is it? And what grandiose plans do you have for her, Mr. Bookmaster? Casting her as Scarlett O'Hara in a remake of *Gone With the Wind*?"

"We thought about that, Colonel, but we're having trouble getting the good fathers of Atlanta to allow us to burn their city." Donovan again marked Bookmaster's untypical playfulness. "No, we're projecting something a bit more modest. But only a bit. I'd like to see Jennifer host a weekly series of personality profiles and interviews based on the magazine *Faces*."

The Colonel was silent for a moment. Even allowing for the ruinous salary Bookmaster would extract for Ms. Blade, he knew that the concept was brilliant. He fenced with Bookmaster to conceal his own interest.

"Assuming that you can bring your *considerable* programming experience to bear in getting such a program ready in the unheard-of time span of ten weeks, Mr. Bookmaster, I've no place to put it. We're set for the fall. This season's schedule is the strongest in fifteen years."

"Oh, yes you do. You're carrying a white elephant, Colonel, and you know it. *CBN Reports*. Eight P.M. Tuesdays. An hour of news and public affairs in prime time, against NBC's Movie and two strong sitcoms. It's going to drag your entire Tuesday schedule into the swamp, Colonel. A laudable but misguided gesture toward enlightened broadcasting. Nobody'll watch."

Donovan's brow furrowed. Bookmaster was right, of course. *CBN Reports,* he reflected, was one of the examples of public-spirited programming he had planned to cite in his speech.

As though reading his mind, Bookmaster persisted:

"You could yank it off the schedule at the last minute—back to the drawing board for fine tuning, on the air in January sort of thing. Look. Colonel. Bob Swallows, the publisher of *Faces*, is flying in day after tomorrow to talk nuts and bolts. We'd be delighted to have you join us at Ma Maison. Of course, if you are firm in your resolve not to reach into your schedule at this late date, we'd be happy to approach another network with the concept . . ."

And Jennifer Blade along with it, thought the Colonel. He heard himself saying:

"I'll be there."

It was only after he had replaced the receiver that the Colonel realized how thoroughly, how skillfully, and in how shockingly brief an instant, had Mal Bookmaster exchanged roles with him. It seemed that the impudent West Coast hustler was suddenly in a position to call some very important shots.

He looked down at his speech.

"Are we professionals," he mouthed silently, "or are we a bunch of self-apologetic little clerks . . ."

"That was impressive, Mr. Bookmaster. Two telephone calls, one new television program. Not a bad start."

He reached from behind her to cup a heavy breast in one hand.

"Not a bad *career,* Jenny, for most people."

She turned her head to nuzzle his cheek with her full, soft lips. Just before plunging her tongue into his ear, she hissed:

"For most people. Not me. Make me a network anchorwoman, Mal."

"Did you see this?"

Richard Fetteridge, the CBN vice-president for news, tossed the copy of *Time* down on the desk of L. Malcolm Bass.

Theoretically, Fetteridge's presence in Bass's office was an aberration in the natural order, the lion deferring to the wolf. Network brass did not normally call on local-station brass.

Theoretically.

The reality, and Fetteridge knew it, was that Bass was the power man in Colonel Donovan's highly informal chain of command. He was, in fact, Donovan's surrogate, speaking the CNB network's official policy from his position at the helm of the flagship station. It was only a matter of time before Donovan got around to appointing Bass, the outsider, to a key network position—most likely Fetteridge's. Fetteridge dreaded the likelihood not only out of consideration for his own skin, but because he was a news executive of the old school, had covered World War II alongside the likes of Cronkite and Collingwood and Murrow. He retained what he liked to call, drawling the phrase out with sublime irony, "a lingering affection for the Bill of Rights and the canons of journalism." The deterioration of standards—at his own network, in particular—sickened him.

Nevertheless, as long as he was titular head of network news, he was determined to try to keep at least a veneer of respectability.

Bass lowered his heavy lids to the page in *Time* that landed in front of him.

Then he raised his eyes to meet Fetteridge's. His horse face was deadpan.

"What of it?"

"Well, for Chrissakes, man—"

The newsmagazine was opened to the Press section. Under a reprint of *The New York Messenger* photograph of Jennifer Blade and Schein there was an item captioned PUBLIC AFFAIRS?

The item began:

> Not since then-Sec.-of-State Henry Kissinger buttered Barbara Walters' bread in Washington bistros has the issue of socializing between reporter and news subject flared so hotly in eastern press circles.
>
> The principals in this season's media ménage are two of New York's most attractive young personalities—hot young comic Robert (Boy Was My Face Red) Schein and TV newswoman Jennifer Blade. Their romance, while confirmed by neither party, is rumored sizzling by friends and the press alike (see photo above).
>
> While it's true that this dalliance does not raise deep questions involving objectivity in political reporting, critics contend that the electronic press's image is being tarnished nonetheless. Blade, daughter of Hollywood made-for-TV'er Sterling Blade, hosted a recent five-part look at Schein's skyrocketing career on the "CBN Evening News." Earlier, on CBN's New York-owned station, WRAP, Blade had conducted a flattering interview with the comedian.
>
> Newsmen from rival networks grump that such fawning coverage blurs the precarious but vital line between news and show business—a line that network news, until now, has honored. Some say Blade should have disqualified herself from the appearance of special-interest reporting.
>
> CBN's crusty anchorman, MacGregor Walterson, is said to privately concur with this view. But the normally available newsman refused to comment . . .

Fetteridge realized that Bass was still gazing at him blankly.

"Well, don't you find anything *embarrassing* about a piece like that?"

Bass pretended to study the article again.

"Yes," he mused. "That's an awful photograph of Jennifer—several weeks old, lifted from a newspaper—"

Fetteridge puffed his cheeks and put his cards on the table.

"What I'm trying to say, Malcolm, is that I *agree* with that damn piece. If a newspaper called me for comment, I couldn't deny we've been hit below the water line. That series damaged our credibility, there's no way to say it didn't.

"Now, dammit, I'm not clear whether Jennifer Blade is working for the network or working for your shop. But I'm telling you right now—" Fetteridge's voice was trembling—"she doesn't get on my *Evening News* again on the topic of Robert Schein. *Ever. Is that understood?*"

Bass picked up the newsmagazine with a thumb and forefinger, held it over the wastebasket beside his desk, and let it drop. For some reason the gesture sent a chill through Richard Fetteridge. Bass pursed his lips and gazed at the network man through drowsy, hooded eyes. When the career market-research man spoke, it was in the tones of an elder counseling a brash, naive youth.

"Don't let it worry you so much, Dick. Hell, publicity's publicity. Been a long time since our store's made *Time* magazine. My guess is, the Colonel will be delighted with the ink and will want Jenny back on the network as soon as possible."

Fetteridge fought to keep the rage and frustration out of his voice.

"Not on the subject of Robert Schein, Malcolm! That's ironclad!"

"You've been burning the midnight oil lately, Dick. You're a fisherman, aren't you? I wouldn't be surprised if the Colonel sent you out for some R and R before long."

As Fetteridge stalked out of L. Malcolm Bass's office, he knew that he had signed his own pink slip.

A copy of *Time*, open to the Press section, was tacked up on the *WRAP-Around* newsroom bulletin board. But no one ribbed Jennifer Blade about it. A subtle formality now marked the news staff's relationship with her. On the surface, nothing had changed

—the phony democracy of the newsroom still applied to her; she was the butt of Cazzini's teasing and Murphy's mock overtures as she had been (to her delight) when she arrived. Now the horseplay continued, but it had a brittle edge. Schein's name was never —but *never*—invoked. Since her return from California, Jennifer Blade bore the stigmata; the stigmata that everyone in the caste-conscious newsroom recognized as though they had been carved on her forehead. She was a superstar, an entity apart. The staff was detaching itself from her, as though it knew instinctively she had been marked for higher things.

At first, the "queen bee" deference saddened her. She had enjoyed the rough give-and-take in the newsroom. Being "one of the boys" appealed to a part of Jennifer that was lonely for uncomplicated friendship—had been since childhood. Her adult relations with men had almost never been free from sexual overlay, a fact that burdened her more than she was willing to admit. Thus the WRAP newsroom-playground had been an unexpected bonus to her job. Doing an impromptu parody of a press conference with Tony Cazzini, clowning on top of a desk, matching cynical digs at the day's news events—it was all wonderful and free. It satisfied some of the secret urge that gripped her at times, the urge to be "one of the boys" in literal fact—to be a man.

But she got used to the deference. If her career proceeded as planned, she would be a queen bee for the rest of her professional life. What were a few wisecracks stacked against the Continental Broadcasting Network anchor desk?

When she saw the *Time* item, she flew into a characteristic rage. She telephoned Bookmaster in California, shrieking for instant revenge, threats, and sanctions against the writer.

"Relax." It was a word Bookmaster seemed to use often. "Learn to ignore that stuff, Jenny. It can't touch you. Hell, it's good for you. Every time you're linked with Schein in some supermarket rag, three more TV critics are gonna take gas and X thousand more voyeurs are gonna tune in to watch the Scarlet Lady.

"When are you gonna understand it—you *need Robert Schein?*"

The Carson appearance was a smash. Schein's routine was brief, tight, and polished. It contained just the right seasoning of political material—a dig at foreign aid and a topical slap at the use of cocaine on Capitol Hill, which drew a hard burst of applause from

Carson's polyestered audience. In the sit-down session with Carson, Schein was modest, polite, respectful, and shy. And boyishly handsome on the frequent close-ups. He seemed content mostly to react to Carson's own gags, which endeared him further to the audience.

"Bobby Schein. He's quite a guy. We gotta do this." The camera faded on Carson turning toward Schein, to slap a ratifying hand on his shoulder.

"Is he ready for Vegas? The Palace wants him, so does the Sands." Marvin Reed, sporting a trendy safari suit complete with epaulets, stood before Bookmaster's black desk.

"You can't quite believe it, can you, Marvin? How anyone as personally bland as Robert Schein could have the hold on the American public that he does?"

Reed shrugged. "I plead the Fifth. I love it here."

"And you resent it, don't you? Because the guy puts you down."

"The Fifth. Hey, what is this? I'm a good soldier, Mal—"

"How would you feel if I told you the world is about to see the last of Robert Schein, comedian?"

Reed's glasses masked any expression of his eyes. But the lips jerked in an involuntary smile.

Then the pragmatic side of Reed's nature took over.

"At this stage? Jeez, Mal, you know what you're doing, but I'd be sort of loathe to interrupt the giant orgasm that's now going on between the guy and America." Reed still couldn't bring himself to refer to Schein by name.

"But he's a lousy comedian," said Bookmaster tonelessly. "Oh, he does all right in controlled situations. He does a good *imitation* of a comic, Marvin. An excellent imitation. That's the secret I'm going to ask you to share with me. In situations where we can control the response to Schein, we are dealing with some kind of instinctual genius. I think the guy has memorized everything he's ever seen on television. That's it, really—he *impersonates* the medium."

"Which in turn impersonates life." Reed was pleased with his little aphorism. He plumped himself into a chair beside Bookmaster's desk. This was rare. His boss rarely confided in him. Reed glowed.

"I'd say the Carson show was Schein's outer limit," Bookmaster went on. "Truth be known, Marvin, I was squirming during his stint on the couch with Johnny. That may have been the biggest risk I've taken with Schein so far—*not* his opening at the Session, as I am aware some of my friends believe."

Reed blushed. That was aimed at him.

"From now on, Marvin, we control every contact that Robert Schein has with the outside world. Particularly the press. He will never give an interview without one of us present. Audiences, too, if we can. Fans. That's why I'm not booking him into Vegas. Two nights there, he'd be pitifully destroyed. One heckler is all it would take. He's a delicate mechanism, Marvin. That, by the way, is why he doesn't relate to you. It's not that he dislikes you. It's more like he doesn't know how to relate to you. Me, he recognizes as the authority figure. He understands—remembers, I don't know —that it's important to relate to authority figures. But with you it's nothing personal."

"Nothing personal is right." Reed shuddered. "Christ, the way you talk about him gives me the creeps. I feel like we're doing a scene from *The Beast That Ate Television.*"

Bookmaster shrugged. "I'm no shrink. God knows. But I think I understand Schein. I also believe he's not that rare as a type. Maybe a little extreme, but—God, Marvin, do you realize how many hothouse people there are out in that strange world beyond the Mojave—people who's only contact with reality has been through the tube?"

He brought himself upright, shuffled some papers on his desk.

"The hell with it. We're not in the philosophy business. The point is this, Marvin: Robert Schein's career is now in a transition stage. The people at CBN may think they're showcasing a new comedian two weeks from tonight. They're wrong, as usual. Behind the times. They're actually closing out a comedian's career and introducing a powerful new dramatic actor."

And beyond, he added silently.

A news item in *The New York Messenger:*

A shake-up of top news executives at the Continental Broadcasting Network yesterday has added fuel to speculation that CBN is radically revising its concept of television journalism. The shake-up was expected to have far-reaching effects, not only within CBN but at rival networks as well.

CBN president and founder Col. Eddie Donovan announced that L. Malcolm Bass, 49, the wunderkind chief executive of flagship station WRAP the past two years, had been named vice-president, CBN News.

Bass succeeds Richard Fetteridge, 60, who had commanded CBN's news division since 1963. Fetteridge's unexpected resignation was accepted 'with surprise and deep regret' by Col. Donovan earlier in the day.

Replacing Bass as acting station manager at WRAP will be Edgar Kurtis, 53, the stations' news director.

Bass's appointment is considered a bombshell development in network news circles. Not only is he without professional journalistic experience—a lack that one rival executive termed 'astounding'—but until he assumed command at WRAP, Bass had never served a day in broadcasting.

Previous to his position at WRAP, Bass was a senior vice-president at Pierce, Wightman and Barnes, a prestigious New York market-research firm. His style at WRAP was marked by a heavy involvement in motivational research as a framework for programming news; for razzle-dazzle techniques including expensive new sets and "happy-talk" journalism plus an emphasis on "personality" reporting.

Although criticized heavily in some sectors of the media, these techniques brought WRAP into its greatest period of prosperity. Under Bass, the UHF outlet forged into parity with its VHF competitors for the first time in history. Channel 26 is presently in a virtual tie for second place in overall adult viewing audience in New York.

In a prepared statement, Bass praised his predecessor and promised 'no major changes in the excellent CBN news tradition.' Skeptical observers, however . . .

"I think things are going to be different around the station now, Elizabeth. Kurtis is a good man. He's no Einstein, but he's decent. Maybe some of the craziness will be over now. Maybe you'd even think of coming back. Cazzini's no good at weekend anchor, and they haven't hired anybody else . . ."

They had run together in Central Park on a glorious green morning. Teller had admired the way she kept in stride with him around the reservoir, their feet crunching the cinder track together in perfect cadence. Her legs were long and white and lovely, slim but nicely muscled. Her skin radiated a glowing healthfulness. Now, across from him at a small coffee shop on Madison Avenue, a scrap of colored cloth tied about her head, her blond hair streaked with perspiration, she had the vital beauty of an athlete. She appeared as though she had never wilted a day under television studio lights.

"I hope you're right about Kurtis, Mark." She smiled without looking at him and cradled her coffee cup with both hands. "I think that craziness has seeped into the walls over there. I don't see how Kurtis can avoid it."

He suddenly dreaded leaving her to go to the station. She was right; there was poison in the very fabric of the place. But aside from that, he wanted the morning with her in the coffee shop to go on and on.

It was the first time he had seen her since dinner in Little Italy. He had called her apartment several times without success. When he had reached her, he detected the same note of unspoken hesitation in her voice. But she had accepted a date for an early-morning run.

"Say." She smiled at him. "You get around that track in pretty good time. You're in shape for an old pundit. You ever do this sort of thing in college?"

He smiled at her, recalling Jennifer's dossier on him with the stab of pain that always accompanied references to her.

"A little. Where I come from we had to outrun grizzly bears on the way to the schoolhouse and back. It was even farther west than Pittsburgh, if you can imagine that." He reluctantly checked his watch. "I have to go mold public opinion pretty soon. How are you going to while away the balance of your day? Join the nearest breadline?"

Elizabeth's answer was interrupted by a woman who suddenly thrust her face close to Teller's in the booth. With her gigantic sunglasses, her powdered-white face, and her lipsticked scar of a mouth, she resembled a giant insect. Teller jerked back in surprise.

"Excuse me, Mistah Tellah," the insect said in a nasal Manhattan accent, "but I had ta tellya how much I admiah ya movie reviews. You awlways put da-own the Communist movies. I nevah go see one dat you don't recommend."

The insect was gone.

"It's nice to know one's work is appreciated," said Teller. "I've never reviewed a movie on WRAP yet. Communist or otherwise."

Elizabeth smiled, but her distaste at the incident was evident. In a flash, Teller saw his work with great clarity through Elizabeth's lens: mouthing trivialities to people who didn't listen. He pushed the image from his mind. Elizabeth turned the subject back to his question.

"As a matter of fact, I'm going to be car-shopping. I'm going to visit every jalop shop between here and Brooklyn. I want a heap that will hold together for a year on the road—nothing fancy. You got any ideas where I should start?"

"I don't want you to go." Her blue eyes flashed at him. He kicked himself mentally. *Go slow! Don't try to swamp her all at once.* He changed to a mock-broadcaster's baritone. "I'm on a mission to recruit you for an exciting career in *WRAP-Around News.* Did anybody ever tell you that with your looks you ought to be on television?"

This time she looked at him without smiling.

"I like it better the way it is, Mark. No autograph seekers. No getting recognized in restaurants. No 'face to meet the faces that you meet.' Just total possession of my soul. Happy lady. Free. Everybody ought to try it."

Her gaze lingering on his told him there was a message there somewhere.

"You've got to scram, buddy. Unless you plan to go on the air in your old college T-shirt."

"Ah, yes. 'Measuring out my life in coffee spoons,' " he matched her Eliot reference. There was a bitterness in his voice that he hadn't planned. He took her hand to help her from the booth. When she was standing, she withdrew it, again unobtrusively.

"Dinner soon?"

She gave him a smile that was almost melancholy—the same note of unspoken reluctance.

She didn't say no, he reminded himself as he jogged through the park toward his apartment on the West Side.

"In about twenty minutes, Robert, there will be a young lady from the *Los Angeles Times-Washington Post* News Service to interview you. Think you can handle it? I'll be with you, of course." Bookmaster's voice was at a whisper.

"The *Post-Newsweek* Syndicate? Gee, that's two hundred fifty papers. Sure, Mr. Bookmaster. Happy to oblige."

Bookmaster raised his eyebrows. Schein amazed him at times. How would he know how many newspapers were in the *Times-Post* Service? And if he knew, how likely was it that he would volunteer the information?

But then, Bookmaster had noted, Robert Schein seemed somehow more fully human when he was in a television studio or on a stage. Just now they were sitting on two folding chairs, a section of the audience bleachers, facing the cavernous sound stage at Continental Studios, CBN's West Coast programming plant. It was the third day of taping the July Fourth special, *The Many (Red) Faces of Robert Schein.* Just now the producers were taping a scene that didn't involve Schein. A dance routine. Another of Bookmaster's clients—the sister half of the "wholesome" singing duo that had captivated family audiences for the past three years—was doing a solo guest-shot. She was portraying a giant firecracker—a cherry bomb, to be exact. (The symbolic significance of that particular piece of ordnance, to Bookmaster's relief, had escaped the network censor thus far.) A circular crimson globe, perforated hopsack reinforced by wire ribbing, covered her head and body—except for her legs, which were encased in fishnet stockings. The sexiest fifteen-year-old legs on television, Bookmaster thought.

The young woman was attempting a routine that called for her to tap-dance her way through an obstacle course while being pursued by the quarterback-turned-country-singer, who was dressed as Uncle Sam and brandishing a lighted torch. The show's producers were not opting for subtlety.

So far, the scene had been interrupted three times due to hysterical crying jags by the "wholesome" teen star, who thought—perhaps with some justification, Bookmaster allowed—that what she was doing was stupid.

Bookmaster just hoped that the *Post-Newsweek* reporter would not walk in during a crying jag.

"Let's just stroll out toward the corridor, shall we?"

Schein mopped his face with a handkerchief. "Sure."

He was drenched with sweat from three hours under the lights.

He was wearing a black T-shirt and jeans. Bookmaster, in his customary three-piece black silk suit, hoped that the reporter would be turned on by the early Brando approach.

So far, the taping had exceeded everyone's hopes. Schein had adapted to cue cards, retakes, and the illusion of relaxed intimacy under pressure with his usual uncanny feel for the moment. In fact, Bookmaster decided, the guy was better in front of a TV camera than he was on stage. He seemed to understand instinctively how to drop the pitch of his voice and the range of his gestures down to the understated scope required by the TV camera. The director, an emotional type who let everyone know he did these things only as a means to making "serious cinematic statements," had rushed onstage after the first taping sequence and thrown his arms around Schein in full view of the cast.

"This man is my ba-a-a-a-y-bee," he had shrieked.

"Boy, is my face red," someone in the cast had cracked.

Now they walked toward the green doors that led to the corridor. Behind them echoed the manic crash of studio-orchestra trumpets.

"You know my signals," Bookmaster murmured, his hand on Schein's shoulder. "If I reach inside my suit pocket, that means I don't want a direct answer to the reporter's question. If I take off my glasses, don't say anything. I'll speak for you."

"Got it, Mr. Bookmaster."

As they neared the door the studio orchestra suddenly stopped. An assistant director on the floor could be heard yelling, "Stop tape! Stop tape!"

Bookmaster and Schein wheeled around. "If that little twat—" began Bookmaster.

On the far side of the stage a cluster of men in dark business suits had entered through another door. They did not look like show-business types. The director had run toward this alien group waving his arms, as if in danger. Now he turned, made an equally frantic beeline toward the orchestra conductor. He whispered something in the conductor's ear, then sprinted for center stage, waving his arms above his head for attention.

"Ladies and gentlemen of the cast," he trilled. "It is my great privilege to welcome our most distinguished guest star into our midst. Ladies and gentlemen, I give you—" the director was in an orgy of obeisance—"the former President of the United States, His Excellency, Mr. V.W. Olds!"

The studio band struck up a somewhat elliptical rendition of *Hail to the Chief*. Actors and technicians onstage raised their hands in applause as the former President, tall and beaming, strode a bit vaguely toward stage center.

Come on, muttered Bookmaster. The two of them hurried back through the empty rows of bleacher seats toward the ex-President's entourage. A young woman in a tailored suit hung on the fringes of the small group: Mary Ellen Olds, the former President's daughter.

Bookmaster arrived onstage just in time to save an awkward moment. No one seemed to know quite what to do with the awesome visitor. Olds had appeared without notice. He was not scheduled to tape his segment with Schein for three days. Now the director, assistant director, cameramen, technicians, actors, and dancers—everyone stood in a sort of live freeze-frame, grinning and racking their brains for protocol. Most uncomfortable of all was the "wholesome" teen-age star, who stood silently sobbing with humiliation under her crimson hopsack. She was about to meet one of the most famous men in the world dressed as a goddamn cherry bomb. She'd need a phenobarbital to come down off this one.

For their part, the ex-President, his daughter, his bodyguards, and aides stood closely knotted together like a group of Rotarians who had become separated from their Disneyland tour group. Olds's shiny dome gleamed under the hot arc lights.

"Mr. President, welcome!" Bookmaster seized Olds's hand.

"Mal! Good to see you!" the familiar authoritarian tenor boomed across the sound stage. Bookmaster was pleased; it would do his stock no harm to be seen on personal terms with V. W. Olds.

"Why, we thought we'd just come out here and have a look around," Olds remarked in his stiff, somewhat artificial manner. He was making a valiant attempt to appear spontaneous and fun-loving, Bookmaster knew. Olds had as yet made no announcements concerning his desires for a second full term of office, but the choice was constitutionally open to him.

Bookmaster knew the former Chief Executive was trying to appear spontaneous and fun-loving because Bookmaster had advised him to do so. The talent manager noted that Olds had even made some sartorial concessions to West Coast informality: the middle button of his business suit was unbuttoned.

"Make yourself at home, Mr. President. I'm sure you know many of the cast members already." An allusion to Olds's easy familiarity with the world of show business, part of the retailored image; actually the man was hopeless outside his narrow circle of bankers, generals, and automobile manufacturers. "Here's someone you haven't met, sir. The star of the show and one of America's top young comedians, Robert Schein."

The actor who had wandered into Stitch's clasped hands with the former President of the United States. A publicity-department photographer recorded the moment with a flash. Instinctively, the ex-President expanded his grin and clung to Schein's hand for the retake.

"It is a very great honor indeed, Mr. President."

"Robert, our whole family counts you as their number one fan. That is, you're, they're *your* number one fan. Fans." The ex-President's tongue had jammed in his throat, as usual. He glanced toward the silent mass of assembled actors, many of whom were trying to suppress titters.

V. W. Olds was seized with sudden inspiration. "Booooooooy," he boomed, "is myyyyyyy faaaaaace reeeeed!"

The cast burst into delighted applause. Bookmaster rolled his eyes skyward. *Jesus*, he murmured to himself with relief. He spoke again, to move the situation along. "Robert, I don't believe you've met the President's daughter. Mary Ellen Olds, may I present Robert Schein."

As the two of them shook hands, Bookmaster caught the P.R.-photographer's eye and inclined his head. The flash strobe flared again.

"You're a superfunny guy," said Mary Ellen in her reedy, breathless voice. "Gareth and I saw you on Johnny Carson and we really laughed a lot." She was a docile woman of twenty-seven. What intelligence there might have been in her attractive but elongated face had been worn thin by too many years of beaming in vacant, fatigued bewilderment before crowds of insanely cheering strangers, by posing with fixed smiles for TV cameras and still photographers, by being told, on too many occasions, how to dress, what to say, what to think. She had long since surrendered any impulse toward self-determination to the strong, forceful men who always seemed to know what was best for her.

"Thank you, Miss Olds. That is the nicest thing anyone has said to me all week."

Bookmaster raised his eyebrows again in astonishment at Schein. There was a gentleness in the man's voice that he had never heard before. Was there no limit to his acting potential inside a TV studio?

He turned back to the small knot of dark suits. "Mr. President, I'm sure that you and Miss Olds would enjoy a tour of Continental Studios. Mr. Henderson here, of the publicity department, will conduct you. Remember, we tape on Friday."

V. W. Olds turned at the edge of the stage to favor the cast with a large, sweeping campaign wave. "Break an arm, everybody!" he called merrily.

The studio orchestra played "The Bear Went Over the Mountain."

Bookmaster and Schein turned away from the ex-President's departing entourage to find a small, dark-haired woman smiling at them. She seemed to have at least three shoulder bags slung about her shoulders. There was a jaunty yellow corsage clipped to her blouse, which bore a print design of crossed tennis rackets.

"Looks like you and Vic Olds are old friends, Bobby," she chirped. "I'm Alice Samuels of *Times-Post*." She held out a hand.

"Pleased to meet you," said Schein. Bookmaster slipped a hand into his breast pocket and smoothly withdrew a pair of dark horn-rims that he kept handy for just such occasions. Alice Samuels, he noted as a matter of course, was the kind of journalist who concealed her star-struck nature under a veil of familiar first-name references and "in" usages. Schein's first formal encounter with the big-league press was going to be a piece of cake.

"I'm Mal Bookmaster. Why don't we all find a place to sit over in the bleachers," he suggested, adroitly including himself in the interview. He propelled Alice Samuels forward with a hand in the small of her back before she could protest.

"I hope you don't think this is going to be just another celebrity interview, Bobby," said Alice in a businesslike voice as she found herself hurtling toward a metal chair. "I'll warn you in advance, I have a reputation for bearing in with the hard zingers. I've no-

ticed you include political material in your act. *What is your reaction*," she demanded as they sat down, changing into an efficient
press-conference tone, "to the former President's warning yesterday against loosening our ties with the oil-producing nations?"

Schein's eyes went opaque. There was a treacherous beat of silence. He opened his mouth to give a reply. Bookmaster perceived
the slight curl to Schein's lip—trouble—even as he whipped off his
horn-rims. Schein held his tongue.

"Bobby's too modest to repeat this himself, Alice," Bookmaster
leaned toward the reporter with a confidential air. "But I was with
him at lunch yesterday when he read that, and he got off a *very*
funny line."

Alice Samuels's brow had furrowed at Bookmaster's interruption, but at the mention of a "very funny line," she poised her
ballpoint over her notepad. *Now let me think of one,* Bookmaster
prayed. His mind raced.

"He said—how'd you put it, Bobby?—he said, 'Vic Olds is right.
If we loosen our *ties* any further, it's our *necks*." Alice Samuels
gave a delighted yelp and scribbled. "Now, what *I* as an average
layman got from that remark, correct me if I'm wrong, Bobby—"

Forty-five minutes later, Alice Samuels, her notebook full of
Bookmaster's one-liners and her own descriptions of Robert
Schein's "boyishly animal charm," stood and shook hands with
both of them.

"If I was hard on you, it was for your own good," she purred to
Schein. "I think you can handle yourself in this league."

"You sure kept me on my toes," said Schein. "Boy. My face was
red there for a while."

Alice Samuels gave him a coquettish look. "*Love* it," she said.
"Just *love* it."

"I saw the P.R. photographer take a shot of Bobby with the
President," remarked Bookmaster, as though the thought had just
struck him. "Those are usually network property, but if you like,
I'll see if I can pry a glossy loose for you."

"Oh, that would be *wonderful*."

"I'll see that it's at your hotel by three o'clock today. Better yet,
we'll messenger it directly over to the syndicate bureau here in
town."

"Lovely. Don't think I'll do you any favors in return, though." She wagged a finger at them.

You'd write the piece on Malibu beach with your tongue if we asked you, thought Bookmaster. Aloud, he said, "Be gentle. It's our first time."

"Oh, *you* . . ." she scurried out through the green doors, shoulder bags flopping.

"It won't always be that easy," said Bookmaster.

Mark Teller and Elizabeth Scott were among the fifty million Americans who watched the CBN special *The Many (Red) Faces of Robert Schein* on the Thursday evening of July Fourth. The total was a record for CBN prime-time programming, and one of the twenty largest viewer totals in television history.

"Okay," Elizabeth had said when Teller called to invite her over. "But no throwing shoes at the TV set, or I split. I'm not into tantrums."

"Are you kidding? This will be 'an hour of flags, frolic, and fun that the whole family will salute. Plus exciting guest stars.' Said so in the paper. What are you, unpatriotic?"

"Wary."

"I'll level with you. I need a friend to get me through this one. It's either you or an acquaintance of mine named Jim Beam."

"That's not only unfair, it is utterly unworthy of you. Give me your address."

The audience size was bolstered by a heavy promotion campaign —critics were barred from the customary advance screenings—and by Alice Samuels's fawning profile on Schein that appeared in two hundred fifty newspapers the day before the program.

"Hi. It's me. I brought along a jug of dago red, to keep your mind off Mr. Beam."

She was wearing a flopping denim shirt, wrap-around shift, and sandals. Her smile was light and radiant, as always—sexy in its very absence of sexual allure. She seemed to bring light with her; there was a quality in her of unassailable serenity, an implacable denial of pain. He was impossibly glad to see her.

His eye was drawn to the reflected hallway light on her arm as she held the doorknob, and the monsters surfaced again. Her serenity was blotted by a dark image of faded jeans, striped polo jersey, white sweat socks, and an overnight bag.

He pushed the monsters aside, but not before she caught a glimpse of them in his eyes.

"Well, have a seat." He gestured into the living room. "Show time."

The record-setting audience was due partly to a CBN programming gamble that paid off: scheduling an important show on July Fourth. Relatively few Americans are in front of TV sets on July Fourth. On that traditionally safe assumption, the other three networks did not bother to offer strong counterprogramming. Thus the most controversial entertainment special of the 1970s ran against a seven-year-old Burt Reynolds movie, the fifth rerun of a "jiggly" situation comedy, and a droning "Special Report" on injuries and deaths due to fireworks.

The CBN audience marveled to a versatile, even an incandescent Robert Schein: wisecracking and pratfalling in the familiar stand-up style that had first brought him to fame; hilarious as a befuddled wide receiver in a skit with the ex-quarterback (who proposed, naturally enough, to run the "Statue-of-Liberty Play"); fetching in a brief soft-shoe routine with the "wholesome" child star (dressed up as a reincarnation of Shirley Temple); and smooth in his introduction of the guest stars. (His obligatory fake on-camera breakup with the Las Vegas country star was a masterpiece of the genre.) The Uncle Sam-quarterback chased the "wholesome" teen star-cherry bomb. There was a special "salute" to Bobby Lee Cooper, "whose music so eloquently captured the spirit of this great land of ours," with the Las Vegas country singer, in white jump suit, lip-synching snatches from several Cooper hits.

Skyrockets burst. The flag waved. The special star-screen filter on the camera lenses made everyone's teeth gleam like searchlights. The laugh machine roared and roared until its sides burst.

And the dish ran away with the spoon, thought Teller.

They had watched silently through most of the program—Teller sprawled on the floor, shoulders against the sofa; Elizabeth, declining his invitation to join him, perched on the sofa, her legs curled under her.

"I'd say you have to give him one thing, Teller," Elizabeth broke a long quiet spell. "He's a polished TV performer. I mean, you can't kick yourself too hard. Maybe if you hadn't spotted him, someone else would have."

"Wonder if you'd give me one thing." Teller waved an empty glass up and behind him. "Little lov'ly dollop of dago red. Estimable dago red."

He knew that he was being disgusting. He didn't have it in himself to care. A self-destructive fury had deepened in him as the program went on. Elizabeth Scott didn't have enough light to drive it away.

After a long hesitation, she filled his glass.

Schein's comedy alone would have sustained *The Many Faces* as a respectable television special.

But the vignette that emblazoned the program in the mind of America—that would touch off a firestorm of controversy in Congress and on editorial pages in the weeks to come—had nothing to do with comedy.

It was the audacious concluding segment: the unprecedented dramatic sketch between an actor-comedian and a former president of the United States.

There was a commercial break. Then the screen went dark. All sound faded.

After a moment, the legend appeared onscreen in simple white lettering:

A CRISIS OF CONSCIENCE

That lettering faded, to be replaced by:

THE PRESIDENT

Fade.

Played by the HON. V. W. OLDS

Fade.

THE SENATOR

Fade.

Played by ROBERT SCHEIN

The screen faded again to black.

Lights came up slowly on a dark, bare stage. Gone were the bright colors, the zany costumes, the upbeat theme music that had marked the previous fifty-two minutes of the special. The solemnity of the mood was underscored by occasional coughs and clinks in the dark background—suggestive of a quiet, reverential audience gathered for a Serious Cultural Event.

" 'S bullshit," Teller muttered from the rug. " 'S no audience. Sound effects're a dub."

Two figures gradually became visible in silhouette, the outlines of their forms silver with backlighting. One, THE PRESIDENT, was seated in a leather chair. The other, THE SENATOR, was standing.

Soft lights filled in their features.

PRESIDENT (meditatively)	'The charm of fishing is that it is the pursuit of what is elusive but attainable . . . a perpetual series of occasions for hope.'
	(smiles)
	I don't recall who said that. But it could apply to the presidency, I suppose, just as well. What brings you here, Senator?
SENATOR (obviously distracted)	I—I didn't expect to find you in your office today, sir. The Fourth of July and all . . . I thought you'd be making speeches . . .
PRESIDENT (with a wave of the hand)	Speeches. Too many people making speeches on this day. I'm always reminded of the late Hubert Humphrey. Wonderful speechmaker. Talking to a crowd in Iowa during a campaign. Somebody nailed him with a tomato. Splat! Just like that. Didn't bat an eye. Said, *'Speaking* of *agriculture . . .'*

(They laugh. Backgrounds of sporadic laughter, coughs.)

No. Too many speeches. Wanted to be here, in this office, on just one July Fourth. Feel the . . . *history* of these walls, these floors.

But you didn't come here to talk about—*speeches*, son.

close-up on
SENATOR (agitated)

No! No, as a matter of fact I've—well, I've come to ask your advice, Mr. President. I'm thinking of *quitting the Senate!*

close-up on
PRESIDENT (concerned)

Quitting the Senate! That's walking in pretty tall grass, son. Suppose you simmer down a tad, and tell me what this is all about.

c.u. on SENATOR
(sitting in leather chair)

Well, I—I don't know exactly where to start, sir . . .

c.u. on
PRESIDENT (gently)

Suppose you start at the beginning.

c.u. on SENATOR
(running hand
through hair)

I guess that's as good a place as any. Well, it's—it's not only my wife's miscarriage . . . the assassination attempt . . . those are things that any senator has to expect.

(suddenly frantic)

Sir, there are times when I feel the walls of that Senate office building closing in around me! When I feel *wild*, and *rebellious* and . . . and I want to just get on my motorcycle and chuck my briefcase into the Potomac and be an *ordinary man again* . . . *free* . . . (He breaks off, sobbing silently.)

c.u. on PRESIDENT
(thoughtfully lighting
pipe)

I guess we've all felt that way from time to time, Senator. You may be surprised to learn that you're not the first elected public official to feel the awesome weight of your duties. Some-

times as I sit in this office, I feel as
though Lincoln himself—and *Eisenhower*—were looking right over my
shoulder.

c.u. on SENATOR
(looking up)

You—you too, sir? You feel that, too?

c.u. on
PRESIDENT (nodding)

I feel it. And I feel that you feel it.
And I'll tell you one other feeling I
have. I feel that your present anguish
may have something to do with that
crucial *Senate vote* that's coming up—
the one where *your ballot* could decide the issue one way or another?

c.u. on SENATOR
(breaking into
abashed smile)

I should've known better than to—
well, 'jive' you, sir, as my generation
puts it. Yes. It's the bill that would
deny our television networks the right
to broadcast those . . . *glorified footraces* they're having behind the Iron
Curtain. And—well—this is my fresh-
man term and all, and the arguments
seem so . . . so *airtight* on both sides,
I . . .

c.u. on PRESIDENT

That's often the way. Remember, son
—the color of truth is—well, it's gray.

c.u. on SENATOR

But it's ripping me apart, sir! In my
guts I know the Commies would love
to get their hands on our airwaves so
they could slip their poisonous propaganda back into every living room,
bar, and college dormitory in the
U.S. But the public opinion polls, sir
—they show that the people who
elected me *want* to see those footraces.
I'll tell you, sir, I get so *alienated* that
I want to drop out of the *system!*

c.u. on PRESIDENT
(broodingly)

Yes . . . public opinion polls. The
public opinion polls, Senator, well,
they're rather like children in a garden, don't you think? Digging things

up all the time, to see how they're growing?

(scattered laughter, coughs in background)

c.u. on SENATOR
(grinning)

You have a way of putting it all in human terms, Mr. President. Sort of makes me feel there's hope for a hot-headed, brash young idealist some-where on Capitol Hill. But—the news-papers, sir. They're all solid *against* the ban. They say it'd be tampering with our First Amendment freedoms. Like . . . *speech!* And *Freedom of the Press!*

c.u. on PRESIDENT
(ruminating)

H'mmmm. Newspapers. (Chuckles) A good newspaper is the nation talking to itself. But there are times, son, when we jokers who are running this old Democracy are—well, we're privileged to certain areas of information that . . . not even the press is privy to. Like —*propaganda.* Or *secret deals.*

c.u. on SENATOR

(who smiles, with a new dawning of understanding)

c.u. on PRESIDENT
(sternly)

I'm not going to tell you how to vote . . . *Senator.*

c.u. on SENATOR

I wouldn't ask you to, Mr. President. Hey—did I come in here blathering something about quitting the Senate? I must have been standing too close to a Fourth of July firecracker!

wide shot
PRESIDENT

(Rising, clapping arm about shoulder of SENATOR)

Could be, son. Tell you what. Let's see if the pair of us can go lobby that First Lady of mine into *stirring up* something . . . like a big frosty pitcher of *lemonade* . . .

"America the Beautiful," up and under
FADE TO BLACK

A moment later the screen brightened again. Robert Schein, in black tuxedo, gold hair gleaming, brandished both arms to stop what sounded like a thunderous ovation by an ecstatic studio audience.

"That's our show . . . thank you very much . . . that's our show for tonight, thank you . . . thank you . . . ladies and gentlemen, wasn't he grand? *President V.W. Olds* . . . (the manic applause swelled to a crescendo as the grinning former Chief Executive bounded out, sweeping his arm in a wave) . . . thank you, thank you very much . . . safe holiday . . . and remember *it's a grand old flag!*"

Teller reached the "off" switch with his foot.

He looked up and over his left shoulder. Elizabeth Scott returned his stare, still curled on the sofa.

A torrent of thoughts came cascading into his head; they jammed there. He couldn't speak.

He decided a little dollop of dago red might go well.

He gestured toward the jug on the table beside Elizabeth.

It seemed to be empty.

"That . . ." he began, turning back toward the empty screen.

"Incredible," Elizabeth said in a small voice.

"Something . . . screwy, Elizabeth. Somebody's got a hold of him . . . pattern going on here . . . that was weird, bizarre . . ."

"I think you might safely say that."

He pulled himself up and around, so that he was sitting cross-legged, facing her. His head hurt. The monsters were everywhere.

"What are you going to do about it?" her voice was crisp, almost impersonal.

He'd been thinking about that. He grinned a sly grin at her.

"Not to worry. Not tooooo worry. I'm tight with Ed Kurtis. He's not gonna make me review this one. Bass, maybe he would have made me review this one. Not Kurtis."

"I was think—hoping, that maybe—" she didn't finish. He didn't ask her to.

She rose to go, smoothing the wrap-around shift with the palms of her hands.

"Don't bother to see me to the door, chum. You look comfortable."

"Dinner next week?"

Her voice was behind him. "I won't be here next week, Mark.

I'm leaving. On my odyssey. Didn't tell you, I found that jalopy. Sublet my apartment. Everything's set. If I don't see you—"

He sat motionless, his back to her.

Until he heard the door close.

Then he turned himself off, like a television set, felt the glow diminish to a pinpoint in his brain, then disappear; and he slept that way, cross-legged, in a solid state, until morning.

Jennifer Blade had flown back to the West Coast—officially, to tape an interview with V. W. Olds on his show-business debut; unofficially, to visit Schein.

She was seated next to Bookmaster at the large cast dinner party upstairs at Chasen's on the night the special aired.

"No need to ram the Fun Couple down the public's throats," he had said, pulling out the chair to the right. "It's good to keep a little ambiguity; keep 'em guessing. If you don't sit together, that fact alone is probably good for an item in a couple of big columns."

She marveled, as usual, at the thoroughness of his calculations.

"Besides," he had added, in his barely audible voice, "I am in the process of violating professional ethics in seducing my star client's woman. I may want to work on that some more during the course of this evening."

She had wrinkled her nose at him. "There probably isn't a professional ethic you've left unviolated."

She enjoyed the intrigue. It wasn't much of an intrigue, really. Bookmaster seemed indifferent to her sleeping with Schein. Schein was not aware of her new affair with Bookmaster, but she doubted that he would react to it. In the meantime she had abandoned herself to the accelerating pace of her life—a fast-growing national reputation (it would be considerably bigger in the fall); the glamor of cross-continental assignments, Los Angeles and New York as the glittering hubs of her activity; the delicious, wicked knowledge that she herself was a star as well as a journalist, a celebrity, the object—in many ways—of her own reporting. She even enjoyed the scandal attached to her alliance with Schein, had learned to laugh at the earnest criticisms directed at her coverage of his career. It hadn't hurt her ratings, it had helped them. In the popular mind, where distinctions between journalism and any other form of entertainment are forever an amorphous blur, she was a goddess—envied, admired, coveted. She had come to have an absolute faith in Bookmaster's use of mind over media. With him calling the shots, nothing was too outrageous, too unprincipled, too risky. They were all immune from consequence—Bookmaster's genius was that he realized how laughably attainable that state was.

She floated on the twin streams of power—Bookmaster and Schein. She belonged to both of them and neither of them. They belonged to her, in a way. Bookmaster's power was more discreet, more invisible, but ultimately more absolute. Schein's power was mystic, strange; visible yet inscrutable, derivative yet self-generating. The differences in their power marked the differences in their lovemaking: Bookmaster subtle and skillful, endlessly inventive, disdaining the tired, conventional Hollywood clichés of abandon— the mirrors, creams, incense, drugs, things that hum—controlling the action, channeling the currents into himself. Schein, direct and primitive, intense in his thrusting but the eyes detached, apart —what fantasies in his mind during the act of love, what hopes did he bring to bed, what fulfillment did he reach?

Bookmaster was the man for a party such as this—a suave complement to her beauty, at ease with fine clothes and famous people and quick minds and champagne.

But she needed Schein. In a way she could not explain, she knew that her destiny was tied to his.

Still, the moment was wonderful. The handsome, vital people at the tables, the laughter, the pretentious waiters, the violinists, the discordant dour knot that was the ex-President's party at one end— wonderful.

Teller would love it.

She covered the thought by making conversation.

"Look at them." She nudged Bookmaster. She nodded toward Robert Schein and Mary Ellen Olds, isolated from the party even as they sat in its midst, talking quietly.

"I tried to talk to her during cocktails," Jennifer went on, sampling the crock of chili that was de rigueur at Chasen's. "She's as spaced out as Schein is. I can't believe she's engaged to the Governor. He's a hunk."

Bookmaster let that observation slide.

"She hasn't had the easiest time of it. Never a day of privacy since she was tiny. A real familyoid. Human prop for that old horsethief of a father all her life. It's a wonder she can stand upright without the Secret Service."

Jennifer studied the pair thoughtfully. She had never seen Bookmaster volunteer so much conversation before.

"They're like—what's that Nelson Algren book—*Lonesome Monsters.*" She turned suddenly to Bookmaster, talking beneath the general uproar. "Mal, what are you doing with Schein? Just what the hell was that sappy skit supposed to mean, anyway?"

"Spend the night with me and I'll pour out all the dark secrets of my heart and mind."

"Can't. Tonight's Robert. I haven't really seen him for weeks. Come on, Mal. Something's up. You're spending too much time and energy with Schein just to develop one more TV comic. What do you have up your sleeve? You can tell me. I'm in on this, too. And I'm a good enough reporter that I'd find out anyway."

Bookmaster turned his glittering, black reptile eyes on her and gazed at her for a long time.

"Yes. You are." In the cacophony of the room, she read the words from his lips, rather than heard them.

His lips moved to form another single word.

"What?" She inclined her ear to his lips.

"Senate."

It was a few moments before the word registered with her. When it did, she stared at Bookmaster through widened eyes.

Then she burst into a shriek of laughter.

"You *bastard.* You're insane!"

The celebrants around them paid no heed. In these circles, the remark was a standard observation.

Jennifer indulged herself in a thorough fit of laughing.

"But I mean *insane,*" she gasped when the convulsions were under control. Then she turned serious. A chill of horror had come up under her mirth.

"Mal, you *are kidding.*"

He was staring back at her with a stony fixation. The black eyes glittered.

"Come with me. We're going someplace where we can talk."

He led her by the hand out of the echoing hilarity of the upstairs party, down through the celebrity-rich main dining area of Chasen's. With a nod to the maitre d', he hurried them through an unobtrusive side door, to avoid the paparazzi out front.

They half-ran to Bookmaster's limousine, which was parked on Doheny.

"Take a walk, Mario," Bookmaster instructed his chauffeur.

In the cool interior of the darkened car, his face thrust toward hers, pale intense face, a pool of light in blackness—eyes, sideburns, tuxedo—Bookmaster's full sinister menace gripped Jennifer as it had not since that first day in his office.

He began talking in a rapid monotone, his words barely audible even in the utter silence of the limousine.

"Now get all of this the first time, Jennifer, and get it good, because this is the last conversation you and I have on the subject, and if I hear one smart-ass giggle like I heard upstairs, I swear to God I'll break every finger on both your hands."

She caught her breath.

"Number one. Point number *one*. You said in the restaurant that you're 'in on this.' Well, sister, you're in on it now. Like you wouldn't believe. Up past your eyebrows. If you are smart enough to continue as you have until now, in your own self-interest, allowing me as your manager to make the right career decisions for you, you will be a wealthy and famous woman and we will all be the better for it. All of us.

"If . . ."

She could feel the word coming; feel the chill of it like a razor blade at her throat . . .

"*If* you ever breathe a *syllable* . . . a fucking *syllable* of what I am about to tell you, Jennifer—on the air—to a friend . . ."

He paused, his body frozen, an index finger suspended between their faces . . .

"Then I'll ruin your father. Like that." He snapped the index finger. "Then I'll come after *you*."

Her jawline hardened in the darkness. She allowed herself a long intake of breath.

"This sounds as though it might develop into an interesting conversation. You mind if I smoke?" She unclasped the purse that she carried with her on a gold shoulder chain.

"Don't smoke. I don't want to open a window."

"Yes, *sir*." She closed the snap on her purse.

How she had managed to find the guts to slip two fingers inside and activate the small portable tape recorder she always carried there, she would never know. If it jammed, whirred, or clicked, she was as good as dead.

His cologne filled her nostrils as he leaned toward her in the blue darkness of the limousine.

"Robert Schein is going to run for the United States Senate in November. As an independent candidate from the State of New York."

She forced herself to treat this statement as though it had some grounding in rational thought.

"I wasn't aware that Robert Schein had strong political feelings."

"He doesn't. In fact I haven't told him that he's running yet." Bookmaster's voice was nonchalant, but his greedy gaze betrayed him. He waited to savor Jennifer's genuflection to his authority.

"Well, I think that makes sense, Mal. You wouldn't want him peaking too soon."

His slap was light, but it stung her lips. His fingers clamped around her wrist, arresting her return blow.

"I told you this is not a joke, Jennifer."

"Sorry."

"All right. You keep that smart mouth of yours shut and you listen to me and you'll learn some things that can help you make some very attractive career decisions of your own. Because I'm going to take care of you, Jennifer; you're part of the plan. Unless you cross me. And then I'll just squash you like a bug."

He released her wrist.

"Now listen to me. There is a consortium of businessmen who are interested in creating a certain kind of candidate for the Senate. The founder and leader of the consortium is your boss, Colonel Eddie Donovan.

"It's a secret organization, actually. They call themselves the Phaëthon Society. They have money. I could tell you names that would make your eyes boggle. I'll tell you one: V.W. Olds. They want to run him again for President in two years. It's part of a very coherent political vision they have. These people deal in hard realities, Jennifer. They are on the right end of the political spectrum. They are disturbed by certain trends that they see developing in our foreign policy as well as in certain key areas of domestic economy and law enforcement. Whatever. That's not my concern."

"What is your concern?"

"My concern is as a businessman, a professional, offering a service. The Phaëthon Society has purchased my expertise to create a product for them. The product is a candidate for the U.S. Senate from New York. They have given me a list of specifications, a general blueprint. The blueprint includes young, it includes attractive, it includes popular, it includes a highly developed talent for following instructions. Your friend Robert Schein is spectacularly qualified in all of those categories. It's funny—we had spotted him as a potential subject before you brought him to us. We knew he had the appearance. We weren't sure about his following instructions, but in that category he turns out to be something of a primitive genius. I'm prepared to reward you with a 'finder's fee,' of sorts, Jennifer, in the form of some extremely attractive options in news broadcasting—if you don't manage to sabotage it with your sarcastic mouth. But I'm off the point. I have agreed to deliver the product to them by a certain date. I supply the candidate, they supply the ideology. What you saw on the air tonight was the product nearing its final development."

Jennifer had the claustrophobic feeling that she was locked into a very small space with a very mad man. Striving, again, to keep her voice conversational:

"No disrespect intended—isn't there a difference between a make-believe senator on a television special and a real senator in the—the Senate?"

"Yes." Bookmaster looked thoughtful. "The difference is that the real senator has to be elected. I'm working on that."

"May I ask another sincere, respectful question?"

"Shoot."

"Do you really think you can get a nightclub comic elected to the Senate from New York?"

The white face pressed even closer to her.

"Jenny. Have you been following the major-party candidates in this election? Do you know who they are? Do you know who is challenging the incumbent—who's ahead in every poll so far? A basketball player."

Jennifer nodded. "A basketball player who was a Fulbright fellow."

Bookmaster pursed his lips at this and nodded. "Fulbright fellow," he repeated. "Yes. That's what has them all excited, isn't it?

That's what's captured the public's imagination, got the TV stations all in an uproar, that's what they're pounding away at in the columns. That he was a Fulbright fellow. God, they're just wild in New York about the way that son of a bitch can analyze Chaucer."

He made a web with his fingertips.

"I have a piece of startling news for you, Jennifer. The essence of this guy's senatorial campaign is that he averaged twenty-three point five points a game for twelve seasons."

He raised an eyebrow. Jennifer said nothing.

"I mean, shit, if he'd ever learned how to play defense, he'd be running for President."

They were both silent for a while.

"I mean," said Bookmaster, "so what's the difference? A basketball player. Running for the Senate against a nightclub comic. It's the fucking American way."

"One difference that occurs is that the basketball player made his own decision to run."

"You sure of that?"

She didn't answer. She would have had to admit that she was not. Perhaps it was the moonlight and the champagne and the imitation of surrealistic power beneath Bookmaster's tomblike calm—but the idea of Robert Schein as a Senate candidate grew in her mind as a sort of perverse plausibility. Power, however likely or however dark in its origin, held a fascination for Jennifer Blade.

She had to test the thoroughness of Bookmaster's scheme.

"The press will destroy him."

"The press won't get near him."

"He's not going to campaign?"

"He's campaigning already."

"Tonight?"

"Yes."

"And that's his issue?"

"What?"

Jennifer made a circle with her hand. "The one on the skit. Whatever it was. Keep the Summer Olympics off television or something."

"*Oh*, yes. That's his issue."

"You don't think—no disrespect, now—you don't think you might have gone for something a little closer to the mainstream?

Crime. Porn. Taxes. I mean, who the hell is going to get excited over keeping the Summer Olympics off TV?"

Bookmaster's eyes gleamed. "I give you my solemn word of honor. In one month it will be the most controversial issue this nation has debated since the Panama Canal."

A vague chill gripped Jennifer. She shook her head. "I'm missing something."

"Didn't you learn anything about television and politics at WRAP, Jennifer? It's the *perfect* issue. First, nobody knows anything about it, so we are not going to be exactly encumbered with a record of established fact. Secondly, Schein will attack with it— which will help keep him from having to defend his position on other issues. Like crime, porn, taxes. And thirdly—"

Bookmaster paused. For the first time since they had entered the limousine, a look of suspicion crossed his face. Jennifer went cold inside. Was he hearing the faint squeak of the cassette tape in her purse?

"Thirdly," she prompted.

The scowl deepened. "I don't know whether I should tell you any more," he said.

She didn't respond, but held his gaze, wide-eyed.

He shrugged. "It doesn't matter. You can't get wetter than wet. And you're wet, my dear. You're one of us whether you like it or not. You may as well hear the whole story.

"The Summer Olympics issue is not a red herring. It's real."

Jennifer wrinkled her brow. "You're saying Colonel Donovan really believes the American public will catch Communism like swine flu if they watch a telecast from Moscow?"

Bookmaster shook his head. "Nothing that simple. The Colonel is a virulent anti-Red. No question. But I don't think even he would go that far. What the Colonel wants is a candidate who can persuade the *public* to think that way. Create a national furor. He wants a popular figure who will strike up an orgy of flag-waving that will last until the major networks get dizzy and say the hell with it, they'll drop their negotiations with the Soviets for rights to cover the games."

"That's a tall order."

"That's *minimum*. Optimally, we'd like a create a senator who could effectively introduce a bill making it *illegal* for an American over-the-air network to transmit from a Communist country. That would automatically preclude coverage of the Summer Olympics."

"You still haven't told me why."

"So the Colonel can cover the Summer Olympics."

Jennifer Blade slowly reclined her head on the back of the seat and stared for a moment at the ceiling of the limousine. Then she closed her eyes and massaged her lids with a long forefinger and thumb.

"Again," she said quietly, "with the usual disclaimer concerning disrespect . . . you have totally lost me. You just said—"

Bookmaster was smiling now, like a wicked child charmed with its own cunning. "I just said the Colonel wants to preclude *over-the-air* coverage of the games. The airwaves are vulnerable to legislation because the government has always regarded them as limited monopolies. That still leaves closed-circuit theaters and the cable system—which transmit by wires."

Jennifer, still massaging her eyes, began to nod slowly. "Would I be straying too far into the realm of conjecture if I guessed that the Phaëthon Society is in the closed-circuit business?"

"You're starting to think like a communicator, Jennifer. You're close. The Phaëthon Society isn't into closed circuits *yet*. They want to be. Most of the members are bankers, investment men, owners of big independent broadcast stations. They know which way the winds are blowing in this country. It is their opinion that communications technology is changing faster than most people realize. They think the days of the big networks are numbered. We're on the threshold of a new broadcast society—a new broadcast world. I'm talking about two-way cable—hell, they *have it right now* in Columbus, Ohio. Systems where the audience can talk right back to the programmer. Do you understand what that means, Jennifer? Instant polls. Instant surveys. Instant ratings. Instant *elections*. My God, people are bitching about celebrities running for office. Christ! Can't they see the future in front of their noses? We're looking at the day when you'll have to *be* a celebrity to get elected . . . when there won't be any difference between entertainment and politics . . ."

"Wait!"

Jennifer held up a hand.

"Pardon my plodding, linear mind. This is all fascinating. But I don't see what in the name of God this has to do with Colonel Donovan and the Summer Olympics."

"All right." Bookmaster framed Jennifer's face in the palms of his hands. "I'll spell it out for you, Jenny.

"The Phaëthon Society needs an apparatus. A structure. They need a system of closed-circuit outlets, a *wired network* around the United States . . . *now!* In anticipation of the day when the flow changes, when the Columbus System goes national. They think it's coming soon. They have money—a lot of it. But not the kind of billions it's going to take to wire up the kind of broadcasting machine they're talking about. They need a *big strike*—a guaranteed blockbuster viewing event to supply them with a captive audience . . . so they can lease closed-circuit theaters all over the country with a reasonable guarantee to pay off the lessors . . . charge usurious admission and still play to capacity . . . build an instant identity, so that when the time comes, when the flow changes, when Future Tube arrives . . ."

"The Olympics. They want to close-circuit the Summer Olympics!"

"*Exactly.* And to do that, they've got to get the bidding out of the hands of the networks."

"What if they miscalculate? What if they get the rights and nobody pays to watch?"

"What if the sun comes up over Santa Catalina? Why do you think the networks are flashing a hundred million bucks apiece at the Soviets? Don't you think they know something? Don't you realize the biggest conditioning campaign in the history of television is going on right now, *on each network?* Whipping this country into a frenzy, a froth-mouthed fucking *estrus,* over events they've never *heard of* before? Getting people to idolize athletes they haven't even *seen yet?* It's all *free advertising* for the Colonel if he pulls this thing off. I think he's a goddamn genius for thinking of it. A goddamn *prophet!*"

Bookmaster's upper lip was beaded with perspiration, and he whipped a white handkerchief out of his pocket to mop it. He stared at Jennifer, his eyes shining with an excitement she had never seen there before, not even in the heat of his sexual passion.

"I take it, however, that you're not involved in this out of any deep-dyed political belief."

"Me? Hell, no. I'm a Kennedy liberal." Bookmaster seemed surprised at the question—a non sequitur.

"I hate to sound like such a spoiler, Mal. It all does sound mind-boggling. But there seems to be one basic contradiction—a rather important one."

"*What's that?*" Bookmaster all but grabbed at Jennifer's shoulders in his intensity.

"As I understand it, the Colonel expects everybody in America to pay to watch the Summer Olympics in his theaters. Right after his man in the Senate has convinced everybody that the Summer Olympics will give them Commie cancer or something."

"Oh! That!" Bookmaster threw back his head and gave a high nervous giggle. "Shit." He daubed at his upper lip. "God." He looked out the window and giggled again. "Christ, Jennifer. You sounded like you had something. For a minute there you made my pulse go up."

"Well?"

He ran the handkerchief over his mouth again—the temperature inside the limousine was rising—and stuffed it back in his pocket. He ran a hand through his thinning hair.

"We're covered on that, from several angles. Number one: What Schein will emphasize—hell, what the conservative columnists are hitting at already—is that whichever network gets the winning bid is going to have to make a deal with the Russians. *Quid pro quo.* The Reds will insist on a certain amount of favorable news coverage to sweeten the pot—upbeat propaganda about Soviet life. Pretty shots of the Volga. Bolshoi in action. Maybe worse. 'Worse' is our assumption in Schein's campaign.

"But if the networks drop out and the Russians have to sell to closed circuit, their options for propaganda go down to almost ground zero. No news on closed-circuit. No documentaries. Just the big broads with all the steroids throwing the javelin. You follow?"

Jennifer nodded.

"Number two: the Colonel and his group, the Society, will not be identified as Schein's campaign backers. We already have a front group set up, a Schein for Senator Committee, we have its chairman, prominent investment banker, member of the Society. That's all we need for the filing papers. So the Colonel doesn't talk out of both sides of his face in public. Am I right?"

Jennifer shrugged.

"Point three. A little insight into nonlinear psychology. *Television hasn't got a memory.* There's no past in television. Only the present. The medium just doesn't encourage reflection. What that means is, not that many people are going to make the equation between watching the Olympics on closed circuit and being contaminated in their living rooms. Okay?"

Jennifer sat impassive.

"Point four. Biggest point of all. *Nobody really gives a fuck.* Biggest point of all, Jennifer. Key to any campaign strategy. People will get all hot to throw out the Commies because some good-looking, blond, blue-eyed TV senator is saying they ought to. They'll form all the committees, they'll bury the networks in letter campaigns. Then, shit, they'll go across the street and pay to watch it. You mentioned porn a while ago. How the hell do you think porn survives in this country? Same principle."

Jennifer Blade folded her arms and looked at Mal Bookmaster now with the undisguised admiration that he had sought from her a few minutes earlier. She chewed on her lower lip. She reflected over all that he had said.

"Damn. You must have poured a lot of champagne down me at dinner. I'm sitting here thinking you might be able to put a catatonic comedian in the United States Senate three and a half months from now."

Bookmaster consumed her gesture of admiration with suppressed glee. "Give me two months," he whispered, "and I guarantee you, people are going to barely remember Schein the comedian. Give me two months, the son of a bitch is going to look more statesmanlike than Lincoln. Hell, he's going to look more statesmanlike than Cliff Robertson. The skit with Olds was the beginning, the kickoff, Jenny. Read the papers the next few weeks. The fanzines. Not the big heavyweight critics. They'll murder us. Read the people that count. Read Liz. Rona. Read *Faces*. Read the *Enquirer*. Listen to the radio call-in shows. Watch the TV news. Watch Johnny. Watch Merv. You're gonna see the Robert Schein bandwagon building, Jennifer. You're gonna see it building before it even *knows* it's building!"

Bookmaster's voice was trembling as he finished. Jennifer found herself almost hypnotized by the rhythms of his words. A thought, which had been working at the back of her mind, suddenly flashed into cohesion.

"But you already *have* a client you could run for the Senate. Gareth. He's a proven commodity, and nobody can figure out what the hell side of the spectrum he's on. With him engaged to marry Olds's daughter, he ought to be a natural. Why didn't you—"

Click!

Her tape recorder.

"What the fuck was that?" She could feel Bookmaster's body go hard as a coil next to her.

She had an instant to answer. She fought panic. She wheeled around in the seat and craned her head, peering through the window.

"I think somebody's outside the car!" It worked; Bookmaster was as jumpy as she. He grabbed the door handle. Then he wheeled back to face her.

"Remember, Jennifer. One syllable. One fucking syllable."

She lay awake next to Schein's sleeping body far into the night. He had seemed glad to see her—strange, how she had accustomed herself to thinking about him that way, detached, "seemed glad to see her," as though he were a particularly intelligent and responsive chimpanzee—and his lovemaking had been as always savage, direct, physically tumultuous. Her orgasms with him were like electric circuits fusing.

But, as always, there was the vacuum of emptiness that slipped back over her after the lovemaking. Like a cathode tube cooling. She had wanted to ask him so much: how it was with him, what were his feelings, was he excited, pleased, what was it like to perform with a former president? Did he know, goddammit, that any of it was happening? She had tried, as she often did. He had listened—deferentially, neutrally. His replies were vague, uncomfortable—an adolescent chewing on the Meaning of Life in humanities class.

She had ached to share her trepidations with him, her horror of Bookmaster's plan—to warn him away. But he would not have understood. Besides, to warn him away would be to disconnect the plug to her own future.

At length, she slept.

Teller awoke slumped against the sofa. His mouth felt caked, dry; each intake of breath brought with it a sour taste that he associated with a troubled sleep. It had been a night of demons.

His shirt clung to his back and ribs; perspiration steamed off his body. When he moved his head, lasers of white pain throbbed at his temples.

He rolled to his left and squinted toward the window. The morning light still slanted, glowing against the curtains.

Early yet.

He turned his painful gaze back to the room. An empty wine jug sat on the table by the sofa. Shafts of sunlight brought up evil green highlights in the glass. He had never learned to drink and never would—a serious drawback, he considered, for one who was a failure in all else as well.

The wine jug reminded him that Elizabeth had left, that he would not be seeing her again. Odyssey. Happy Independence Day. First considerations first. Get the foul dryness out of his mouth.

He shuffled on hands and knees to his television set, snapped it on. He clicked the dial away from Channel 26—CBN did not have a morning news show. Channel 2—CBS—was the first channel to come up after the UHF band. He left the selector there and stumbled toward the refrigerator. He had an enormous craving for orange juice.

Already the apartment was hot with sunshine. He had not turned the air conditioning on last night. He stripped off his shirt and stood with the refrigerator door open, letting the cool air play on his chest. The bright refrigerator light hurt his eyes. He groped for the orange juice.

From the muffled sound of the TV set back in the living room, he thought he heard a familiar name. He grasped the bottle of orange juice, closed the refrigerator door, and padded back toward the living room.

John Hart's face filled the screen.

" . . . Already spokesmen for the other networks, including CBS, have taken the unprecedented step of jointly rebuking CBN for, quote, 'allowing a patently partisan political message to be broadcast on its airwaves in the guise of entertainment.' "

Teller put down the orange juice and slowly sank into the sofa.

"While the nation's major television critics mocked the skit on esthetic terms," Hart continued, "—*The New York Times* assailing 'Moo-cow sentimentality'—bipartisan committees in both the House and Senate were issuing various calls for a censure of CBN by the Federal Communications Commission, and for air time to rebut the point of view that restricting coverage of an international sporting event could be justified in ideological—"

Teller switched the dial to Channel 4.

Tom Pettit of NBC was interviewing the president of NBC News.

"I quite frankly don't know which was more offensive to me," the news president was saying. "CBN's allowing a potential candidate for the Presidency a forum in which to sell his politics wrapped up in a pretty entertainment package—or CBN's rather shameless proselytizing in its own business interests."

"What do you mean, 'business interests'?" No soft touch for his bosses, that Pettit.

The NBC executive coughed into his fist. "I mean it's been obvious to everyone for weeks that Colonel Donovan's network just doesn't have the financial resources to bid with the rest of us on securing the Summer Olympics coverage. Now, you add those two factors together, Tom, and what you've got is a pretty dark moment in the history of—"

Even through the haze of his hangover, Teller sensed instinctively that the NBC executive was following at least one false trail.

"It's not Olds you have to worry about, buddy," he breathed. "It's Schein."

He clicked to Channel 7.

Geraldo Rivera was standing in front of the Commerce Center— framed dramatically between two of the Six Captains.

". . . those of us who take our profession *seriously* as *jern*alists," he was saying in his familiar arrested-adolescent tenor. "Now, Aw-ie may get in trouble with maw-ie *baw*-ses at ABC for *sighing* this—" roguish half-winks, defiance at the fates— "but *Aw*-ie *feel* that when *Establishment rip-offs* of the *media* like this one occur, they endanger the *fray*-dom of each and every—"

Teller switched off the set. It was going to be a gruesome day at WRAP, he knew. And he was in no condition for an *average* day.

He gripped the orange juice bottle by the neck and took it into the bathroom. He felt around the medicine cabinet for the aspirin.

We'll let the stomach bleed a little, he thought. There'll be plenty more bleeding before the day is over.

He read the newspaper accounts of the Schein special in the cab en route to the studio. The *Times* played it on page one, below the fold. The other morning papers, the tabloids, had it up near the front.

The news accounts followed the CBS news report: industry outrage, critical derision, angry blusterings from Democrats in Congress. Apparently, reaction had mobilized as soon as the Schein special had left the air.

He turned to the inside pages of each paper. The *Times* review was predictably judgmental and overwrought, as Hart had indicated. Teller was intrigued to find, however, that the other papers reviewed Olds and Schein's performance in purely television terms.

The *Daily News* called the skit "Welby-esque," and remarked that "Redford look-alike Schein dispelled all doubts that he could switch gears from comedy to sensitive drama without a hitch."

The *Messenger* critic, who prided himself on being not so easily taken in, pointed out knowingly that the Olds-Schein combination was "a variation on the hoariest human-interest ploy in television's bag of tricks, the old-cop, young-cop combo, with funnyman Schein playing Michael Douglas to Prexy-turned-thespian Olds's Karl Malden."

"Still," the *Messenger* critic allowed, "the formula worked. Schein brought a surprisingly persuasive sensitivity to his cameo dramatic debut—and as for Mr. Olds, well, it was refreshing to see a politician turn actor for a change, instead of vice versa."

That point of view, Teller suspected, would set the tone for critical reaction out in the heartland.

Well, that was somebody else's problem. Teller's problem was to get to Ed Kurtis before the day heated up, and talk his way out of a review of Schein's performance. He shouldn't have much trouble, he reasoned. Kurtis was hardly the gung-ho organization man that Bass had been. Besides, an in-house laudatory review of last night's debacle would only compound the firestorm of criticism raining down on the Continental Broadcasting Network and its divisions.

The *WRAP-Around* newsroom was in an uproar. Telephones jangled continuously. As Teller entered, the phone clerk brandished a receiver above her head.

"Question about Schein," she shouted above the din. "Is he married? Who wants to take it?"

Nobody did. The staff had assembled more than an hour earlier than usual. It was one of those spontaneous fusions, a collective instinct to gather, that affects any news department after a crisis. Reporters, producers, rewrite people, editors, even technical crew (for whom the newsroom was normally off-limits) clustered in small, noisy knots around the room—reading aloud from the morning papers, arguing, dueling one another with mordant wisecracks.

"This sort of thing would never have happened while V.W. Olds was alive," Sean Murphy announced from his usual position atop a desk.

Tony Cazzini, at Murphy's feet, spotted Teller. "And speaking of Moo-cow sentimentality," he shouted, "here comes the man who first brought Robert Schein to the attention of the people of America. Let's see if we can get through to have a word with him!"

Cazzini moved toward Teller, pointing an imaginary microphone at him, an evil glint in his eye. Teller was in no mood for Cazzini's mouth, and was bristling to tell him so, when a commanding voice cut through the newsroom din:

"*Teller!*"

It was Ed Kurtis.

He was standing in the middle of the newsroom—a squat fireplug of authority at the center of confusion. Teller noticed that he had taken to wearing a suit since his promotion to station manager. Maybe there was hope the old tiger would be civilized, he thought with affection.

He turned toward Kurtis, but the beetle-browed executive was already pistoning toward him.

"You better have your writing hat on today, Teller," he roared as he made his way across the newsroom. "We got our ass in a public-relations sling and we need some of your high-minded prose to help get us unslung." He stopped directly in front of Teller and glared up at him.

"If your piece sings the way I hope it sings, it goes on the network news. The Colonel has requested it and I said I knew you could come through. This might be your big network break, Teller."

Teller gaped down at Kurtis with his mouth open.

"Ed, you know as well as I do that program was a piece of shit, the papers are right—"

Kurtis took Teller's elbow and steered him toward the corridor.

"I had an idea you were going to try and pull this," he muttered. "Let's get out where we can talk."

Outside, Teller wheeled on Kurtis.

"Ed, you're smarter than this. I'll look like a whore, you'll look like a madam, the station'll look like a whorehouse. You've bailed me out of these things before. Goddammit, for *everybody's* good—"

The eyes that stared up at him were the eyes of a stranger.

"I told you a long time ago," said Ed Kurtis, "that you were going to have to make up your mind about this station. *Now don't lecture me about whores, buddy. Or I'll tell you about parasites.* Now you have a script on my desk by noon or you fuckin' don't work here at five o'clock. *Now get outta my way, I got work to do!"*

Teller stared at Kurtis's retreating back until it was lost amid the newsroom jumble. He thought of Elizabeth's words: "Poison in the walls . . ."

Then he shrugged, went to his office cubicle, rolled a sheet of paper into his typewriter, and began:

"It is ridiculous to suggest, as many have, that last night's Robert Schein special produced some sort of obscene blot on the record of American television.

"I discovered Robert Schein, and I've had the pleasure of knowing him both as a comedian and as a human being . . ."

Colonel Eddie Donovan's voice was shouting in Bookmaster's ear.

"Bookmaster, what have you done to my network!"

Bookmaster peered at the illuminated dial on his bedside alarm clock.

"Colonel, you might be forgetting that it's only six in the morning on the Coast. I'll be happy to talk business with you at nine my time, noon your—"

"Have you read the bloody papers! Have you seen the morning news! They're tearing our throat out, Bookmaster!"

"I told you, Colonel, that you'd have to expect some rough treatment from the middlebrow sector of the—"

"Middlebrow! Middlebrow! They're after my station licenses in the Senate! I've been publicly humiliated by my own colleagues! By Christ, I was mad to listen to you, Bookmaster! You've persuaded me to run a saloon comic for the Senate and now you've made my network a laughingstock—" the old man's Irish voice was thick and choked with rage—

"You're fired, Bookmaster! Bloody fucking fired, oh, Jaysus, Mary, and Joseph, you've torn down what it took me twenty-five years to build . . ."

The voice on the other end dissolved into uncontrollable sobbing. The Colonel did not hang up, Bookmaster noted—a fact that confirmed his notion as to the true nature of the call.

He waited, adjusting the silken bedsheets around him, inwardly disgusted, until the choking and gasping on the other end subsided. Then he said, in his quietest and deadliest voice:

"You're overwrought, Colonel. It's Friday. By Monday afternoon, when you have crawled back on your hands and knees to apologize to me, I'll be perfectly happy to forget that this conversation ever took place."

At 10:13 A.M., the *Times*'s second-string TV critic, whose review of the Schein special had run that morning, held up a telegram with his thumb and forefinger, by the very edge of one corner, as though it were a dead rat he had found on his desk.

He deposited it in front of the feature writer next to him. The *Times*'s second-string TV critic was a Williams College grad, whose primary field of interest was post-Impressionist painting. He was not used to the sort of language that was contained in the telegram.

"Would you have a look at this, Robert?"

Robert read:

> YOU FROGFACED LIMP WRISTED FAGGOT YOUR JUST JEALOUS YOUR NOT AS HANDSOME AS ROBERT SCHEIN ALSO HE'S A TRUE PATRIOT AND YOUR KIND ONLY TEARS DOWN THERE ARE THOUSANDS OF US PS I DARE YOU TO PRINT THIS
>
> BETTY SPRING
>
> PRESIDENT ROBERT SCHEIN
> FAN CLUB NY CHAPTER

"Yecch," said Robert. "They're out there, you know. They breed in the sewer system."

At 10:52, a group of five hundred persons with placards and banners formed a line on Fifth Avenue in front of Rockefeller Center. The placards and banners said SOUR GRAPES! and NBC—GET OFF SCHEIN'S BACK, and WHY DOES MEDIA KNOCK AMERICANISM?

By 11:30 the crowd had grown tenfold. It formed a human daisy chain around Rockefeller Center, chanting:

"BOOOOY, IS NBC'S FAAAAAAAACE REEEEED!"

At 11:45, a caller informed a New York radio talk show that there would be a rally of Bobby Schein's fans in Washington Square Park. The caller was a crank; he had no knowledge of a rally.

At 11:56, Mark Teller walked into Ed Kurtis's office and dropped a commentary script on his desk.

"If you like it, send it on down to TelePrompTer," he muttered, and stalked out the door.

"I'm glad you're being reasonable, Mark," Kurtis called after him. "Hey. Stand you to a martini after the show." But Teller was gone.

At 1:34, a New York Police Department squad car radioed for reinforcements at Washington Square. A mob of yelling, prancing, fist-brandishing Robert Schein fans—mostly young, mostly female—had blocked traffic all the way back to Herald Square.

New York's television stations hesitated, for an average of three minutes apiece, and then dispatched videotape crews. Schein was CBN's Folly. That made it a bitch to cover.

On the other hand, there was a mob scene. Television assignment editors ignored a mob scene the way an icicle ignored a blowtorch.

On the fringes of the crowd, an elderly man with a skull face pedaled an armload of red T-shirts at thirty-five dollars a throw. The T-shirts proclaimed, "BOOOOOY, WAS MYYYYY FAAACE RED!"

A roving TV crew spotted the old man.

"No, I don't begrudge Bobby a thing," said Al Gnagy, looking the camera dead in the eye. "Great guy, great talent, I wish him all the best, I'm just happy to be able to say he got his start at Stitch's . . ."

"I just love him," shrilled a blond girl into a microphone. "I think he's great, I think he looks great, I think he's sincere and I just wish the media would leave him alone—" she broke off in sobs, inspired more by the sudden overwhelming whiff of her own profundity—certified by the attentive camera, the respectful mike—than by any feeling toward Robert Schein.

A cameraman twisted his lens for a zoom close-up of her heaving tear-streaked face.

By 2:30 P.M., the wire services reported collective expressions of support for Robert Schein in Chicago, Los Angeles, Atlanta, Pittsburgh, and South Bend. In Saint Louis a group of Playboy Bunnies called a press conference to announce "White Tails for Ol' Red Face."

At 3 P.M., L. Malcolm Bass walked into Colonel Eddie Donovan's office.

"Colonel, I'm getting reports from all over the country that people are getting *silly* over Robert Schein—uh, that is, they're expressing great support for him. I think we have some kind of popular ground swell on our hands." He handed the Colonel a sheaf of wire service reports.

When the old man looked back up at Bass, there were tears in his eyes. "I thought we were ruined," he whispered.

"Malcolm—" he pointed to the wire copy—"*this* is your newscast tonight."

At 5:39 P.M., Mark Teller finished pinning the lavaliere microphone to his lapel, stacked his script copy on his knee, and waited in the trumped-up intensity of the studio lights for the commercial break to end. Mom, Dad, and the Kids were singing life-insurance hosannas. The seconds oozed. There was something about the studio lights that not only intensified color and movement, but made the senses themselves seem to leap ahead of time. Teller always found himself possessed with the ability to think more clearly and quickly under the studio lights than he could otherwise. It was as though his mind, charged with the artificial energy of the arc lights, could pry apart the frames of time itself; expand, isolate, linger on instants.

Perhaps it was that strange property of the arc lights—and not just the thirst for fame—that drew sojourners such as Lon Stagg to a life under these lights. Reality expanded here, welled and paused like brookwater in a deep pool. *WRAP-Around* as the Fountain of Youth.

He stole a glance at Lon Stagg, slumped a few feet away beneath a macrame pot, idly drumming his fingers on the anchor desk-surface, absorbed in the commercial on the monitor screen. The Fountain of Youth hadn't worked for Stagg. False promise. The flesh was sagging at lip and chin. White-ringleted child, he of the shoulder moues and the beguiling pouts, was growing old.

"Ten seconds," called the floor director.

Stagg glanced up and caught Teller's gaze. He favored Teller with a wink—hell, no harm in keeping up personal public relations, even with the egghead element—and made a circle with thumb and index finger.

"Read your script," he mouthed. "Outtasight."

"*And* five."

Stagg's eyes shot to Camera One, and he leaned his shoulder in like a gossamer fullback hitting the line.

The director pointed; the camera light went red.

"Over the last ninety minutes we've given you a comprehensive report on the controversy that erupted last night between our station, our network—and some elements of the press—over that Robert Schein special."

Stagg paused, and lifted a corner of his mouth in an ironic smile.

"Perhaps the one man in America best qualified to put the Robert Schein affair in perspective is sitting next to me."

Camera One pulled back for a wide shot of Stagg and Teller.

"Our commentator Mark Teller is an expert on Robert Schein —after all, Mark spotted his talent before anyone else—and he's a media specialist as well." Stagg pivoted.

"Mark."

Time slowed. Teller was conscious of the universe around him, every particle in it—the glint of light in a cameraman's glasses, a script girl's slouch, the electric halo of light about Lon Stagg's smiling face.

"Thank you, Lon."

He saw his TelePrompTer copy come up full and clear, like a sunrise, on the transparent Plexiglas screen over the camera lens.

He began reading:

"It is ridiculous to suggest, as many have, that last night's Robert Schein special produced some sort of obscene blot on the record of American television."

Teller dropped his eyes to the script in his hands, and continued in the same detached, professional tone of voice:

"The record of American television is covered with obscene blots. One more could hardly be said to produce much of a separate stain.

"What happened on the Continental Broadcasting Network last night was business as usual. The business is selling. The selling never stops. Potato chips, presidents, personalities, pills, politics, points of view, pet food. It's all the same package. And the friendly folks at CBN—and the other networks as well—are betting you're not bright enough to know the difference."

In the control room, Teller's face appeared on six monitor screens—four in color, two smaller ones in black and white. Two banks of editors, directors, and technical personnel sat facing the screens, talking in a low-key babble, checking clipboards, making on-the-spot decisions as to which of Lon Stagg's upcoming news items had to be shortened, or tossed out, to conform to the constantly fluctuating rule of the stopwatch.

A lone assistant director sat frowning at Teller's image on the screen. He peered down at a carbon of the commentator's script.

"Hey," he said aloud, but to no one in particular. "I don't think Teller's following his 'PrompTer copy."

Several faces glanced up sharply.

"So why all the furor over last night? Well, CBN has created a wonderful new product to sell—an instant personality called *Robertschein*. All you do is add words."

"He's gone off his nut!" yelled the assistant director at the control panel. He wheeled around to face his superior, the new news director, a man named Phillips. "YOU WANT FADE TO BLACK?"

Phillips froze. His mind raced furiously, clawing at the alternatives. If he faded to black—Teller wasn't being obscene—he'd catch hell for censorship. If he didn't fade, it was his ass. He had to decide.

"Stand by," Phillips instructed the control room. "Stand by . . ."

"What does this product do? An amazing thing: It—sells— *products*! It sells itself, of course. And it sells T-shirts . . . and magazines and newspapers . . . it sells the CBN Network, which in turn can sell more potato chips, pills, and pet food. And personalities. Perhaps you begin to perceive a pattern."

In his new office on the thirtieth floor—Bass's old one—Ed Kurtis stared at the screen transfixed, the sauerkraut from a Reuben sandwich dangling unchewed from his lips. He shook his head, spat the mouthful onto his desktop, and fumbled under his tundra of papers for the white hot-line telephone that connected to the control room.

"Last night the makers of *Robertschein* used him to sell you a political product called *Instant Ban-Games*. Perhaps they were selling another product as well—*Family Style VicOlds*. Perhaps *VicOlds* was selling *Robertschein*. Perhaps they were selling each other. It was hard to tell."

"PHILLIPS, YOU FUCKING IDIOT, GET THAT BAS-
TARD OFF THE AIR!"

Phillips replaced the telephone carefully. Had to remain calm.
First rule of an emergency.

"Stand by . . ." he instructed the A.D. "Stand by . . . stand
by . . ."

In the studio, light was dawning on Lon Stagg. He had come out
of the stupor he normally sank into while Teller was talking. He
listened, incredulous, for several seconds. Then he began yelling
at the floor director:

"FADE TO BLACK! FADE TO BLACK!"

His screams were audible off-mike as Teller proceeded through
his commentary.

Teller inclined his head toward Stagg.

"Lon was correct. I did discover *Robertschein*. I regret it and
repudiate everything I might have said in his behalf."

From the corner of his eye, he saw Stagg coming out of his
chair.

"But in the end, *Robertschein* is not the enemy. He's neutral. *It
is the people who have programmed and packaged him . . . invisible people, but powerful . . .*"

He was racing now, trying to get it all in, trying the old trick of
breaking down time, freezing the frames. It astounded him that
the red camera light was still on. But now Lon Stagg was on top of
him, lunging at him with a roar . . .

Teller leaped to his own feet and thrust out his long arms,
blunting Stagg's charge. He braced himself, planted both hands on
Stagg's chest, and gave the anchorman a savage shove.

The shove propelled Stagg back into his swivel chair with
trajectory force. The chair, with Stagg in it, careened on its rollers
down the long shiny causeway that was the *WRAP-Around* anchor
module—upsetting Tiffany lamps, shooting under flower pots,
until it reached the edge of the raised platform. It crashed among
cables and light standards, sending Stagg sprawling in a backward
somersault.

The Camera One cameraman, like the trained professional he
was, swiveled his lens around to follow Stagg's flight.

Then—there was nothing else to do—he focused back on Mark
Teller.

Teller said what he always said at the end of a commentary.

"Over to you, Lon." He unfastened his lavaliere mike and walked off the set.

"FADE TO BLACK!" Phillips had reached a decision in the control room.

Teller flung open the heavy door to the corridor and strode down it at a measured pace. He was headed for the elevator. Nothing important on his desk anyway, not now. If they wanted him they knew where they could find him.

He heard the footsteps clacking, running. Ed Kurtis and L. Malcolm Bass rounded the corner at the same time.

"AAAARRRRRRRUUUUUUUGGGGGGGGHHHHHHH," roared Bass, and reached out his hands. Spittle swung from his lip and jaw.

Teller ducked his first lunge easily.

"Ed, for you I am truly sorry," he declared, keeping his eyes on the network news chief. "You're a good man, but . . . ."

Bass had regained his balance and was readying for a second charge.

" . . . poison in the walls . . ."

Bass plunged at him.

Teller stepped aside, cocking his right arm as he did so. He drilled Bass under the corner of his right eye, letting the executive's own momentum supply most of the damage. Bass went down in a rumple of seersucker.

"And for you, Mr. Bass, I'm happy. You're finally in on the genesis of a news event."

He started down the corridor, then stopped and turned back.

"By the way, Ed—I'm thinking seriously of quitting."

He walked outside the main entrance to the Commerce Center, into the blazing late-afternoon sun. This was the time of day he had always liked best, the time when the sunlight did its magic on the bronze busts of the Six Captains; cupreous needles of sunlight . . .

He had met Jennifer Blade out here once. For dinner and a show. He remembered the night.

Nowhere to go now but home. Hang around town for a few weeks, catch a few ball games, run some, get back into top shape, close down the apartment—then he'd see. Maybe back to the Ozarks.

Big joke. Big joke of being *here*. An Ozark boy in New York, telling the most sophisticated people in the world about themselves, about celebrity*hood*.

Well. He'd told them.

It was funny, he thought in the taxicab. There was no exhilaration in playing the hero. No sense of having given comeuppance to the rascals, none of that Johnny Mack Brown, Hopalong Cassidy *noblesse* he used to get off on as a Saturday-matinee kid. Riding off into the sunset was not that big a deal. He'd made a major fool of himself on live television, punched a guy out—maybe a lawsuit in that, could claim self-defense; probably gotten three or four guys fired, including Kurtis, poor bastard—ruined his own career—and he hadn't dented the surface of what tormented him.

The villain was too big, too elusive. Villain was the airwaves themselves, he guessed.

He disembarked from the taxi a block from his apartment and walked slowly up Riverside Drive in the suppertime heat. Windows were open above his head; he could hear the murmured cadence of the evening news.

Ten steps from his doorway a woman called his name.

"Mark? Mark Teller?"

He turned around.

She was large, white sleeveless blouse above meaty arms, turquoise pants, white sandals. She fluttered a hand at him, smiling gaily.

"Are you Mark? I thought so. I watch you on the news." She was hurrying toward him, panting from the exertion.

"I saw what you did tonight on Robert Schein. And you know what I thought?" Her smiling face was under his; her eyes gleamed up at him.

The woman spat in his face.

"That's what I thought, you homosexual nut for tearing down Robert Schein . . ."

She waddled hurriedly down the street, her voice diminishing.

Teller wiped the saliva from his cheek with the sleeve of his suit jacket. He entered the apartment. His body felt heavy, old, going up the stairs.

He turned the last level, toward his apartment.

"Hi. Gee, you looked terrible on the news tonight."

She was perched cross-legged in front of his door. Cotton scarf holding her hair back. Baby-blue jeans, pretty white ankles, floppy sandals.

"I brought you this." She held up a jug of red wine. "I thought you had a free binge coming."

She was on her feet, turning her lips up to him, closing her blue eyes as he reached out to her . . .

"What about your odyssey," he murmured into the hollow of her neck, several minutes later.

"Oh, that. That's off." They kissed again, her mouth sliding sweetly open under his. Her back was warm and damp under his hand that pressed her to him.

She broke away and traced his lips with her tongue.

"There's only one problem," she whispered. "I gave up my apartment."

Teller told her how he thought they could solve that problem.

Schein.

The name entered the language. It was spliced into the cluttered stereo track of American consciousness. Robert Schein. *Robertschein.*

Robert Schein? Gee, I think he's terrific. He's like really funny and in real life, you know, he's this really serious guy. He's like into politics.

Citizen of the late-afternoon talk shows and the morning game shows, *Robertschein* lived on that mythical block between Monte and Merv. Cut-up on *Beverly Hills Bonanza.*

"What is *Delphi*, Bobby?"

"Delphi, Delphi . . . town on Mount Parnassus . . . beautiful town . . . in fact I'd say it's the *Athens of Greece!*"

(laughter)

" . . . *Then we rented a car at Budget and we drove from Vegas to L.A. and stayed at Holiday Inn in Hollywood? And we saw the taping of the Griff Michaels show, and you know who was on it, that Robert Schein? And Herb hates me saying this but I will anyway he is a gorgeous man his hair is just as yellow in person as it is on television I got one shot of him that's him you can hardly make him out in the corner . . ."*

His face looked down on cities for Natur-Pak Orange Drink Mix (artificially flavored) and in television commercials, business-suited, he told Americans that:

"I'm *Robertschein*. And I won't lie to you. Professional entertainers like myself make money. Good money. In the short run. Long-range financial security? Well, that's something else again. That's why . . ."

I won't lie to you. . . .

"Our next guest is a guy who's getting to be more of a regular on this show than *I* am." (laughter) "Tommy just woke up, he thought I said *more regular*." (laughter) "Tommy's idea of a good time is to get high on a six-pack of *prunes*." (laughter) "Will you welcome please, Mr. *Robertschein*."

THE SEXY NEWSQUEEN IN BOB SCHEIN'S LIFE

In this Issue:

Robert Schein on
What I Look for in a Woman
(Hint: It Isn't Just Looks)

". . . Sentinel Insurance understands guys like me . . . understands we care about security the same way we care about this great land of ours. So whether *you're* a celebrity in Hollywood . . . or back in your own backyard . . . investigate Sentinel Insurance. That way, you won't *ever* have to say . . ."

BOOOOOY WAAAAAAAS MYYYY FAAAAACE REEEEEED
Nation's New Hit Catchphrase

I won't lie to you. . . .

"*Robert Schein? He's a Libra and he's a comedian who's really serious on the inside and he's single and I bet if you went out to Hollywood where he's at he'd be a really nice guy, like down to earth.*"

"Can I say something? One thing?"

"What?"

"Something serious? Just . . . one serious thing."

"What."

"I know people are not supposed to get serious on your show."

"Are you kidding? Thus far tonight we have made *Lowell Thomas Remembers* look like *Saturday Night Live.*" (laughter, applause) "What's on your mind?"

"Well—I know Hollywood types aren't supposed to have opinions. Right? But—you know, you hear all this talk about how our leaders are *losing their resolve* in terms of, you know, military superiority."

"Yes, I always wondered exactly what it means to *lose* your *resolve*. I mean, how does . . ." (scattered laughter)

"I lost mine when I was twelve." (oohs, ahhs, laughter, applause) "Just kidding, folks. Really.

"No, but seriously. I read the papers a lot—and I just want to tell you about a group of guys—about a hundred sixty-*two* of them —and they're in Congress—and they've formed a committee to make sure that the U.S. of A. stays *one notch ahead* of our friends in the Soviet Union when it comes to those big skyrockets and popguns. Right? And I wanta say—" (interrupted by prolonged applause)

"—*I* wanta say that *I can dig it!* I come from New York. Right? And when you grow up in New York, you know it doesn't do any good to be the *second* baddest kid on the block. I had a buddy named Knuckle Eddie. Right?" (laughter) "And he . . ."

"Take these tapes, Robert, and just run them through when you have a . . ."

Cover Story:
TV'S SCHEINING LIGHT

He is a comedian who thinks serious thoughts. He is a darling of Hollywood sophisticates, whose favorite meal is a Florida orange. He is a private person whose rumored romance with a network newswoman became the talk of the country. He is an open sort who refuses to discuss his family or background. He is an affable soul who drove a New York TV commentator into an on-air frenzy. He is . . .

The Cover:
SCHEIN ON, SCHEIN

He is that rarest of specimens of *comedianus Hollywoodus*: the topical jokesmith who also confesses to deep political beliefs. He is a figure family-familiar to millions of Americans, but whose personal background remains shrouded in ambiguity. He is a fashioner of facile catchphrases who, in personal conversation, sometimes lapses into helpless silences. He is a pop phenomenon in a cutthroat milieu who can behave off-camera like a little boy lost. He is . . .

"Robert Schein? He's handsome, witty, sexy . . . and when he talks about America's place in the world market, I feel that he's talking to me."

"Twice the impact of any other leading personality."

"Looks . . . brains . . . a way with ideas. Yeah, I'm switching to Robertschein."

And I won't lie to you. . . .

"The Tonight Show Starring Johnny Carson. Johnny's guest host tonight . . . *Robertschein! . . ."*

Six weeks after Mark Teller left WRAP, the station sent him three large brown envelopes—the accumulated mail in response to his attack on the Schein special.

He opened the first envelope and sifted through the letters. Of the first ten he opened, five were unsigned. Three were death threats.

Contained among the more readable letters were such sentiments as:

"If Robert Schein is as bad as you say he is why is he a famous star and your only on the news."

"You must be ashamed of yourself for haveing scarred his soul for life. I pray for you in my prayers."

"I think your choice of words were very poorly chosen."

A television column in *The New York Messenger:*

"One of the worst-kept secrets in television as the fall season nears is CBN's decision to dump its Peabody Award-winning prime-time newsmag, *CBN Reports,* and replace it with a video version of *Faces* magazine.

"CBN Network Correspondent Jennifer Blade, the ravishing reporter who cut her teeth in the hard-news arena at WRAP, will neither confirm nor deny reports that she will host the celebrity-interview format.

"CBN insiders, meanwhile, are privately bitter over the junking of a public-affairs vehicle that in the past uncovered such major scandals as . . ."

Teller's violent exodus from *WRAP-Around News* had made him an overnight celebrity.

The New York papers splashed the story on their Saturday front pages. Typically, the accounts skimmed over the substance of Teller's commentary and dwelt instead on his scuffles with Stagg and L. Malcolm Bass.

A *Daily News* photographer had happened to be watching Teller's commentary in the photo lab. When he heard the critic begin to lacerate his own network, the astonished photographer grabbed a nearby camera on a hunch and aimed it at the TV screen. One of his clicks caught Teller shoving Stagg into his swivel chair.

The *Daily News* ran the photo, massively blown up, across two inside pages, almost palpably savoring the caption:

HE'S MAD AS HELL AND HE'S NOT GOING TO TAKE IT ANYMORE.

The photograph was subsequently nominated for a Pulitzer prize.

By Sunday, digging reporters from three papers had triumphantly arrived at a "motive" for Teller's "on-air rampage." Each quoted a "highly placed but anonymous" WRAP source (who had white-ringleted hair and a sybaritic pout) that the outburst was triggered by jealousy.

CRITIC TANTRUM TIED TO BLADE TRIANGLE

Slurped the Sunday *Messenger.*

When Teller's eye fell on that—at breakfast with Elizabeth—he hurled his coffee mug against the living room wall.

"I'd try to control that," observed Elizabeth idly. "They have more dirt than we have mugs."

"*I want the bastard.*" The words trickled between clenched teeth. Teller was standing now, facing the window, twisting the *Messenger* into an ugly, clublike roll.

"I know. We went through that Friday night. Among other

things. You're not going to get him with coffee mugs. Coffee mugs are out of season, anyway."

Teller turned around slowly to face her. His features, so boyish and carefree when she had first seen him more than a year ago, now were strained, and somehow old.

"I'm way past kidding about this." His voice was a snarl.

She kept hers light, gently chiding.

"So I gathered from watching you on television that day. That's one big reason I decided to stick around. Remember? For a nice divorced lady from Pittsburgh, I do enjoy a good fight. But not with coffee mugs, Mark."

She was glad to see some of the tension, the anguish, drain from his face. He walked, lanky and smooth in his cutoff jeans, back to where she was perched on the floor by the coffee table in a pink half-slip.

She teased him with her tongue as he leaned down to kiss her. One of his big hands slid along the silken inside of her leg. She welcomed the touch. The strong fingers, so gentle now, could squeeze her flesh in a painful vise if Teller willed it, and she liked knowing that. She had watched Teller at the station before that day they became acquainted, the day she left, and although he had attracted her, there were times when the fantasy of his caress would have been distasteful. Those were the days when Jennifer Blade's name was first being linked to Robert Schein's; when Teller's "secret" affair with the beautiful reporter was unraveling in full view of the WRAP newsroom. Teller had shriveled. His attraction for her had waned. The thought of his fingers on her skin would have produced an association with cold scales.

But now the strength was back in Teller's veins. The fingers could caress or crush, and she liked that. Their potential frightened her at times, but it thrilled her. She knew the fingers were waiting to close around a certain quarry.

"Sorry, Elizabeth," he murmured after a long, lingering kiss. "Shouldn't take it out on you." He dropped down beside her, his hand slipping around her back and under her arm to cradle her breast.

She shrugged. "Just remember who the primary target is." She twisted in his arms so that her blue eyes were peering into his. "That, by the way, is important. Above and beyond my own health and welfare. Remember what you said on the air that

Friday. Just before you did your Richard Widmark number on Stagg. 'Robert Schein is not the enemy. It's the people who have programmed him,' et cetera."

"The way I feel right now, Robert Schein is the enemy." He stared at the ceiling, lost in a mood.

After several minutes, he said:

"All right. Schein is not the enemy."

"Now you're talking like a grown-up."

"But somebody close to him is. Even if I didn't hate the bastard personally—"

"Watch it—"

"—I think I'd still have the notion he's dangerous. It's almost like he's leading a charmed life." Teller sat upright. "I mean, look. Look at Friday. I only throw away a freaking television career for the privilege of saying that somebody is pulling Robert Schein's strings so that he can pull ours. And what comes out of it? What gets played up in the papers? Not my big speech. No. *Not* anything about the issue of mass mind-fucking on TV. Nossir. What gets played up is that Mark Teller pushed X and punched out Y; Mark Teller's *jealous* of Robert Schein. Thumb-sucking stuff. And the bastard comes out of it looking even better than before. *Free publicity!* I throw my *job* at that zombie and it comes out *free publicity . . .!*"

He was up and pacing the living room, fingers dug into his cutoff jeans pockets.

"Aren't we straying from the subject?" Elizabeth extended a white arm toward him.

"Are we?"

"I thought you wanted to get at the, uh, enemy."

Teller gestured in a circle with his hand. "The enemy," he repeated.

"Maybe I have a clue for you."

He turned, his features instantly composed and attentive.

"The guy who's supposed to be managing Schein? Bookmaster?"

Teller shifted his gaze to the rug, instantly disappointed.

"Yeah. Big mover in Hollywood. Jennifer probably got them together. What of him, he manages half the famous people in this country."

"Didn't you ever wonder why a man of his stature would take on somebody as marginal as Schein?"

Teller lifted his eyes. She had his interest again.

"Another clue," she said.

"Lay it on me."

"I believe that this Bookmaster is a close friend of Colonel Donovan's. I mean a *very* close friend."

He dropped down in front of her, searching her face intently.

"How do you know that?"

"What's the matter, Teller—you think I'm just another pretty face? Hey, I was a reporter and weekend anchorwoman at that sweatshop. I was in Donovan's office a few times. I'm nosy, Mark. I know things about that station that'd make you—"

"*Why didn't you tell me that before?*" Some of the mottled strain was returning to his face. She smoothed his cheek with the backs of her fingers.

"Haven't had a chance. Do you remember yesterday? I hardly came up for air." He was beginning to grin, despite himself. "In fact I've been meaning to talk to you about setting down some written agreements on the limits of my obligations around here, you sex maniac." She nibbled his lip.

"How about oral?"

"You goat." She giggled. Then she pulled back. "But really, Mark. If you're going to follow through with this thing, that might be a place to start looking."

But he was already looking, she noticed as she lifted her face toward the ceiling, in another place.

The Monday following his walkoff at WRAP, Mark Teller was contacted for an interview on *Good Morning, America*. He accepted eagerly.

"Are you self-destructive?" was the interviewer's first question.

Teller was unprepared for the question. "What do you mean?"

The interviewer gave him a knowing smile and tossed her hair.

"People are saying that your outburst on the air last Friday was triggered by jealousy that Robert Schein had taken your girl away from you. And by *girl*, of course, I mean Jennifer Blade. I guess I can use that name on this show. Really, Mark. Is *any* woman worth a career?"

Teller swallowed his astonishment and indignation.

"I don't think my personal life is all that interesting," he made himself say in a neutral voice. "What I was getting at—and what

I'd like to get at here—is the whole question of prepackaging an *idea,* a point of *view,* and selling it to the American—"

"Pardon me for interrupting. But you're changing the subject. What *I* want to know is, is it true that Jennifer Blade and Robert Schein are—"

"You are totally missing the point—"

"The point *is,* how could a man in your position throw away a promising career—"

"I was trying to draw people's attention to the issue of—"

"Do you believe that love and a career can mix?"

After that, Teller did not accept any further invitations to be on television interview shows.

"I thought somebody might at least offer me a job," he admitted to Elizabeth. "You know—'See the Krazy Kommentator Lose His Mind every Monday, Wednesday, and Friday right here on our show.'"

"I assume you've wised up. No, you're more valuable as a walk-on than walk-off. You're a two-headed cow now, Mark. Better face it. A curiosity. You and the Plant Doctor and the Astrologist."

He wrote to newspapers, offering his services as a columnist. Most did not bother to reply. One that did—a large Eastern paper of impeccable reputation—confined its rejection to a single question:

"Do you think we are morons here?"

The invitations for him to *be* interviewed, however, continued in a steady stream.

Faces magazine was among those Teller refused.

Then one day in August Teller received a query from a small monthly journal of opinion, *The Eidolon,* published in Washington. The editors were intrigued with the implications of Teller's embroilment with CBN "as they relate to the question of social control." Would he consider contributing an essay to *The Eidolon* on the subject? The managing editor would be in New York the following week. Perhaps if Teller were available for lunch, they might further discuss . . .

Teller telephoned the *Eidolon* office in Washington to accept the invitation.

"We can't pay you more than a pittance." The *Eidolon* managing editor, a twenty-five-ish youth named Rothberg, wore a shiny herringbone tweed jacket despite the sweltering August heat. They were in the dim dining room of a declining hotel on Madison Avenue.

Rothberg seemed apologetic. "I mean, we're operating on a shoestring, so we can't really make it worth your while monetarily. What I'm trying to say is—"

A waiter snatched up their menus and hovered over them, pen at his pad. He gave no sign of recognizing Teller. Rothberg ordered the chef salad. Teller, taking the cue, held it to a grilled ham and cheese sandwich.

"What I'm trying to say is—" Rothberg seemed uncomfortable. He drew his thin lips illogically back in a grin, revealing pale gums.

"What you're trying to say," prompted Teller, "is how can you be sure a big-name television news stud like me will do any more than drop his by-line on you with some scribbling under it, to pick up a little easy prestige. Is that it?"

Rothberg shook his large head nervously. "Something like that. It's just that we can't afford—"

"I've read your magazine. You guys don't pull any punches. I respect what you do. I'll make you a deal."

Rothberg nibbled on a bread stick and listened.

"I'll give you my best shot on why I think the Schein affair is as important a public issue as, let's say, a political election. What it implies about social control, to use your phrase. I'll postulate some connections in it that I can't prove right now, but my instincts tell me exist. Connections between a network and partisan political interests. I'm afraid you guys will have to stick your necks out to publish it. But you're in the habit of doing that anyway."

Rothberg did not answer, but gave a slight nod to show that he was interested.

"Here's the deal. If you think my conclusions are too far-fetched, or if you think they'll get you tangled up in a libel suit, then don't run the piece; we'll forget about a kill fee.

"If you use it—use it gratis, and make me a contributing editor of your magazine. Put my name on the masthead."

Rothberg stared at Teller from behind his thick glasses. He considered himself sophisticated in the ways of Washington maneuvering, but he did not have much contact with people from the world of television—the world of show business, as far as he was concerned. He could not puzzle out Teller's angle.

"You don't have to make any commitments right now," Teller told him. "But if you use my article, the condition is that my name goes on your masthead. And that you'll issue me a card verifying that I work for *The Eidolon*."

"Of all the magazines you could have gone to work for," said Elizabeth that evening, "you choose one that pays you in leftover McGovern buttons. I'm sorry, but I don't understand."

"I could look for six months for a publication that would risk hiring the mentally unbalanced. Or I could take an opportunity that's shoved under my nose. I'm not interested in getting rich right now. I want credentials. When I go out and try to dig for information—or go to a press conference—I want to be able to say that I represent somebody, and I want to be able to prove it."

"I think that even the *Children's Express* pays off in Milk Duds."

"Elizabeth, I need a favor from you."

"A small loan?"

"I want you to go to Ed Kurtis and ask for your job back."

"Oh, come on, Mark. Have a heart. I'm really getting into *The Young and the Restless*. And it's such a pleasure being able to walk into Zabar's without everybody going, 'Oh, hi, Miss Savitch!' "

"On second thought, forget Kurtis. I want you to go right to Colonel Donovan."

"You're serious, aren't you? If it's money you're worried about, I told you I had some stashed."

"I don't want your money. I want you back in that station. I think Donovan is tied in with Schein somehow and I'd like you to help me find the link."

Elizabeth set down her coffee cup and cocked her head. She put a hand on Teller's arm.

"You're a lot of fun to live with lately. Why didn't you just pin the request on the refrigerator door. It would have saved you the trouble of having to talk to me."

Teller had been staring fixedly out the window. Now he turned to face Elizabeth as though he were noticing her for the first time.

"You're right, Liz. That sounded cold and I know it. I'm sorry. It's . . . look, it's nothing personal."

"What a relief. What a comfort. What a wonderfully romantic thing for you to say. 'Dear Diary: Tonight Mark told me it was nothing personal . . .' "

"All *right!*" He had jumped to his feet and begun to pace, but when he saw the rueful smile on her face, he ran a hand through his curly hair, grinned, and nodded.

"Yeah. I had that coming. Jesus, I'm glad one of us still has a sense of humor."

"Do you like it? Do you think I should go on television?"

"That's exactly what I—" he saw that she was still putting him on.

"Smile, Mark. Laugh a little."

He came to her and took her hands.

"Don't expect miracles. It's enough that I've stopped throwing coffee mugs. I think I have you to thank for my sanity, you idiot." He shook his head, and some of the pain eased from his face. "And I always thought beautiful blonds didn't have the brains to be funny."

"It's an image that comes in handy at times. Which, I gather, brings us back to the subject."

"Elizabeth." His tone was serious again. "Nobody in this country is taking Robert Schein seriously. Except the people who are going to vote him into the Senate."

"Mark, when you put aside your own feelings about Schein, do you honestly believe—"

"*Yes, I do.*" There was a terrible darkness in his face now—a darkness that Elizabeth had learned not to trifle with.

"I've seen him up close and I've seen the effect he has on people. I don't understand it, but I know he's uncanny. He's a chameleon. He can be anything he wants to be, and when he isn't being anything, he's like *switched off*, he's like a machine that nobody's using. You'd have to be around him, Elizabeth, to know what I mean. But I *know* he wouldn't be making the moves he's making now without some kind of incredible organization behind him. That Hollywood agent of his, Bookmaster—he's brilliant, but, God, he's hardly a political kingmaker. There's got to be somebody else."

"Who?"

"Donovan, of course! You said it yourself. Everything points to it. That's the premise of my *Eidolon* piece. But I've got to have more proof. I think something's going on."

She studied his face. Memories of him, defeated and depressed at WRAP, came back to her. She decided to play the devil's advocate —to test the extent of his resolve.

"Mark—if that's all true, maybe there's nothing you can do about it. You took it as far as you could. You said what you had to say on the air. It cost you your job. You don't have anything left to prove to yourself. Why don't you drop it?"

Teller stared for a long moment at his hands, rubbing them together.

"Elizabeth—what drives me crazy, what keeps eating at me, is that I gave the guy his start. *I created him.* Whatever happens, I'm partly responsible. Do you understand what I'm saying? I'm not a world-saver. I'm not the goddamn Lone Ranger. I'm trying to get a monkey off my back. Robert Schein is my fix. He's all I think about. I've got to rip him off me."

"All right. I understand that. How do you suppose my going back to WRAP is going to help you? Assuming I can get rehired in the first place."

"It may not. It may not help at all. I just think there's a connection between Schein and Donovan. Donovan's an old right-winger, America firster, a flag-waver from way back. He was a big hero when I was growing up. I'd always heard about him. This Summer Olympics issue would have been something he'd come up with. I don't know why, exactly, but maybe it's just that—a handy issue. It sure isn't hurting CBN network any—I don't think they have the resources to bid on the Olympics at the last level I've heard."

"God, Mark. Anybody who'd manufacture a U.S. senator just to sandbag his business rivals has to be a little dangerous."

"I'm sure it's been done before. I don't even know if it's true. But damn, Elizabeth—either WRAP or CBN has been right there at every big turn of Schein's career. *And nobody's noticing it!* The big heavyweight political pundits are treating him like a harmless freak. The TV critics are treating him like a rock star. *Nobody* is writing about him as a serious candidate, and nobody has investigated who's behind him."

"So that's what you want me to do. Get my job back and expose Robert Schein—when? During lunch break?"

"I want you to get to know Donovan. Get to be his friend. Protégée. Come on to him if you have to—not heavy, just enough to get his glasses fogged. Flatter the old coot. Make yourself a fixture in his office if you can. You know, you're new in this business, you want to hear how it was when he was blazing all the trails; you want to hear the old stories. Make it so that he's used to having you in there. Then if you're ever alone in his office *for a minute—*"

His hard nails bit into her flesh.

"—Search the place. *Ransack it!* His desk. Shelves. Drawers. Wastebasket. For *anything*, a memo, a scrap of paper, page on a calendar—anything that will *give us a link!*"

She looked up at him, transfixed. She was fascinated, against her will, at the savage mask his face had become. The boyish Ozarker, the lean runner with the whimsical wit, the playful self-mocker, fashioner of charming jokes at the expense of the pop-cultural scene, was gone. In his place stood a martinet. A man obsessed; a man willing to burn up her, himself, anyone else, to smash the object of his obsession.

As she watched, the hateful mask softened somewhat. A hint of the old gentleness returned to the eyes. His hands relaxed their painful grip on her shoulders, the fingertips feathering her bare arms with caresses.

When he spoke again, his voice was tender.

"Look, I'd do it myself except they'd see through the blond wig." He smiled at her.

"I'm using you, Elizabeth. I know that. And if you say no I still want you here."

She nodded faintly.

"Give you something to do," he prodded. "We can't just hang around this place and make love till the—" his voice trailed away.

"—Money's gone," she finished.

"—Cows come home," he corrected in her ear. "Or maybe we can." His lips were at her neck.

"I'll do it," she breathed.

The face that instantly loomed in front of her was the face of the martinet.

"I think you can swing it. Kurtis likes you. He always did. It would make the station look more stable to have a familiar face come back to it. Nobody knows we're living together. It'll be perfect. Work fast, Elizabeth. I need a Watergate in two weeks."

Later, she couldn't help wondering whether it would have been better if she'd simply agreed to support him. Let him fight his holy war alone.

But the next morning she sucked in her pride and telephoned Ed Kurtis.

And Teller took a plane to Los Angeles.

The Continental Broadcasting Network organized a junket of television "editors" from sixty of the country's largest newspapers. CBN flew the "editors" to Los Angeles and checked them into the Century Plaza Hotel, where the TV "editors" were to cover the gala party to celebrate the forthcoming premiere of *Face to Face*, featuring Jennifer Blade as "chief correspondent."

CBN had announced that *Face to Face* would premiere at Continental Studios on September 25. Thereafter, the hour-long show would be telecast "on a modular, free-flowing point-of-origination basis, moving from city to city with the same dynamic flexibility as the Now People whose lively pulse it will record."

"Makes us sound like the road company of *Emergency!*" Jennifer muttered.

They were in "executive conference" in Bookmaster's office. In bed. The sofa that was grouped with the Eames chairs folded out into a comfortable kapok playground—not the Ritz, but not bad for trysting. Jennifer hated it when the typists and receptionists glanced sideways at her with pursed lips when she emerged from an "executive conference." Apparently Bookmaster had, at one time or another, sought the earnest, private counsel of most of the secretarial pool.

"It's beautiful prose," retorted Bookmaster. "I wrote it."

The network press release went on to explain that *Face to Face* would "utilize CBN's far-flung video-technology resources: mini-cams, airborne studios, mobile vans, and the latest transistorized gear, operated by crack CBN production crews deployed through-out major American cities, to achieve unprecedented immediacy in covering celebrity trends from the worlds of cinema, rock, the theater, sports, politics, Beautiful People, and the arts."

"What for? All I'm going to be doing is asking a bunch of dumb twenty-three-year-old kiddie porn-stars if they've discovered the meaning of life."

"Get the smart-ass out of your system right now, Jennifer. You're going to be holding a group interview with the TV editors at ten in the morning, and I want to see *bright-eyed*, I want to see *enthusiastic*, I want to see *committed*, I *don't* want to read where the star of American network television's most revolutionary new concept in personality journalism thinks it's all a piece of shit."

She was in a petulant mood.

"Why do you call them 'editors,' anyway?" she asked. "I always thought they were called critics or columnists or something."

Bookmaster snorted out a laugh.

"Wait till you see them," he said, with a rare grin on his face.

"Why? Do they wear green shades and sleeve garters?"

"Not quite. Actually they are TV critics. At least that's what it says at the top of their columns. But you'll never hear a network flack call them 'critics.' It's one of the unwritten rules of the indus-try. 'Critic' is an admission that these people have the right to think for themselves, and a few of them actually can. 'Critics' write columns with points of view. 'Editors' are like visiting firemen. They wear the nametags the flacks give them, they put the sou-venir T-shirts in their American Touristers, and the souvenir tape recorders, and the souvenir expense money, and they lap up the Bloody Marys, and they crawl to the typewriter long enough to compose their own by-lines at the top of the press releases, and then they fall in the pool and go back home to East Jesus and write columns bragging to the Great Unwashed that 'Jennifer Blade confided to me over cocktails in Hollywood . . .' and they neglect to mention that there were fifty-nine other confidees present and a transcript would be available on request.

"That's why they call them TV 'editors.' "

"I see." Jennifer shuddered and reached for her cigarettes. "Why bother to hold a press conference? Why not just hand them out a package of quotes?"

"We'll do that. The press conference is so they can describe in their own words what your hair looks like."

"I can hardly wait till ten A.M. tomorrow."

"Come over tonight. Pass the time quicker. I'm having a few people you ought to meet anyway. Couple of producers. I'm showing *Saigon Journal*."

"*Saigon Journal* hasn't been released yet." She'd read about the forty-million-dollar Vietnam War masterwork.

"This print, uh, escaped. Come on. Dress black pajamas. I'm barbecuing a whole goddamn yak afterward, sort of a tie-in with the theme. Had to dig up my whole backyard. Might be a fucking wipe-out. Oughta be fun."

"Sounds like it. If things get dull you can all go put a Zippo lighter to the thatched roof at Trader Vic's. Maybe lay down a little napalm on the coolie car attendants at the Beverly Hills. I love theme parties." She touched a match to her cigarette.

He indulged her sarcasm. He reached a hand around to caress her lean, smooth thigh under the hip. He was growing hard again.

"So I'll expect you at eight. Maybe we'll all get weird."

"Start without me. I'm seeing Robert tonight."

The hand withdrew. Bookmaster's dark eyes crackled with annoyance.

"What the fuck do you see in that stiff?"

"What do you see in him?"

"Don't smart-ass me . . ."

"I see me in him. How about you, Mal? Don't you see you in him? We all see whatever we want to see in Robert. He never disappoints, as long as you never ask him to be anything except what you really want. I love him because I love myself. And you're never going to get me away from him, not entirely away, any more than you can separate me from myself. He's my happiness machine, Mal. Don't try to take me away from my happiness machine."

That night Schein talked to her.

She would never be able to reconstruct what he said, not word for word. It was nothing memorable, couched as it was in his flat,

unremarkable sentences. But long afterward, she tried to reconstruct the night itself, tried to recall the exact sequence of movements, remarks, interactions, that might have amounted to some
sort of mystical unlocking of Schein's terrible reticence, his overwhelming loneliness. She could never find it. The best analogy she
could think of, long after the night, was that of a clock radio
coming on by itself in the dark, after hours, years, of dull, mute,
orange glowing. But who had set the dial? And what did the radio
voice say after startling her to wakefulness, terrified for a wild
instant that a third entity had invaded the dark hotel suite? Time,
temperature. News, weather, and sports. Nothing really. Nothing
but—the impulse to say *something*.

It had to do with his daily routine, impressions he'd had of the
game-show studios, the talk show studios. In his flat, hesitant sentences Jennifer caught—lying frozen next to him in the dark,
fearful that a move would send him skittering into silence—caught
the sense of something like a memory; caught a haunting res-
onance of thought. It was as though in entering those studios
Schein were *returning* somewhere, to a landscape familiar from his
childhood. To nothing more than a dream, perhaps—an old and
half-articulated dream, fed by endless days of watching television,
of what the insides of those studios must be like.

It must have been the same random volition that had propelled
him into Stitch's in the first place, on that long-ago August night
of Bobby Lee Cooper's death, when she and Teller (Teller . . .)
had first seen him.

What did it matter what he said? What did people have to say to
one another anyway? Television said everything for everyone, before anyone had to bother thinking.

When he was silent again, quickly, and sleeping, she lay for
hours awake in his arms, happy for one of the few moments in her
life.

He would talk to her again, and together they would harness the
silent moon.

The conference suite was cool with air conditioning. Jennifer
sat on one of three swivel chairs on a raised platform facing six
rows of ten folding chairs side by side, with an aisle down the
middle. Seated on her left was the executive producer of *Face to*

Face, a ruddy, fair-haired man of fifty named Ericson. (Ericson was the *Face to Face* producer in title only. Mal Bookmaster had created every facet of the show from behind the scenes.) On Jennifer's right, his blue blazer stretched over a yachting tunic of broad blue-and-white stripes, sat Bob Swallows, the publisher of *Faces* magazine.

A tanned CBN public-relations man, a dapper symphony of lemon-and-lime patterned jacket, lime slacks, and white shoes, all sharp creases and tight knots, inspected his Pulsar watch.

"Nine fifty-seven, people," he said through his fixed grin, which he had begun to unlimber five minutes ago after twenty minutes of various high-pitched tantrums. "They should be on their way up in the elevator at this minute."

Jennifer reached down for a glass of ice water on the coffee table in front of her. She looked across the rows of empty chairs toward Mal Bookmaster, who had managed to make himself nearly invisible by lounging in front of a sunlit window. There were two or three men hanging near Bookmaster—large, beefy types in tight suits. CBN West Coast brass, she supposed, or colleagues of Bookmaster's that she hadn't met.

This would be her first press conference—from the answering end. It would be vital to the initial publicity push for the show, she'd been told. Quickly reviewing all the wicked little press-conference tricks that she had learned in her year at WRAP, she felt a case of nerves coming on.

She glanced at Swallows, whose lips were moving as he studied a grubby page of handwritten notes. He seemed to be praying. Ericson, on her other side, appeared to be asleep with his eyes open. Not many questions would be directed at Ericson. He was the parsley on the side of the gourmet dish of Big Names that Bookmaster had arranged for the "editors."

At Bookmaster's suggestion, Jennifer had dressed Strictly Business Newswoman—tailored beige suit, simple accessories. Also at his suggestion, she was made up like a high-priced call girl. Her generous lips glowed with a softening lipstick, the hollows below her stunning cheekbones were subtly accented with shadow. The Strictly Business skirt was tugged back from the knees just enough to allow the editors a businesslike appraisal of the famous Jennifer Blade legs.

She heard a ululating of voices from the corridor, and the editors filed in.

Jennifer was incredulous. The people shuffling into the room looked like refugees from a stagecoach holdup. A stream of confused-looking white people, festooned with name tags, flaunting every conceivable extreme of tourist dress. Tortoise-shell sunglasses rampant. Body shirts stretched over soft bellies. Go-to-hell paisley pants topped off with white belts. Leisure suits. Bermudas over white toothpick legs. Polyester blazers draped over arms. Here a sleeveless white dress, revealing this season's eye-catching cellulite, accented with merry bursts of crimson strawberries (complete with seeds). There a floor-length muumuu.

The entourage arranged itself matter-of-factly among the folding chairs. Now and then an editor would glance up at Jennifer and her two colleagues, casing them with the bemused incomprehension one might lavish on three mechanical crocodiles at Disneyland.

Once in their seats, the editors became absorbed in disentangling themselves from a Byzantine network of straps: Instamatics, portable tape recorders, handbags. Jennifer noted that most of them dutifully carried small red canvas travel bags, emblazoned with the CBN logo, over one shoulder. The travel bags had been distributed by the network's public-relations staff. They contained the *"Face to Face* Press Kit," a prefabricated "package" of the show's technological marvels, a bio of Jennifer, a page of credits, glossy photographs of Jennifer, plus several pages of upbeat "quotes" and "tidbits" relating to the series.

No editor had to worry about being too strangled on hospitality to make it to the press conference—or being too fuddled to make sense of it, once there. The network had given each editor his own story kit—each with some nugget "Exclusive to You in Your Area" —ready for easy assembling.

The conference suite suddenly smelled of suntan lotion and gin. From midway back in the folding chairs, the drawling voice of a woman "editor" was audible:

"Had m' hair done this morning, cost me fourteen ninety-five. Gawd, m' whole *head* isn't worth fourteen ninety-five." Snickers.

These, Jennifer realized, were people who actually had some standing in the cities and towns where they wrote—who were looked upon as arbiters of taste and values in the American broadcasting system, who were themselves considered celebrities by the uncounted millions who depended on them for a comprehension, however vague, of the forces at work on the airwaves.

Flanking the "editors" as they trudged in had been a couple of young CBN P. R. staffers, insolently natty in their institutional blazers. The green-and-lime confection was obviously their leader —a toady himself, Jennifer understood, but obviously a minor eminence in the eyes of the herd. When he stood and held up a manicured hand for silence, sixty pairs of sunglasses flashed in his direction.

When the buzzing and snickering had ceased, the green-and-lime P. R. chieftain delivered what he called "some housekeeping" announcements—optional tour of the movie lot in the afternoon, meal schedules, dress "suggestions" for the gala party that night on the patio behind the Century Plaza. The group alternately cheered and whined.

Then the public-relations man introduced Ericson, the producer, who gave a "rundown" on the *Face to Face* "concept":

"Our primary goal is to duplicate on the air the enormous chemistry and creativity that Bob Swallows here has brought to *Faces* magazine in print: we will focus in on the hottest names in the country in a particular week, let the viewing audience see them doing whatever it is they do, and subject them to the incisive and distinctive interviewing technique of the woman you'll have the pleasure of meeting in a moment—whom I consider the premiere practitioner of the art in America."

Jennifer faked embarrassment to scattered applause. From the right, someone wisecracked: "Don't tell that to *Bawbwa*." There were snickers and the smack of a hand on an arm. *What a zoo*, Jennifer thought.

Bob Swallows said how pleased he was to be part of such a dynamic and creative step forward in the history of broadcast journalism.

The public-relations man reminded his charges of the many interesting technological implications involved in switching a major show from city to city each week. He said Ericson was geared up to handle all inquiries on that score. He said what a great pleasure it gave him to introduce one of the truly brilliant young personalities on the "television-journalistic horizon," a woman who had "earned her wings in the crucible of deadline news," the daughter of a famous Hollywood name and now a superstar in her own right, a lady with both brains and beauty, Ms. Jennifer Blade.

The editors stood and applauded as though Miss Jane Pittman herself had entered the room. An Instamatic flashbulb popped. And another. Jennifer gave a crisp and businesslike rundown on why *Face to Face* was not going to be "just another personality puff show." She said how she hoped to "cut through the show-business facade of some of these people and really get at what is making America tick." She listed a few Serious Issues that she thought a show like *Face to Face* might "productively explore."

The public-relations chieftain threw it open for questions.

"Who does your hair?" tied with "Are you and Robert Schein an item?"

Jennifer found herself staring at the woman who had asked the "hair" question—hers was blue.

"I do it," she said coolly. The woman seemed crestfallen. Jennifer glanced quickly into the cobblestone plaza of sunglasses on her right.

"Did I hear someone mention the name Robert Schein?" she asked with mock severity.

The editors all but threw their hands over their mouths to suppress titters.

"What was the question again?"

An elderly man bobbed his Adam's apple.

"I say are you and Robert Schein an *item*?"

An item? She glanced at Ericson, who shrugged.

"A twosome!" someone offered helpfully.

"He means, *do you date?*"

"Aaaaaaaah!" More giggles. Jennifer was beginning to feel like the Story Lady.

The public-relations chief raised both hands and moved toward the platform. "Just a minute now, folks. I don't think Jennifer should be expected to . . ."

Jennifer waved him back. "No, no. Fair's fair. If I'm going to ask tough questions on *Face to Face*, I should be able to field them myself." (It was a little pageant worked out beforehand, in anticipation of the inevitable query.)

There was a ripple of applause from the editors. Somebody

mumbled, "Right *on!*" Jennifer Blade, Friend of the Working Newsman.

"I'm glad to be able to clear up an annoying rumor," she said, and paused momentously.

Sixty ball-point pens poised above sixty pads.

"The facts of the case are that Robert Schein and I are . . . *very good friends.*"

A reverential silence descended upon the room while sixty minds digested this revelation.

The group scribbled in unison.

"Will Robert Schein be a guest on your first show?"

"We'd planned to keep that a secret (*like shit,* she thought) but since you asked me, I'll give you a little scoop: Robert Schein *will* be on our premiere."

Applause.

"What was the turning point in your career?"

"What does your father think of all your success?"

"Do you want to get married and raise children?"

"What's your sign? What's Robert's sign?"

"Do you call him Robert or Bob?"

"How did you come to be born in Los Angeles?" This from a bald man in a Hawaiian shirt, who had been gazing in stupefaction at Jennifer's bio sheet. "I wanted," she replied evenly, "to be near my mother at the time." Several editors wrote this information down.

"Who was your hardest interview?"

From the corner of her eye, she noticed that the door at the rear of the room had opened and a lone figure had entered. She thought she knew him, but she couldn't quite make him out.

Besides, her attention was engaged just now in a long-winded, self-important question from a member of the editors group whom everyone else seemed to find loathsome.

He was a strange piece of work—short, dark, scowling, with his hair piled high over his forehead in a quaint pompadour. He had a nervous habit of squinting his eyes alternately as he talked. For a moment Jennifer had thought he was *winking* at her, but realized it was a tic of some sort. He was dressed in a style that would have been fashionable on *Hullabaloo* in the late sixties—sleeveless vest over a shirt with puffed sleeves, bell-bottom denims with high cuffs, two-tone platform shoes. The kind of smoothie, Jennifer conjectured, who might order a champagne cocktail.

". . . Ever since the era of Nixon's gang of white-collar thugs," the editor droned in his nervous staccato, "network honchos have been performing behind-the-scenes midseason surgery on no-holds-barred public-affairs shows. . . ."

She scanned the back off the room. But the new arrival had taken a seat somewhere.

". . . Can you promise us your show won't degenerate into mindless gutlessness . . ."

There were hoots and catcalls around the squinting, blinking editor, who ignored them.

God, deliver me, thought Jennifer. *This is from Marat/Sade.* She had no idea what the man was driving at.

The P. R. man grinned at the editor. "Uh, you're sort of making a speech, Horace. Does anyone have a question for our panel?"

The editor stopped talking, squinting, and blinking all at once. He looked deeply offended. Somebody said, "Siddown, ya little germ."

There was a moment of awkward silence.

"I have a question for Jennifer Blade."

The voice came from the rear. Jennifer knew the voice. It carried a tone of challenge, of authority, that cut through the confusion and made the editors whip and crane their heads around to see who had spoken.

"Jennifer, you are being managed by Mal Bookmaster Associates, a firm that also controls Robert Schein. Schein has been the subject of your news reports several times and I understand he'll appear on the first segment of *Face to Face.* Would you tell us why this is not a conflict of interest?"

Jennifer sucked in her breath. *It wasn't possible that he'd be here!* God, he looked worn and somehow desperate in his faded jeans and cheap polo shirt. A lot had come down on him . . . she felt irrationally glad to see him, suppressed an impulse to call, "Mark!" before her iron self-discipline clamped down. He was the enemy now. And he had come to torpedo her.

The public-relations man beside her was going into a little paroxysm of waves and gestures: "Sir . . . could you identify yourself, please? This is a closed press conference . . ."

"I'm opening it. Mark Teller, representing *The Eidolon.*"

Two of the beefy studs had fallen into step with Bookmaster as he moved around toward the back of the room, toward Teller. *Bodyguards,* Jennifer realized.

"Question two!" The three men were closing in on him. "Would Mr. Malcolm Bookmaster, who is in this room—who is, uh, walking *toward me,* would you explain, sir, why your client Robert Schein lent his reputation to an overtly partisan political harangue in the guise of . . ."

A goon grabbed Teller under each arm. It was a smoothly professional move, designed to look innocuous. Jennifer stifled a scream. "Sorry, my friend, gotta have CBN credentials," she could hear Bookmaster saying in a loud, jovial voice as they hustled Teller out the door. "Credentials are just down the hall. We'll be glad to show you . . ."

They were gone.

Jennifer shut her eyes. *Don't let them kill him,* she thought.

Several editors in the crowd had begun to hiss at Teller during his questions. When he disappeared through the door, there was yet another round of applause.

"I guess people in my line of work should suffer cranks kindly, but frankly, Mr. Teller, I'm getting a little tired of you. You tried to embarrass one of my clients on television and now here you are disrupting another client's press conference. What do you envision that I am supposed to do—beg for mercy?"

They had "escorted" him, a goon-hand under each shoulder, into a suite down the corridor. The small, black-suited man in front of him had closed the door and was now speaking softly to Teller, so softly that his lips barely moved. It rankled Teller—as he knew it was intended to—that the man looked away from him as he spoke. The phrase, "tried to embarrass," did not escape Teller. He found the condescension infuriating.

"You're Mal Bookmaster?" He tried to keep his voice even.

The small man glanced at one of the goons and lifted an eyebrow, as though Teller had asked him for an autograph. Still keeping his gaze elsewhere, he continued in a bored monotone:

"I mean, what is it with us, Mr. Teller? Did I insult you at a party once or something? Cut you off in traffic? Maybe I didn't return one of your phone calls. God knows what sets off the press these days . . ."

Teller started to take a step toward the little man, but two hands slapped against his shoulders, restraining him.

"The press wants to know what you're up to with Robert Schein and also what perversion of journalism allows a newswoman to be represented by the same firm as the people she covers?" Teller was shouting. The small man was studying his digital watch; he gave no sign of being aware that anyone in the room had spoken.

"I mean, I'm happy to answer any of your questions, Mr. Teller," he said softly, "but I have neither the time nor the temperament to indulge an obscure vendetta. I don't believe in threatening people. But if you step on my toes again I'll have your lights knocked out." He shot his cuffs, and his tone became a parody of courtesy. "I'm sorry I can't be of any more help to you, Mr. Teller. Jerry, Phil, see that Mr. Teller finds his way out of the hotel."

The two thugs propelled Teller toward the door.

"Just a moment, Mr. Teller."

He turned his head to find Bookmaster staring at him. For the first time he noticed the serpent-like malice in the black eyes.

"You said 'the press' wanted to know a couple of things about my clients. You were wrong. You meant the unemployed press, which can get fucked as far as I am concerned. The *press* wants to know who does Jennifer's hair."

"Any other questions?" asked the lime-and-lemon public-relations man through his fixed grin.

"Yoo-hoo." It was the lady with the fourteen ninety-five hairdo.

"Any chance we can have *less serious stuff and more entertainment* on television? I think we're all sick of . . ."

Her colleagues drowned her out with laughter and cheers.

The editors returned to their home cities and wrote picturesque columns about the gala CBN party celebrating the premiere of *Face to Face*. They named the top celebrities who were there. They reported snippets of witty conversation. They described the torches that illuminated the patio. They named the orchestra. They provided copious lists of the types of hors d'oeuvres on the white-linen tables beside the goldfish pond. They passed along personal tidbits that various stars had "confided" to them in the course of the long, fairy-tale evening.

None of them mentioned the two questions that Mark Teller

had tried to ask at Jennifer Blade's press conference. Most of the editors felt it would be impolite to do so, in light of CBN's extraordinary "hospitality." A few others feared that the lime-and-lemon public-relations chieftain would be mad at them, and would not call them by their first names on the next junket.

Four or five editors felt it their duty to report what had happened; they were, after all, independent journalists and not in anybody's hip pocket.

These four or five courageously printed the fact that "a heckler" had "marred" the proceedings at one point.

Only Horace, the squinting, blinking iconoclast who was openly contemptuous of his colleagues, had taken coherent notes of Teller's attempt at a showdown.

But Horace did not publish the item either.

Teller had asked the question that Horace was trying to ask. And Horace was jealous.

By late August, the wave of rebuke against the Continental Broadcasting Network for its "disguised political statement" of July Fourth was all but forgotten.

The unprecedented joint-network censure of CBN fizzled into disregard. Most people did not read about it, or did not understand it, or shrugged it off as "jealousy" over Robert Schein.

The senators and congressmen who had fulminated for an FCC investigation found they had no real basis for such action. Neither of the actors in the skit was a declared candidate for office; therefore, CBN had no equal-time obligations. Everyone seemed to agree that CBN had done something distasteful; tawdry, even—but what were you going to do? Make the U.S. Government the final authority on what a TV network could and could not broadcast?

Prestigious newspapers and serious-minded magazines published a wave of alarmist columns and articles. Some of the pieces called for citizen-license challenges of all CBN-owned or affiliated stations. Other essays trenchantly analyzed the skit as the latest surfacing of television's Big Brother tendencies, and called for Congress to examine anew the proposal to dilute the networks' vast monopolistic power by forcing them to relinquish control of their owned stations.

Most Americans did not read these articles. Those who did clucked and nodded soberly; they agreed with every word. The situation was shameful. When was someone going to do something? Thank God *they* didn't depend on TV for information, but rather on papers and magazines like the ones they were now reading . . .

In any case, another media story came along to overshadow the boring July Fourth controversy: C. W. "Hoss" McCullum, Bobby Lee Cooper's old manager, announced plans for a monster Bobby Lee Cooper Anniversary Concert to be held at the Houston Astrodome. The concert, scheduled for the date on which Cooper had died, would bring together all his leading imitators, as well as his closest friends in the recording industry. There would be fireworks, a marching band, a daredevil cyclist, and a patriotic speech by the Governor of Tennessee, in which he would declare Bobby Lee an Honorary Posthumous Governor. The country's most widely publicized psychic would attempt to communicate with Bobby Lee's spirit, right on live TV.

The network that would telecast these proceedings flooded the nation's press with almost daily disclosures of this kind. The press glutted itself. Bobby Lee was back on magazine covers, in the gossip columns, and on people's minds.

Even Robert Schein was pushed into the background temporarily (until it was announced that he'd be among the celebrities on hand).

The nation looked forward to a deeply enriching orgy of morbidity.

Nothing else mattered.

Teller did not mention his confrontation with Bookmaster to Elizabeth upon his return. No reason to upset her more than necessary.

"Not terribly productive," he conceded to her. "I got off a couple of hostile questions at Jennifer's press conference. And I met our man, Bookmaster, briefly. Unpleasant bastard. And I did some snooping around. A lot of Hollywood people have a theory that Bookmaster has a political scheme involving Schein, but nobody takes it seriously. They all think it's a big joke."

"All in all, a rather extravagant vacation for an unemployed newsman. Did you get to swim?"

"Are you kidding? The San Andreas Motel didn't have a pool. It did have an ice machine—directly under my window. How'd the week go for you? What was it like back at the old sweatshop?"

She had been waiting for the question; she savored the moment.

"Have you ever heard of the Phaëthon Society?"

"No. What is it? Group of snake-lovers? New series this fall on CBN?"

"It's the organization I think you're looking for."

His tone changed. "Tell me about it."

"It was a name I'd heard before at the station. I'm surprised you didn't. There's always been this rumor that the Colonel belonged to some lunatic fraternity for aging moguls. People joked about it, nobody knew much about it, there was just that name—Phaëthon."

"I remember the rumor," muttered Teller. "But I never heard the name."

"You were not a connoisseur of office minutiae, like I was. Anyway, I heard him use it one day in his office. Or rather, I heard his secretary use it. I was in there doing what you asked me to do, and feeling pretty *ulterior* about it all, I can tell you."

"Go on." The voice was expressionless.

"Well, I mean, the point is, it *worked*. I went in there my third day back and laid this god-awful line of crap on him about how foolish I'd been to leave the station and how glad I was to be back on board, and how I'd always *admired* him, and that seemed to just make him glow. So I lied some more. I told him how fascinated I was with his career, and wondered what it had been like in the early days when he was setting the world on fire. That phrase made him do a double-take. But it got him to reminiscing, and he started telling me about his first trip to Hollywood, and how I reminded him of this movie star he met out there; I think he must have been in love with her or something, because he started getting *very* romantic. And mellow. I don't think the Colonel has many real friends around him, Mark. He seems so lonely, like nobody ever asks him any questions about himself."

"I am deeply touched. Go on."

"Well, while he was in the midst of his reverie his secretary opened the door without knocking—you remember Lillian, she's been with him for about the last hundred fifty years—anyway she just barged right in and told him that the Phaëthon Society called, they were meeting that night. Then she saw me and her face got white and she turned around and made tracks out of there. I guess she wasn't used to the Colonel having a visitor."

"She didn't see you when you came into the Colonel's office?"

"She wasn't at her desk."

"All right. So what happened next?"

"I just assumed my most innocent expression, which for me is not at all difficult, and I asked the Colonel what a 'Phaëthon' was. He seemed a little flustered at first, but then he sort of leaned back and put his fingertips together and told me this long anecdote out of Greek mythology."

"Phaëthon was a Greek god?"

"In a manner of speaking, I guess he was. The story comes from Ovid. It seems that Phaëthon was a real-live boy who found out that his father was the Sun."

"Whose father was . . . the *son?*"

"The *Sun*. The *Sun* up in the sky. So Phaëthon wonders what it would be like to be up there in his father's chariot, guiding the horses along the heavens, giving light to the world. He goes to the Sun's throne room and the Sun tells him it's true; he grants the boy one wish. The boy cries out, 'I choose to take your place, Father! Just for a day—a single day! Give me your chariot to drive!'

"Well, the Sun tries to talk him out of it—no mortal could drive his chariot, the climb into the heavens is too steep, the descent is so dangerous that he might fall headlong into the sea-gods, the heavens are full of beasts of prey—the Bull, the Lion, the Scorpion, the great Crab. He promised the boy any of the earth's treasures instead.

"But Phaëthon had his mind made up, and the Sun had given his word. So Phaëthon mounted the chariot and started off. The horses felt the weak hands on the reins, realized the Sun was not there to command them, and soared recklessly into the sky. They descended so fast that they set the world on fire. Phaëthon was burning. Jove threw a thunderbolt and killed him, shattered the chariot, and plunged it into the sea. And the way the Colonel told it—it was so beautiful—the naiads pitied Phaëthon and buried

him and carved a legend on his tomb. I tried to memorize it, and I
think I did. It goes: 'Here Phaëthon lies who drove the Sun-god's
car./ Greatly he failed, but greatly had he dared.' "

Elizabeth sat back and drew a breath.

"Isn't it beautiful?"

The face staring back at her was twisted with impatience and
confusion.

"Will you kindly tell me what you think that has to do with a
secret political organization and Robert Schein?"

"I'm coming to it. The Colonel told me that the Phaëthon
Society was a group that he belonged to. He said that it was dedicated to the *ideals* of Phaëthon—the ideal of seizing the Sun-god's
chariot, of taking the reins, of trying to shed one's own light on
the world . . . and that even though Phaëthon failed, that was all
the more reason for enlightened men to try, and try again.

"Mark, don't you see—that's the perfect parable! If the Phaë-
thons are political, it describes what they want to do! They want
to *seize the reins*! They want to *drive that chariot*, Mark! Spread
light, enlightenment . . . to set the world on fire!"

"And Schein is their torch man." Teller's face was impassive, his
voice still toneless.

She suddenly felt ridiculous. She had allowed herself to get so
carried away with Teller's obsession that she identified with it, and
now her own imagination had swept her into a foolish cloak-and-
dagger fantasy.

"You think I'm crazy, don't you?" she asked finally, in a small
voice.

"No," said Teller, his body frozen in thought. "I think you are
absolutely on target."

The Houston Astrodome was in apotheosis.

C. W. "Hoss" McCullum was in his finest hour.

Standing in a glass broadcast booth overlooking the empty
sports cathedral's parabolic sweep, watching workmen unfurl the
acres of red, white, and blue bunting on the infield, listening to
the distant tacking of hammer against scaffold wood, "Hoss" Mc-
Cullum allowed himself a wet moment of profound emotion.

On'y thing thass missin', he thought tenderly, *is Bobby Lee
hisse'f.*

Hoss McCullum conceded in the next instant that if Bobby Lee had been present there would be no such spectacle for him to complete. Never in Bobby Lee Cooper's spangled lifetime had his legendary promoter promulgated a single event approaching this scale.

The Bobby Lee Anniversary Memorial Salute had struck a chord in the national polyphony unsounded since the death of Valentino. Perhaps since the journey of Lincoln's funeral train. It produced a spasm that rippled through the American consciousness, that brought a lump to the Republic's throat, that paralyzed Ticketron circuits (twenty-five dollars a person, man, woman or child) and started a nationwide run on mid-August vacation requests.

They had been streaming into Houston for ten days, and now, on the third night before the concert, the stream had become a flood. The Astrodome's sixty thousand seats had long since been sold, but still the people came, to look, be near, to *watch* the ones who *watched*, to buy souvenirs, to gaze upon the Astrodome itself as though it were Lourdes.

The Astrodome had never drawn such a throng. Not for the Billy Jean King-Bobby Riggs match. Not for the Lord of the Universe. Whatever confluence of dark, unspoken drives the chord had touched—self-pity, boredom, superstition, necrophilia, the simple unfocused yearning to *worship*—it brought the Bobby Lee faithful to Houston like the Shrine of Our Lady of Guadalupe brought Mexicans crawling across the blistering plaza on bloodied knees.

The parking lots that ringed the Astrodome were already shimmering seas of silver and glass. The license plates told of pilgrimages from all over the South, from California, from Idaho, from New York, from as far away as Ontario. They came to mourn their dead television idol swathed in the vestments ordained by television: they came in their decorator-finished VW Campmobile buses with optional pop-up tops, and their Dodge Street Vans with the built-in forty-channel CB sets; they came in their Plymouth Arrows (Miles and Miles of Heart) and their Rabbits and Civics and Fiestas, they came on their Toyota SR-5s and their BMW 733s and their Yamaha X5400s; they came in Jeep Cherokee Chiefs with Willie Nelson on the AM-FM stereo; they came in CJ-7s and 124s, 2000s and RX 7s and YZ400Es; they hit Houston in a wave of two-barrel, four-cylinder, twelve-valve, four-wheel-drive, rack-

and-pinion-steering, steel-belted-radial, single-overhead-cam-vertical-twin-state-of-the-art-shaft-drive *frenzy* . . . wearing their Sears Thumbs Up jeans (washed thirty times) and their DO IT T-shirts and their Wrangler CorduWroys; they came with their Kodak Tele-Ektras and their Colorbursts, Ban Super Solid under their arms and a Bucket o' Chicken in the Styrofoam cooler (Good-Bye-Ho-Hum!), with their BMX crash helmets and their Adidas sneakers, drinking oceans of Bud and Miller Light, sucking Sno-Cones: Mom, Dad, and the Kids incarnate, geared up and ready for some serious mourning and some rock'n'roll, and those who mocked them did so at their peril.

A newspaper columnist in far-away Detroit made the foolish mistake of poking satirical fun at the *Cooper Memorial Salute*. He was pounced on as he left his office and beaten to a stupefied pulp.

The city fathers of Houston issued a nationwide plea, on the seventh day of the pilgrimage (six days before the *Salute*) for those who did not have tickets for the event to stay away from the sweltering city. Hotels, motels, and city parks were overflowing; a health hazard was feared.

Still they came. The procession had all the exterior trappings of another Woodstock, or perhaps another Altamont. But an examination of the pilgrims showed that this was not so.

"For one thing," noted Howard K. Smith, standing at the side of Interstate 610, as a glut of automobiles inched along in the background, "this is not exclusively a cavalcade of the white and the young, although white and young there be. Look closely at these people and you will see short hair, sensible shoes, respectable coats and ties, all the badges and effluvia of America's solid Middle Class. There are few drugs—albeit plenty of beer and not a little sour mash—and it seems on the whole that this requiem for Bobby Lee Cooper, conceived with modest expectations, has produced a cross-section of American passions and hopes that any politician would be happy to harness."

Indeed, the national media seemed nearly as thick in Houston as BOBBY LEE souvenir guaranteed-sweat-stained scarves. Cameras and correspondents were everywhere. Only the network telecasting the *Salute* sent correspondents in at first, but within three days its envious rivals—who would have preferred to ignore the phenomenon—yielded to the inevitable.

The rival networks knew they would be boosting a competitor's potential ratings by giving national publicity to the delirium in Houston.

On the other hand, it was a ready-made news event—a pre-assembled study in "secular religion" or "grass-roots totems of the folk culture," or whatever the hell label the assignment editor felt like hanging on it. With visuals.

When the Big Media arrived, it arrived with a vengeance. The networks didn't bother with local talent or second-string stars. They pulled their heaviest hitters, the White House corps itself; the Boys on the Bus swarmed Houston as though they were covering a political campaign.

"Why did *you* come to Houston?"

"To pay my respeks to the luvliest soul that Gawd ever put on this great airth."

Gray-suited superstars, pale with a White House pallor under their pancake makeup, stood on street corners and racked their brains trying to explain the human deluge in terms of "America's hunger for tangible values," or "a reawakening of the Town ethos."

Truth to tell, none of the correspondents had the slightest idea why the people were there. As for the people, they kept a darkly suspicious distance from the media whenever possible: they heard condescension in the questions.

On the day of the concert the hot city of Houston was a tinder-box. Patrolling National Guardsmen told one another they sensed hysteria in the people that could trigger a rampage on the Astrodome at any time. In the late morning a rumor had swept the city that Bobby Lee Cooper had never died at all; that he'd been alive and in hiding all this year, and would make a triumphal re-appearance at the *Salute*—possibly bringing with him the living but vegetated remains of John F. Kennedy.

A weekly national magazine appeared on drugstore shelves in the morning, its cover teasing an inside story.

The Question That Must Be Asked:
DID LOVE KILL BOBBY LEE?

By noon, the issue was sold out citywide; one youth was in critical condition with stab wounds resulting from a fight over a copy.

Yes, thought C. W. "Hoss" McCullum. *Yes, sir.* It was his finest hour as an impresario:

—An all-time record viewing audience expected to watch the show (which had been expanded from an hour to two hours at the last minute).

—Gate and concession receipts, combined with telecast authorization rights, that would make him a millionaire one more time.

—His picture on the cover of *Newsweek*.

His finest hour.

Or could have been.

Except that he didn't have a damn thing to do with it. This fellow Bookmaster had thought the whole thing up in the first place. And allowed McCullum to take credit for it.

Ordered him to, in fact. Under the threat of things that C. W. "Hoss" McCullum didn't even want to think about.

McCullum sighed. Show business had certainly changed since he was a young fellow starting out in it.

"You know the script? You know exactly what I want you to do?"

"Yes, sir, Mr. Bookmaster."

They were in the Presidential suite of the Hyatt-Regency Hotel. Bookmaster sipped from his champagne glass.

"I'm sorry there is no way we can rehearse this. But I have complete faith in you, Robert. You haven't let me down once in all the time we've been working together. I wish I could say that for any other client of mine."

"Thank you, sir."

"You're sure you won't be nervous. There'll be sixty thousand people in that stadium. Have you ever seen sixty thousand people in one place before?"

"No, sir."

"Bother you?"

"No, sir."

"In a way," said Bookmaster, "it will be a piece of cake compared to the Anaheim thing you did. With the flag. There you had an element of risk. You had to jump down over a wall and run out onto a field. A lot of things could have gone wrong. Here, all your moves will be anticipated. The cameras will be right on you. It's only what you say that will depart from their script. And nobody's going to yank you offstage. Not with fifty million Americans watching on television."

"No, sir."

"I think you're more nervous than he is, Malcolm." Jennifer Blade stood with her back to them, gazing out a window, arms folded, cigarette smoke rising over her left shoulder.

"Robert, why don't you go into the bedroom and change into your costume? I'd like to see how it looks on you."

"Yes, sir. Jennifer—excuse me?"

"Of course, Robert." He was *making contact—more than ever!*

When Schein had left the room, Bookmaster spoke without turning his head to Jennifer.

"Don't start with me. I thought you were supposed to be out with a film crew someplace. Taping celebrity interviews."

She shrugged. "Our friendly rivals who are telecasting this circus are getting uptight. They don't want our people siphoning off their glory. I don't blame them."

"Getting awfully benevolent now that you're a star, aren't you?"

"Malcolm, I know it's against the rules to say things like this, but I don't like what you're doing. I'm afraid of it and I think it's wrong."

He twisted the stem of the champagne glass between his thumb and finger, his narrow eyes regarding the bubbles spiraling up from the vortex.

"So who the fuck asked you if you like it?" The voice was menacingly pleasant.

"If something should go wrong, you know, you are ruined. So are a lot of other people."

"Nothing's going to go wrong. There is no way anything *can* go wrong. And who's going to ruin me? You, Jennifer? You think maybe you're big enough and famous enough now that you could bring down Mal Bookmaster and expose Robert Schein and take a shortcut to that precious anchor job?"

She thought fleetingly of the tape, then forced it from her mind as quickly as if she'd been caught holding it.

"No."

"Because I'll tell you why that's unproductive. Number one, you'd have to topple the Colonel along with the rest of us, and then where would your anchor seat be? Number two, I'd kill you."

"I don't like you to use that kind of language on me, Mal. You know I'm not going to do anything to stand in your way. Now stop threatening me."

He grinned with half his mouth, black eyes still lowered into his glass.

"Hey. I'm not such a bastard with you, Jenny. Christ, I'm a pussycat with you. Don't I let you have it off with our man Schein whenever you feel kinky? Don't—"

"*Mal, I'm warning you.*"

"Don't ever warn me about anyth—"

"*I want Robert Schein,* Mal. I don't expect you to understand that, but I do, and you're not going to keep me from having him. If you want to know the truth about it, *I think I have more power over him than you do . . .*"

She had blurted out the last statement. She immediately wished she hadn't. The room was suddenly very, very quiet. She turned from the window and stole a look in Bookmaster's direction. He was sitting with his back to her, idly gazing at the stem of his champagne glass. She saw the tops of his shoulders, encased as usual in a tailored black silk suit jacket; saw the ridged quarter-profile of his white face.

Several moments passed. Bookmaster was absolutely silent.

"What I meant was that I think he wants me too . . . needs me . . . Mal?"

His voice was so low she was not sure she heard the words. But she heard the hatred.

"I'm very happy for both of you."

Schein came out of the bedroom.

Jennifer took one look at him, then turned quickly back to the window.

He was dressed in a grotesque parody of a country-western singer: Iridescent skin-tight blue pants tucked into fire-engine red cowboy boots. An enormous studded belt with a buckle in the shape of a guitar. A metallic-silver tunic shimmering with tinsel-like buckskin; rhinestone workings across the front. A red bandanna knotted around his neck. A white Stetson with exaggerated brim.

He looked like an extra in a particularly campy Bette Midler production number or a male carhop at a gay drive-in.

"How do I look?" One of the few questions she had ever heard him ask.

"Great, Robert."

"Just fine, Robert. Really. Terrific."

"Well," said Schein. He rubbed his hands. "Hardly wait till tonight. Huh?"

He's making an effort, thought Jennifer. She kept her face toward the window so that no one would see the tears. *God, it's like watching a cripple try to walk. You want him to, and when he tries you don't want him to.*

She stood there considering the consequences of turning the tape over to someone—Teller, of course—and doing exactly what Bookmaster had dared her to do. Not so much to ruin Bookmaster. Nor even to advance her own career. But to save Robert Schein from the monstrous exploitation that Schein couldn't even know was propelling him.

She realized she would never do it. It wasn't that she was afraid. No. She *wanted* Bookmaster's scheme to succeed. She wanted to see Robert Schein at the top.

Because that was the surest way for Jennifer Blade to reach the top. Right behind her happiness machine.

Schein had left the room to change back into his jeans and black pullover.

"Mal, I'm really sorry for what I said a minute ago . . ."

He wheeled around, all smiles and sweet reason.

"Hey. It never happened. We're all a little strung out. Just stick with me, Jennifer. Follow my plan, I'll put you in that anchor chair so soft and nice you won't even know it when you touch down."

In the darkly opulent drawing room of a private midtown Manhattan club, twenty-three of the country's wealthiest and most influential broadcast executives and financiers gathered over brandy and cigars for a highly improbable reason:

An evening of watching television.

More improbable still, their choice of viewing was not some foreign-policy debate or landmark cultural presentation on the public-TV station.

Nor was it even a sporting event of the kind that occasionally draw such men together.

No, the program was a lurid two-hour live telecast from Houston, Texas—a crassly commercial, overbearingly slick "salute" to a dead popular singer whom many of the businessmen had never seen, or had heard of only fleetingly.

The businessmen puffed their cigars in stiff silence as the Mistress-of-Ceremonies, an overdeveloped woman in a skin-tight sequined dress, a hideous wig, and a nasal squeak, welcomed them to "A Hie-ppie Remembrance of a man Amurica tuk tew its heart —who's pra'bly lukkin' down on us na-ow from Gawuhd's hivvinly kwar—th' immortal BABBAH LEE KEW-PUR!"

The cathode glow of the giant color screen flickered over twenty-three unsmiling, granite faces as a symphony orchestra played the opening notes from a song the announcer described as "Polecat," while the TV cameras panned up from the busty woman to an astonishing genuflection to bad taste: twin billowing banners, each reaching from the foot of the centerfield wall to the mists near the top of the dome—one banner a vertical American flag, the other a gargantuan blowup of Bobby Lee Cooper's face.

It was two hours of television that none of the Phaëthon Society ever forgot. (For some of them, it was a chance education in the kind of programming their own stations were feeding the public.)

They saw an unearthly mixture of sex, sentimentality, self-promotion, pop patriotism, painfully contrived spontaneity, music that was hideous beyond belief, and a bewildering succession of introductions to people all of whom apparently were familiar to the crowd.

They pursed their lips in distaste as a succession of men in spangled jump suits, greased pompadours, and silk scarves gyrated in front of a standing microphone while mumbling lyrics that the businessmen found incomprehensible.

They raised their eyebrows as a heavy-maned girl in red-and-white-and-blue hotpants belted out a song that seemed to involve being mistreated.

They gasped as a motorcyclist, dressed in a red crash helmet, blue cape, and white asbestos suit, attempted to leap his cycle over twelve automobiles, parked end to end, that the announcer said had belonged to Bobby Lee Cooper. The cyclist miscalculated his approach and went flopping like a rag doll until he struck the edge of a raised platform containing members of Cooper's family.

The crowd howled its approval.

The businessmen gaped at rhyming prayers offered by singers on Cooper's behalf. They allowed themselves to chuckle at a woman psychic with platinum hair who, after pressing her temples, announced into an echoing microphone that she had "made contayect with Bobby Lee, an' he sends his eternal luhv to all-ayew here." That drew a standing ovation of five minutes.

They chortled outright when a spotlight played on a tall, blue-suited, balding man making his way along the main platform while waving a Stetson. Former President V. W. Olds embraced the overdeveloped Mistress of Ceremonies, turned to wave again at the crowd, caught his wrist on the Mistress's arm, dropped his Stetson, bent to pick it up, and inadvertently plunged his face into one of the woman's billowing breasts.

"Looks as though Victor has graduated from kissing babies to kissing tit," remarked a baritone voice in the semidarkness.

There was murmured laughter.

The one element of the program that did engage the Society was the repeated panning of the TV cameras to the crowd. The close-ups revealed slack, often tear-streaked faces, mothers comforting daughters, Instamatics raised against the boundless Astrodome sweep—unmistakable evidence of a throng transported.

The lights inside the Astrodome dimmed. The giant stadium fell dark, except for vast tubes of white beams directed on the billowing flag and the blowup of Cooper next to it.

A TV camera suspended from the Dome's superstructure played on a tiny pool of glittering blue far below—the Mistress of Ceremonies in her sequined dress, illuminated by a single spotlight. The cameraman twisted his powerful Telephoto lens, and the Mistress of Ceremonies came hurtling across space into a full-screen closeup. Her forehead was streaked with beads of perspiration. Some of the excessive lipstick had begun to smear around the corners of her mouth, and her stacks of bouffant curls were slipping low on her forehead, giving her the appearance of a large marzipan doll left to melt in the hot sun.

The Mistress of Ceremonies was clearly trying to bring her emotions under control.

"Y'all please rise."

A vast sigh of moving bodies was audible.

The Mistress of Ceremonies drew herself into what she evidently considered a posture suitable to the gravity of the moment.

"An' nay-ow, a momint thet I'm sure Bobby Lee's minny friends an' relatives will treasure in their hawrts forever. Ladies an' ginnilmin—may Ah pra-owdly presint the Guhvuhnuh of Tinnissee—Th' Honnable Mr. Erstel DeMent!''

Polite applause rippled across the Astrodome like wind across a lake as a small, grinning man in wire glasses made his way to the podium—pausing only to grasp the hand of former President V. W. Olds.

The Governor made a brief speech praising Bobby Lee as "a great American artist, a world humanitarian, a poet whose work will live on wherever man gathers to sing and to love," snuck in a quick pitch for Tennessee as a fine family tourist state, and proclaimed the late singer an Honorary Posthumous Governor of Tennessee.

Then the camera shifted down to the darkened Astroturf surface of the infield, where the famed Tennessee Twirlers, each holding a lighted candle, stepped off in a formation that spelled out the dead hero's name.

As they marched in stately cadence, a soundtrack filled the Astrodome with the actual recorded sound of Bobby Lee's voice singing "America the Beautiful."

The television screen showed the juxtaposed images of the marching Twirlers and the billowing flag.

"I wouldn't have believed it," breathed a member of the Phaëthon Society. "It's barbaric."

The screen faded to black. The Phaëthon Society sat stone-faced through commercials for panty hose, leg hair remover, denture adhesive, and home insurance.

When the scene returned to the Astrodome, the stadium was again lighted. The Mistress of Ceremonies, smiling now, announced that the crowd would now meet a few of Bobby Lee's "closest and dearest friends from the world of entertainment."

The first "close and dear friend" was Robert Schein.

"I believe this is what we came to see, isn't it, Colonel?" asked a member of the Society.

Schein trotted to the podium in his flashy red, white, and blue cowboy outfit, acknowledging the cheers with a broad wave of his Stetson. He took the hand microphone from the Mistress, gave her a deft show-business kiss on the cheek, and turned to face the crowd and the camera.

The camera angle on Schein was from below the podium, so that he seemed to tower over everything like a golden, blue-eyed statue. Behind him were visible the red and white stripes of the giant American flag.

"*My fellow Americans.*"

The words echoed through the stadium.

"You all know me as a happy-go-lucky kind of guy, a comedian, a fellow who always has good reason to say . . . BOOOOY, WAS MYYYYYY FAAAAAAAAACE REEEEEEED!"

Hoots, cheers, and laughter from the crowd.

"But tonight I didn't come to you in the role of comedian. I consider it a privilege to be here in the humble role of . . . *friend of Bobby Lee Cooper* . . . a role that I share with each and every one of you here, and (nodding down toward the camera) those of you sharing this wonderful Memorial Salute at home."

Applause.

"And I think that there is no better way to honor the memory of this immortal artist than to share with you something that . . . Bobby Lee shared with me not long before he died."

At the network control panel, a director checked an agenda sheet. "This guy's goin' past his time limit, isn't he?"

"I think that Bobby Lee had some advance inkling of what was going to happen to him. Don't ask me how. Perhaps it's beyond science. But he said one day when we were out walking in his rose garden behind that beautiful Chattanooga mansion that he built for his mother and father . . . he said . . ."

Schein's blue eyes darted about the stadium; he paused, like a preacher priming his flock for the heart of the Gospel message . . .

"He said, '*Robert, there are certain foreign powers . . . Communistic foreign powers* . . . who want to *worm their way* into our free-enterprise system of life!' "

"What the fuck is he tryin' to pull?" groused the director at the control panel. Then, reflexively: "Camera Two, stand by." Camera Two was trained on the enraptured face of a middle-aged woman in the crowd.

"Take Two. *And* hold."

"He said, 'They want to get on our airwaves and spread their propaganda filth into *each and every American home!*' He said, '*Robert, don't you let it happen if you can help it!*' "

"Camera Eight, stand by." Camera Eight was a wide shot on a section of the crowd.

"Dissolve to Eight. Pan Eight. Camera One, in tight on Schein.

Tighter. Stand by One. Who the hell does this jackass think he is?
Take One."

"Ladies and gentlemen, my fellow Americans, and friends of
Bobby Lee Cooper: I am here to tell you tonight that I am no
great thinker or world leader or anything like that. I am an ordinary guy from the world of show business . . ."

Cries of *No, no, no!*

"And I can't carry out Bobby Lee's last wish alone. I need the
help of all of you. Each and every one of you who were Bobby
Lee's friends just like me!

"Won't you join me! Won't you stand with me tonight! Won't
each of you make a pledge in your hearts that the first thing you'll
do tomorrow morning is, you'll *write a letter* to each of our great
television networks! You'll remind them how wrong it would be
to take their cameras to Moscow, Russia, and cover the Summer
Olympics under terms dictated by the International Communist
Party!"

Whistles, cheering.

"If we all do this, then by God—*and I do mean by God*—*with
God's help*—we can prevent the takeover of our American airwaves—"

An animal roar from the crowd drowned out Schein's words.

"Three! Wide on the crowd. Pan. Stand by. Take Three. *And*
Six, in tight on that majorette, I want to see the tear, that's it,
stand by Six, *and* dissolve to Six, Camera One . . ."

"To keep the Russians or anybody else from selling their im-
moral system of life to the families and the children of this mighty
nation of ours . . . *so help me God!*"

The Astrodome erupted in a wild cacophony of cheering,
stomping, weeping, hugging, and whistling. On the podium,
former President V. W. Olds had broken from his seat at Schein's
last words to rush toward the young comedian, arms outstretched.
Olds's daughter, Mary Ellen, was at her father's side.

The Mistress of Ceremonies, her face a stunned mask of bewildered ecstasy, was trying to stretch over the former President and
smooch Schein. One large breast obscured all but the top of Olds's
bald head from the camera's view.

Three major celebrities from the movie world, whose time
Schein had usurped, and hating the bastard from the depths of

their souls, elbowed and clawed their way forward to be seen congratulating their "close friend" on national TV.

And the band played, and the crowd roared.

In the darkness of the Manhattan drawing room, someone flicked off the big television set. Someone else switched on the overhead light.

"Well." A sallow owner of three independent television-radio combines dipped the end of a fresh cigar into his brandy snifter.

"He seems to have a way with crowds."

"Yes. But do we want a senator in aluminum buckskin?"

"Anyone who's in aluminum is all right with me."

The executives neighed low laughter to cover their embarrassment.

"Well, Colonel. I hope your friend from California can draw out this fellow's statesmanlike qualities in a hurry. We have an election in, uh—three months."

By the next morning, America's radio call-in shows were flooded with questions and opinions on whether a U.S. television network should be allowed to risk national security by covering the Summer Olympics.

Most callers felt that telecasts of the games should be forbidden.

Within three days, public-opinion pollsters were finding that Summer Olympics coverage was among the ten issues Americans regarded as "most serious." Sentiment was running roughly 60–40 in favor of telecasting—although in the Deep South and in the Midwest Bible belt, anticoverage sentiment held a slight edge.

In New York, anticoverage opinion was surprisingly strong, although a majority of respondents were in favor of allowing the networks the freedom to telecast. More than thirty-five percent of the respondents answered "Don't Know."

The strong showing of sentiment against telecasting the Olympics puzzled the pollsters. But more mystifying than the breakdown of opinion was the presence of the issue itself.

It had never before shown itself as a matter troubling the American people.

Citizens queried their senators and congressmen to find out where they stood on the issue. The senators and congressmen, totally unprepared for the question, directed their staffs to hammer out official statements as equivocating as possible.

Letters poured in to newspapers. The newspapers wrote editorials treating the Summer Olympics telecast question as a serious, weighty issue. Some papers supported telecast rights. Others opposed.

But they all took a position.

"We have our Panama Canal," said Bookmaster with a tight smile, putting aside the morning news digest that Marvin Reed had prepared for him.

"Get him on the talk shows."

Reed didn't have to strain himself to carry out that order.

The talk shows were coming to Schein.

"Ground rules?"

"None."

"Robert, this is Dave Tellander of our organization, I don't think you've met him."

"How do you do, sir?"

"Robert."

"Dave runs our in-house interview training seminar; it's a little service we have for clients who do lots of talk shows. Now I know you're a talk show veteran, but you're going to get hit with some brutal interviews over the next few weeks. Dave here's going to help you gear up for them. He's going to ask you some of the hardest questions we can think of, you're going to watch yourself on videotape—and you're going to look at tapes of people we think handle themselves well. We're going to teach you how to counterpunch. Questions?"

"No, sir."

"Dave, you've got him till Friday."

While talk show producers were eager to book Schein, their bosses at the network level agonized.

On the one hand, they were pitted against one another in a desperate bidding war to secure exclusive telecast rights with the Russians. At stake were hundreds of millions of dollars' worth of profits in the future—the network carrying the Summer Olympics invariably enjoyed an overall surge into first place for months,

even years following the event. Why risk tilting public opinion
against them by giving free air time to a dangerous opponent?

On the other hand, Robert Schein's presence on a TV talk show
was automatically worth a great deal of extra cash right away: the
spot sales division could virtually auction off the time slot in
which he was scheduled to appear.

Besides, each executive reasoned to himself: if we don't have
him, the other guys will.

Each network hit on the "perfect solution" almost simultaneously: place a "qualified spokesman" on the segment along
with Schein, to gently and politely shoot down the populistic
bombast of this opportunistic Hollywood hack.

"Robert, I respect your concerns about Communist propaganda
very much. I assure you that all of us at this network are very
much aware of the Soviets' willingness to manipulate us."

"Then why don't you drop out of the bidding?" (asked quietly,
blue eyes blinking, suit-and-tie man now, no Hollywood epaulets
for Schein)

"Let me finish. They're willing to manipulate us—*if we let
them*. Which of course we have no intention of doing. The point
is . . ."

"How can you stop them?"

"The *point* is . . ." (studio applause) ". . . the *point* is that the
American people *want to see the games*."

"Not the American people I know. Not the sixty thousand
American people I saw in Houston. How many American people
do you know, Mr. Albright? How many American people can you
get inside the first-class cabin of a 747 jetliner?" (mischievous
smile to show he's not really mad at Mr. Albright; whistles and
cheers from the studio audience)

"Whoa, ho, hold, hold—let Mr. Albright have his say."

"Robert, you're a terrific comedian; one of the best we've got.
Hell, you're my favorite entertainer. The whole Albright family
loves you. So I hate to come down hard on this, but—Robert, are
you familiar with the Communications Act of 1934?"

"No, sir."

"Well. You really ought to read it sometime. I think you'd be
impressed with its careful emphasis on protecting our American

airwaves from control by any sort of partisan faction in this country . . ."

"Mr. Albright, my friend Bobby Lee Cooper probably never read the Constitution. But that didn't stop him from singing 'America the Beautiful.' And my not reading . . ." (ovation from the studio audience)

"Rob—you mind if I call you 'Rob'?"

"No one else does, but you go right ahead, sir."

(laughter)

"Heh-heh . . . well, *Robert*, I've listened with interest to what you have to say about the Olympics, and I must say you've performed a public service by putting this debate out in front of the American people."

"Thank you, sir. And you could perform an even greater one by pulling this network out of the bidding." (laughter, scattered applause)

"Well, of course that's a matter of . . . I mean, the thing I hear you *saying* in all this is that the American people are going to tune in the Olympics and catch Communism the way they catch measles. Now that simply isn't realistic. I mean, after they watch you, people don't turn into *stand-up comics, do they?*" (silence from the audience)

"No, sir. (answering the question with icy seriousness) But I would like to ask you one question. Your morning show spent a week in Russia this spring, didn't it?"

"Yes, it did, and we're quite proud of—"

"You showed the Bolshoi, some pretty scenes from the Volga River, isn't that right?"

"Well, yes, and we also—"

"Did you interview any Russian dissidents?"

"Robert, if you understood Russian diplomacy, you'd realize that's—"

"One of your reporters talked to a Soviet jurist. Did the question of human rights come up?"

"*All* I'm saying . . ." (studio applause, hoots)

"Mr. Schein, pardon me for being blunt, but it seems to me that you are willfully misrepresenting the integrity of the three networks who are bidding on the Summer Olympics, and you're turning this nonissue into some kind of platform for a particularly sleazy type of demagoguery. Now you let me ask you some questions: *Who's behind you and what do they expect to get out of all this?"* (reflexive ripple of studio applause, shocked silence)

"The American people are behind me, sir."

"That's not what I'm—" (whistles, applause)

"And they expect to get, uh, their message across to responsible TV executives like yourself: *'No Russian propaganda on our airwaves.'*" (more applause)

Mark Teller completed a five-thousand word essay called "The Selling of Schein: A Study in Television and Social Manipulation."

He reviewed the beginnings of Schein's public notoriety, sparing himself no embarrassment as the inadvertent catalyst.

He traced Schein's increasingly frequent appearances on WRAP and later on CBN, isolating Jennifer Blade's legitimizing role in presenting him as an experienced and popular American entertainer. He established Mal Bookmaster as the common link between Jennifer and Schein—his most damning point in the article.

He examined the subtle transformation of Schein's style from topical wisecracking into jingoist sloganeering. He noted how Schein always delivered his political thoughts in an entertainment context—never on the home ground of seasoned political reporters.

He remarked the sudden appearance of the Summer Olympics coverage as an overnight issue, timing it to the *Bobby Lee Cooper Memorial Salute* telecast.

He reviewed the broadcast career of Colonel Eddie Donovan, famous for his unabashed right-wing political homilies in the forties and fifties, and compared Schein to Donovan as a personality-proselytizer.

He established the existence of the Phaëthon Society, reported its philosophy as articulated by Colonel Donovan, and drew the parallels between Phaëthon's mythic quest and the plausible goals of a secret society hoping to seize political power. He concluded with an open challenge to Colonel Donovan to dispel "the appearance of a grave conflict of interest" by publicly disassociating himself from Schein and deploring his network's "possibly inadvertent" role in creating a parapolitical figure.

He sent the manuscript by registered mail to *The Eidolon* in Washington four days ahead of the deadline. If Bookmaster were planning some sort of move with Schein in November, the piece might have some impact. He wondered how safe his life would be when Bookmaster read it.

He decided he'd face that problem when the time came.

A week later, he received a call from Rothberg, *The Eidolon*'s managing editor.

"Loved your piece, Mark. Real dynamite. We're holding it for the December issue."

"You're *holding* it?"

Rothberg's voice became apologetic. "Fact is, something came up, Mark. We just received a very heavy by-line piece from Governor Gareth Rice of California on cleaning up water pollution. Frankly, we'd like to use his name on our November cover, it'll be dynamite for sales, and your piece can hold . . ."

Teller hung up the phone.

"That about tears it," he said.

Studio "A" of Continental Studios was a field of flowers.

Fans from all over America had sent bouquets to Jennifer Blade, wishing her success in the debut of *Face to Face*.

The show's producers had heaped as many of the floral arrangements as possible onto the set. Roses, orchids, jonquils, chrysanthemums glowed and gleamed under the hot studio lights. In the center of it all, looking radiant, a yellow corsage pinned to her dress, facing Camera One, was CBN correspondent Jennifer Blade.

The normal studio "look" for *Face to Face* was to be business-like, even a trifle severe—a news anchor desk "environment," the Hawthorne Collective had decreed, to lend "authority" and "substance" to a program that would generate little of either on its own.

But for tonight, for the live premiere out of Los Angeles, a festive touch was permitted. The Collective hoped that the visible flowers would establish Jennifer as the "Favorite Daughter" in the imaginary "national family."

There would be no studio audience for *Face to Face*—the better to carry out the Serious Business ambience. But a small group of well-wishers stood outside camera range.

Sterling Blade towered above them all. The big old lion fairly burst from his unaccustomed tuxedo. Silver locks combed, tears at the corners of his eyes, Jennifer's father stood in awkward pride, feet planted apart, big hands clasped in front of him, trying to stay out of the scurrying technicians' way.

Mal Bookmaster was there, of course—friend and benefactor. No tears in Bookmaster's black eyes. Dapper in his customary black Wall Street lawyer's suit, controlled smile on his lips, Bookmaster seemed to melt into the haze of arc lights, unobtrusive, nearly invisible, evanescent as the light itself.

A beaming former President V. W. Olds was on hand, comradely paw on Sterling Blade's shoulder. Olds's daughter, Mary Ellen, clutching a bouquet, stood timidly beside him.

Jennifer was touched by Olds's presence. She understood his political motives for being there. But in his bumbling way, the former Chief Executive had proved an affable, considerate friend. Even his Rotarian attempts at flirtation she had found endearing. And he had been an invaluable ally for Schein.

If only she could fathom his daughter, so reticent and vague . . .

Schein himself was present, of course—backstage with the other guests for the *Face to Face* premiere. It was a stunning lineup of celebrities by anyone's measure:

—The glamorous, alcoholic wife of a United States senator, a woman who had confessed her "secret" on the cover of every important national magazine;

—The country's most celebrated mass murderer (on videotape, to be sure, from his prison cell) playing a song he had composed in honor of the *Face to Face* premiere;

—The author of a best-selling biography of the deceased celebrity cat;

—A "ruggedly handsome" Catholic priest specializing in exorcism and Pentecostal healing;

—Two bitterly feuding executives of rival chocolate-chip cookie companies;

—A Middle Eastern leader (via satellite hookup) who had promised a major policy announcement "for my good friend Jenny-fer";

—And, of course, Robert Schein.

All in all, not an entirely lackluster premiere.

"Thirty seconds. Quiet, please."

Hot lights, frigid air—the deadliest half-minute in television.

"Jenny, honey—tuck in that chin just a *teensy*—that's it!"

"*God*dammit, her dress top's coming up fucking *mauve* on the monitor."

"Whaddaya wanna do about it, Shelley—cancel the show?"

"Take gas."

"Ten seconds." Like a gazelle, the floor director suddenly pounced onto the set and planted a kiss on Jennifer's cheek.

"Make it sing, baby!" He leaped backward.

"Goddammit, he *drooled* on her left cheekbone."

"*And* five."

"Wipe it off—no, never mind! *Stand by!*"

"*And!*"

"Cue the theme."

"Roll tape!"

Throbbing electronic music surged through the studio. All eyes fastened on a monitor screen above the set, to watch the sophisticated *Face to Face* title graphics unfurl: a lightning-fast montage of famous faces, every tenth face frozen on the screen for an extra beat. Every eye watched save Jennifer's, which were fixed on her TelePrompTer.

"Coming up on One."

The red light winked on.

"Alcoholic Senate wives. A major policy statement from the Middle East. A priest who chases devils . . . a strange musical love note to *us* from a maximum-security cell . . . a 'Schein'ing star . . . and the cookie crumbles. Hello, I'm Jennifer Blade, and you'll be seeing all of that and *more* tonight . . . *Face to Face.*"

Fade to black.

"Clear."

"Nice, baby." This from Sterling Blade.

"Two minutes."

"Beautiful, Jenny. Keep it singing."

"Is Mrs. Schoenemann in the studio? Will someone please seat her at the interview table."

"*Or under it. She'll be more at home there.*" (sotto voce)

"Jenny, you have four minutes on this next segment."

"Somebody wipe Larry's smooch off her cheek, for God's sake. This is a family show."

"I'm still getting mauve."

"Maybe you're just a *mauve person,* Shelley. Ever think of that?"

"Thirty seconds to air."

America sat down for just about five minutes to watch.

"Come on in here, Fred. This is good."

"She don't look like an alky does she?"

"She's had a facelift. I read it somewhere. Her birthday's the same day as Marlene's."

America put its tired feet up on the coffee table and had a beer and watched.

"Can you imagine putting a killer on like that. Pass me some of those Frito-Lays."

"I read where he's homosexual."

"They all are. In prison. He's got cute eyes though. I read where he had something to do with the Kennedy killings. Carries a tune, I'll say that."

America rubbed its varicose veins and dreamed.

"I wonder how much they pay her to do that show."

"Be still a minute. That Arab's the one that married the debutante."

"Is that the one that had the affair with Jennifer?"

"Be still, he's makin' a policy statement. No that's Robert Schein that's having the affair."

"I guess you can have more than one affair. If you're Jennifer Blade or any of them."

"You wish."

"Is that on live?"

"Will you be still? Course it's live, it's a satellite hookup. I wonder if he bought that suit in Arabia."

America loosened its belt and got involved.

"Is that that lady that wrote the cat book?"

"Yes it is now just say something smart about it . . . Timmy I'm gonna smack you in about a minute."

"Are you actually watching an interview with somebody who wrote a cat book?"

"You make fun of everything you don't have any feelings I don't care if you laugh I cried my eyes out when that cat died."

"Christ when Bobby Lee Cooper died I thought you were going to join a convent or something."

"You say just one word against that man I'll lay this lamp up alongside your head now be still a minute would you like it if I got my hair cut the way she has hers?"

"I read where she has it done by a fag up in Beverly Hills."

"God you're prejudiced. I read where she's a Capricorn."

"Let's see the last part of *Project U.F.O.*"

"You leave that set alone. Robert Schein's on next, he's the one that's having the affair with her."

"How do you know?"

"I read it."

"Two minutes to air, Jenny. Beautiful show."

"Is Mr. Schein in the studio?"

"Switchboard gal says she's jammed up, Jenny. About ten thousand calls. They love you."

"You're going to be bigger than *Sixty Minutes*."

"This way Robert. Right here."

"Hi, Robert."

"Jenny."

He looked so real under the arc lights. The blue eyes were alive. She saw life in them. He was growing into a personality—his personality—she knew. Television was making him real. This moment would make him real. This was the moment she had known instinctively was going to happen from the first night she saw him, felt the power in him. This was the moment when their destinies would fuse, meld, join in the common collective fantasy; made more real, more binding, because it was happening *on television*, his realm, his sanctuary. The biggest television news event of the year was about to happen on her show, her scoop, her exclusive, his triumph (her mind tripped madly ahead, hurtling clear and precise through the light-years of thought made possible by the time-freezing properties of the studio lights) and she wanted to laugh, cry, orgasm, hug him; the smile on his lips was a secret smile for her, he was out of Bookmaster's power, she would have him, her happiness machine, she would ride him forever and they would harness the silent moon . . .

". . . Glad that you brought up that question. Because, yes, I am aware that many people, many *well-meaning* people, believe that I have adopted this issue as a means of keeping my name before the public and furthering my career as an entertainer—"

Nod, Jennifer thought, *look thoughtful, don't give it away with a squeal of joy, you're skeptical now, probing . . .*

"—and I know some people find it hard to believe that a young urban guy out of the, let's say, very liberal-minded comic's milieu, can identify with *traditional* values, with basically *conservative* issues . . ."

Tap your finger on the desk, you want to break in, hit him with a high hard one, but don't quite because he's going on . . .

"—well, I'm not going to just *tell* you how strongly I feel about these things, Jennifer. I'm going to demonstrate to you. And to the people of America. I have the highest regard for you as a member of the press, and so I'm going to spring a little exclusive on you tonight, an announcement that I have pondered carefully for some time and which I fully believe to be the most satisfying and challenging decision of my life."

Look deeply interested now; he has your full attention but you are still detached, still the probing, critical journalist . . .

"I am very pleased to announce my engagement and forth-coming marriage to Miss Mary Ellen Olds, the daughter of the man I respect more than any other in public life—"

The moon swung down and exploded in Jennifer Blade's face.

"—and together we are going to launch my campaign for United States Senator from the State of New York—"

In a Malibu beach house, a male scream rent the twilight air. The voice screamed and screamed and screamed; it wafted down the evening wind, across the crashing surf, and people heard it, and froze in what they were doing, but made no move to investigate nor to call for help, because some pretty bizarre sounds had come out of the Governor's place . . .

"—I'm happy to say that my campaign workers have secured the necessary twenty thousand signatures, and that my name was en-tered one week ago, within the September nineteenth filing deadline—"

She was having trouble breathing; her lungs heaved for oxygen in the sudden vacuum; the grinning blue-eyed face before her had sucked the oxygen out of the universe like a vampire. The face, the set, the cameras, the flowers, swam and yawed before her. They were all in a fun house, a house of mirrors, and she wondered how she looked to the viewers—had the warp of glass caught the white of her eyes, making them bulge and bug in her astonishment? Or had the mischievous glass toyed with the hollows of her cheeks, sucking and pulling them in, making a hideous pucker?

She was dimly aware that there were other people around them; they had been joined by fresh grotesqueries—the former President of the United States, V. W. Olds, his bald head shooting up in bobbing balls of skin, and his daughter, Mary Ellen, whom the glass made to seem like a shimmering snake.

"They're here, Jennifer, this is our little surprise for you and our way of wishing you a very successful reign on *Face to Face*."

Through the ringing of all that was broken, Jennifer Blade heard as from a distance a woman's voice, flat and professional, a voice very much like her own:

"Ladies and gentlemen, a major political development—as well as a surprising personal announcement. Robert Schein, comedian, seeking to become Robert Schein, United States Senator from New York. As for his totally unexpected wedding plans—well, what is there to say but—" turning to the beaming couple flanked by proud Papa—"my very best wishes to you both." Off the set, a disembodied hand was describing a circle—the signal, it struck her, that someone had gone cuckoo.

"That's it for tonight's premiere edition of *Face to Face*. Thanks for watching—I'm Jennifer Blade."

There were voices all around her, hands reaching out of the ringing universe to touch her, clasp her, men's lips at her cheek and mouth and neck. She did not push them away as much as melt through them, formless as an image in a fun-house mirror. She felt her way, hypnotized, down off the set and toward the darkness, senses suspended, not daring to feel, not daring to think lest the screaming begin.

Two black eyes, hard as serpent's, loomed at her. And a very quiet voice hissed:

"Who has the power over him, Jennifer? H'mmm? Who has the power?"

And somewhere in America, a yawning voice spoke up out of torpor:

"I thought you said those two were having an affair. What's on at nine o'clock?"

Robert Schein was a phantom candidate, waging a phantom campaign.

He did not walk among the voters, as did the Democratic candidate—the liberal ex-basketball player—or the Republican incumbent—a respectable moderate Republican, gray and dour and competent.

No shopping center debates for Candidate Schein, none of the probing round-table discussions on Channel 13, no teas in influential east side apartments. No pressing of the flesh.

His commander, Bookmaster, preferred an air war.

Candidate Schein haunted and harassed his opponents from above, from the airwaves, incorporeal, chimerical, taunting: a campaign by talk show. When his opponents fired back, they found themselves shooting at . . . thin air. Schein had said nothing, argued nothing, made no challenges, proposed no concrete solutions for any of New York's problems—juvenile crime, mass transit repair, education, health, state aid for civil service salaries, the New York City budget. Nothing, save his single, relentless, monomaniacal, and infinitely repeated promise, his *idée fixe*, his seemingly sole premise for a Senate campaign:

"I will, if elected, immediately introduce a bill in the Senate making it illegal for a licensed American broadcast station to transmit program material from a sovereign Communist state."

Which was distilled to a popular slogan.

"BOOOOOOY, DO I HATE REDS!"

His opponents laughed at this—in the first week. In the first week both major camps reached the quick conclusion that Robert Schein was a crank candidate, running on an idiotic (if expensive) delusion.

Stranger things had happened.

"I mean look, he's comin' in six weeks before election day. Crazy bastard's not even a blip in the polls. He needs six years to match our guy's identity factor. I don't care if his name's Robert fucking *Redford*."

Such caprice led to costly blunders.

Responding to a Schein jibe launched from a New York City radio call-in show, the Republican incumbent—distracted and anxious over the very real challenge being mounted by the basketball star—waspishly dismissed Schein as "*The Gong Show* candidate."

The following morning the Senator's staff was presented with a petition containing 5,000 signatures demanding a public apology.

The Senator—a courteous man—apologized.

"BOOOOOY, was hiiiiiiis faaaaaaace reeeed," Schein triumphantly cracked to Stanley Siegel the next day.

Schein's blitz of radio and TV appearances produced equal-time requirements, of course—but his opponents quickly found that the opportunities were not worth taking: not cost-effective. Even compared to the lean and telegenic basketball star, Robert Schein —handsome, clean-cut, modest, witty, and earnest in his single-minded crusade—ruled the turf of the TV studios.

His opponents decided to ignore him and concentrate on one another.

Mark Teller watched Schein's phantom campaign develop with the helpless rage of a man in a dream. His worst suspicions had come true. Something ghastly was happening; if he could only lift his arms, he could prevent it. But he could not lift his arms. They were mired in syrup. Every circuit of his brain throbbed for action, but his body could not respond. He could not even scream a warning to the people around him, the people who could not see the ghastly danger unfolding. His voice had been taken away. No one listened to him.

Only he could see the horror taking shape. Only his eyes could discern the substance that had fallen into the shadows of public scrutiny, the shadows between informed, serious political journalism and pop-gossip idolatry.

He wondered whether he had gone paranoid. Maybe his obsessions were deluding him. Maybe Robert Schein was nothing more than a harmless sideshow, a preposterous futility, an embodiment of half-coherent delusions, one of the countless buffoons and pretenders who pranced on the peripheries of so many American elections, mocking the essential hollowness of all the "serious" candidates with their intimations of perfectible man—a necessary clown, but nothing more.

Maybe. Maybe.

And then came the first New York public-opinion poll since Schein entered the race.

"I don't fucking believe it."

"It isn't possible."

Twenty-seven percent of those sampled said they would vote for Independent Candidate Robert Schein.

On October 10 Mal Bookmaster released The Ad.

It saturated the New York TV channels from dawn until sign-off. It became as familiar to viewers as Cronkite's mustache, as the Pillsbury Dough-Boy's ticklish belly, as David Hartman's simple blazer, as the Dorito Crunch. Compared to his opponents' "scientifically researched" spot-ads—blinding montages of tousled heads, rolled-up sleeves, indefatigable grins, stretching arms, snappy quick-cut quotes—The Ad shimmered with the guileless simplicity of a Golden Oldie Original Artists album offer.

It seared itself into the collective political consciousness.

The Ad was nothing more than a thirty-second cut from Robert Schein's famed July Fourth CBN skit with former President V. W. Olds.

The sound overlay was the voice of Bobby Lee Cooper singing "America the Beautiful."

At the very conclusion, over a freeze-frame of Schein smiling up at Olds, an announcer's quiet voice said:

"*His* face. Not the Reds. Robert Schein. For the U.S. Senate."

By Halloween Robert Schein commanded the preferences of thirty-one percent of New York's voters.

His opponents began to sense a terrible, clammy panic—the panic that descends upon soldiers who suddenly realize they have been flanked.

The eccentricities that had reduced Schein's campaign to a joke, a sideshow in the "respectable" media, were now unveiled as a cool and cunning strategy—an electronic end run around the conventional electoral process.

The eleventh-hour entry into the race, so much the object of ridicule by the major-party professionals: it wasn't a liability at all. Robert Schein did not need time to establish his "identity." Robert Schein *was* "identity"—pure identity. His late declaration simply reduced his margin for error; compressed the time frame in which he was vulnerable to accountability on the broad range of issues.

The lack of a complete platform was, in fact, a liability in the eyes of informed, serious voters. At the same time, it attracted Schein to people who yearned for a simple perception of things, who yearned to reduce the bewildering complexity of issues into one easy slogan—the way they saw it done on TV.

There were a lot of those people around.

Too late, the "major" candidates and the "respectable" press reacted.

They found themselves turning slowly, too slowly, like Teller's dream-self, mired in the syrup of their own fatuity, agonizing, to defend against the sudden horror emerging from the shadows.

The New York Times unleashed its most astute political reporters to probe Schein's background, search out his backers—they were unsuccessful, save for Bookmaster, whom they pilloried—lay bare his barren political thought-structure, savage his insolent isolation from the voters, and question again the dubious role of the Continental Broadcasting Network in launching him into political prominence.

The Village Voice lampooned him and the voters who were stupid enough to take him seriously.

The problem was—and everyone knew it—that not too many of Robert Schein's followers read the *Times* and the *Voice*.

On the cover of *Faces*, by contrast, Robert Schein was THE CANDIDATE-COMIC WHO ISN'T KIDDING.

At ten o'clock on the morning of November 1, Mark Teller was hunched over his typewriter, cold coffee at his elbow. Elizabeth had left for work. He was feverishly redrafting his *Eidolon* piece for submission to the *Times*. At this point, he guessed, it was a matter of going through the motions. But something more was at stake for him. He sensed that if he stopped trying to deflect Robert Schein, he might go mad.

The telephone rang.

"I'm in town, I've got to come right over."

His blood froze at the shock of her voice. How like her, to make it sound as though she were picking up a conversation begun five minutes ago.

He fought to keep his voice even.

"You can go to hell, Jennifer." He'd been wanting to suggest that to her for a long time. He replaced the receiver on its cradle.

Now his concentration was exploded. She was the last person in the world he needed to hear from. All the old emotions—hurt, lust, anger, jealousy, frustration, despair—surged back into him, water held back too long, bursting its dam, returning to its natural level.

He clutched the sides of his typewriter, lowered his head onto the carriage, and sobbed.

The telephone rang again.

He looked at it. Let it ring. He felt his temples throbbing. His teeth were clenched.

It rang.

He tore the phone from the cradle and drew in his breath to roar at her.

"Don't hang up!"

Something in her voice made him contain his rage.

"God's sake Mark don't hang up!"

"I'm listening."

"I've got to talk to you about Schein, it's important. Can I come see you?"

"Lover's quarrel?" He couldn't resist it. "Want me to talk some sense into his head, get you two crazy kids back together?"

"Don't—I haven't got time—listen to me—"

"I'm busy."

Her voice rose to a shriek. "You weren't too busy to fly out to Los Angeles last month and try to humiliate me in front of a room

full of newspaper people! Do you think I'd be calling you if I
wasn't *desperate*?" Her voice lowered, became almost wheedling—
a quality he'd never thought he would hear in her.

"Mark, I'd like to be friends with you. I know you want to get
Schein. I have something you can use. Please, Mark? Let me come
over?"

He thought about that.

"About our exalted friendship, let me get one thing straight
with you, Jenny. I hate your guts. Now if we can operate on that
understanding, come over."

There was a moment of silence. And then he heard the line
click.

Twenty-five minutes later, his buzzer rang.

A different Jennifer Blade stood in his doorway than the bold,
magnetic young temptress of a lost golden evening. Teller thought
of the overnight bag, the white sweat socks. He was stunned to
look into her drawn face. Aside from his brief confrontation with
her from across the interview suite at the Century Plaza in September, he had not seen Jennifer Blade eye to eye for nearly a
year.

She was thin. The hardness that used to appear at her jawline
had spread over her face, drawing it inward. The light mockery in
her eyes, the hint of absurdity that used to modify some of the
sharpness of her tongue, was gone—replaced by a gray, wary, flat
film.

Makeup and the television camera masked most of what had
happened to her face. But looking at it now, he realized he could
never imagine her as a child. It was the most utterly, irrevocably
adult face he had ever seen, a face that could not escape its own
consequences, turn away from the enveloping forces it had helped
generate.

And she was still a beautiful woman. And all of the knowledge
that he had of her came back in a flood, and he knew that he was
still susceptible to loving her, even through his hatred.

It was a chamber he would never open again.

"Come in."

She did something sudden with her head, something that might
have been a move to kiss him on the cheek, and then pulled back.

She walked past him into the living room, her quick eyes taking it in.

"I see you have a roommate now."

He didn't comment.

"Somebody who's good enough for you, I hope. Homecoming queen? Cheerleader?"

A joke from their relationship.

"What exactly is it I can do for you, Jennifer?"

"Would it make any difference at all to you if I told you I've missed you? I mean, I've missed talking to you . . . Teller . . ."

If he so much as moved a muscle, he sensed, she would be in his arms.

He didn't move.

"Can I offer you some coffee?" He was polite, neutral.

"Come on, give me a break." Forced playfulness in her voice. "I meant what I said on the phone, Mark. I think we should be friends . . ."

She was making him crazy. He suddenly felt a murderous impulse toward her; the wild wish to crush, punish, retaliate.

He smiled.

"I believe you also said something about Schein, something that I can use. I assume you're going to tell me about it."

There had been the beginnings of a softness at her mouth, a wistful smile, an easing—but now her face collapsed again into a hard mask.

"I have a tape." She thrust a hand into her shoulder bag and withdrew a miniature recorder. "I recorded this one night in L.A. Bookmaster didn't know I was taping him and he spilled the whole machinery behind Schein. He implicates Donovan. He ridicules Schein's followers. He pretty much takes the credit for mind-fucking the voters with a fake candidate, for the voters' own good. If enough people heard this tape, I can't imagine Robert Schein getting elected dogcatcher. I don't care how devoted his fans are."

"Play it."

Jennifer pushed the "play" button.

"Consortium of businessmen . . . product is a candidate for the U.S. Senate . . . I supply the candidate . . . so the Colonel can cover the Summer Olympics . . . two-way cable . . . instant elections . . . Society needs an apparatus . . . *Television hasn't got a memory.* . . .

give me two months, people are going to barely remember Robert Schein the comedian . . . the Robert Schein bandwagon building . . . before it even *knows* it's building . . ."

She clicked the tape off.

Mark Teller sat for a long time with his fingertips pressed into his chin.

"The smoking pistol," he whispered finally.

Jennifer ejected the tape cassette and lobbed it over to him. It landed in his lap.

In his lap. There it was—a miracle. The one weapon that might work against Robert Schein: an attack on the gullibility, on the self-esteem *of his followers.*

For what was Robert Schein if not his followers? At every crucial step of his career he had advanced—rather, had been nudged ahead—on the impetus of the self-interested needs of others—from himself, Mark Teller; to Al Gnagy at Stitch's; to Jennifer's career hopes; to WRAP's ratings requirements; to Bookmaster's scheme; to the competitive needs of the magazines and reviewers and gossip columnists; to the self-flattering approval of the Hollywood crowd; to the ideological interests of a political cabal; to the random inchoate mooning delusions of an entire society . . .

A whole system of usings—and Schein had floated to the top on it, like a cork in an ocean of narcissism.

And now, ironically, the ultimate using: one whose usage of Schein had been thwarted, using him, Mark Teller, to bring Schein down.

"Why did you bring this to me? If you want it broadcast, why didn't you broadcast it on your show?"

She shook her head violently; he saw the pain crease her features.

"I couldn't. I couldn't do it to him myself. God, Mark, I can't explain it to you. It's like I love him, but it's not the kind of love you'd understand; I don't think I can put it into words. I don't know who he is, or what's going on inside him, or if he has any insides. I don't know him. I'm sure there's a psychological explanation for his kind of personality; he's only real when he's inhabiting somebody else's thoughts, somebody else's ideas. *You saw it, too, Teller.* I don't need to explain it to you, you saw it. You sensed the same thing in him and you needed it and you reached right in and grabbed it. You got what you wanted. *You turned him on.* I just wanted more of it than you did. I looked in there past his eyes and I kept looking until I saw myself looking back. Or something that I wanted to be myself. And I just knew that if I looked long enough, if I stayed close long enough it would come true, it would come real. He's like watching television, Mark. You watch just a little bit, you're okay, you're not hooked, you're still your own person. But people can't watch just a little bit. They watch a little longer and a little longer and pretty soon the goddamn tube has become their whole identity, it's like the tube has traded identities with them, it has their personalities locked up inside. Well, I looked so long I got sucked in just like I hoped I would. Right through his eyes. Now I'm television, too, and I can't get off it, and Bookmaster's pulled my plug and I've got to have it back and if I don't get it back I'll have to destroy it, only I can't do it myself . . . *you turned him on, Mark! You have to turn him off. Nobody else can! Do it for me! Please!*"

He would have thought she was crazy.

Except that he understood every word she said.

But now another thought intruded.

"If this tape airs, Bookmaster will kill you."

"He already has."

"No, he hasn't. But he will. He's vicious. He will literally destroy you."

"I don't care. Look, I can take care of myself. I'll handle that problem. Let me worry about myself. *Please get that tape on the air, Mark. Please!*"

Teller turned the cassette over in his hands. He could get it on the air this evening. By tomorrow morning it would be a national scandal. Schein finished, Bookmaster in disgrace, Colonel Eddie Donovan and his opportunistic little network ruined. A salutary object lesson to the country in the perils of celebrity-worship. All of Teller's resentments laid to rest in one stroke; his obsession satisfied, his self-respect vindicated. He'd be a hero. Might be a political future in it for him, in fact . . . the legitimate way, of course . . . clean up the airwaves, reorganize the FCC, new master plan for the network structure . . .

And if Jennifer wanted to take her chances with Bookmaster? Her problem. He owed her nothing. She had caused him greater anguish than he would have believed a woman could.

The moment was his. In the silence of his living room, with

Jennifer Blade watching him wide-eyed from the sofa, he let the moment engulf and lift him, the warm liquid rush of power, of satisfaction, of the sense of control returning to his life after a year in hell. He gripped the cassette in a hard caress, wedged it in the hollow between his thumb and forefinger, feeling the small impersonal plastic rim digging into his flesh.

He let his head slip back, drew himself together, and unleashed a yell of ecstasy, a yell that came all the way from his boyhood, from the Ozark Hills, from the exuberance of an age not yet defiled by heros.

And skimmed the cassette across the room toward Jennifer, where it hit her in the breastbone with a *crack!*

"Take it. I'm not your executioner."

She was up at the door in an instant. Hand on the knob, she turned back and looked at him, and for just a moment her face was filled with the lush softness he used to love.

"Gutless," she said. "Gutless, Teller."

And she was gone.

 The chairman of the Schein for Senator Committee—a Wall Street investment banker (and a member of the Phaëthon Society) —announced a rally for Robert Schein on the night before Election Day. The rally would be held at a location of particular sentimental importance to the candidate, the campaign chairman announced—in front of Stitch's, where Robert Schein originally came to the attention of New Yorkers. The master of ceremonies for the evening would be Al Gnagy, proprietor of Stitch's and "longtime friend" of Schein.

It would be the candidate's first appearance in front of a public gathering. Accompanying him would be his fiancée, Mary Ellen Olds, and her father, former President V. W. Olds.

Jennifer Blade strode into Lon Stagg's office without knocking. The anchorman looked up from his desk in surprise. He flushed and hastily attempted to sweep away a sheaf of papers that he had been reading when Jennifer burst through the door.

She thought for an instant that she had caught Stagg in the act of reading porn. But she glimpsed a page before it disappeared into his middle desk drawer and realized that Stagg had been absorbed in the week's ratings totals. Lon Stagg read ratings pamphlets with the same furtive enjoyment that other men experienced from flipping through *Penthouse*. On the walls of his office were pinups of ratings sheets from weeks in which he had done especially well.

"*Jenny!*" He stuck out a hand, but did not rise—probably trying to cover an erection, Jennifer thought. "Hey, I thought you were in the Golden State, big-time lady!"

She mentally crossed her eyes. "I came into town to cover Schein's rally. We're going live on the network with it and I'll get some extra footage for *Face to Face*."

"What brings you over *WRAP-Around* way?" His face cracked open with his best lopsided little-boy grin.

That man should not be permitted to open his mouth without a TelePrompTer, Jennifer decided silently. Instead of replying right away, she fixed him with a long gaze and a mysterious smile.

Then she turned around and walked back to the door, letting her hips undulate in a parody of sensuality that Stagg undoubtedly perceived as a woman's rightful style.

She pushed the door to his office closed and slid the bolt into place. She turned around to face him and slid her hand deep into her shoulder bag. The motion was somehow carnal.

When she withdrew it—from Stagg's expression, he might have been expecting a garter—she was holding the cassette.

"I have two surprises for you," she said softly. "One of them is this."

Stagg squinted at the object.

"What's the other one?" he asked. He thought he might know—but he didn't dare believe it. Stagg had had the "hots"—as he liked to call them—for Jennifer ever since she had first showed up at the station. But something about her decisive, authoritarian manner inhibited him from approaching her with the line that he found sure-fire among stewardesses and cocktail waitresses: "How's your sex life?"

Was she about to come on to him? Jesus, think of the time he'd wasted . . .

"This," she said. She was wearing a suede skirt that came to mid-calf. Under the skirt she was wearing boots. She seemed to be undoing the buttons that held the skirt together down the side.

Stagg couldn't believe it! It was just incredible what being with an anchorman did to women in the eighteen-to-thirty-four age group. They couldn't leave him alone! But now came a moment of decision. The beautiful woman stripping in his office was between him and the clothes hanger. On the one hand, he wanted to tear off his clothes and ravish her right away, before she somehow came to her senses . . . changed her mind . . . on the other hand, he was wearing a brand-new Adolfo three-piece charcoal chalk stripe . . . elegant set of threads . . . really ought to get those pants on a hanger . . .

Unbuttoning his vest (the jacket was already hung, thank God) he began moving away from his desk, circling Jennifer, holding her gaze over his left shoulder. His best side. He got the vest off—she was down to bra, panties, and boots, *incredible body*—and reached for his belt buckle.

His boots! He was wearing the damned Botticelli pull-ons, they came practically up to his knees, he'd have to get them off first or the pants would get snagged; he liked his pants tight, especially in the ass, women liked a guy's ass, he'd read that in *Viva* . . .

Still holding Jennifer's gaze, Stagg reached down carefully, bringing the heel of his right boot up across his left leg, and tugged.

The boot slid off.

Now the other one.

Jennifer was moving slowly toward him, her hands at the clasp of her brassiere. *God, she was going to keep her boots on!* What a turn-on! He felt his excitement surge; it made his knees weak, made it hard to stand on one leg . . .

He had to get to the clothes hanger behind her. Not to make it obvious! Tugging now at his left boot he began to hop, carefully, one hop at a time, trying to circle her, trying not to spoil the mood of her sudden desire . . .

"Hey, baby, I'm a great big bunny rabbit. Come get me." Maybe if he made it a game. She was smiling now—almost laughing, it seemed. Funny how women react when they get their juices up . . . some of 'em are screamers . . . he hoped Jennifer wasn't a screamer . . . still, it wouldn't be bad for his rep if the word got around the office that he was banging Jennifer Blade.

She was stalking him now, and in his haste he lost his balance. Still gripping his right boot, he went hop-hopping backwards, toward his desk, like some demented Scotsman doing the Highland fling. She was on him as the small of his back hit the desk, and

together they went plummeting back across the surface, and her
expert hands were at his trousers, and he was free, and they slid
back further still, down the other side, in a tangled heap of tanned
skin and Adolfo fabric and hot mouths sucking . . . his hand
grasped at the top of a file cabinet as he went down, her on top of
him, honey-blond hair cascading, and a stack of ratings sheets fluttered down around them, covering them with the sweet sticky
musk of *demographics*, and all the statistically concupiscent ladies
of the eighteen-to-thirty-four age group coated him like a Xerox
harem as he came and came . . .

Afterwards, after she had finished undressing him and lay with
her legs entwined with his, her hand gently massaging his satiated
member, Jennifer Blade pressed her lips to the base of Lon Stagg's
ear and whispered to him:

"I've been dying to do that for months . . . I wouldn't let myself
while I worked here . . . I make it a rule never to get involved at
the office . . . but after I left I couldn't stop thinking of you . . .
your hair . . . that fabulous smile of yours . . . those sexy looks you
give . . . those *clothes* . . ."

"Hey," he whispered back. "I can dig it. But don't let yourself
get involved, Jenny, I'm not into deep commitments . . ."

She snickered into his ear—she didn't believe him, he guessed.
None of them did. What the hell . . . but she put a finger over his
lips to silence him.

"Lon . . . I have something else for you . . . remember the first
thing I showed you, that cassette tape . . . Lon, it's got dynamite on
it . . ."

After she had dressed and gone, Lon Stagg sat at his desk in his
snakeskin-pattern Jockey undershorts (the same pattern Lydell
Mitchell of the Baltimore Colts wore in that full-color ad) and
tried to figure out all that had happened in the last thirty minutes
of his life.

One: He had Done the Trick with one of the foxiest women in
the United States.

Two: He had been presented (by this same chick) with a piece
of news material that could give him the instant national renown
he longed for.

Three: He had ripped the bottom of the best pair of suit pants
he had ever owned.

Three did not matter for the moment. Stagg turned the cassette over in his hands and frowned at it. Jennifer had said she wanted to see him as a network anchorman. (So did he.) And not on a low-rent network like CBN, either. (He'd had the same thought.) But one of the Big Three, one of the blue-chip networks, a quality organization that a man of his stature and reputation deserved. (Exactly.)

Don't waste this bombshell on WRAP or even CBN, she'd urged him. Play it. Listen to it. See if he agreed with her that it was major-scoop, dynamite stuff. Then call her at the Hilton . . . she'd explain who the guy was that did all the talking on the tape . . . and from there, they'd figure out how to get it, and him, on a network news show. He'd be an instant star, she said . . . it was a revelation on a par with Woodward and Bernstein . . .

Why waste another minute? He pulled a cassette recorder out of his desk drawer and played the tape.

It was dynamite, all right. Even Lon Stagg, with his limited understanding of politics, grasped that. Robert Schein a stooge for a secret businessmen's cabal! Everything arranged behind closed doors, like in that television movie a couple of years ago.

In a way, Lon Stagg felt almost personally betrayed. He'd been a big Robert Schein fan. Used a lot of his jokes at parties, in fact. Thought he was terrific. But if all this was true . . . bugger Bob Schein, it was Lon Stagg's ticket up!

He wondered who the man was. Obviously the guy who pulled Schein's strings. The voice sounded awfully familiar, but Stagg couldn't quite place it.

His course of action was clear: Call Jennifer at the Hilton and get the ball rolling. The sooner the better.

No. One thing to do first.

Call his agent. His new manager. The new guy he'd hired just before this incredible windfall, to help him out with what he felt was a stagnating image. No pun intended.

The guy who'd been recommended to him by the Big Boss himself, the Colonel, Eddie Donovan.

California guy. But he was in town, too, Stagg recalled. Be good to run over this thing with him first. The guy had made it clear—he expected to know every last detail about Stagg's life. Professional and personal.

So be it.

He dialed the Hilton and asked for the suite of Mal Book-master.

Stitch's was ablaze in the cold November night air.

Spotlights and television lights seared into the seedy little establishment, turning its dark facade into a glowing ember of garish red.

The police had reluctantly agreed to cordon off this block of Second Avenue, sending traffic into confusion throughout the Upper East Side. But even this cleared space was not enough for the throng of fifteen thousand people that surged and pushed into the area to see Robert Schein return to the point of his first fame.

The street was already clogged with police cars, mobile vans from New York television stations, and a brass band that played from the platform of a truck. Scaffolding had been erected in the street directly in front of Stitch's; it was upon this surface, piled with bunting and backed with a giant, billowing photograph, that Candidate Schein and his fiancée would greet his supporters.

The rally had been scheduled for eight P.M., but the crowd had started gathering as early as six. Now the streets around Stitch's were a nighttime wheatfield of straining humanity. Bookmaster, nearly invisible near the base of the scaffolding, noticed expensive leather coats, angora turtlenecks, fashionable scarves. This crowd was not rabble. These were the cognoscenti, the people who waited in lines around a city block in freezing rain for the latest Woody Allen. Hip. Serious fans. A killer crowd. He had selected these people out of their separate lives as surely as if he had lifted them up by tweezers, and set them here. There was a bright moon, and the crowd's faces were bright and cold with a skittish intensity. They pressed in on the scaffolding, their collective voice high with manic chatter. Bookmaster permitted himself to feel very proud.

Because of the national interest in Robert Schein's phenomenal climb to the threshold of political power—the latest poll showed him the slight favorite, with a scant plurality of voter support—the four networks had decided to pre-empt prime time programming and telecast Schein's rally live. The networks and the New York stations agreed to share four "pool" cameras, due to the shortage of space. Three of the cameras would be at fixed points. The fourth would be a roving minicam.

Among the reporters present would be Jennifer Blade. Bookmaster kept glancing toward the shiny, roped-off area where the silhouetted cameras stood mounted like machine guns; where correspondents and crewmen flitted in and out of the harsh light like sentries in an armed camp.

There was a matter he had to settle with Jennifer tonight. Here, in the midst of the crowd. It would only take a minute.

At seven thirty, the band on the truck bed swung into a series of Sousa marches. The guests of honor began to pick their way up the metal stairs to the top of the speaker's platform: a few independent candidates for lesser offices. A sprinkling of New York entertainers and celebrities who claimed longstanding friendship with Schein. Bodyguards.

As each new arrival emerged at the top step and crossed into the field of arc lights toward the folding chairs, the moiling crowd set up a howl of recognition. They were deep-throated howls, animal roars, and they carried a suggestion of something deeper, darker, more urgent than mere campaign fervor.

The personalities on the platform felt it, and shivered. Stepping into the arc light's glow was, for many of them, like stepping into a field of fire. The crowd's intensity rolled up onto the platform in hot waves, dispersing the pleasant chill of the November urban night. Under the moon, their white glistening faces waited, slack and grinning.

A cheer greeted the arrival of Colonel Eddie Donovan, president of the Continental Broadcasting Network.

The loudest roar came as former President V. W. Olds reached the top step, stumbled briefly, and swung his arms in a jaunty winner's wave toward the wheatfield of people. The crowd—most of whose members had ridiculed Olds in their private lives— unleashed a great cascading roar that swept down Second Avenue like a tidal wave, crashing into Midtown.

Olds ushered his wife, a terrified woman in a pink coat, into the cross-hairs and across the stage. The band played, "The Bear Went Over the Mountain."

Teller could hear the *wheep* of the public-address system from as far west as Lexington Avenue. As he ran toward Second down 68th he could feel the crowd begin to thicken and slow, like stream water rushing into a deep pool. He was breathing hard, concentrating on his pace, on the running, breath coming in regular gasps. He didn't want to think what was going to happen once he reached the rally. He didn't know. He didn't really have a plan. Avoid Bookmaster and his goons . . . keep from getting killed if he could . . . *get to Schein!* Dismantle him. It would have to be that way, he saw. Somebody would literally have to take Schein apart in front of a crowd. He could not be destroyed by the media. He ate the media. Every one of Teller's attempts to ruin Schein on the air had failed—worse, had been turned into fuel to further propel Schein's phantom image. Schein was impregnable in the studios, invincible on the airwaves. After tonight, Teller knew, after the election, Schein would vanish from corporeal presence forever. He would ascend on the airwaves, he would rule on the airwaves. It would be the beginning of a new order: medium and messenger forever intertwined, indistinguishable.

So the confrontation, if it was ever to take place, would have to be in the flesh. A primal reckoning under the November moon, on a temporal street, under the witnessing eyes of human beings.

Teller's pace was slowed by jostling bodies. He had not expected the crowd to be on this scale. Could he worm his body through it? He sensed the hysteria in the collective temperament around him. He should have arrived hours earlier. But that would have left him open to Bookmaster . . . he could hear the echoing voice of the Schein for Senator chairman as the man began to make introductions. The platform and the red facade of Stitch's were small bubbles of light across an acre of human flesh.

He came to Third Avenue and sprinted uptown for four blocks, across the current to 72nd. At that intersection he encountered an immobile mass of humanity, a blackening pond.

Like a swimmer about to plunge into dark and icy waters, Teller hesitated, took a breath, and knifed into the crowd.

"WHAT WE ARE HERE TO CELEBRATE TONIGHT IS NOTHING LESS THAN A REVOLUTION IN THIS COUNTRY'S ELECTORAL PROCESS . . ."

Jennifer Blade drew the lapels of her coat close around her. Despite the heat of the crowd and the warmth here in the TV pit, she felt a deep-winter chill. The crowd frightened her. She had seen madness in the faces. The crowd had come here not just to cheer, not just to worship, but to devour something. There was the kind of ecstasy that she had seen in sweat-soaked faces at Tennessee churches when she reported the Bobby Lee Cooper phenomenon a year ago. But this ecstasy was tempered with something else—a kind of crackling current of raw power, undirected, capable at any moment of whipping out of control.

"—WE ARE ON THE EVE OF A NEW ERA IN THE SYMBIOTIC DIALOGUE BETWEEN A PUBLIC OFFICIAL AND HIS PUBLIC—"

They were all mad. She was, certainly. She had come here to devour something, too. Schein. But she had come unarmed. The tape—what had happened to Stagg? Gutless bastard. Like Teller. Covering his own ass, probably. The men she had turned to were ineffectual. She would have to carry it out herself.

But how? If she'd had the tape, she might rush onstage and stick a recorder in front of a microphone, let it play until they dragged her away. But she didn't have the goddamn tape.

"—A NEW WEDDING OF COMMUNICATIONS TECHNOLOGY AND THE HUMAN COMPASSION NECESSARY TO PRESERVE OUR TRADITIONAL VALUES—"

Perhaps she would rush the stage anyway, seize a microphone, blurt the connection that linked Bookmaster and Schein and Colonel Donovan's foolish group . . .

It wouldn't work. The papers would play it the way they'd played Teller's outburst on the air. A lover scorned. A sideshow.

And Bookmaster would kill her.

In the first heat of his betrayal of her, in that first wrenching knowledge of Schein and Mary Ellen Olds, and for weeks afterward, she had felt that death would be an insignificant price for revenge on Schein and Bookmaster. She wasn't sure she felt that way now. Death was heavy around her in this crowd, unconscious perhaps to the crowd itself, but palpable to her. It made her sick with horror. She wanted to live.

"—AND NOW, BEFORE WE MEET THE CANDIDATE HIMSELF, IT IS MY VERY GREAT PLEASURE TO—"

But what of this crowd? How to explain its stench of death? She recalled old conversations with Teller—he would talk earnestly about the things one gives up in one's adulation of the famous. It's impossible, he would say, to identify so heavily with someone else, and not lose a corresponding measure of your own identity.

Was this crowd an ultimate expression of that truth?

No time for such thoughts. She turned her gaze to the base of the speaker's platform. There in the shadows stood Bookmaster like a coiled snake on a rock. The sight of him filled her with dread and loathing. But he had said to look for him there—he had something for her.

Something, perhaps, that she could use, a scrap of information she could twist around in some way to hurl at him and his hideous puppet.

She glanced at her watch. Ten minutes until eight.

"Back in a minute," she called to her producer.

She headed for the shadows.

Al Gnagy was at the microphone now.

Dressed in a robin's-egg-blue tuxedo, his eyes as wild and distended as the crowd's eyes, Gnagy clutched the microphone close to his mouth, popping his *p*'s like gunshots as he rambled on about his early association with "this man of genius, this populist visionary." Gnagy's spittle glittered in the arc lights; there were rivers of sweat on his skull face despite the cold air.

The crowd gaped at him with a large loon smile. He was the warm-up act before the main rock'n'roll show.

Teller was deep in the crowd by now, wedging and squeezing his way forward. It was a nightmare journey. People turned around to see who was pushing them from behind. Some of them recognized him as the man who had tried to destroy their idol on television, and these people were not kind. A red welt had opened under Teller's left eye from an elbow thrown there. A hand had come across his mouth, bruising his lips. He had been shoved, tripped, cursed, ridiculed. The crowd hated him. Teller sensed that it was capable of killing him at any moment. He fought claustrophobia, fought the terror of sinking deeper into a mass of human quicksand, and pushed on.

"MANY'S THE TIME AFTER HIS ACT, BOBBY SCHEIN AND I WOULD SIT LONG HOURS HERE IN THIS ESTABLISHMENT YOU SEE RIGHT BEHIND ME . . . 'AL,' HE'D SAY, 'THE PEOPLE OF AMERICA NEED A NEW VISION, THEY NEED SOMEONE TO HELP THEM REDIS-

COVER THEIR ESSENTIAL HONESTY AND DECENCY AND COMPASSION . . ."

"Hello, Mal." She had virtually to scream to make herself heard above the din from the crowd and from the speakers over their heads.

Bookmaster gave a jump. He turned flashing serpent's eyes on her.

His mouth formed the word, "Jenny."

She put her mouth to his ear. "You said you had something for me."

The crowd had somehow broken past the rope barrier around the scaffolding; bodies pressed in on them.

She saw Bookmaster smile; saw him nod his balding head in vigorous affirmation.

He reached a hand inside his overcoat.

He withdrew it, clutching a small, thin rectangular object.

He brandished it in front of her eyes.

It was a tape cassette. She recognized it: the cassette she had given Stagg.

In that instant Jennifer Blade knew that she was about to die.

The fixed smile was still on Bookmaster's face. His eyes glittered. His free hand was sliding back into the pocket of his black outer coat.

She knew he had a pistol inside.

In a flash, Jennifer understood that Mal Bookmaster had picked the perfect setting in which to kill her. No one would hear the pistol go off. In this crush of humanity, she would not even fall. No attention would be drawn to her. Her body would not be discovered for hours—another random, senseless incident of gunplay in New York. It could even happen to a television personality!

With his usual thoroughness, Bookmaster had thought of everything.

He had even created the crowd—Schein's crowd—to absorb her murder.

The crowd!

Jennifer thrust her mouth into the moonstruck face of the fan nearest her and screamed at the top of her lungs:

"THIS MAN'S GOT A GUN HE'S GOING TO SHOOT ROBERT SCHEIN!"

Faces turned.

"—LIKE MY OWN SON—" Gnagy droned on the platform.

"Hunh?"

"What the fuck!"

"Grab him!"

Hands reached out for Bookmaster. Something glinted at his waist and then was lost in the shadows. In the instant before the crowd closed on Bookmaster, his wild eyes met Jennifer's.

"*Who's got the power?*" she mouthed to him.

Then, in the loudest shriek she could muster:

"THERE! HE'S THE ONE! STOP HIM HIT HIM KILL HIM KILL HIM KILL HIM KILL HIM!"

She could feel all the animal lust in the crowd coalescing into the small group of people who had now encircled Bookmaster and flung him to the pavement. The energy surged into them at the speed of light. Men, women, middle-class; there were perhaps a dozen of them. She glimpsed expensive leather overcoats, tweed jackets, a woman's handbag rising and falling. But some mania now gripped these people. Their teeth bared, their voices cursing, laughing, snarling, they seemed to have absorbed the collective electric frenzy of the animal crowd. She could almost see the currents flashing from body to body, in a gigantic but ever-receding V, until they grounded in the twelve or so men and women who were now beating Mal Bookmaster into a bloody sponge.

Even through the din of the loudspeakers and the general crowd noise, Jennifer could hear the rhythmic, oddly monotonous sough and thog of fists and boots slamming into Bookmaster's flesh. There were splotches of blood on some of the leather coats now. Jennifer realized that if she did not get herself out of the way she could be drawn into the melee and crushed along with Bookmaster.

Her back pressed against the scaffolding. She felt along it with her palms, gripped the cold metal tubings that formed a network below the platform. Spinning around, she reached as high as she could and pulled her body up. Her arms trembled. She could feel the entire speaker's platform sway with her weight.

Her feet found purchase on a crossbeam. Turning carefully, she gripped the beams behind her and looked down at the murder taking place beneath her.

Bookmaster's face was a scarlet, pulpy sausage. The crowd had formed a perfect circle around him now, kicking and smashing him with an almost ritualistic precision. She wondered whether he could still see, could make out her form on the scaffolding above him.

"Who's got the power?" she screamed down at him. "*Who's got the power, Mal?*"

A heavy face turned from its work to stare up at her, like a sheepdog with blood on its chops. What if he thought she was Bookmaster's accomplice? He'd pull her down and kill her.

On impulse, she waved merrily at the suspicious face.

"Jennifer Blade," she called into a cupped palm. "CBN News!"

The murderous face split into a grin. "Hi, Jenny!" The man flipped her a jaunty salute and turned back to his labors.

"—GIVES ME GREAT PLEASURE TO INTRODUCE THE NEXT UNITED STATES SENATOR FROM NEW YORK—"

The metallic voice above her brought her out of what had been a hypnotic daze. A cold wind whipped down from dark Uptown, above the crowd, and stung at her eyes.

The horror of what had passed beneath her knifed in on the wind. She turned her face and retched into the scaffolding—once, twice, three times. Her body convulsed, and she was seized with the fear that she would faint and tumble back into the feral crowd.

She tightened her grip, and held. She was sobbing.

Above her, they were introducing Schein. Spotlights swept over her head. The crowd let loose a roar that made her ears ring, a roar that she could feel in the palms of her hands as it coursed along the metal girders. She saw the silhouetted TV cameras swivel and pan, and she remembered that she had deserted her station. The Continental Broadcasting Network was covering Robert Schein's ascension without her.

She became aware that there had been a small noise at her side for the last several minutes—a persistent *pip-pip-pipping*.

Her beeper. They were paging her on her beeper.

Directly above, she knew, Robert Schein was advancing toward the microphone. People were screaming, sobbing, embracing one another, waving their arms like sinners about to be redeemed.

She forced her gaze again to the foot of the scaffolding.

She saw that the horror was not yet over.

A curious thing was happening. She gazed in stupefied fascination. The hideous red wreckage that had been Mal Bookmaster's body had begun a macabre journey back into the bowels of the crowd.

It had been an isolated killing.

Most people in the vicinity had scarcely torn their eyes from the speaker's platform long enough to comprehend more than a scuffle.

It was as though the crowd itself had unconsciously detached a portion of itself, a set of jaws, to do the necessary work.

But now, even as Robert Schein's hand caressed the microphone above her, Jennifer could see the pattern of rippling awareness, the turning of heads, wheatstalks touched by a gust of night wind.

It was a chain reaction—an outward impinging of information, a combustion of turned heads, *like the airwaves*, Jennifer imagined. And behind the widening ripples floated the corpse of Mal Bookmaster—passed back along the crowd from hand to hand, quietly, without panic, until the body disappeared into the maw, and Jennifer could follow its passage only as a receding oval in the darkling field of humanity, a gray blip on the screen of heads . . .

The crowd was *digesting* Mal Bookmaster.

She clung to the metal scaffolding, her consciousness fading into the collective deafening whisper of the crowd.

From another direction, another small oval of movement was pushing its laborious way toward the platform.

"—FULFILL A PROMISE TO YOU THAT . . . I MADE MORE THAN A YEAR AGO AT THE DEATHBED OF ONE OF THIS NATION'S IMMORTALS . . ."

"He looks a little distracted," observed the pool director, a CBS man. "Stand by, Two."

"You'd be too, in his position," muttered the technical director.

"He keeps looking back onto the platform."

"—NEVER BEFORE HAS THIS COUNTRY STOOD, stood . . . STOOD AT THE THRESHOLD OF SUCH GRAVE DANGER OF SATURATION BY SOVIET PROPAGANDA

... uh ... DELIVERED NOT THROUGH ENEMY CHAN-
NELS BUT ON OUR OWN MISGUIDED, uh ..."
  "Why's the bastard keep looking around? *Take* Two."

  Teller's ribs and shoulders ached from a constant pounding of
elbows, hands, bodies. He was drenched in sweat. The closer he
pushed toward the platform, the more resistant the crowd became.
Now he was nearly at a standstill. The figure in front of him, a
beefy stud with a Fu Manchu mustache, was refusing to budge.
  "I don't give a fuck who you are, fuck off, you fuck."
  Now there was a pressing in from their left. People jostled
against him. He fought for breath in the sudden crush. Something
heavy was passing back through the crowd alongside him. People
were turning and stepping backward, onto his feet, against his
shins, to clear the way.
  The man ahead of him turned a half-step—and gave Teller six
inches of open space. Teller plunged into the opening.
  It was like stepping out of heavy underbrush into a creek bed.
The line of people in the wake of the heavy object seemed somehow more pliant, more willing to step aside, clear room. He was
within thirty yards of the platform now. He could see Schein's
face illuminated in the spotlights and the TV lights, could pick
up the glint of his ice-blue eyes. Even in his preoccupation with
the crowd, Teller could sense that something was not right with
Schein. The voice was hesitant. He kept pausing to sweep the
speakers' chairs behind him with searching glances.
  Bookmaster would have him off the stage in no time. Teller
lowered a shoulder into the pliant crowd and bulled his way
ahead.
  "—AN AIR ATTACK NOT FROM ENEMY ... from enemy
... MISSILES BUT AN AIR ATTACK ON AMERICA'S
OWN AIRWAVES ..."
  The chairman of the Schein for Senator Committee had been
scowling intently at Schein, arms folded, from his seat behind the
candidate. Now he leaned toward Colonel Donovan and asked in a
rasping whisper:
  "What the hell's the matter with him? Is he drunk?"
  Donovan shook his head. "I don't see his manager anywhere. I
think the boy is at a loss without him."

"Well, I'm going to stop this thing before he pisses away the election."

Donovan nodded.

The chairman cursed under his breath and sprang up from his seat, arranging his face in a jaunty television smile as he did so.

He strode up the aisle until he was directly behind Schein. He clapped a hand on the candidate's shoulder.

"LADIES AND GENTLEMEN—" the campaign chairman began.

He felt Schein's shoulder tighten like a steel coil. Schein spun around as though he had been attacked from behind in a dark alley. The campaign chairman found himself looking into the panic-stricken eyes of a stranger.

He tried to salvage the instant. "HA-HA, SCARED 'IM! BOOOOY, IS MY FACE RED!"

Scattered boos from the crowd.

"LADIES AND GENTLEMEN, THIS MAN HAS HAD A HARD AND EXHAUSTIVE MONTH OF CAMPAIGNING! I THINK IT WAS A MARVELOUS TRIBUTE TO YOUR SUPPORT THAT BOB SCHEIN IS HERE WITH YOU TO-NIGHT! I KNOW HE'D LIKE TO BE HOME RESTING UP FOR THE BIG DAY TOMORROW! I THINK WE SHOULD ALL GIVE HIM A BIG HAND, A BIG SHOW OF OUR SUP-PORT—"

Cries of, "No!" "No!" "Let him speak!"

Teller crashed through the last remaining rows of people and burst upon the small clearing at the base of the scaffold.

He threw his bruised head back and stared upward. His quarry was directly above him. Robert Schein looked like a waxen dummy on a high shelf, a doll that Teller could not quite reach. The platform was more than twice his height. The steps leading to it, on the side to his right, were ringed with policemen. The facade directly in front of him was a hopeless arrangement of vertical steel tubing. He saw that he could pull himself partway up by standing on crossbeams that were four or five feet above the pave-ment. But his stretching hands would still fall a couple of feet short of the platform base.

He had the strangling sensation that he was living in a night-mare. He had clawed and battered his way this far, absorbing the blows of the crowd, only to stand helplessly at the feet of the monster, his monster, while the last seconds of hope ticked away.

"WE WANT TO THANK EACH AND EVERY ONE OF YOU WHO HAVE BEEN A PART OF THIS MAN'S PHENOMENAL SUCCESS STORY—AND WHO WILL DEMONSTRATE AT THE POLLS TOMORROW THAT THE PEOPLE OF AMERICA CAN BREAK THROUGH THE ESTABLISHED POLITICAL MACHINERY AND SPEAK WITH THEIR OWN VOICE—"

The frustration, the futility of his quest washed through his body and left him limp. The ringing idiot voice in the loudspeaker pounded and mocked at his skull, a funhouse shriek lulling the gullible to their pre-assigned complicity in their doom. There was nothing more he could do. He wanted to seize the steel girders with his hands and shake the platform down. Instead he grabbed at them as though they were prison bars, hung his head, and gazed stupidly at the rotting newspapers and food wrappers in the Second Avenue gutter.

"Mark!"

The voice came at him from above, to his left, apart from the general murmur of the crowd. It seemed to float in under the platform, through the scaffolding—a familiar woman's voice calling his name.

He raised his head and looked to his left.

The silhouette of a woman clung to the girders on the far end of the scaffolding. Her feet rested on the crossbeams.

The voice was Jennifer Blade's.

He scrambled to the left side of the structure and rounded the corner. Jennifer looked down on him from above.

"You want up there?"

"Yes, goddammit!"

She held down her hand.

He took it, grabbed a beam with his other hand, and pulled himself even with her.

"Lock your fingers!"

He placed a foot inside the sling she had made with her hands and, as she lifted, pulled himself upward on the vertical beam with all his strength. His hands felt the smooth edge of the speaker's platform. Jennifer's hands were above her now, and he felt her arms tremble under his foot. He placed his palms flat on the platform, elbows high, and pushed with all his might. The center of his gravity shifted, and he rolled onto the stage floor.

He found himself looking up at the pink coat of the former First Lady of the United States, who screamed.

He smiled up at her husband, who was frantically fumbling to free his foot from its entanglement in his metal folding chair so that he could spring into action . . . escape . . . somehow cope with the welt-faced intruder who had rolled in out of nowhere.

"Mark Teller, *WRAP-Around News*," he said, as conversationally as possible.

"Yes," said the former President, breaking into a broad smile of relief. "How are you? Uh, no comment at this time." He reached an arm around his wife, who was in hysterics.

"—AND SO WE WILL SAY GOOD NIGHT TO YOU ALL, AND WE'LL GREET YOU FROM OUR WINNING HEAD-QUARTERS IN JUST ABOUT TWENTY-FOUR HOURS, TO USHER IN A NEW ERA—"

Teller got his feet under him. There was a clear path between him and Candidate Robert Schein. Down a long row of chairs filled with dignitaries, the path was free. He was on his feet now. The dignitaries had turned their horrified faces to him, their expressions frozen into masks of bewilderment and fear. Beside the former President and his wife, there was Mary Ellen Olds, open-mouthed and uncomprehending. There was Colonel Eddie Donovan, his old boss—caught in a rigid stare of scowling indignation. For all his immobility, he might have been one of the Six Captains festooned on a stake. There was Al Gnagy, the Master of Ceremonies, serene in his blind moment of stardom. Several other people whose faces Teller had seen on TV and on billboards—candidates. Two melon-faced giants who could only have been bodyguards. Behind them on the platform, a receding sea of pink, prosperous faces.

And, of course, Robert Schein.

Teller absorbed the whole scene in an instant—in that elongated beat of time that expanded under the TV lights. Bathed in that harsh white glow, the dignitaries in the folding chairs seemed permanently frozen in the pop of some giant flashbulb.

Teller's throbbing eyes swept the platform for the one man who could unfreeze the tableau and send all these statues into a frenzy of action that would engulf him, smother him, kill him perhaps, certainly keep him from reaching his final goal. Bookmaster was nowhere to be seen. Surely he was there. Teller had to act in the second or two of grace before the superagent spotted him and willed his destruction.

He sprinted down the platform, crashed into the chairman of the Schein for Senator Committee, and sent the beefy man staggering. Teller snatched the microphone from the man's hand as he shoved.

In their respective studios, the four network correspondents had already begun their analysis of the Schein rally.

MacGregor Walterson of CBN put his hand to his earpiece and glanced at his monitor screen.

"Something's happening up on stage," he told his viewers.

"Let's go back live."

The other three networks followed suit.

"Camera One, get on this!" yelled the pool director. "We're still in business! Where the hell's that minicam crew? *Take* One!"

Mark Teller was alone on the platform with Robert Schein.

He gazed into ice-blue eyes that seemed to fill the universe. His own eyes throbbed. He fought against the sudden fascination, the rush of hatred and exhilaration, that threatened to hypnotize him.

He drew a breath and shouted into the microphone with all the volume his heaving lungs could master:

"MARK TELLER, *WRAP-Around News!*"

It was a lie, of course—but it didn't matter. The amplified echoes of his voice boomed off the buildings around, and sent shock waves through the crowd.

The reaction was instantaneous. The shock waves came rolling back in a thunderous wash of boos. This was the man who had tried to bring down their hero!

Teller's eyes darted around the platform again. Still no Bookmaster! Without him, the people onstage—even the bodyguards—seemed confused, paralyzed. Time was ticking by in milliseconds, freeze-frames. Schein's face, inches from his own, was a heaving landscape, a convulsion of skin, the blue eyes distended, the features a flickering, snapping screen of long-dormant emotions flickering to tormented life.

"I HAVE A QUESTION FOR THE CANDIDATE!"

Again the thunderous echoes boomed out over the crowd. The boos continued, but the volume abated. The shiny faces turned upward in renewed fascination. The man confronting their hero might have been a hated enemy—but he was a *celebrity*.

The crowd waited to see what would happen next.

Teller turned once again to stare into the universe of blue eyes. There was fear in the eyes now—an emotion he never expected to discover in Robert Schein. Fear clouded the eyes like static.

Milliseconds.

Teller drew in his breath again.

"WHO ARE YOU?"

Schein flinched. His mouth flapped open, unhinged, hung there, in the shocked expression of a man who has just received an unspeakably withering insult.

(*"Tighten that shot, One! Tight! Tight!"*)

"Who ARE YOU?"

The words boomed out of the loudspeakers again, over a crowd that had now fallen silent. Teller thought he heard a stirring on the platform. But he did not allow himself to take his eyes off Robert Schein.

Could it be his maddened imagination . . . was he already hallucinating . . . or had Schein begun, in some strange and subtle way, to disintegrate before his eyes? Teller's own senses expanded. He felt the collective fascination of America watching through the camera lens, watching something that was very much like a murder.

He knew that he had only seconds left before somebody on the stage snapped out of it and sent the goons to yank him into oblivion as though he were a piece of gristle that had landed there . . . and even now he heard the heavy footsteps behind him; he planted his feet, waiting for the blow to come down . . .

"Get away from him!" . . . the hiss belonged to the Colonel . . . "Can't you see *we're on television!*"

The footsteps stopped. Teller spun around, smiled through his bruises into the melon faces of the bodyguards. He looked at the Colonel. The old man's entire life had come down to one split-second decision—and he had opted for decorum. He would not, in the end, violate the imperatives of the airwaves. The moment had to be played out. Now his whitened face was turned imploringly to Schein.

Teller was about to show the old man what a hideous thing decorum could be.

He turned back to Robert Schein and placed the microphone to his lips. In the background he was aware of men with earphones moving quickly toward him—the minicam crew.

Jennifer Blade hurried along with them.

The air was white and cold with the essence of arena. The crowd was absolutely still. All the ruinous questions that Candidate Schein had not been called upon to answer—could now be laid down upon him like bludgeon blows.

The minicam's snout hovered over Teller's shoulder, leering into Schein's quivering face. A fresh pool of light spilled upon the golden hair, the ice-blue eyes. The very pores of Robert Schein's skin filled the screens of shocked America.

Teller opened his mouth to deliver the first question—and handed the microphone to Jennifer Blade.

Something persuaded him that it was her moment.

Their eyes met. She nodded almost imperceptibly. And then Mark Teller withdrew, out of the arena, out of the light—back into the far shadows of the stage.

"ROBERT SCHEIN, THERE ARE A NUMBER OF ISSUES WHICH YOUR OPPONENTS CLAIM THAT YOU HAVE AVOIDED ADDRESSING YOURSELF TO . . ."

Teller let his attention drift away from the scene, down to the people below the scaffolding. He scanned the individual upturned faces—confused, frowning, not quite making sense of it all. Fathers with small children perched on their shoulders. People smoking, eating things, focusing Instamatics. The collective feral personality seemed to have flowed out of the crowd; seemed to have broken up, to have rediffused itself into all the fragmented impulses, the inner preoccupations, the transient passion, of strangers gathered on a common ground to view something—a juggler, a woman with a boa constrictor in her purse, a body that might be drunk and might be dead, a candidate, a beautiful child. A crowd. An audience. The same audience that had waited down the generations, down the centuries, for television to take its mind off the pain of being human for a while.

"—CAN YOU, FOR INSTANCE, TELL THE VOTERS OF NEW YORK HOW YOU WOULD RESPOND TO THE

QUESTION OF A PROPOSED FIVE PERCENT ACROSS-
THE-BOARD CUT IN FOREIGN ASSISTANCE—"

The crowd was not following the strange dialogue onstage. Its
evening, begun in such high spirit and pageantry, was trickling
away in anticlimax. Some confusion up there, reporters asking
questions. The band wasn't playing. The night air was cold. It was
time to go home.

The crowd began to dissolve, hands in its pockets.

Teller turned back to the stage. Most of the assembled dignitaries had fled the platform like thieves in the night. The little
lighted pool of people left in the center—Schein, Jennifer Blade,
the minicam crew—seemed somehow private, inconsequential. It
was hard to believe their conversation was being watched by most
of the households in America. Perhaps it wasn't. Perhaps the
cameras were no longer even transmitting.

And then as Teller watched, a horrible and spellbinding thing
happened. As Jennifer Blade held the microphone to Schein,
Schein's entire body began to tremble. His yellow hair shimmered
in the harsh light—for a moment, a trick of backlighting made it appear to Teller that a shower of sparks had erupted around his head.

The convulsion lasted only a moment. And then Schein became
unnaturally still. He froze like an appliance whose cord had been
snatched from the socket. Even from where he stood in the shadows, Teller thought that he could see the brightness in Robert
Schein's ice-blue eyes recede into twin pinpoints of light, then
disappear, leaving his face a blank screen.

He watched as Jennifer nodded to her crew and began to gather
in the microphone cord. The light man switched off the beam that
had bathed Robert Schein's face. Down below, in the television
pit, the big cameras and lights had already shut down.

He listened to the clear footsteps as Jennifer and the crew made
their way down the stairs at the far end of the platform.

The interview, he imagined, had assured Jennifer of her network anchor job. Somewhere. Biggest political pulldown since
Watergate. If Robert Schein still lived, he lived in Jennifer Blade.

Teller walked past the husk standing immobile in the darkness
and descended the stairs of the platform. The moon was high and
there was a cold energy in the air. No wonder, he realized, glancing at his wristwatch.

It was Prime Time.

Powers, Ron   N/E
Face value   cop.3

Public Library
South Bend, Ind.

Central Building
122 West Wayne Street